The Bowl of Souls: Book Four

The WAR of STARDEON

By: Trevor H. Cooley

Cover art © Renu Sharma | www.thedarkrayne.com
Map by: Michael Patty

Trevor H. Cooley

The Bowl of Souls Series:

Book One: **EYE of the MOONRAT**

Book 1.5: **HILT'S PRIDE**

Book Two: **MESSENGER of the DARK PROPHET**

Book Three: **HUNT of the BANDHAM**

Book Four: **The WAR of STARDEON**

Book Five: **MOTHER of the MOONRAT** *(2013)*

Dedication

To my father, Wayne Cooley, who has been one of the greatest supporters of my writing, reading every chapter as I finish it and giving me his thoughts and opinions. He is an inventor and musician. It is his universal card game that is used by the characters in my books. Of all the influences in my life, he has been the one who showed me how to dream.

This one is for you. Thanks, dad.

Acknowledgements

Once again, there are many who helped and supported me during the writing of this book. Special thanks go out to my beautiful wife and editor Jeannette. My brother Jared edited the Bowl of Souls series review trailer and is currently directing a live action trailer for the series. He is also the face of Ewzad Vriil on this cover, a fact which gives me an endless amount of glee and amusement. Renu Sharma took my ideas for a cover and once again made them a beautiful reality. Also a special thanks to Michael Patty, who designed the map in this book. Check out http://trevorhcooley.com/ for a high resolution version.

Also thanks to all the readers who have visited my site and the Trevor H. Cooley Facebook page. Please join us. There are many exciting things to come.

Table of Contents

Author's Note

The events in this book have been a long time coming. I have been eagerly waiting to write many of them for over ten years. Now that I have, I find a great weight off my shoulders and an excitement at the thought that you, dear reader, are about to experience them. In addition, if you have not yet had the chance to read book 1.5: *Hilt's Pride*, please do so. The events in that book tie directly into this book's narrative and you will have a greater understanding of the characters and motivations that take place herein.

Thank you for reading,

Trevor H. Cooley

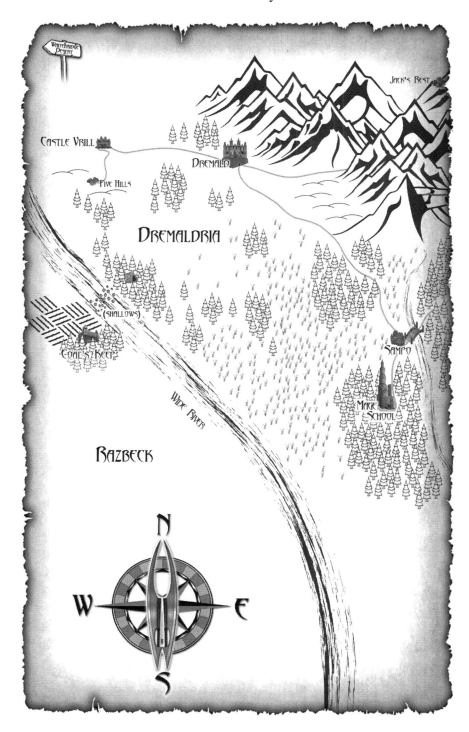

Prologue

"You truly expect us to believe that Lord Protector Vriil is behind this siege? Hmph! Preposterous," said a man Willum had never seen before. The man stood with arms folded and spoke with calm measure but his round face had grown quite red. It was not a good look for him. His nose had been bulbous and dark when Willum had started his report and now it looked positively purple.

"This is what my father said, yes," Willum replied. He looked around the Battle Academy council table but no one leapt to his defense. The reason he had been brought in was to retell his story for the members of the newly assembled War Council. He hadn't expected to be interrogated. The first time he had told the council of his father's warning, the table had been supportive and full of questions. This time they just sat quietly and listened. Even Tad the Cunning said nothing. He was watching the stranger's reaction over steepled fingers, his elbows resting on the council table.

The War Council was put into effect whenever the academy came under attack. The members were comprised of the leaders from the different factions held within the academy's walls. The members included the regular Battle Academy council, the Training School Council, and Demon Jenn, the mayor of Reneul.

"Hearsay. And it comes from a man living in another kingdom. That is what the Queen would say if I told her this rubbish," the stranger said. He was short and stocky and wore an expensive puffy shirt of silken brocade with collar and cuffs made of flowing lace. Willum thought the outfit looked itchy. Perhaps the man was a noble or merchant or something. But that still didn't explain why everyone was listening to him.

The stranger sat down in his chair and leaned back, placing his hands behind his head. "Why are we even considering these accusations?"

"Master Coal is a named wizard and a friend of the academy," said Hugh the Shadow, head of the academy's Assassin Guild. "We have no reason to doubt his word." Hugh gave Willum a pointed look as he spoke and Willum felt his face flush with embarrassment. The council hadn't exactly been happy with him when he had revealed his father's identity. Hiding the identity of one's father wasn't uncommon, but it was frowned upon, especially hiding it from the council. He had been keeping it a secret, determined not to let Coal's status be part of the factor determining his entrance into the academy. He had wanted to succeed on his own. Willum was just glad that they didn't know the identity of his birth father. That would have complicated things greatly.

"And Master Coal has with him sworn witnesses to Ewzad Vriil's actions," said Sabre Vlad, head of the Swordwielder's Guild.

"Oh, right. The witnesses. An elf, a dwarf, and an ogre. An ogre? Please." Despite his nonchalance, the mystery man's nose was getting even purpler.

"There is also Sir Edge," Willum added. "He is the named warrior who was imprisoned by Ewzad Vriil for a time. He saw Ewzad Vriil use magic. He even saw him call an army of goblinoids to fight for him."

"More hearsay. Tales from a named warrior no one has ever heard of, talking about a battle in the Lord Protector's keep that supposedly released hundreds of prisoners and yet no one has heard of the incident!" There was definite anger in his voice now and he was scowling. A vein throbbed on the man's temple and his nose had become so engorged Willum feared it might burst.

"What I think would help is if you could show us the letter in your father's hand," said Demon Jenn. "Or perhaps you could produce some kind of signed statement from the witnesses?" Jenn was an academy graduate, as most of the mayors of Reneul had been over the years. She had earned her name on the battlefield and was well respected, but the years had not been kind to her. Her face had been disfigured by a goblin dagger while protecting a caravan in her youth and as she had aged, the scar had shrunken and puckered, leaving one lip pulled upward in a permanent sneer.

"I am sorry, ma'am. That isn't possible," Willum said. "My-."

"Hmph! Again, the lack of proof." the stranger said. "I still don't see why we are listening to this."

"This information didn't come by letter," Tad the Cunning said, speaking up for the first time since Willum had entered the room. His eyes remained on the fancily dressed man as he spoke, "Willum, please explain to everyone how you received your father's message."

"Of course, sir."

Willum couldn't tell them of the true nature of the bond he had with Coal. Bonding magic was rare and unknown to most of the wizard community and the rest of the world was completely ignorant of its existence. Instead, he recited the story Coal had concocted the first time he had asked Willum to pass a message on to the council.

"When I left home, my father wanted to be able to keep in contact with me, so he used a spell to set up a . . . mental connection. Even though he is very far away, if we are both concentrating, we can communicate to each other with our minds. It's not easy. I-I can usually only accomplish it at night, sir. When I am laying in my bed after all my tasks are complete, for instance."

The story wouldn't have held up if a wizard had been in the room. As far as Willum knew, no such spell existed within the realm of elemental magic. There were objects enchanted to carry people or items over long distances, but to send one's thoughts was a more difficult task. Only spiritual magic could accomplish that.

The man smirked and opened his mouth to retort, but Tad spoke first.

"I have a piece of evidence to back up his claim." He picked up a scroll and slid it over to Demon Jenn. "This scroll arrived from the Mage School not long before the attack. They had received a similar communication from Master Coal and urged us to heed his warnings. They vouch for his words and his methods."

The mayor opened the scroll and nodded appreciatively. For a woman that made her name in battle, she seemed to put a lot of trust in paperwork. "This is signed by Master Latva himself." She directed her gaze to the stranger. "This eases my mind."

"So one wizard vouches for another? What does that change? Let me see that. Do they include any new evidence to support his claims?" The man snatched the scroll away from her and poured over it with his eyes.

Tad cleared his throat. "You are ignoring another fact. Many of Master Coal's claims have already proven true. His witnesses knew of the army amassing in the mountains. He warned us that an attack could be coming. If he had not warned us through his connection with his son, we may have been caught unawares."

Willum's shoulders sank in relief. Finally Tad was backing him up. The tension in the room had been giving him a headache.

The man stood, his face twisted in anger, more purple than ever. "I-!" He paused and closed his eyes for a moment. His shoulders quivered briefly and he blinked a few times before clearing his throat. He raised one shaking hand and smoothed back his thinning hair. He saw everyone staring and smiled apologetically before sitting down. Much of the extra color had drained from his face.

"Are you okay?" Tad asked. "Can we get you some water or something?"

"No, I'm fine, fine. Uh, your point is well taken, Tad. However, just because this Master Coal was right about the invasion does not mean that his witnesses are right about everything else. A man can be right in some cases and wrong in others. I for one still refuse to believe that Lord Protector Vriil had anything to do with this attack. I will need to see better evidence than this if I am to send a message warning the queen."

"I understand your position." Tad's eyes left the man and moved to Willum. "Has your father told you anything new to report, Willum?"

Willum hesitated. He was already dreading the stranger's reaction to his news. "Yes, he has gathered a small band of . . . warriors and along with Sir Edge is traveling here to help in whatever way he can. As they began their journey, they were attacked by several of Ewzad Vriil's altered beasts. They lost one of their number but were able to defeat the beasts and have since continued on their way."

"And when was this?" Tad asked.

"Two days ago, sir."

"Beasts made by the Lord Protector? Surely you don't expect us to believe- . . . Never mind," the stranger said with a shake of his head. The color was flooding his face again and his voice was loaded with sarcasm as he asked, "Well, why don't you describe these horrible creatures for us?"

Willum swallowed. He knew that his description would sound outlandish to say the least. "There was an armored orc that spat acid, a large plant-like beast with razor sharp whips, and a huge red beast that flew like a dragon and radiated heat from its very skin. Father called it a bandham."

The stranger laughed in derision, though to Willum, it seemed that his eyes weren't laughing. The man's eyes were watching him with calculating intensity. Thankfully no one else in the room found it funny.

"Thank you, Willum, son of Coal," Tad said with a nod. "Please keep the council informed of any new developments." He looked back to the rest of the council. "I believe Stout Harley has a report on our current supply situation. If you will excuse me for a moment?"

Tad smiled and stood from his chair. He nudged Willum on his way to the back of the chamber and Willum followed him out the rear door of the council hall.

Willum followed Tad down a hallway and passed several

rooms whose purpose he had no clue about. He knew that the rear of the building contained the personal apartments of the council members but this was the first time he had been there. They walked down some stairs and headed down a dimly lit corridor. At the second junction, Tad stopped and grabbed Willum's shoulder. He kept his voice low.

"I am sorry I had to put you through that."

"Who was that man?" Willum asked, relieved that his teacher was acting more like normal.

"He is Dann Doudy, the new Dremald representative to the academy."

"The new representative? What happened to Proud Harold?" Willum asked. Harold had been the Dremald representative on the council for over a decade. He was a jovial man and well liked by the students. When King Andre had died and his sister Elise had been crowned, Harold had been summoned back to Dremald along with the rest of the Dremald troops that were usually assigned to the academy.

"I don't know and that concerns me. This . . . Dann Doudy, showed up the evening before the attack. He had papers from the queen announcing him as Harold's replacement. He says Harold had grown weary of his duties and wanted to retire."

Willum's brow knit in concern. If his father's suspicions about the situation in Dremald were correct, something bad may have happened to Harold. "What do you know about this new representative?"

Tad frowned. "Not much. He is a minor noble. The Doudy family has been in Dremaldria for generations, but why the queen would choose him is a mystery. She didn't list any of his qualifications."

"I understand," Willum said. Tad's behavior in the conference room was making sense now. He had been watching the man's response to his father's warning to gauge his reaction. "So do you think he was sent here to keep an eye on us?"

"If he was sent here by Ewzad Vriil as a spy, he isn't a very effective one." He stroked his chin. "He definitely hasn't been trying to make any friends since he arrived. No spy worth his spit would have acted so bothered by our information. His actions were so bizarre it makes me wonder if he was acting the avid Vriil supporter to throw us off. A pretty clever ploy, I must say. I'm interested to see what Hugh thought of his act."

"And what if he is reporting information to the enemy?" Willum asked. "He will be in every council meeting. He could tell the enemy how many men we have, how the men are positioned, what our food supplies are . . ."

Tad patted his shoulder. "Good. You are thinking this through. I can tell you have been paying attention in my class. But don't worry. I have archers posted on the wall looking for birds. We are watching any possible form of communication. We are safe unless he was somehow able to get out of the academy, but we are surrounded by tens of thousands of goblinoids, and we have soldiers at every possible exit. There is no way he is sneaking out."

"Good to know, sir." Willum said with relief.

"Unless, you think . . . Could Ewzad Vriil possibly use a spell like your father has been using to communicate with you?"

Willum swallowed. "I don't think so. It is a spell of my father's own creation." But what if he could? Coal had told him that Ewzad Vriil had the rings of Stardeon and that those rings used spirit magic. What if Ewzad Vriil had found a way to make a mental connection with this noble? He would have to ask Coal that night through the bond.

There was a sound down the corridor and Tad looked to make sure that no one was coming. "Now you must keep this conversation to yourself. I do not want doubts about our new representative being passed through the students. They have enough to worry about. The only reason I told you about my concerns is that I need you to pass them on to your father. See if he has any information about Dann Doudy. Get his opinion. And one other thing . . ." He looked into Willum's eyes. "I want you reporting directly to me from now on. Your father is our only pair of eyes outside the academy right now. Any new information he tells you, bring it to my attention. No matter how small, you understand? Tell no one else."

Willum nodded, "But-."

"I mean no one. Don't even tell the other council members. Report to me only. I don't plan on bringing you back before the council unless it is absolutely necessary."

"Yes sir," Willum replied. But why the secrecy? Was Tad worried about the loyalty of the other academy teachers?

"Good. Now it is time I returned to the council. You should go about your duties." Tad gave him a confident smile. "Don't worry too much about our new representative. We are watching him."

"Of course, sir."

"Just head down the corridor to the left and you'll reach the entrance."

"Thank you, sir."

Tad the Cunning turned and walked back towards the council hall and Willum turned up the joining corridor as instructed. After a short distance, it opened into the long high-ceilinged foyer at the front of the building.

As Willum walked towards the outer doors, he looked at the tapestries depicting the glorious battles of the academy's past and wondered if the current siege would be depicted on these walls some day. He supposed it would, if they survived.

When he reached the doors he nodded to the two guards at their posts on either side of the doors. He took a deep breath before grasping the handles.

"Going out's always the hard part, ain't it, Willum?" said one of the guards.

"Yeah, Zhed." he said. "It's nice and quiet in here."

The architect that had designed the council building had put it together so that all sound from outside was cut out. His teacher had told the class that the effect was caused by the cunning way the blocks of stone had been put together, but Willum was pretty sure the architect had a wizard's help. Whatever the case, it was effective.

The other guard snorted. "Quiet? I call it boring. I'd rather be on the wall looking down at the goblinoids. It's all I can do to keep from falling asleep."

Willum shrugged. "I would suggest you enjoy the quiet

while you can."

He pushed open the doors and walked out into a wave of sound. The academy was packed with people and the high walls caused even small sounds to echo. Students were training, smiths pounding away on anvils. Citizens rushed back and forth on errands, shouting to each other, and behind it all was the low drone of the goblinoid army surrounding them.

The Dremaldrian Battle Academy usually held around two thousand students and close to five hundred faculty and graduates waiting for jobs. When the incoming attack had been confirmed, the Training School had been halted and all trainees brought inside. Reneul was evacuated. Those who had somewhere else to go fled, but anyone who wanted to stay was brought inside the academy walls. The end result was that they now had over four thousand people crammed inside.

The dorms and outbuildings were overflowing. Cots and tents had been set up in the yards. Even many of the seldom-used tunnels underneath the academy had been opened up for people to sleep in. The council building was the only structure not packed with people.

Willum hurried along, weaving his way along the congested pathways that crisscrossed the grounds. He was late for his shift on the academy wall. This time of day he was supposed to be on the northeast corner. So far the enemy hadn't attacked and seemed content to marshal their forces as more goblinoids joined their ranks from the mountains every day.

The faculty switched up shifts a few times a day to keep the students alert. Each wall had its own perils to watch for. It seemed that in order to stave off infighting, the leaders of the enemy army had split it into racial groups.

The eastern wall looked out over the Training School grounds where the gorcs were camped. The training tents still stood, along with the barracks and marketplace and several small arenas. When on watch there, Willum could see the gorcs crowded around them. Fighting for sport seemed to be their favorite form of entertainment.

The north wall overlooked the Scralag Hills, which had been mostly overtaken by giants and ogre tribes. They seemed to make a game of getting as close to the wall as they dared and throwing jagged rocks. The students and graduates on the wall shot arrows to keep them at a safe distance and most of their throws fell short, but every once in a while one would clear the top. The large beasts roared and hollered when one of their rocks made it over. Luckily, there had only been a few injuries so far.

The western wall looked out over what had once been empty farmland. Now it was covered in goblins. They were the most numerous and unruly bunch, always yelling and hollering, making obscene gestures and fighting amongst each other. They were more a source of entertainment for the watchers than a source for concern.

The southern wall shift was the trickiest. It overlooked the main city of Reneul which was full of buildings for the enemy to hide in. The western half of the city, which included the huge academy arena and the majority of the working class homes had been taken over by orcs. They seemed the most organized part of the army, always marching around in units and busily taking buildings apart to build siege engines. In the short time since the siege had begun, they had already constructed several catapults, battering rams and trebuchets.

Eastern Reneul had been overtaken by trolls and other monsters. Strangely, they seemed to mill about peacefully, only screeching and attacking when the orcs threw them food. At night, while the other parts of the army were aglow with torches and camp fires, Eastern Reneul would be scattered with the glow of yellow and green moonrat eyes. The unsettling sound of their chittering moans made night on the southern wall the most dreaded shift on the wall.

Willum groaned as he approached the duty desk at the base of the wall. Roobin was in charge of check-in again. Roobin wasn't a bad guy; he was good-natured most of the time and not bad with a sword, but he had recently graduated and loved giving Willum a hard time about it.

"Willum, son of Coal, reporting for duty."

"Oh, the mighty son of Coal, eh?" Roobin chuckled, though it was only a few short weeks ago that he had been known as Roobin, son of Roobin the Knuckle.

"Just sign me in, okay?"

"You are kind of late, aren't you? Tsk-tsk, students shouldn't be tardy." Roobin dipped his quill and looked down at the log-in sheet. His smirk faded. "Lucky you. Go on to station twenty eight. I guess I don't have to report you."

"You were gonna report me?" Willum said in disbelief.

"Of course, except that it says here that Tad called you away. So you have an excuse."

"Oh, so it's just 'Tad' now, is it?" Willum said, getting in a jab of his own. "Just because you have graduated, you two are on a first name basis? Should I be calling you, 'Roobin, the Well Connected' now?"

Roobin's eyes narrowed. "Shut up, Willum. Just go on up. You're relieving Swen, son of Rolf, the Fletcher."

"Yes sir!" Willum said with a salute, and grabbed a bow and quiver from the rack next to the stairs. Some students carried around their own bows, but that wasn't Willum's forte. He was okay with a bow, but his specialty was his scythe and throwing daggers.

He headed up the stairs pleased with the irritation on Roobin's face, but as he reached the top of the wall, his pleasure faded. A mix of his fellow students and academy graduates lined the walls looking down at the massive army that sprawled below. The dull roar of the enemy was much louder up here. It was rough and rhythmic.

Willum was careful not to touch anyone as he walked to his station. The top of the wall was wide enough for three men to walk side by side and there was an abdomen high barrier on either side, but no matter how many shifts he took, it always made him nervous if someone brushed against him while he was at the edge.

Swen was at post twenty eight, bending over the edge and staring down unconcerned at the height. Swen was a tall man, maybe six foot four and the wall's edge only came up to his waist. Though he was only a few years older than Willum, his face was angular and weathered, with wrinkles at the corners of his eyes from squinting in the sun. He was also the best archery student the academy had seen in decades. Swen made all his own arrows and the other students had started calling him Swen the Feather. Willum thought the name was going to stick.

"Swen I'm here," he said. "Sorry, but Tad the Cunning called me away for a while."

"Yeah, that's fine." The tall man barely gave him a glance as he spoke. His eyes were focused on the army below. "I've been up here for eight straight hours, what's another one or two?"

"What's the problem?" Willum looked down, trying to see what was bothering the man. The base of the wall was clear of enemies for a good two hundred yards on this side of the school as the army tried to keep out of shooting distance. But there was one group of goblinoids that were gathered in a bit closer than the others. They were the chanters. There were groups of them all around the wall. A mixed group of orcs, gorcs, and goblins sat cross-legged on the ground, slightly swaying back and forth, chanting loudly. They had been at it for days. Every once in a while one of them would pass out and be dragged away, but they were always replaced.

"I don't like the sound of that grunting down there," Swen said, his voice a low monotone.

"Yeah, it gives me the shivers."

"What do you think they are doing?" Swen asked.

Willum had asked Coal the same question the night before. He had relayed his memory of the chant and had Coal pass it on to Bettie. Her answer had been unsettling.

"They're chanting a prayer to the Dark Prophet," Willum said. "They ask him to bring the wall down."

"Oh." Swen's face paled. The big man lifted his massive bow and pulled a long arrow from his quiver. Swen's bow was nearly as tall as Willum and as thick as his forearm. Swen had named it Windy. It had been reinforced with runes to keep it from weathering or cracking and most of the other students couldn't even string it, much less shoot with it. Even Mad Jon, the archery teacher, had difficulty with firing it.

"Be careful," Willum said. "You know the rules. We

aren't supposed to waste any arrows. Only fire if they come in range."

Swen looked at him in surprise. "Have you ever known me to miss?" He focused on the group chanting below. "I figure the one with the black feathers on his armor is the leader."

Willum peered down and located the orc Swen spoke of. It wore some kind of headdress bristling with something like feathers and walked among the rows of chanting orcs waving its arms about as if to encourage them to chant louder. "He does look the most energetic."

Swen pulled the arrow back to his ear, the muscles on his arms taught with the strain.

"It'll just . . . make it." Swen grunted. Willum heard the wood creak as he gave it an extra pull. Swen sucked in, then slowly released his breath as he fired.

Willum saw the arrow arc out, but lost track of it for most of the distance until he saw the black-feathered orc squirm and squeal. The arrow had struck it in the belly. The chanting stopped and the goblinoids pointed urgently at the top of the wall. Swen waved. Several of them grabbed their dying leader and they retreated back another fifty yards.

"Great shot!" Willum said.

"Hit it in the belly," Swen said with a slight frown. "I was aiming for its neck."

"Can you hit another one?" Willum asked. They were startled now. If another went down, they might not be able to chant so freely.

Swen shook his head. "Just out of range."

"Well I'm here now. You can go rest if you want," Willum said. "Unless you want to move further along the wall and see if you can disperse some more chanters."

The tall man smiled. "Good idea." He pulled another arrow from his quiver and walked down the wall looking for more targets.

Willum took his place and looked down at the mass of beasts below. A cool breeze blew and the smell that wafted up was horrible. The air on this side of the academy used to smell of tilled earth and pine trees. Now it stank of beasts and filth and cook fires mixed with an underlying rot.

Willum shuddered. It was hard to believe that this was all the work of his uncle.

Chapter One

"Ewzad Vriil is Willum's uncle?" Justan said, mouth agape.

"That's what he dag-gum said." Lenny's mouth too had fallen open.

Fist watched both of their reactions and scratched his head.

They had been standing around the evening cook fire as the sun neared the horizon and Coal's announcement had come out of the blue. The wizard looked as though he had expected this sort of reaction. He wore a weary smile. "Yes, Ewzad's older sister was Willum's mother."

Fist didn't understand why this mattered. From the surprise in Justan's mind, it seemed that the information was pivotal, but Fist was still confused by the importance humans placed on blood relationships. In an ogre tribe, family relationships did not matter. An uncle was only as close as any other tribe member. One's father was the only important distinction.

"Why didn't you tell us before?" Justan asked.

Master Coal bent and warmed his hands next to the supper pot. Lenny's pepperbean stew was just starting to bubble and from the expression on the wizard's face, it didn't look like he found its appearance very appetizing. As flavorful as the stew was, Lenny's pepperbeans did strange things to one's system over time.

"I didn't tell you because I did not see how it made a difference to our current situation. This information changes nothing and besides . . . it was not my secret to tell. I have spoken with him about it before, but until last night, Willum wanted this information to remain a secret."

"I can't blasted believe it!" said Lenny. "Yer Willum's a dag-blamed Vriil!"

"Why do it matter?" Fist asked.

"'Does', Fist." Justan said, correcting the ogre out of habit. "Why 'does' it matter."

"Oh. Right." Fist nodded. He had asked Justan to correct him anytime he spoke the human tongue incorrectly. He still struggled with verb tense sometimes. "Why does it matter?"

"Fist has a good question." Justan sighed and rubbed his temples in an attempt to stave off a headache. "You are right, Master Coal. This changes nothing. Willum is who he is no matter who his parents were."

"I musta missed a dag-gum story here, Coal." Lenny said with a scowl. "I thought Willum was yer son. How'd you end up bonded to a Vriil?"

"It ain't none of your business, you ornery cuss," said Bettie, who was unsaddling the horses. Lenny always had been an irritable sort and his moods were all the grumpier after a long day of riding.

"I didn't mean nothin' by it!" Lenny retorted.

"Couldn't tell by looking at you! You look like a baby dwarf who got in a tussle and found out he dropped his lolly in the dirt."

Fist had to admit Lenny looked a sight. Half of the dwarf's handlebar moustache and one eyebrow had been singed off during their fight with the bandham just a few days prior. Lenny had been forced to shave off the other side of his moustache to match and it had taken decades off of his face. Bettie had told him pointedly she didn't like the look and it would be months before he looked like his old self again. On top of that humiliation, Gwyrtha had taken up burying him in the night once again and though he tried to get all the leaves out of his hair, he had missed one that stuck awkwardly out the top of his head. Bettie found it amusing not to tell him.

"It's fine Bettie! It's fine," Coal said placatingly.

"Willum told me last night that I should tell Sir Edge and his bonded everything."

"Yeah, but he didn't say 'tell the nosey dwarf about it'," Bettie jeered. "Hear that, Lenui? Butt out, ya oaf!"

"Dag-blast it, woman! Would you stay offa my case fer one toad-hoppin' minute!" Lenny shouted, hopping up and down in anger.

Fist watched the two bicker in puzzlement.

She's a half-orc, he's a dwarf. Justan said through the bond as if that should explain it. *They like each other.*

If they like each other, why do they yell? Fist asked.

Neither one of them is comfortable showing their affection for one another. So this is the way they do it, Justan sent. *Usually I find their banter kind of cute, but right now it's just getting on my nerves.*

"Enough!" Justan said aloud. "If you two want to have a lovers' quarrel, do it somewhere else. Master Coal was trying to tell us something."

"Lovers?" Bettie shouted, her face red.

"Sir Edge is right, Bettie," Coal said and from the way he stared at her, Fist could tell that they were communicating further through their bond. Finally Bettie scowled and went back to her work. "Lenny, you are more than welcome to listen. But I am quite tired, so please let's keep the interruptions to a minimum if possible. When I finish, perhaps you will understand why Willum has wanted it kept secret until now."

"Uh-sure," Lenny said, his face flushed as red as Bettie's had been. "Please go ahead."

Fist felt a nudge in his side and looked back to see Gwyrtha's large shaggy head. He smiled at her customary greeting and scratched behind her horse-like ears the way he knew she liked. Squirrel chose that moment to leave his pouch at Fist's side. The little beast had been asleep and wondered what all the fuss was about.

Coal is telling a story! Fist sent, scratching Squirrel's back so that he wouldn't be jealous.

Squirrel scurried up over Fist's shoulder and down his

arm to sit on Gwyrtha's broad back. Squirrel had taken a liking to the rogue horse and whenever Justan wasn't riding her, she had become one of his favorite places to sit.

Justan greeted Gwyrtha's approach with a smile, but his eyes wandered to the bundle of leather tied behind her saddle. His smile faltered. Gwyrtha had insisted on being the one to carry Qyxal's body until they could get it back to his people. As a result, Justan rode with Qyxal behind him every step of the way. The elf's death weighed on him. It was the first time one of Justan's close friends had died and Fist knew he felt responsible for it.

Coal continued on, oblivious to the somber change in Justan's feelings, "I'll tell you what I have been able to piece out from the things I know of the family Vriil and Willum's memories, vague as they are.

"The Vriils are one of the oldest of the Dremaldrian noble families. Their lineage has a rather tarnished past that I won't go into very much, except to say that they have been censured by both the Mage School and the royal family multiple times over the centuries. This has happened so often in fact, that they are now considered relatively minor nobility. Willum's grandfather Ruprect Vriil had two children. The eldest was Willum's mother, Jolie. His second child was Ewzad, who was born of his second wife.

"It was considered a major coup when Ruprect married his daughter to the second son of one of the major houses, the Prosses. Jolie's husband's name was Nedney Pross. From all accounts, the two had fallen in love and Nedney had forced the marriage upon his parents. With his legacy assured, Ruprect sent Ewzad off to be raised at the palace in Dremald, content to let Jolie and her husband take control of the family lands once he died.

"Jolie gave birth to Willum several years later and he became the pride of the Vriil family. When Willum was four, Ruprect and his wife died under mysterious circumstances. An inquiry was held and Willum's parents were found guilty of their murders. They were sentenced to death."

"I remember that," Lenny said, his stubbly eyebrow

raised. "Happened when I just done moved into my shop in Dremald. It was all anyone was talkin' 'bout back then. Them Vriils got their gall-durn heads chopped off right in front of ever'body an-." Lenny noticed everyone looking at him. "What? I didn't go to the dag-blasted thing! I was back at my forge makin' swords."

"A public beheading?" Justan said. "That's not a common punishment in Dremaldria. Not even for murder."

Master Coal nodded sadly. "In this case, the finding of the inquiry was that Willum's parents had sacrificed Ruprect and his wife to the Dark Prophet."

There was stunned silence for a moment until Justan finally asked, "Were his parents really guilty?"

"I don't know. Willum has never in his heart believed it to be true. He has shared his memories of them with me and I have never seen any actions that would lead me to believe it was possible. However, the inquiry claimed to have proof."

Fist didn't understand the humanoid system of laws, but he understood the necessity of punishing a crime, even unto death. In ogre tribes, when one ogre brought an accusation against another before the chief, a fight was the only way of proving guilt or innocence. But only the crime of betraying the tribe was punished by an execution. In such a case, it was the chief's job to kill the betrayer. It was the only time when the guilty ogre did not have the right to defend himself in battle. Fist had seen his father punish two such betrayals. One time it had been his responsibility to hold the ogre's arms back while his father killed him. Fist knew how humans felt about their families and could see how sacrificing one's parents to the Dark Prophet might be one such punishable offense.

"So how'd you end up with Willum then?" Lenny asked.

"I happened to be in town during the execution. The bond struck us just as his parents died," Coal said. "I bound the men guarding Willum with a spell and took him back to Razbeck with me that very night."

"Ewzad Vriil had to have been involved," Justan said.

"I have wondered the same thing," Coal said. "With his

parents dead, Willum would have technically been the heir to the Vriil house. That would have made him the only thing standing between Ewzad becoming the last remaining Vriil and the sole inheritor of its fortunes."

"Getting rid of a four-year-old wouldn't be so hard for a person like him," Justan said with a frown.

"At the very least, Willum would have been placed under his uncle's care. Ewzad would have been the one in charge of the Vriil estates until Willum came of age, plenty of time for Ewzad to decide what to do with him," Coal agreed. "However, he was at the palace with Prince Andre and Princess Elise at the time of Ruprect's death. He couldn't have killed his parents. At least not personally. And he was only seventeen at the time. No one had a reason to expect he could pull something like that off."

"I still think Ewzad had to have been responsible," Justan said with grim certainty. His anger towards the wizard had been constant since their battle with Kenn.

"Why did Willum want us to know this?" asked Fist.

"Last night Willum told me that there was a new Dremald representative at the academy. He showed up just hours before the siege began and Tad the Cunning thought he might be a spy. When Willum showed me his memory of this man, I recognized him at once. He is Dann Doudy, the noble that was in charge of the inquiry against Willum's parents. He was the one who presented the evidence that convinced King Muldroomon to sentence them to death."

"Dag-nab son of a hoop-skirtin' camel!" Lenny said. "Didja' tell him?"

"I couldn't hide that kind of information. He deserved to know," Coal replied with a sigh.

"So what is Willum going to do?" Justan asked.

"He is in a delicate position. We agreed that it wouldn't be wise to tell them the truth of his lineage at this point. I told him to stay away from Dann Doudy, but to tell Tad how the man had been associated with the Vriils."

Justan opened his mouth as if to reply, but paused for a moment and Fist knew he was communicating with Deathclaw.

From the stern look on his face, it seemed that they weren't agreeing. This happened quite often. Deathclaw didn't understand Justan's reasons for making decisions.

"Fist," Justan said. "Deathclaw has found some meat to go with our dinner. Would you go help him with the kill?" *I would go myself, but he seems more comfortable around you than Gwyrtha and I. Perhaps it's because you have already fought together.*

Fist had an idea it was more than that. Justan was a puzzle to the raptoid, and Gwyrtha . . . Fist didn't understand it, but there was something about her that Deathclaw found infuriating. The reason Deathclaw preferred his company most likely had to do with the fact that they were both new to humanity. That and their shared hatred for Ewzad Vriil.

"Yes, I will go." Fist said. Actually he was glad to have something besides Lenny's stew to eat. He had gotten more and more used to it, but the stuff still sat like rocks in his stomach. "But will I miss Master Coal's story?"

"That's alright, Fist. I have already told you most everything there was to know," Coal said.

"Listen, ogre," Lenny said, pointing a menacing finger at him. "Whatever you and that lizard bring back, it'd better be good eatin'. No more cats or giant bugs or nothin'."

"It will be good," Fist replied, though he didn't understand the dwarf's preferences when it came to food. His philosophy was that if it couldn't talk back to you, it was okay to eat.

He felt a slight click in the bond as Justan connected his mind with Deathclaw's. The raptoid was only a short ways into the forest, shadowing their prey. From its smell, Fist instantly knew what it was. Lenny was not going to be happy.

Ogre, the human wants you to come, Deathclaw grumbled. He didn't like being told to hold back.

Justan worries for us. He wants you to be safe, Fist explained.

Deathclaw gave a mental hiss. *Safe? I have killed much worse.*

Fist shrugged. Justan had become both more cautious and more reckless since Qyxal's death. He was far more concerned about keeping his bonded from harm, yet at the same time eager to rush to the academy and do battle with thousands of goblinoid troops. He and Master Coal argued about their course of action constantly. Justan favored a direct route, wanting to get there as soon as possible, while Coal thought it best that they take a slower approach.

The wizard felt that the academy was in no immediate danger. They were well stocked with provisions and well defended and the goblinoid army did not have the means to mount an efficient assault. He thought it best that they act as scouts going from village to village learning what was going on in the land and letting Willum tell the council their findings.

Justan understood the wizard's reasoning, but feared that the army could decide to assault the academy at any moment. Fist knew that if Justan's mother or friends were killed, he would blame himself for not being there. He was a named warrior now and felt that meant that he had the responsibility to protect them.

Fist would have felt the same in Justan's place. He had not been able to stop the wizard's goblinoids from killing Tamboor's family and though he understood that he had done everything in his power to save them, he still felt guilty at being unable to stop their deaths.

So far, Fist hadn't confronted Justan about the way he was acting. It was alright for a leader to mourn, but Justan was letting his emotions rage out of control. If he didn't come to his senses soon, Fist would have to talk to him.

Faster, Ogre! Deathclaw said impatiently. *Daylight is fading.*

Fist rolled his eyes. The raptoid recognized that he wasn't the leader of their tribe, but that didn't stop him from bossing Fist around all the time. Fist didn't think that he did so intentionally. Deathclaw had been a leader his whole life. He expected others to follow. Unfortunately this also meant that he chafed under Justan's orders.

Fist headed into the forest in the direction the bond told him, slogging around leafless trees just beginning to bud and trudging through deep piles of wet leaves. He was tired of the cold nights and wet days that were spring in the lowlands of Dremaldria. Summer could not come fast enough.

Silence, the prey is near, Deathclaw hissed. *Your stomping is loud.*

I know how to hunt, Fist replied.

He reached for the mace that Lenny had made him. The weapon was long and ugly, with runes carved into the length of the shaft. Spikes covered one half of the mace's head for piercing, while the other half was covered with ridges for bashing and gouging. As he pulled the weapon free from its place on his back, his muscles sped up in reaction to its magic. While he held his mace, he was twice as fast, but he also used up twice as much energy.

Fist crept through the leaves as quietly as possible, not an easy task for a four hundred pound ogre on any occasion, but even harder when his movement was increased. It was something he was still getting used to. He wished he had a way to switch off the magic until he was ready to use it, but that wasn't a function the dwarf had built into the weapon.

Deathclaw chirped out a command through the bond and Fist recognized that the raptoid wanted him to circle around. Deathclaw sent him an image of the prey and Fist was impressed. This was a big one. He pulled the massive oval shield from the harness on his back and called out to Squirrel through the bond.

A battle comes, Squirrel. Fist couldn't help but grin. Though he had enjoyed farm life for a time, his warrior instincts were heating up. He was ready to hit something.

Squirrel left its leather pouch and scrambled up to Fist's shoulder. It leapt onto a nearby tree branch and cocked his head, questioning Fist on how long this battle was going to take.

Not long. We will kill it quickly. Since Justan had discovered that Fist was a bonding wizard, he had been teaching the ogre more and more about how the magic worked. Now Fist's understanding of Squirrel's thoughts had gotten even better.

She smells your scent, Deathclaw sent. *Come now before*

she flees.

Fist knew what the raptoid wanted. He was to dart in and get the beast's attention so that Deathclaw could leap in from behind and strike the killing blow. It was as good a plan as any and had worked for the raptoid for decades. Fist moved forward through the trees with swift strides, no longer trying to be stealthy. Soon the prey came into view. She was looking right at him.

The bear was standing on its hind legs, a full foot taller than Fist's eight feet. She was a mountain grizzly. Fist had faced their kind before. Back when he lived in Jack's Rest, he had killed a few that had come too near the human's territory. He had no idea what one was doing this far south, though. Perhaps it had fled the goblinoid army.

The bear roared and came at him on all fours. Fist met her advance, stepping forward and swinging the dull side of his mace at her head. His strike was fast. He put all his muscle into it and the impact rocked her head to the side, shattering the bear's jaw, sending teeth and blood flying. The bear's momentum carried it forward into him and he shoved its bulk aside with his shield. It crashed to the side, unable to move, but still breathing.

Fist swung the spiked end of the mace this time, finishing its life with a crunch. When he looked up, Deathclaw was standing next to him. Fist could feel the raptoid's disappointment at not being the one to strike the fatal blow. He wrenched the mace free and smiled. "I killed it for you."

Deathclaw stepped forward and lifted the bear's rear leg. With a few precise cuts of his claws, he cut the leg free from the knee down. He tucked this portion of the kill under his arm and regarded Fist with his head cocked.

You are useful, ogre. Take it to the others, Deathclaw sent, then slunk into the trees to eat his dinner alone.

Fist snorted in disbelief. *You are not going to help?*

You killed it without my help, Deathclaw replied. *You are big. You can manage.*

Fist frowned and looked down at the enormous bear. Deathclaw had a lot to learn about being part of the Big and

Little People Tribe. He hefted one of the beast's remaining legs over his shoulder and began to drag it back towards the camp.

Squirrel leapt back to his shoulder and skittered down to sit on the bear's hide as they went. He chattered his opinion of the hunt, informing Fist that he should have killed it in one hit.

I will do better next time, Squirrel, he replied.

The bear was heavy and hauling the kill through the forest in the dim light was a struggle. Luckily Squirrel's eyes were sharp and he saved Fist some grief by pointing out various obstacles in the way. To Fist's relief, Justan noticed his discomfort and asked Gwyrtha to come help the ogre with his burden.

When they arrived back in camp, Lenny was the first one to see the kill. The dwarf jumped up and down. "Gall-durn it! A dag-gum bear? Again?"

"Good one, Fist," said Bettie, who was standing by the fire. The half-orc had a smile on her face. "Maybe a tough meal will shut the dwarf up."

While the dwarf sputtered in protest, Bettie came over to help Fist skin the kill. She tossed him a knife. "Why is this thing missing a leg?"

"Deathclaw is eating it," Fist explained.

"Raw?" Bettie asked, then shook her head and smiled. "Never mind. What am I saying?"

They were efficient and had the bear cleaned in minutes. They then cut away several large portions to go with dinner and took them over to the fire, leaving the rest for Lenny to deal with. The dwarf grumbled as he brought over leather wraps and divided up the rest of the carcass, rubbing the meat down with salt and ground spices before packing it away for later.

Bettie chopped some of the bear meat and combined it with Lenny's stew, then set the rest of the meat to cooking on spits. It would take some time before dinner was ready to eat, so Fist walked over to join Justan, who was unsaddling Gwyrtha while having a very animated discussion with Master Coal.

"I am sorry, Master Coal, but I still don't see how waiting around and visiting towns is helping the academy," Justan said.

"At least not down here. We are far too far away from Reneul for any local information to make a difference."

It was the same discussion they had been having for the last few days, and Master Coal looked even more tired than before. Fist knew that the wizard could have cut Justan off or dismissed his concerns out of hand, but he was impressed by Coal's restraint. The wizard listened patiently and waited for Justan to finish before replying.

"The city of Filgren is only a few miles east of here. It isn't a large city, but it is one of the major crossing points of the Wide River. Most people leaving Dremaldria for Razbeck will cross there. It is a perfect spot to gather information on the current goings on in Dremald."

"Alright, fine. We gather information. And then what?" Justan asked. "Once we leave Filgren are we traveling to the academy?"

Coal sighed. "I will send the information to Willum so that he can tell Tad the Cunning. We will then see what Tad thinks our best course will be."

Justan frowned. "So we spend tomorrow at Filgren. Tomorrow night you speak with Willum. Then we wait around another day so you can speak with Willum again that night and see what Tad says?"

"That is the current plan, yes," the wizard replied.

"Argh! That's just more delaying!" Justan said. "What if something were to happen? What if Ewzad Vriil were to give the order for the army to attack? There is no way we could get there in time to help."

"Tad is convinced that the army will not attack for some time." Coal reminded him. "Ewzad Vriil is waiting for something. He has to know that the academy is well prepared. With their current forces, even a sustained attack would not overcome the walls."

"Goblins and orcs might not break the academy, but Ewzad has more than that!" Justan said. "Surely you haven't forgotten what he made Kenn into? How many bandhams would it take to bring the academy down? Three? Four?"

Fist shivered. All he knew of the academy came from Justan's thoughts and memories, but the thought of four of those creatures flying down into the packed mass of people behind those walls was horrible. Even the best soldiers in the world wouldn't stand a chance.

Coal shook his head. "I doubt that is possible. The way the Rings of Stardeon work, he would have to have bandham bodies to work with to make more monstrosities like Kenn. Bandhams are too rare a creature for that."

"We wouldn't have thought it possible the first time it happened to us either," Justan argued. "The truth is we don't know about all the beasts Ewzad Vriil has created. Deathclaw showed me some of the creatures he fought in the dungeons and if he hadn't been there to fight them, we may not have made it out alive."

"You are right," Coal said. "We don't know. Which is why we are scouting out the situation before we barge in."

Fist could tell that Justan was having difficulty restraining himself. "Then what if we split our forces? I could take my bonded and go now and while we make things harder for Ewzad's army, you could continue to gather information. Our small group could attack their supply lines, assassinate their leaders-."

"No!" Coal snapped, and this was the first time Fist had seen anger in the wizard's eyes. All other talk in the camp ceased as everyone's attention focused on the wizard. "The Mage School put you under my care and until either the High Council or Valtrek say otherwise, you must stay with me."

Justan was startled by the intensity of Coal's reaction, but Fist felt his surprise turn to defiance. Justan's eyes narrowed. "And if I were to leave anyway?"

"I am your master. If you ran off against my will, you would be in breach of contract," Coal said, his expression unchanged. "You promised the school two years. You have just over eight months left."

"I understand that, and I would return as soon as the siege was over," Justan said.

"It wouldn't matter to the council. A contract breaker is rarely given a second chance. Do you know what happens when student's breach contract?"

"Yes," Justan said, looking down. Fist felt a hint of fear come from him. "They hunt down contract breakers and quell them . . . but could they do that to me? Could they take my bonded away?"

Coal shook his head. "I doubt it. Most of the wizards don't even know spirit magic exists, much less how to take it away. They could take away your elemental magic, however. You would lose the ability to heal your bonded or protect them from spells."

Justan swallowed. "But they wouldn't know unless you told them. With my family in danger, would you do that to me?"

"It would be my duty," Coal said, his stern gaze unforgiving. "Not that it matters. If you were to run off now, you would most likely die anyway, you and your bonded versus thirty thousand goblinoids. Still, if you did survive, the Mage School would hunt you down."

"Justan," Fist said. "Maybe-."

"Not now, Fist." Justan took a deep breath and tried to push his anger down. "Look, Master Coal, I know that you aren't doing this out of fear, but-."

"I am very much doing this out of fear," Coal said. "Not fear for myself. Fear for you. Fear for Willum. Fear for all of us. If we do not act smartly, we will simply die fighting that large army and that will not help the people in the academy."

Justan's eyes were closed and his hands clenched at his sides. "I am sorry, Master, but what we are doing isn't enough."

"It will have to be, at least for now." Coal said with finality. "And that is all I will say on the matter tonight. It is time I spoke with Willum and then I really do need to sleep. I need to have my wits about me when we go into Filgren tomorrow."

Justan nodded and sat by the fire sullenly, unwilling to talk to anyone on the subject. Even Lenny was rebuffed with a firm shake of the head. When the meat had finished cooking, they ate, but even though his mouth burned from Lenny's spices,

Fist didn't taste anything. He was too concerned about Justan. Justan's bitter feelings sat like coals burning in the back of his mind.

They bedded down for the night shortly thereafter and Fist eagerly fluffed up his pillow. He had left the leather cover on as Miss Becca had commanded even though it took some of the soft squishiness out of the pillow, but he could still smell the faint scent of the honstule blossoms it was stuffed with. The smell brought back memories of his brief time at Coal's Keep and the home he had made there. Thinking of the place made him feel both sad and happy at the same time.

"You are missing the farm," Justan said from his bedroll a few feet away.

"Yes. It was a nice home for me," Fist said. "Do you not miss it too? Just a little?"

Justan thought for a moment. "It was a good place, but I don't have room in me to miss it right now. What I miss is the surety of knowing what I'm doing. I miss having some sort of control over my life." *And I don't like being threatened.*

He would not really do it, Fist sent in what he hoped was a comforting manner. *Master Coal would not tell on you. He is too kind and he is our friend.*

Probably not, Justan agreed, though his feelings still said he was uneasy about the wizard's threat. *But I hope I don't have to risk it.*

If you decide to leave, I will follow. All of us will, Fist sent. He believed in Justan, Gwyrtha adored him, and Deathclaw would much rather be fighting the wizard anyway. *Still, I hope that you will wait until you have to.*

I will, Fist. And I probably need to go and apologize to Master Coal in the morning, but I hate this waiting. I feel paralyzed.

It can be hard when you are not the one in charge-, Fist began, but Justan cut him off.

"No, it's not that. It's just . . ." *My family is in danger and . . . I am just tired of doing nothing!* Justan sent. It was the same thing he had been saying, but Fist knew there was more to it than that.

Maybe the reason you feel like you are doing nothing is because you are doing nothing, Fist replied, finally saying what he had been feeling for the last few days. *Since Qyxal died, you have not studied with Master Coal. You have not trained with your swords or bow. You have not even exercised. You just sit on Gwyrtha and feel bad all day, and when you feel bad the rest of us feel bad. I yelled at Squirrel earlier today.*

Justan's body tensed and Fist felt a twinge of anger, followed by realization coming through the bond. After a few moments, Justan took a deep breath and those feelings settled down to acceptance.

"You are right, Fist," Justan said aloud. "Thank you and . . . I'm sorry. I wasn't thinking about how my moods were affecting the rest of you. Please tell Squirrel I am sorry too."

Fist nodded, content that he had delivered his message, and closed his eyes, inhaling the soft scent of honstule blossoms. Squirrel soon joined him, crawling under Fist's shirt and curling up in a ball on his broad hairy chest as they both drifted to sleep.

Justan did not find sleep so easy.

Chapter Two

The man burst into a million pieces. The queen's small audience chamber was splattered and the royal guards standing at either side of the unfortunate messenger fell to the ground in shock. Arcon and Hamford who stood next to the throne were pelted with gore, but neither one flinched. Arcon's face dripped red but his expression was as void of feeling as usual. Hamford if anything, just slumped a little further, still radiating sorrow after hearing of his brother's demise a few days prior. Queen Elise, who had been sitting on the throne behind Ewzad was the only one untouched.

"My tapestry!" She ran over to the wall and began picking bits of messenger off the priceless family heirloom. She frowned and took a step back, then gave Ewzad a reproachful look. "Blood stains are so hard to get out."

The wizard didn't notice her displeasure. He still stared at the spot where the messenger once stood.

"Insolence!" Ewzad spat, his outstretched finger still writhing madly. He threw the letter he had been reading to the sodden floor and stomped on it repeatedly. "I will not stand for it. No-no-no!"

Elise sighed. It was hard to stay mad at him. Ewzad was still furious over the death of his beloved servant Kenn. Or was it his bandham . . . or Kenn the Bandham, she wasn't sure. Ewzad alternated whatever he called the thing that had died. But what he called it didn't matter. He was angry.

She had known it would only be a matter of time before someone would say the wrong thing and take the brunt of his fury. This was why she had been taking audience in her personal audience chamber instead of the throne room. If he had destroyed a man in front of the nobles, there would have been a much bigger mess to clean up. This way at least, the damage was contained. The royal guards had taken an oath and wouldn't talk and the servants that would clean up afterwards were loyal to her. They had cleaned worse messes in the last few weeks. She just hoped Ewzad had gotten this behavior out of his system for now.

"Ewzad, darling! You are a mess!" Elise said and rushed to his side. She plucked at his blood-soaked shirt with distaste. "Take care of this, would you?"

Ewzad turned on her with a sneer, then blinked as if noticing her standing there for the first time. He looked down at his clothes. He giggled and his familiar radiant smile reappeared. "Yes-yes, oh my, what a mess." Ewzad waved a finger and the blood and gore simply fell off of him, leaving his garments with their black and golden thread sparkling. "Is that better, my dear Elise?"

"Beautiful," she said and leaned forward on her tiptoes to kiss his cheek. Ewzad was so sweet. Sweet and handsome. She breathed in deep, taking in his scent. His smell was so clean and manly . . . It was intoxicating.

Ewzad's face twisted again. "So you say, horrible witch, but I can still do as I please, yes!"

Elise drew back, her eyes widening briefly, but she realized he wasn't speaking to her. It was that dreadful woman that ran their armies. She was talking to Ewzad's mind through that hideous eye the Dark Prophet had placed in his arm. The witch was always interrupting, always arguing. Elise knew that she was useful, but part of her wished Ewzad would just crush the woman. Another, far smaller part of her was screaming in terror, but she had learned to ignore it. To listen to that part would mean going completely insane and who would raise the heir then?

"What did the message say, dearest Ewzad?" she asked, pointing to the torn and bloody parchment under his foot.

"The fools want you to send the Dremald army to help break the siege at the Battle Academy." Ewzad snorted. "As if I, the Lord Protector, would allow such nonsense, no. I've already told them they belong here, protecting you, sweet queen. Yes-yes they do."

"Which fools, dear?" she asked.

"Oh, the noblest of families of course. Yes, the heads of Pross, Roma, and Tensow. Even Earl Preen signed this filth." He stomped on the torn and bloodied letter once more and it burst into flames. "I so want to kill them."

"I know you do, dear," Elise said with a pouting lip and caressed his angular jaw, but inside she was concerned. Those were four of the most powerful houses in Dremaldria. "But don't worry about the nobles. They will not act without my approval."

Not yet, were the words she did not say. Her grasp on Dremald was more tenuous than Ewzad cared to know. All of the noble houses chafed under Ewzad's commands. Despite the flowery praise they spouted when in his presence, none of them respected him. None of them forgot his past behavior.

"The commoners are getting more and more vocal in support of the academy, that's all," she said. "This message was just an empty gesture meant to placate the crowds."

"Oh, my. Placate the crowds? No, what they are doing is making me look bad. That's what they're doing!" Ewzad said. Then he snarled and Elise knew that the moonrat woman was speaking to him again. He pulled back his sleeve and glared at the shriveled moonrat eye embedded in the inside of his forearm. "Yes-yes, I know of the importance of your plans, you nasty harlot! And, no. NO! I refuse to speak to you further! The Dark Voice may not let me remove your toy, but I don't have to listen to it. Arcon!"

"Yes, Lord Protector Vriil," the young mage said, taking a step forward. He hadn't bothered to wipe the blood from his face.

"You tell me what she wants, yes? I refuse to speak with her any longer!"

Ewzad's fingers writhed and his arms swayed snake-like. The vein on the side of his temple was bulging again. These things only happened when he was losing control and Elise knew that this meant trouble for Arcon. Ewzad didn't trust the man and he was likely hoping for an excuse to kill the moonrat woman's pet. From Arcon's reaction, she was sure that he understood the danger.

Arcon nodded and licked his lips before speaking. "My mistress . . . humbly requests that you turn your attentions to the war at hand." His face twitched slightly and sweat began to bead under the drying blood on his forehead. Elise could see that the moonrat woman was hurting him. She wouldn't like to be referred to as humble. "She fears that these local distractions will delay your sending the help her army needs."

"Oh, she does, does she? Ask her this, will you? Has she found out who destroyed my sweet Bandham Kenn? Hmm? Ask her!"

Arcon swallowed. "She . . . she is very sorry it has taken so long, but she has no children in the area you indicated . . . and has been v-very focused on the siege."

"It was the demon, Master," Hamford said from his post by the throne. "He killed Kenn, I know it."

"No-no, Hamford. Even your sweet demon could not have destroyed Kenn and my orc-spitter and my whip-beast! No-no, someone else did it."

"That is true, My Lord," Arcon said. "A-as I was saying, my mistress has heard some news regarding this from her spy within the academy."

"Oh?" Ewzad's brow rose with interest. "Do tell me. Do tell."

"Sh-she . . ." Arcon was still trying to talk but no sound was coming out. A trickle of blood fell from his right nostril.

"She doesn't wish you to tell, yes? I can destroy you, you know," Ewzad's face turned to a slight grin. He giggled. "Or better yet, I could twist your body and transform you into my new chair. Yes-yes, I would like that. My Arcon throne. Would the witch like that?"

"That sh-should not be necessary my Lord. She was merely taking the time to tell me the tale." A capillary burst in Arcon's eye as the statement left his lips and Elise felt sorry for the man. Both of them were furious at him now. No matter what he did at this point, it was not going to turn out well for him. "Her source inside the academy has heard that a named wizard called M-Master Coal and another man called Sir Edge, came upon your servant and . . . m-murdered him, sir. Th-they are on their way to the academy now."

"Edge? Hmm, that sounds familiar, yes," Ewzad said thoughtfully.

"My mistress' spy says that the man claims to be one of the prisoners that survived the . . . battle in your castle, My Lord."

"Oh-oh! That Sir Edge? The fake that claimed to be named warrior and wizard? How delightful." Ewzad's eyes grew angry and his grin turned fierce. "Perhaps I should go destroy them myself. Yes. Yes, I would like that!"

Arcon gasped and doubled over. "L-Lord Protector, sir. I-I . . . my mistress suggests that it would not be . . . preferable for you to tend to such a thing personally."

Arcon looked close to passing out. Elise was impressed. It was obvious that he was heavily editing his mistress' words and she was punishing him, but he continued to do so wisely, knowing that Ewzad was the bigger threat. She decided to keep an eye on the mage. If he survived this ordeal, he could be useful.

Ewzad raised one swaying arm. "She does, does she?"

Arcon's nose was now bleeding from both nostrils profusely. "Sh-she suggests that since you can no longer c-create a portal to the place, the journey would take too much time. Now is a c-crucial time for your army!"

Ewzad's face twisted and he made a squirming fist with one hand. "Oh? The more your horrible mistress speaks, the more I want to go myself!"

Elise winced. Since the Rings of Stardeon had fused to his body, he no longer had the raw power needed to create portals from place to place as he once had. It was a sore subject and he complained about it every time they had to take a carriage ride.

"Darling," Elise offered, running one hand across his

shoulders soothingly. "I don't want you to leave me now. I can't handle all these nobles by myself."

Her statement wasn't quite true. She had manipulated nobles all her life. It would be much easier to handle them without Ewzad's constant presence riling them up. However, she couldn't bear the thought of him being away from her that long and besides, if he left now, the populace would undoubtedly start believing the rumors that he was involved with the army besieging the academy.

Ewzad lowered his arm and gave her a pouting glance. "I suppose you are right, dear Elise. I couldn't leave you now, could I?"

"Send me!" Hamford said, stepping forward, his eyes wide and wild. "Let me go and kill them and avenge my brother. I-I'll take some of those weapons you made and maybe even one of your beasts and I'll . . . I'll do it for you, Master!"

Ewzad snickered. "You? You, Hamford? I think not." The big man slumped. "I have someone much better to send. Yes-yes I do."

"One more thing . . ." Arcon gasped, bent over, blood flowing from his nose and ears. "Y-you stu-stupid . . ."

"What? What is it, you fool?" Ewzad snapped.

"Sh-she . . . Just kill me!" Arcon fell to his knees and looked up to Ewzad pleading. "Kill me, you worm-fisted freak!"

Elise gasped, one hand to her open mouth. Hamford's eyes widened. Both looked at Ewzad and waited for Arcon to meet the same fate as the messenger.

"Worm fisted . . .?" Laughter erupted from Ewzad's lips. "Do you hear that, witch? Oh, how droll! Sweet Arcon! You must be just as eager to be rid of her as I am!"

"Do it!" Arcon growled.

Ewzad's smile faded. "No. I think not. No-no. I think that your mistress' punishments will be far more gratifying than anything I could do to you. I will leave you to them. Come-come Elise."

Elise walked forward and placed one hand on Arcon's head. She bent and whispered something quietly in his ear, then gave the mage a sad smile before rushing to Ewzad's side. He linked one snakelike arm through hers and strode out of the audience hall through the back of the room.

Once they were out of earshot he shot her a glance and crooned, "My-my, dear Elise. That was a touching gesture, wasn't it? What exactly did you say to the boy, hmm?"

Elise smiled at him. "Why darling, aren't I allowed my own little intrigues?"

"Intrigues?" Ewzad giggled, then his face grew serious. "Why no."

"You're no fun," She pouted. "I merely told him that I was quite impressed with his bravery and that if he should ever be free of his mistress, I would happily have him on my staff."

"Him? Brave?" Ewzad giggled again. "Well I suppose he was, wasn't he? Yes, sweet-sweet Elise, your insight is impeccable as always. Still I do sometimes wonder what you are planning with these little whispers of yours."

He was playing closer attention to her moves than she thought. Elise quickly changed the subject. "Ewzad, darling, where are we going?"

"You will love this, dear Elise. Yes, I think you will. I am taking you to my sanctuary."

Elise beamed. She had been begging for him to take her to his sanctuary for weeks. He had been spending so much time away from her down there that she was burning to know what he was up to. "Oh, Ewzad, you spoil me. Thank you!"

"I can keep nothing from you, dear Queen." Ewzad's eyes were sparkling and she was glad that the death of the messenger and Arcon's punishment had put him in a good mood. "There is no need for you to stay away from my creations any longer. They are all well behaved."

To her surprise, Ewzad led her to the door to her own chambers. Once inside, he walked to a place in the far corner of the room next to her favorite wardrobe. He reached out a hand and with a curl of one finger, a section of the wall swung inward revealing a narrow passageway beyond.

"Here? A passage in my own room?" The thought sent

chills through her. All her life she had been afraid that someone was in her room while she was gone or standing by her bed at night. What if it were true? "Seal it up, Ewzad. I want this passage destroyed."

Ewzad saw the fear in her eyes. "Oh my, don't be troubled, dear Elise. The passage was old and dusty when I discovered it years ago. No one knows of it but me."

"I still don't like an entrance I cannot lock. Please, my love?"

He patted her arm and kissed her cheek. "I have it warded, my dear. Yes-yes, if anyone but I were to try to enter this passage, they would suffer the same fate as that messenger. Do you trust me, love?"

The small part inside of her that had been screaming earlier was sobbing and pleading now, but she shoved it down a deep dark hole and locked it away. "Of course, dear Ewzad."

"Good-good, now follow along." He led her into the dark narrow passage. .

The way was so tight that the walls slid along his shoulders as they walked and there were sections where they had to hunch over to avoid cracking their heads on the ceiling. They passed several alcoves that Elise could only see because small beams of light pierced the darkness from peepholes in the walls.

"Yes, I learned so much in these passages, dear Elise. Listening in on council meetings, hearing the deepest secrets of the nobles. This, yes, this is where I learned the secrets we used for the games we played as children."

Elise remembered those days well, Ewzad was her closest friend and confidant then. While others would fawn over her and bore her with crocheting and music and proper etiquette, Ewzad had more fun games to play. Games of intrigue. Together they disrupted the plans of nobles and household servants alike. They would steal items and plant evidence. Make an innocent remark or two. Matrons were fired, nobles stripped of rank, and none were the wiser. Her father though, he suspected something. Perhaps that was why he disliked Ewzad so.

"Why didn't you show me these passages back then?"

she complained.

"Why I had to have some secrets of my own, didn't I? Yes, I had to be mysterious for you, didn't I dear?"

He led her to a small alcove and they descended a ladder that must have gone on for several floors. They were deep under the castle when they finally left the ladder and he opened another door into a corridor lit with glowing orbs.

"Yes! We are almost there, Elise. I am so excited to show you! Come-come." He clasped her hand and pulled her down the corridor with him, taking swift strides.

Ewzad's fingers squirmed in her hand as they walked. Elise didn't find the squirming repulsive. Not anymore. She had chosen to see them as one of his adorable little quirks. Nowadays his fingers only misbehaved when he was excited or angry or casting a spell. The fact that they squirmed now told her how excited he was to show her this place and that pleased her greatly.

The corridor ended at a thick iron door that was locked shut in several places. Ewzad paused a moment once he had opened the locks. "Now, my dear, please stay behind me as we enter. There is no need to fear, no. But I must make some proper introductions first, yes? You remember my dear Talon? Yes, well I have made some more changes since the last time you saw her. Oh, she is so near perfection!"

She nodded with a hesitant smile, but inside her heart began pumping faster. She remembered Ewzad's pet all too well. The way it looked at her, she could tell that it was jealous. It wanted to hurt her.

He pushed the door inward and Elise gagged and turned away. An awful stench poured out of the open doorway. It smelled of decay and feces and something hot and musky. She felt her stomach lurch, but Ewzad placed a writhing hand on her lower back and a warming sensation passed through her body. Her nausea died down and the horrible smell went away. It was fine. The room beyond smelled as clean as any other in the castle.

"My-my, is that better my dear? Now follow me, yes?

Stay close now. This used to be one of your ancestors' private dungeon, but someone sealed it away. What a waste, don't you think?"

They entered a long hallway with corridors branching off to the right and left every twenty feet or so. Each long corridor was lined with iron doors that could only be cells. There were hundreds of them and she could hear sounds of movement within; Shuffling and slithering, soft moans and hissing. She wondered how many of the cells were already occupied by Ewzad's creations.

"Ah, you see my dear Elise? When the Dark Voice first told me to turn the power of the rings inward, I was afraid because I knew that their power would be lessened. And it was, oh yes. Some of the things I used to be able to do with ease are now beyond my grasp. But then the Dark Voice gave me knowledge." He placed one finger against his temple. "Yes, now the power of the rings is contained within me but I know how to use it. I can do so many marvelous things and when my creations are finally unleashed, the world will tremble. Exciting, yes?"

"Oh yes, my love," Elise said, clutching his arm. She was so proud of him. When he talked like that, he sounded like a king; the kind of king that could conquer all the known lands. "Please show me."

"I will! I will. Come. I am sure she is just around the corner. Look!"

The corridor opened into a large round room full of tables of varying sizes, some of which had clamps and straps to hold a creature down and many were covered with metal instruments whose purpose Elise could not discern. All of the tables were empty except for one against the far wall on which Ewzad's Talon was curled. She raised her head to look at them as they entered the room.

Talon's head was proportioned like a humanoid, though she had flat drums for ears and her nose was just two slits. However, Ewzad's new modifications had given her large eyes more like that of a cat than a lizard and she now had a set of full pouting lips that pulled back when she smiled at them to reveal a mouth full of curved and sharpened teeth; the teeth of a dragon.

50

"You let her run free?" Elise said, aghast.

"Yes, of course. She is so very obedient. Yes-yes she is. Watch," Ewzad gave her a reassuring smile and crooned, "Oh Talon, my sweet! Come see me!"

As Talon rose, Elise saw some of the other changes he had made. Talon still had the same long slender tail with its cruel barb. She still had a set of long curved claws on her feet, and her hands were still tipped in black talons. But where in the past, she had a vaguely feminine shape, she now looked like a woman. From knee to neck to elbow, she was a lithe, perfectly-figured woman that might as well have been merely wearing a skin-tight scaled suit. That made her all the more terrifying to Elise because Talon walked towards Ewzad with a sultry sway to her hips.

He opened his arms. "Dear Talon, have you missed me, my sweet?"

The raptoid slid into his arms and cooed, rubbing her head against his and licking his ear with a quite human looking tongue. Ewzad giggled and she rubbed her body up against him in a way that made Elise's blood boil. Talon gurgled and ran her long-fingered hands down his back.

"Y-you stop her!" Elise said, stomping her foot. "Stop her this instant, Ewzad!"

He blinked and looked at her with one eyebrow raised in warning. Then his eyes softened and his smile returned. "Don't mind her, dear Elise. She is just being playful. Aren't you, my sweet?" Talon cocked her head at Elise and snapped her pointed teeth before making kissing sounds with her new lips. "Yes, you see? She is playing nice. Aren't you? Yes-yes you are."

Ewzad gently pried Talon off of him, his arms contorting snake-like in order to do so. He stepped back. "Now go say hello to your queen, will you?"

Talon glided towards Elise and somehow her claws made no sound on the floor. She drew near and gave Elise a deep bow. Then Talon paused as if in surprise and cocked her head, sniffing and blinking. She leaned in close and Elise trembled as Talon sniffed along her shoulder and touched her neck briefly with a dart of her tongue. Then she crouched and pressed the side of her head against Elise's belly briefly before chirping and taking a step back.

She knows, Elise thought.

Ewzad called out, "Come here, dear Talon. Come, I have a mission for you. I think you will like it. Yes-yes, I do. Would you like to leave this place for a while?"

She hissed and clapped her awful hands together with glee. "Yess."

Elise's breath caught in her throat. It was the first time she had heard it speak. The sound of the creature's voice was guttural and unnatural.

"Very good, my Talon. Yes! You are learning, aren't you?" Ewzad giggled. "Now I am sending you far-far away and though you know I trust you. Yes, you know I do. I must give you a gift."

He pulled something from his pocket, grasped Talon's hand, and lifted her arm. Then Ewzad pushed something into her skin. She hissed in pain and when he stopped, a small shriveled orb bulged from the inside of her forearm like an unblinking eye. Talon's lips drew back in dismay.

"Oh! My-my. Don't you like my gift?" He lifted his arm and pulled the sleeve back to reveal his own orb. "See, dear Talon? Now we are alike. Yes-yes, I am so sorry about this, but you are a member of my army now and I must ask you to listen to my commander, dear. She will guide you towards your goal. You see, you are to find those who destroyed my dear Bandham, yes? And when you do? Kill them."

Chapter Three

Jhonate watched the goblinoid supply caravan slowly amble down the mountain path towards her position. She counted nearly forty goblinoids, but they were of no concern. Most of them looked to be new recruits from the way they were still dressed in furs and carried only crude weapons.

Goblinoid veterans usually had armor and weapons looted from their conquests of the mountain villages. This didn't mean that the recruits were new to fighting. Goblinoids were always making war with each other. However, this did tell her that they were not used to fighting humans.

Jhonate placed an iron ball in the cup of her sling, swelled the end of her staff around the end of the string, and held tightly to it, waiting for the signal to strike. Her heart beat with excitement and a slight smile lifted the edges of her lips. For weeks she had been relegated to watching over Mage Vannya. Faldon had resisted her complaints at being left out of the fighting, but finally with Wizard Locksher's encouraging, Faldon had relented. Jhonate had even been given the honor of starting off the ambush. She just had to choose her target.

One concern was two heavily armed orcs that were riding mountain spiders. That was something she hadn't seen before. The orcs carried long barbed spears and the spiders were enormous hairy things that dripped something, either saliva or poison, from their fangs. A creature like that should have been ungainly, but these mounts moved with nimble precision, one of them leading the caravan, the other following up the rear. The other goblinoids shied away from the spiders jabbering in terror any time they came near. Perhaps part of their purpose was to discourage desertion.

Her other concern was the two supply wagons near the front of the caravan that were pulled by great ugly giants. The first wagon was covered with canvas and over laden with supplies nearly spilling out the back. The second wagon was fully boxed in, roofed with wooden walls and a door that was locked from the outside. Something important had to be inside, but the thing that caught Jhonate's eye right away was the moonrat riding on top of the wagon.

Moonrats were nocturnal creatures and usually stayed to the shadows, their oversized eyes sensitive to the sunlight. The majority of moonrats had yellow eyes, but this one's unblinking green orbs told Jhonate that it was here to control something. The mother of the moonrats used her green-eyed children to keep the trolls and mountain cats and many of the other wilder and less intelligent parts of the army in line.

At first, she thought that the moonrat was there to control the rock spiders, but soon dismissed the idea. The spiders were being guided by the orcs riding them. They wandered too far from the moonrat for it to keep them under control. She decided instead that it was there to control the huge giant that pulled the boxed wagon it rode upon. Its head was dented in on one side and it was heavily scarred. The giant moved well, but such a ruined beast would be vicious and stupid, likely unable to follow instructions. With a grim nod, she knew which target she would strike first. She whispered instructions to her archers and they readied their bows, waiting for her signal to take aim.

Faldon's forces were spread out along either side of the trail, all of them trained veterans of battle. Jhonate and her five marksmen hid behind boulders on one side, while Faldon and Jobar were perched in the trees at the back of the trail with three more archers ready to take out any goblinoids that tried to flee. The remainder of their group consisted of Tamboor and his howlers, who waited in the trees on the far side of the trail ready to assault the core of the goblinoid forces.

Tamboor's Howlers were comprised of the remnants of the academy's old Berserker Guild that had retired in the mountain villages. The Berserker Guild had been broken up several years ago when the academy council realized that their kind were no longer sought after by the neighboring kingdoms. Tamboor had been the last Berserker Guildmaster and as news of the siege spread, his old comrades began joining Faldon's army, eager to serve with their old guildmaster again.

Jhonate felt the surface of the message stone change in her hand and looked down. Scrawled on the surface was a word. "*Nom*". She frowned until she realized it was supposed to say, "Now". Somehow Faldon had managed to make his w look like an m. She really was going to have to talk to him about his handwriting.

Jhonate crouched and whirred the end of her staff, building up speed and her archers pulled back their bows. She stood and swung forward, willing her staff to release one end of the string, sending the ball hurtling toward her target.

The iron ball caved in the head of the moonrat with a sharp crack, knocking both green eyes from their sockets. As her strike landed, her marksmen fired, their arrows taking out the orcs driving the wagons, then shifted their attention to the spider riders. At this signal, Tamboor's Howlers burst from their concealment in the rocks and waded into the startled goblinoid recruits, swinging their weapons and screaming with battle-fueled fury.

The goblinoid forces were in disarray from the beginning. The ferocity of the berserker attack scattered the ranks and they were mowed down relentlessly. Tamboor was the only berserker not screaming. He mowed through them like a silent demon, his face twisted in rage, dancing through the goblinoids, shearing off limbs and heads with great swipes of his sword, Meredith.

The giants heard the sounds of battle and stopped pulling the wagons. They stood in surprise, staring at the dead orc drivers and the attackers and blinked stupidly. Then the scarred one bent and picked up a heavy rock.

"Keep firing! Take care not to hit our men. Focus on the first giant and the spider riders!" Jhonate commanded and as her marksmen obeyed, she climbed over the boulder in front of her and ran towards the wagons, willing the end of her staff to flatten into a blade.

The giant with the dented head had its back to her and didn't see her coming. It had one arm cocked back ready to throw the large rock when she struck. The razor thin edge of her staff cut through the back of the giant's right leg like butter, severing its hamstring.

As it cried out and fell to one knee, she twirled and reformed the tip of her staff to a spear-like point. She put all her weight into her thrust and pierced the giant's ribs, sinking in a full foot before she pulled it back out again. The giant gurgled, turned and swung its arm around, the rock still clenched in its fist.

Jhonate ducked the blow and slashed upward with her staff at an angle, slicing deeply into the beast's armpit. With her hands now gripping the center of her staff, she turned both ends into blades and whirled, slashing back and forth, carving the giant's fleshy back.

It roared and tried to turn to face her, but she moved, staying behind it, striking its shoulders and the back of its neck. It swung back at her again and again, but every movement now hurt the beast and its strikes were hesitant and more easily evaded. She turned the tip to a spear-point again and jabbed, piercing a kidney. The giant's roars turned to whimpers. It arched its back and fell to the side, reaching out one pleading hand.

There was only one mercy she could give it. Jhonate flattened the edge of her staff like one long blade and jumped over its extended arm, swinging down in a mighty two handed chop to its neck. The giant's dented head rolled from its shoulders.

A roar erupted from behind her. Jhonate turned just in time to avoid the frenzied swing of the second giant. The beast was carrying a large wooden spoked wheel that it had torn from the first wagon. This giant wasn't as big as the other one, but she wasn't catching this one unawares. Its side and back had been peppered by the arrows of her marksmen, but the beast seemed unaffected. Its eyes were full of rage and sadness and Jhonate wondered if she had just killed its friend.

She was forced to dive to the ground to dodge its next

swing. Jhonate rolled to her feet. It was not going to be easy to get in close to this one. Its reach was extended too much by that wagon wheel.

"Marksmen!" she cried. Only one arrow responded, joining several others already sticking out of the giant's shoulder. The giant barely winced. She chanced a glance to the archers' position and saw one of the spiders climbing amidst their boulders, its orc rider slashing about with a long spear. To her relief, she saw that Faldon and Jobar had broken the concealment of their position and were headed their way.

The giant swung again. Jhonate jumped back and almost tripped over the leg of its dead companion. Her feet slid, the ground slick with giant blood, and she realized that she needed a new strategy. The giant was not allowing her to get in close enough to work her staff and she definitely didn't have time to string up her sling. She had to find a way to at least distract it long enough to get in close. Her hand flew to the pouch hanging at her neck.

She opened the end of the pouch and waited until its next swing. As the wheel narrowly missed her, she threw. The open pouch hit the giant in the nose, sending a plume of finely ground pepper right into its open eyes. The pepper was intended for fighting trolls, but for this use it was perfect.

The giant roared, clawing at its burning eyes and Jhonate rushed in. One spear-like thrust pierced a lung, a wide slash opened its belly, and it had more to worry about than its eyes. As it clutched at its stomach, trying to keep its insides in, she slashed a final time. The tip of her Jharro staff opened its throat and the beast gurgled and fell.

The sounds of fighting were still fierce all around. She looked to see if her marksmen still needed help, but the spider rider was nowhere to be seen and arrows were once again flying from their position. Jhonate's gaze returned to the boxed wagon and the corpse of the moonrat on top of it. Why had the moonrat been there? She no longer thought the giant had been the reason. It had seemed coherent enough to obey orders without control.

As if in answer to her thoughts, there was a bang from within the box and the wagon swayed. Was there someone trapped inside? Maybe a prisoner? She took a couple steps towards it and a series of loud knocks rang out getting louder and louder.

The wagon rocked back and forth, the internal blows continuing until one wall cracked and bulged outward. With a hail of splinters, the wagon's occupant burst free and Jhonate saw the reason for the green-eyed moonrat. Green slime dripped from the creature's bulky body. It sniffed the air for a moment, then reared back and roared, exposing a cavernous mouth full of rows of sharp crooked teeth.

It was a troll, but a breed of troll Jhonate had never seen before. Most trolls were tall and lanky. This one was large and wide, not as big as the ungainly giants had been, but maybe seven foot, and with thickly muscled arms and nasty claws. It turned to look at her.

Jhonate gripped her staff, ready to battle the beast, when she noticed its gaze move past her. She glanced back to see one of the giant spiders stepping over the corpse of the second giant and heading towards her. It was riderless, riddled with arrows and missing half of one leg, but still very formidable. She was sandwiched between the two monsters. The troll charged, roaring and mad with hunger.

Jhonate crouched, her heart thundering in her chest and waited for the right moment. When both beasts were almost on her, she dove forward and rolled, turning and swinging her staff as she came to her feet. The end of the staff was solid as iron now and struck the running troll in the small of the back, forcing it into the spider's path.

The two creatures collided together and the troll, as stupid and mad with hunger as trolls usually were, attacked the spider, clawing and biting. The spider struck out with its fangs, plunging them into the troll's stomach, pumping poison. The troll ignored its attack and gnawed at the spider's armored back.

Jhonate grasped the center of her staff and changed both ends to blades. Knowing which was the bigger threat, she began slashing at the troll from behind, swiftly alternating blows and opening deep gashes in its back. The only way to kill a troll was to burn it or pepper its dismembered body to keep it from regenerating. Her goal at the moment was to slow it down and hope that the spider would keep it distracted long enough that she could find her pouch of pepper.

The troll was too frenzied to notice her strikes. It ripped at the spider, its powerful claws tearing deep holes in its chitinous shell. The spider bit at the troll and crawled backwards, trying to get away, but the troll hung on, gnawing until it broke through and began feasting on the spider's soft flesh.

Jhonate felt a jolt of fear hit as she realized that her attacks had been ineffective. Every opened gash began healing almost instantly. She took a step back and looked for her pouch but the spider had backed up until the two creatures were fighting over the second giant's body. The pouch was somewhere underneath.

"Troll!" she shouted, looking for help from her archers. "Fire! I need fire!" The slime that coated a troll's body was highly flammable and their main weakness. "Marksmen! I need fire arrows!"

Nothing came immediately. They hadn't seen any trolls when scouting the supply caravan so none of the archers had fire arrows prepared. The troll was still focused on the spider, but unfortunately, it had already won the fight.

The spider was convulsing, its legs curling in. The troll had climbed on top of it and its face was covered in spider-ichor as it plunged its clawed hands into the spider's abdomen and scooped handfuls into its toothy open maw.

Trolls were single minded creatures. Hunger was their only emotion and it drove them relentlessly. This made them predictable, but this particular troll was an unknown. Hopefully it would continue focusing on gorging itself until they could kill it.

Jhonate smiled in triumph as a flaming arrow arced through the air and plunged into the troll's muscular back with an audible thud. Her smile faltered when the troll's slimy skin did not erupt into flame. The arrow hissed and the flame guttered out. The troll stopped feeding and its head whipped around, sniffing, looking for its attacker. Its beady eyes latched onto Jhonate and it turned to face her.

Jhonate set her jaw as it slid off the spider and screeched at her. Two more fire arrows thunked into its back, but they were extinguished just as quickly by its thick slime. The troll didn't even flinch this time, its complete attention focused on her.

Jhonate took a step back. A troll that wasn't flammable? How was that possible? She looked into its eyes and saw that the hunger was gone. Had it been satiated by the spider? Trolls were never satiated. Then its brow furrowed and its face twisted with rage. She heard a familiar feminine voice in the far reaches of her mind.

"You have been marked for death."

The bulky troll roared, bits of spittle and spider ichor flying from its mouth, and for the first time since her childhood, Jhonate considered giving into fear and running away.

That made her angry.

Jhonate came at the beast swinging a staff made hard as iron. It leapt at her. The end of her staff caught it in the jaw and knocked it stumbling to the side. The beast was healing too quickly for slicing or piercing strikes unless she could hit a critical location. She couldn't let it regain momentum. If it grasped her with those powerful hands, she would be done for. Another blow sent it stumbling further. It tried to dig its feet in, but she kept at it relentlessly with a quick series of blows, striking the troll's hands, knees and head, looking for the right opening.

Finally she had it. She bashed one hand wide, and reversed with an upthrust blow that struck it under the chin, knocking its head back, and the beast was stunned for a mere moment. She sharpened the tip of her staff and sent it upward with all her might, driving it up through soft flesh under the troll's chin and through the roof of its mouth, piercing its brain.

She yanked her staff free and the troll fell to the ground, convulsing wildly. Jhonate shouted in triumph but she knew the victory was temporary. A troll would heal from any wound no matter how severe. Cut one into six pieces and if you didn't burn them, you would end up with six identical trolls.

She ran to the fallen giant and searched for her pouch of

pepper, but where was it? Had the giant fallen on top of it? To make matters worse, the corpse of the spider had collapsed on top of the giant's legs. Jhonate jumped over the beast and looked behind it, but the pouch was nowhere to be seen. She crouched to one knee and began searching under the edges of the giant's body. She saw movement in her peripheral vision and a chill went up her spine. The troll rose from the ground and once again she heard the eerie chuckle of the mother of the moonrat echo in her mind.

"You have been marked for death, Jhonate Bin Leeths."

The troll roared and ran for her, no visible trace of its wound remaining. This one healed far too quickly. What kind of troll was it? She shifted her stance and crouched, ready to launch an upward thrust to knock the beast back again, but the troll never reached her.

Tamboor charged from the side like a mad bull, swinging a powerful two-handed swipe of his sword. Meredith caught the troll in the shoulder, cleaved through flesh and struck bone, the force of the blow driving it to the ground. He ripped the blade free and the beast climbed back to its feet quickly. It slashed at him as he swung his sword again. His blade struck between two of the troll's fingers, splitting its hand all the way to the wrist.

The troll didn't register pain. It held the wounded arm out away from its body, leaned forward, and slashed out with its other hand. His sword still stuck in the troll's other arm, Tamboor was forced to let go of the Meredith's handle with one hand to catch its incoming wrist. He yanked the troll forward and slammed its face with a fierce headbutt.

Jhonate stood to help, but as she was about to leap over the giant's corpse, she saw something out of the corner of her eye. Hanging out from under one of the spider's legs was the drawstring to her pouch. She knocked the leg aside with her staff and scooped up the pouch. To her relief there was still some pepper remaining in the bottom. The troll wouldn't catch fire. Hopefully it wasn't immune to pepper too.

Tamboor grappled with the beast, his back on the ground. He was forced to abandon his sword. His blade had bound in the troll's wrist bone and its flesh had begun healing around it.

Tamboor gripped its right wrist with one hand, its left forearm with the other, and shoved one foot up under its chin, keeping its hideous maw away.

Jhonate darted behind the troll and slashed its back open with a two handed swing of her staff, then grabbed a handful of pepper from her pouch and rubbed it in the wound before it could knit back together. She could feel its flesh, recoil from the spice. The troll screeched and tried to pull from Tamboor's grasp, but he refused to let go. It tried to back away. Jhonate slashed its hamstrings.

The pepper was beginning to take effect. The wounds weren't closing right away. Jhonate honed the tip of her staff to a fine point and thrust at the base of the troll's skull. The tip wedged between two vertebrae. She caused the tip to swell, widening the gap between the two bones until there was a crack. The troll jerked spasmodically and Tamboor forced its head back further with his foot, using its two arms as leverage. Jhonate twisted her staff and with a pop, the troll's head hung limply.

Tamboor kicked the troll to the side and Jhonate chopped down with her staff two times, severing its head completely. She rubbed the last of her pepper into the base of its head and the stump of its neck, then kicked the still moving head aside. She wiped her hands off in the dirt and sighed with relief, knowing the beast could no longer regenerate.

Jhonate felt a hand on her shoulder. She looked back as Tamboor gave her a firm, approving nod. He grabbed his sword by the pommel and had to jerk it a few times before it tore free of the troll's spasming wrist.

It had grown oddly quiet and Jhonate realized that the battle around them had ended. Tamboor wiped off his sword and spat on the beast before heading back to help his Howlers dispatch the goblinoid wounded.

She trotted back to the boulders to check on her marksmen and found that, although two of them had been wounded by the spider rider, all five men under her charge were alive. Luckily Faldon and Jobar had killed the orc and fought the spider off.

The operation had been a success. The caravan had been

wiped out and only one of their men, one of Tamboor's Howlers, had died. But for some reason, as Jhonate found her teacher, he did not look too pleased. Faldon stood apart from the other men. He was talking to Jobar, but when he saw her approaching, he folded his arms, a stern expression on his face.

"I have come to make my report, sir," Jhonate said. "Is there something wrong?"

"Jhonate bin Leeths, why did you leave your men behind and run into battle alone?" Faldon asked.

Jhonate's eyebrows rose in surprise. "They are veteran warriors in a defendable position. I had given them precise orders. They knew what to do. I destroyed the moonrat and left to dispatch the giant I thought it was controlling before it got out of hand, sir."

"That explains it. It was the moonrat." Jobar said with a slight smile and a shake of his head. "You always have to go after the moonrats, don't you, daughter of Xedrion?"

"I do what is necessary." Jhonate narrowed her eyes at her tattooed fellow student. Indeed she had made a point of dispatching every moonrat she came across. They were the witch's children and every one she killed gave the witch some amount of pain. She could feel it.

Faldon did not agree with her assessment. "Part of the reason I put you with the archers is your skill with your sling and the fact that you could protect them if the enemy came too close. Jobar and I had to abandon our position to cover for your absence. The archers dispatched two gorcs trying to escape, but we're lucky that there weren't more. They may not have been able to stop them otherwise. If word gets to the rest of the army that we were here, we could find ourselves fighting off a much larger force."

"A moonrat died," Jhonate said. "Their mother knows that something happened here."

"But she doesn't know how many of us there are or what tactics we used," Faldon replied. "Secrecy is of the utmost importance if we are to strike fear into the goblinoids. You know this."

"I apologize, sir. I thought I was doing what was best." Jhonate said, her cheeks reddening. Faldon had never berated her publicly before. Had she truly been in error? "I left my position to dispatch the two giants and, with Tamboor the Fearless' help, killed a large troll."

Jobar laughed. "I love the way she says it so easily. Took out two giants and a troll? Maybe we should call her 'Jhonate the Giant Killer'."

The blow from her staff caught Jobar in the stomach, doubling him over.

"I have not given you permission to call me by name, Jobar da Org." she said as the muscular man wheezed.

"You know her rules, Jobar," Faldon agreed, frowning at the man. "Respect them."

Jobar scowled but nodded sullenly. He knew to refer to her only as Daughter of Xedrion, which was the proper form of address among her people. Of all the troops in the army, she had given only Faldon the Fierce and Wizard Locksher permission to call her by name. Tamboor deserved the honor as well, but as he did not speak, she had not felt it necessary to tell him.

Faldon returned his stern gaze to Jhonate. "I understand your impulse to act, but I will not look past such behavior in the future. Your first duty is to the men under your command. That is something that all my advanced students should know, and you should know better than most."

Jhonate, along with Jobar, Qenzic, and Poz were the members of Faldon's graduate class, a group of students that had signed on for two extra years of schooling under his direct command to learn leadership and guerrilla tactics.

"Yes, sir. It shall not happen again," Jhonate said. Truth be told, she had not truly thought of the archers as being under her command. She was not a true markswoman. Her sling always shot true, but it was slow to reload and her other skills were far more useful.

"See that it doesn't," Faldon said. "Now tell me about this troll you were fighting. We didn't see any trolls when we scouted the caravan."

"The troll was hidden within the boxed wagon," she explained. "It was unlike any troll I have ever seen, sir. It was wide and muscular and immune to fire."

"A troll immune to fire?" His brow furrowed with concern. "Show me."

As she led him to the beast's remains, Jhonate described the battle in detail. As they passed the corpses of the two giants and the spider, Jobar whistled in approval.

"You weren't kidding, Daughter of Xedrion. You really tore them up," he said before scowling again. "Your whole name/respect tradition really messes with everyone else's traditions. How are we supposed to give you a good warrior name? What are we supposed to call you? 'Daughter of Xedrion, Giant Killer'?"

"It broke free from the wagon there," she said, ignoring Jobar, and pointed out the body of the strange troll. "Look sir, it is still twitching." That was quite odd. When a troll's ability to regenerate was taken away by their body's reaction to the pepper, they usually died just like any other creature.

Faldon reached down and lifted the troll's head by its slimy hair. Its face twitched and its jaw opened and shut as if trying to bite him. He looked into its rolling beady eyes and said, "Jobar, wrap up that troll's body. We need to take it to Locksher."

While Jobar went to find something to wrap the body in, Jhonate climbed to the top of the wagon and retrieved her iron ball from the moonrat's head. She picked up its two green eyes and felt a twinge of anger stir from within her mind. *I blind you yet again, witch*, she thought and crushed them to jelly.

Chapter Four

Jhonate felt the location for their camp had been well chosen. The scouts had found a cluster of ancient fir trees whose upper branches had grown so closely together that their lower branches had withered and lost their needles. In a short amount of time, men with hand axes had cleared away the lower branches a good ten feet above the ground, leaving a rather open and well protected area in which to pitch their tents. The thick pine canopy above hid the light of their fires at night and protected them from the prying eyes of enemy scouts during the day.

They had left Jack's Rest a week prior, taking most of the able bodied men with them. The town was well fortified and since the goblinoid army had left the mountains to wage war on the academy, it was no longer a threat. So they left the town in the hands of the few men that wanted no part in the battle ahead.

There were several hundred men in Faldon's army now, most of them academy veterans and retirees, though there were many refugees from the villages and homesteads around that had joined their cause. The army was orderly, their tents clustered tightly together and cookfires were kept small and as smokeless as possible.

When they returned from the ambush, Faldon ordered the spoils of their victory distributed amongst the army. This mainly consisted of the contents of the supply wagon and the few enemy weapons that were in good enough condition to be of use. Their wounded were brought to the healing tent which was staffed by Vannya, a few herbwomen, and a wife of one of the academy retirees that had been a mage once herself. While these matters were attended to, Faldon, Tamboor, Jobar, and Jhonate went to the command tent to meet with Wizard Locksher.

When they opened the tent flap, a cloud of acrid smoke was released, causing all of them to hack and cough. Faldon peered into the tent with concern. "Locksher, are you okay in there?"

The wizard spent most of his time in the command tent working on various projects. He had his own tent but rarely used it but for the occasional nap. Since the command tent was much larger, he had room to spread out his instruments and conduct his experiments. Faldon put up with it, though it was difficult for Jhonate to understand why.

"Of course. Come on in. Sorry about the smoke, but it is necessary."

Despite the smoky haze, the tent was well lit by glowing orbs that floated in the corners. Locksher was in the back of the tent at a makeshift workbench. A thick set of glasses were perched on his nose and he puffed away absently on a pipe that belched purple fumes. He had laid several instruments out on the table before him and was peering at something glistening on a square of white cloth.

"So how was the ambush?" Locksher asked.

"We were successful," Faldon replied. "The caravan was destroyed and none of them got away."

"Good. Have you found any others?"

"Not yet. Poz, Qenzic, and Zambon are out scouting the mountainside," Faldon said. He peered at Locksher's workbench. "Still working on that moonrat eye?"

The night before, Locksher had begun dissecting a shriveled eye they had found in the possession of an orc captain a few days prior. Jhonate had wanted it destroyed, but the wizard had insisted on keeping it in a pouch that he had prepared with his magic. He had assured them that no sound could penetrate the material and that the spells he had used should disorient whatever signal the mother of the moonrats used to communicate.

"Yes I am and the results are fascinating," he said. He

noticed their coughing and teary eyes and reached down into the pockets of his robes. He pulled out several sets of glasses similar to his own. "Here, put these on. I prepared them just for this sort of occasion."

Jhonate put the glasses on and to her surprise, the irritation went away and she could see and breathe clearly. Before she could ask why, Locksher continued.

"Step over here and look at what I've found." He gestured to the square of white cloth and Jhonate saw that the eye had been cut into several sections. "I always wondered about these beasts, you know. Their eyes are overly large and impractical. I used to think that was because they keep mostly to the dark, but that is incorrect. Moonrats are mostly blind and rely on their sense of smell and hearing to get around. Their eyes are actually intricate receptors and transmitters of energy."

"What do you mean?" Jobar said and Jhonate could see that the man was completely lost in the wizard's large words.

"It was also hard for me to understand at first," Locksher replied. "Let me put it this way. The eyes have two purposes. They gather information and send it back to this moonrat mother and she uses them to send commands back to her army."

"We have already figured that much out," Faldon said and Jhonate noticed that he was tapping his foot impatiently. Faldon was usually a very patient man, which was part of why he was such a good teacher, but since finding out about the siege on the academy, his patience had faded. Jhonate knew he was worried about his wife.

"Yes, but we didn't know how she did it," Locksher said. His lips pursed in frustration and he added, "This would be so much easier if you were magic users. I will try to explain.

"One of the things that intrigued me about the eye was that my mage sight could find no magic emanating from it. I knew she was communicating with them, but how?" A grin lit up his face. "I discovered the answer just an hour ago."

"How does she do it?" Jhonate asked.

"Spirit magic," Locksher said triumphantly. When the only response on their faces was a vacant expression, he added,

"We wizards use elemental magic. Earth, Fire, Air, and Water. Every spell we cast is woven of those four elements. However there is another type of magic that has long been lost to us called spirit magic. We don't even teach about it at the Mage School any more. I only know about it from my research into the deepest mysteries. Some of the oldest tomes in the library mention it. Others hint at it."

"So it's old magic?" Faldon asked.

"The oldest, or so I understand. This is the magic that the prophet uses. This is the magic used by the Bowl of Souls when it names warriors and wizards. It is invisible to even mage sight."

"Then how do you know it is the way she controls her army?" Jhonate asked.

"There are two reasons, Jhonate." Locksher said. "First of all, I had eliminated every other possible option. The second reason is all around you."

Faldon and Jhonate looked at each other.

"The . . . smoke?" Jobar said.

"Brilliant deduction, Jobar." Locksher said. "Indeed, the smoke from the specially treated herb in this pipe makes spirit magic visible to regular mage sight."

"This piece of the eye . . ." He grabbed one shiny metal instrument and gently lifted one tiny clump of tissue from the white cloth. He glanced over at Jhonate and paused. One of his eyebrows rose with sudden interest. "It, uh . . . positively glows with spirit magic. It is quite remarkable, actually. Jhonate, would you care to see?"

"I, sir?" Jhonate said in surprise. "I cannot see anything."

"No, you can't. Because you are not a magic user. If you were, your powers would have manifested in some way by now. However, everyone has some small trace of magic ability." He waved her over. "Come here and I will show you."

Jhonate took a few cautious steps forward. Locksher had the expression on his face that she had come to know meant that he was fascinated by something. She wondered what this had to do with her.

"Now," Locksher reached into his pocket and pulled out a

small triangular piece of metal. "I am going to touch your forehead. When I do, look at this object and tell me what you see."

Locksher reached out with one finger and Jhonate had to force herself not to shy away. The wizard touched her between the eyes and Jhonate's vision blurred momentarily. She blinked a few times and when her vision cleared, she looked down at the triangle in his hand.

"It burns a bright red!" she exclaimed.

"Good! That is the element of fire. This is my kindler. I use it to light campfires. Avoids wasting my magic. Now look at the eye on the cloth. Do you see it?"

Jhonate's leaned over the workbench and her vision blurred a bit more, but she shook her head slightly and it came into focus. "There is some sort of white haze around that part of the eye."

"Yes! That is the spirit magic I told you about. Now look at the staff in your hand."

She looked at the staff to see a silvery haze surrounding it. The staff practically glowed. One white strand led from the staff up along her arm and disappeared into her chest. "What is this?"

"I had wondered how you were able to manipulate that staff of yours to do what it does. Now we have the answer. You are linked with it. The spirit magic connects the staff to your mind." He looked thrilled. "You must tell me more about how you came to have it."

Jhonate's eyes widened. "And what is this?" she asked, lifting the index finger of her right hand, where the ring Justan had given her glowed a dark blue.

"Oh, that ring of yours has magical properties. It is a mix of water and earth magic. If I examined it more closely I could tell you what it does."

"It's a protective charm," Faldon explained. "That ring has been in the family for a long time. Justan gave it to her."

"Amazing. What a rarity," Locksher said. He lifted her hand. "And powerful. Why there is a fine barrier covering your skin."

Jhonate stared at Faldon in shock. "You knew about this and you did not tell me?"

Faldon gave an embarrassed shrug. "Justan wanted you to have it. I didn't know if it really worked, but I was afraid that if you knew what it was supposed to do, you would refuse to wear it."

She grasped the ring and twisted it on her finger. "Then all this time . . . in all these battles . . ."

"You never have a scratch," Faldon confirmed. "Though that may just be your skill."

"No. It makes sense now." She thought back to all the times she had mended torn armor and clothing. With all the battles of the past year, she should have some scars just as everyone else had. The cool blue glow of the ring suddenly made her feel as if Justan was with her at that moment. Part of her wanted to tear the ring off. Instead, she found herself clenching her fist.

"Don't cut yourself short, Jhonate. It was skill," Locksher said. "Just because it has protected you from a few scrapes doesn't mean it would save you from a direct sword thrust. I wouldn't depend on it too much. That ring won't make you invincible."

"This mage sight. Can you teach it to me?" Jhonate asked.

"Well . . ." Locksher's brow furrowed in thought. "I could help you from time to time the way I just did. If you remember the way it felt and focus and practice enough, I believe you could learn to use it at will. I don't see why not. All cadets learn it."

"You can teach this?" Faldon asked. "Mage sight?"

"Well, to some. There are a few like Jhonate that could handle it."

"Then why have we not been teaching this at the academy all these years?" Faldon asked. "Imagine how useful it would be if some academy-trained guards and soldiers could see when an enemy carried some kind of magic!"

Locksher scratched his head. "I can't say that I know the answer to that question. Surely it should have been thought of, unless . . ."

"Unless?" Faldon prodded.

"Well, unless at some point the Mage School High Council decided that teaching such a thing to the masses would be a bad idea." He saw the glower on Faldon's face and added, "I don't know this for sure. I mean, it has never been discussed when I have been with the council. It is a supposition, but one that makes sense. We wizards enjoy a bit of anonymity from time to time. If everyone who had the slightest trace of magical ability was trained to use mage sight, they could pick out our magic. If they learned enough, they could tell what amounts of magic were used, how powerful the spell was, or even who cast it. Why every wizard has their own style, I can pick many out by the spell that was cast . . ."

Jobar was looking hopelessly lost. "Uh, are we going to talk about the troll?"

"Troll?" Locksher said, relieved to be changing the subject. "You have a question about trolls?"

Faldon's eyes narrowed, but he nodded. "Jobar, bring it in here.

As Jobar retrieved the troll's body, Jhonate told Locksher of the events earlier in the day. By the time Jobar returned, the wizard was practically hopping on his feet with excitement.

"Bring it here!"

They laid the body on the floor by his feet and unwrapped it. The troll still twitched, its head continuing its empty gnashing. Though the power of whatever Locker had done when he touched her forehead was fading, Jhonate thought she saw a faint white haze emanating from the body.

"Incredible!" Locksher said. "An inflammable troll. It's just like you said; bulky, muscular . . . it's been peppered and yet it still lives."

He bent down and sliced into its chest, cutting out a chunk of skin and muscle. The flesh writhed as he picked it up. He extended a finger and a small flame sprouted from the tip. He waved it under the troll flesh but it did not catch fire. He held it over the flame a bit longer until the edges began to blacken, then he placed it on a coal brazier that stood beside the workbench and let it sizzle.

He turned back to face them. "Amazing. Jhonate, tell me, what did you see just now as the beast was unwrapped?"

"Spirit magic," she said, looking down at it.

"Right. This troll's body is crawling with spirit magic. The only conclusion I can come to is that somehow this mother of the moonrats has modified its body in some way."

Jhonate felt a chill. "If she can do this to other trolls . . ."

"Then the goblinoid army just got harder to fight," Faldon said. He looked to the wizard. "What can we do to combat this?"

"I am testing that right now," he said, gesturing to the brazier. "We know that it still reacts to pepper. It doesn't kill it, however. It lives, but at least so far its body hasn't regenerated. If we come across more, we should be able to pepper them and dismember them and their threat will be neutralized." He turned the meat over on the coals. "If heat still kills it, we can burn their bodies as usual after the fact."

After a few moments, he took the flesh off the brazier and laid it on the bench. He cut a thin slice from it with his knife and examined it closely. As far as Jhonate could tell, the flesh was no longer moving.

"Aha, see? The flesh is cooked through and the tissues are dead. The spirit magic has left it." He looked at the bit of cooked flesh thoughtfully for a second and to Jhonate's horror, popped it into his mouth and began chewing.

Faldon looked concerned. "Locksher, I don't think that's a good idea. Trolls are filthy. You could get sick."

"Nonsense. It is thoroughly cooked through. Troll meat is perfectly safe if well cooked. It is a bit gamey maybe and cooking it is usually hard because of the way it tends to burst into flame, but there are worse meats out there. Musk toad for instance . . . disgusting."

"I can't believe you just swallowed that," Jobar said,

looking sick.

Locksher shrugged. "I experimented on troll meat as an alternative food source back in my old days at the Mage School. We had a troll that we kept imprisoned in a cage. It was a fascinating study. We would cut off a limb every once in a while to experiment on and the creature would grow it back." Noticing their looks of unease, he added. "Please understand, it was quite necessary. Consider the possible value of a regenerating meat supply. If we could find a way to get people to eat it, we could solve the world's hunger issues. Their flesh has healing properties as well."

"No matter how hungry they were, no one would eat that," Jhonate pronounced, feeling a little queasy.

"There was an old goblin by the name of Honstule that lived at the school back in those days, I tell you he was smarter than half the mages there. The whole concept was his idea. He helped me with the testing for awhile before the impracticality of keeping a herd of monsters that constantly tried to kill you finally brought us to our senses."

"So what you're saying is that fire will still kill it?" Faldon asked impatiently.

"It would seem so. Please leave the head with me and I will examine it further. " He gestured at the head, which was trying to drag itself towards them by its tongue. "But um . . . take the body with you and burn it. Lets make sure I was correct."

"Very well. We shall leave you to it. I for one need to eat. Even if I have lost my appetite." Faldon started for the tent flap, but turned back. "And Locksher, our discussion about mage sight isn't over. I want you to start thinking of a way to figure out who among my men can learn. This could be of great use in our fight against a wizard like Ewzad Vriil."

"Uh, yes," Locksher said reluctantly. "Yes, of course."

The wizard stooped and picked up the troll's head by the hair. He nodded at them and placed it on the workbench, his eyebrow raised as they followed Faldon , dragging the troll's body out of the tent.

When Jhonate arrived at her tent later that evening, a soft glow already shone from within. She ducked inside to see a glowing orb floating against the ceiling. Vannya was sitting cross-legged, looking down at a small mirror and brushing her hair for what Jhonate could only assume was the hundredth time that day. Beside her, neatly folded, was the letter that Justan had given the mage. For some reason, Vannya always liked to mention it when Jhonate was around.

"So you survived the battle without injury?" Vannya asked sweetly without taking her eyes off the mirror.

"Of course," Jhonate said. "Otherwise you would have seen me earlier."

"That's true. When the wounded were brought in and you weren't among them, I assumed you had survived without a scratch. Either that or you were dead. A terrible thought, since I am so used to having you around." She smiled and looked up at Jhonate. "But to my relief, here you are. Alive as ever."

Jhonate forced a smile on her face in return. "I am just glad that you were able to stay behind so that you could heal the warriors that were out doing the difficult work."

"Indeed. Why I did just fine without my babysitter today," Vannya said with a haughty look. "I would have you know that even without you looking over my shoulder, I wasn't raped once."

"Do you really think that is why I agreed to be assigned here with you?" Jhonate frowned. "I am not here to protect you from the other students. They are not so base as that. I am here to protect them from you."

"From me?" Her tone was shocked, but Jhonate was sure that she knew exactly what she meant.

"Yes, Mage Vannya. You are a distraction. The way you strut about and . . . flaunt yourself makes the men unfocused. I stay with you to ensure that your presence here does not get one of my fellow students killed."

Vannya looked down at her full-length robe and looked back to Jhonate. "Flaunt? I am more covered than you."

"You do not need to expose your body to be a distraction.

Your very face is a problem."

"My face? What would you have me do? Wear a mask?"

"That would be helpful," Jhonate suggested.

"You are being completely ridiculous!" Vannya said, and stood as much as their tent would allow, hunched over, hands on both hips. "Why you are just as pretty as I am. Why am I a problem when you aren't?"

Jhonate's face flushed. That was nonsense. "I most certainly am not as . . . I . . . I do my best to discourage any distracting thoughts."

"Oh, it's that easy for you, is it?" Vannya asked.

As a matter of fact it hadn't been. In the beginning, several of the students had been a problem. Qenzic was the perfect gentleman and focused on his studies, but Poz was easily distractible and Jobar still had to be corrected from time to time. "I have needed to be firm for them to understand. But yes, you must put forth the effort."

"Well, sure. If I spent all my time glowering and hitting the boys, maybe they would learn not to see me as a woman too."

Jhonate blinked. Is that how the mage saw her? "I keep them focused on the job at hand, but they are aware that I am a woman."

"Of course they are. Just look at you. They're men," Vannya said and then said more quietly, "I . . . I try not to encourage them."

"You laugh at any joke they say, no matter how stupid," Jhonate pointed out. "And you reach out and touch them as you do it."

"I most definitely do not!" Vannya's face was flushed.

"And you primp yourself and scent yourself, and spend too much time . . . washing."

"That is simple hygiene!" Vannya said with a glower, shaking her fist. "I do no more than necessary."

"You are shaking your brush at me right now," Jhonate pointed out and Vannya looked down at the brush she still had clutched in her fist. "We are at war. How straight does your hair need to be?"

"Y-you! If I don't brush it my hair becomes a tangled mess. You keep your hair perfect so easily." She pointed an accusatory finger. "Why you have just returned from battle and there is not one hair out of place."

Jhonate snorted. She was very aware of the giant's blood, troll slime, and dirt in her hair. "I keep my hair braided in the traditional style of my people. When done correctly, it does not require constant attention."

"Aha!" Vannya laughed in triumph. "You care just as much about your hair as I do! You-!"

They were interrupted by the sound of someone clearing their throat just outside their tent flap. The two women scowled at each other in embarrassment.

"Who is it?" Jhonate asked.

"It's me," came Locksher's voice.

"You can come in, Professor," Vannya said.

"No-no. That won't be necessary. I-uh, just wanted to let you ladies know that your . . . conversation has not gone unheard. You see, um . . . sound travels farther at night and-."

"We understand, Professor," Vannya said, exchanging an uncomfortable glance with Jhonate. The rest of the camp must have been finding their discussion quite amusing. "Thank you. Is there anything else?"

"Uh, no."

"Good evening then, professor."

"Yes, good evening."

Vannya hid her face in her hands as Locksher walked away. "I'm going to sleep now."

"That would be best," Jhonate agreed.

Jhonate waited until Vannya had dispelled her glowing orb before changing out of her battle-stained clothing and slipping into her bedroll. She laid in silence and began preparing her mind for a light sleep. Lately she had been forced to go to bed ready for combat.

"You should have let Professor Locksher take care of it,

you know," Vannya said from her much more plush sleeping pad.

"What are you speaking about?" Jhonate replied.

"The mother of the moonrats," Vannya clarified. "You lost critical information that could have been helpful to us. If only we knew-."

"I am fully aware that I lost the information." Jhonate said. She thought about it constantly, in fact. What that woman thing had done to her . . . she still had headaches from time to time as a result and her dreams were strange. She thought back to the troll attack earlier in the day and the voice she had heard in her mind. Something wasn't right. "Are you attempting to start another argument, Vannya?"

"No . . . I am just frustrated is all. I hate being up here in the mountains, not knowing what we are up against. Not knowing what is happening with the Mage School or with Justa- . . . the rest of the world."

"As do I."

Jhonate's mind wandered from her meditation. She laid in the darkness and twisted the ring on her finger, knowing that the cool glow of its protection covered her body. It was almost as if Justan were there with her. Again she had the urge to take it off, but instead she held it more tightly. If only the ring would protect her from her dreams.

Chapter Five

Race me, Justan sent.

He shivered as he looked into the upper branches of the tree in front of him. The sun had not yet broken the horizon, but with the heightened senses he had gained, Justan saw movement in the branches above. He smiled. His request had caught Deathclaw off guard.

Race? Why?

I need to run, Justan sent, his tone matter of fact. *And I need someone to push me.*

Why would I do this? Deathclaw's tone was suspicious.

Deathclaw was getting much better at communicating. In the beginning, their conversations had been complicated because the human language was so full of foreign concepts to the raptoid. Over the past few days, Justan had started sending along a mental explanation of words he felt Deathclaw would have difficulty with as they spoke. This seemed to help and to his surprise, Deathclaw had begun to do the same when talking to him.

You have raced Fist before. Justan responded. *Why not me?*

You will lose, came the raptoid's response.

"It doesn't matter," Justan said aloud. "Come on. I need someone to push me."

You are the leader. You would lose face in front of the pack? Deathclaw seemed surprised.

"We don't think that way in our pack. We all have our different strengths," Justan replied. "We all know that Fist is much stronger than the rest of us but that doesn't matter. Why should this?"

The leader is the best of the pack. Deathclaw sent. Justan was curious what he meant by his statement, but the raptoid kept his thoughts quiet.

This isn't a raptoid pack, he reminded. "Will you race me or not?"

Deathclaw somehow managed to climb down from the tree so silently that Justan's sensitive ears barely heard the sound of his claws against the trunk. He soon stood before Justan, arms folded, reptilian eyes black in the faint light of daybreak. The sword slung across his shoulders was his only adornment. *Where?*

"Across the ridge. To the base of the hanging cliff." Justan sent an image of the area he had seen when they had stopped to camp the day before. At the edge of the valley they were in, a plateau rose out of the forest. A large section of the cliff face had split away from the side of the plateau and hung outward ominously like it might fall any moment.

It is far.

Justan smiled. It was probably five miles. An easy morning run for a student of Jhonate bin Leeths. "That's why it will be a challenge. Do you have the stamina?"

I will win. Deathclaw sent with confidence.

"We will see." Justan turned towards the cliff face. He could barely see the edge jutting out against the brightening sky. "Are you ready?"

Deathclaw had not moved. *Run then.*

Justan took off in a loping jog, smiling to himself. Fist was right. This was just what he needed; to get his blood pumping, clear his mind. He sensed Deathclaw's amusement.

This is a run for you? the raptoid asked.

Justan turned his head to see Deathclaw running alongside him at the same speed, exerting very little effort. Justan dodged around a tree. *I am pacing myself. Conserving my energy. This is a long run remember?*

Raptoids run all day through the desert. Deathclaw let

out a hissing chuckle. *You are exposing your weakness. Humans tire so easily. The pack leader should not be the slowest member of the pack.*

Justan smiled back at him. There was a time in his life when Deathclaw's remarks would have been right. He had been weak once. A year of training with Jhonate and the increase of abilities from his bonding magic had changed that. *I am not as slow as you think.*

Run faster then, Deathclaw sent, and sped up. The raptoid leaned forward, his tail extended out behind him. He moved with grace, jumping lightly over tree roots and fallen logs as he went.

Justan increased his pace. He suddenly wanted very much to beat the raptoid. Could it be done? Deathclaw was agile and quick, but did he have the stamina as he claimed? Justan knew he was similar to Gwyrtha in some ways as far as the way his body had been changed, but he didn't have that same core of unlimited energy that the rogue horse had.

He caught up to Deathclaw, his legs churning as he dodged trees and watched the ground for obstacles in the growing morning light. Deathclaw's dark eyes glanced over at him. The raptoid thought with the mind of a hunter. Justan could sense his mind assessing his stride, dissecting his movements. But Deathclaw's conclusions were harder to read. Unlike Fist and Gwyrtha, he kept most of his thoughts below the surface of his mind. He still did not trust Justan enough to let him know what he was really thinking and no matter how curious he was, Justan did not pry. Sooner or later Deathclaw would learn to trust him.

You hold back, Deathclaw sent.

Justan jumped over a jutting rock and would have stumbled if he had not corrected his stride at the right moment. *That's how you run a distance race. I am saving some energy for the end.*

Deathclaw gave a mental snort. *You don't know your own body.* He sped up even more, surging ahead.

Justan nearly stumbled again as the raptoid's thoughts sunk in. He had indeed changed much since leaving Reneul. He was older now; nearly twenty; a man grown. And his body had altered more with each bonding. He was taller, faster, stronger. His awareness of his body had increased as had his control over it. But how well did he know his limits? Justan suddenly realized that he hadn't tested them. He had been pleased with the changes, but had been so focused on learning his magic that he had let farm work and light sparring do as training. Perhaps it was time to find out just what his body could do.

He leaned forward and increased his speed, arms pumping, legs churning. His heart rate increased. The increase in awareness that Deathclaw's bonding had given him turned inward. Justan could feel each individual muscle expand and contract with every movement. He could feel the sweat bead on his skin. He was no longer chilled by the cold morning air even as it rushed in and out of his lungs. It was exhilarating.

He caught up to Deathclaw and passed him by, sending out a mental taunt as he did so. The raptoid seemed pleased and veered off into the trees outside Justan's line of sight. Justan could still sense him though, darting through the forest and sharing in his enjoyment of the run.

Justan turned his focus to winning the race. Through a gap in the trees, he saw the hanging cliff face and judged that he was about three miles away. The speed of their progress was quite surprising. The pace he had set would have been a dead sprint back in his Training School days. He hadn't run this fast since the day he encountered the Scralag during the stamina test.

The memory of that day loomed in his mind and Justan lost concentration for a moment. His foot caught on a tree root, sending him stumbling forward and he was barely able to keep his feet under him. He regained control but he could feel the frost encrusted scar on his chest now as if it were a lead weight slowing him down.

He had been trying not to think of the Scralag. With thoughts of the Scralag came memories of the way it had dragged itself out of his chest and the way it had eaten Kenn's frozen heart. Just a few nights before, he had awoken sweating from a dream in which the creature had pulled itself free from his chest once again, but this time it was holding his own beating heart in its talons.

The Scralag was just one in a long list of nagging mysteries that had to be put on hold until after the academy was freed. Once it was over, perhaps he would seek Professor Locksher out again. He had been forced to leave the school before the wizard returned from his trip. Maybe his latest experience with the thing would help Locksher determine what it was. Justan wished desperately to be rid of it.

In the meantime though, he felt Deathclaw pulling away. The raptoid had found a stretch of level ground somewhere in the forest to his left. Justan refocused his attention on the race. So far he had just been running in a straight line towards the cliff, but the way was getting more congested with trees and undergrowth. He had to come up with a better strategy.

What did he have that Deathclaw didn't? He had the stamina gained from bonding with Gwyrtha, but it didn't seem like that was enough. He had strength from Fist, but this was a race . . . A thought occurred to him. Maybe there was a way to use that strength.

He increased his speed a bit more and watched for the next obstacle to appear. A thorny bush loomed in the distance. It was about chest high and Justan knew he had to time his move just right. He lengthened his strides, and just before the bush, he gathered both feet under him and let loose with a mighty jump, putting all his strength into it.

Before bonding with Fist, he never would have cleared the bush. This time he fared only slightly better. For a second he thought he was going to make it, but his feet caught in the thorns. Justan crashed down on the far side of the bush, landing chest first into the wet leaves, one foot tangled in the bush. The air exploded from his lungs and he gasped as he yanked his leg free.

Deathclaw sensed his crash. The raptoid was far ahead, but Justan heard his hissing snicker. Justan climbed to his feet and staggered forward. His vision swam and his legs burned from the deep gouges the thorns had left in his skin, but he didn't dare stop.

Justan berated himself. He should have known it wouldn't work. He was much stronger, but he was still human after all. He had imagined himself bounding through the woods, clearing obstacles like a deer, but Master Coal had warned him that the bond wouldn't enhance his abilities beyond what a human body could achieve.

As soon as he had gathered his breath, he pushed himself harder. He had to make up ground, but the fall had exhausted him and the going was difficult. He knew that he could reach out to Gwyrtha and tap into her energy, but that would be cheating. He forced his body to move faster with pure willpower alone.

Justan kept on a straight path towards the hanging cliff and soon the woods opened up around him. He began to gain on Deathclaw and as the final half mile came into view, he knew he had a chance. Deathclaw's easier route had taken him on a longer path and now they were both about the same distance from the finish. Justan smiled. The last stretch to the base of the cliff was on a slight slope and the trees were spaced far apart. It would all be about speed now.

In the distance he saw Deathclaw dashing through the trees. Justan put every last bit of energy he had left into one final sprint. He extended his body to the limit, pulse pounding, arms and legs pumping. He ran faster than he had ever run before and he could feel the raptoid pushing just as hard.

Deathclaw pulled ahead at the end and when Justan reached the cliff's base, Deathclaw was waiting, hunched over, hands on his knees. It was the first time Justan had seen the raptoid breathing heavily.

You are faster than most humans. But I am the fastest, Deathclaw sent triumphantly.

"Not . . . even . . . close." Justan walked a few feet away before collapsing on the ground. He rolled to his back and lay in the leaves, gasping. *Next time you should try racing Gwyrtha.*

Deathclaw cocked his head and looked down at Justan. *You tried hard. Yet you are not angry at losing.*

Justan smiled. *I knew you would probably win. But I still wanted to see what my body could do.*

Deathclaw thought about that for a moment, then asked, *Why do you lay there before me? Leaders should not show weakness.*

Why not?

Leaders must always look strong. It is the way of the pack.

"Things change," Justan said.

The ways of the pack do not change, Deathclaw replied.

Justan sat up part way and leaned back on his elbows. "You have changed. You are not like other raptoids."

The wizard did this to me.

"Yes, but you have changed more since then," Justan said.

I still follow the way of the pack.

"Really? What about the way you always climb trees? That isn't what raptoids do. There are no trees in your desert memories."

I have adapted. Raptoids adapt. If a raptoid wants to stay hidden, he stays between the dunes. If he wants to see far, he climbs atop the dunes. In trees I can do both.

"But why do you need to hide?" Justan asked.

Deathclaw cocked his head. *Why would I wish to be seen? A raptoid on his own is . . . vulnerable. It is best if a lone raptoid hides.*

"You are no longer alone," Justan reminded. He hadn't expected Deathclaw to fit in with the group right away, but it still bothered him that he didn't socialize with the rest of them. "You have a pack. You have us. You are no longer vulnerable."

Perhaps . . . Deathclaw sent, but the way the thought came across Justan knew that in a way, joining their group had made him feel even more vulnerable.

"And what about your sword?" Justan pressed. "Do raptoids wield swords?"

Another adaptation. Deathclaw replied and Justan sensed irritation stir within the raptoid's thoughts. *Why do you ask these things?*

"I want to know you better," Justan explained. *You are a part of me now. I wish to know why you think the way you do.*

If you want to know so badly, why not just search my mind? You could do that with your magic. It would be easier for you. Why not take my thoughts?

There was no emotion emanating from Deathclaw's thoughts this time. Justan could not tell if he was serious or not. *Your thoughts are your own. They belong to you. I wouldn't take them without permission. I respect your wishes.*

You lead the pack. The pack leader takes what he wants. Deathclaw genuinely seemed puzzled. *You have done it before. In the beginning.*

"I . . . I am sorry about that, Deathclaw. I was still learning and . . . I shouldn't have done that." Justan said with a twinge of guilt. "Can you forgive me for that?"

Deathclaw paused as he digested the meaning of Justan's request. *More weakness? Why do you ask this? Why does it matter what I feel?*

"You are my bonded." Justan explained and tried to send emotions conveying what that meant to him. *You are a part of me and I am a part of you.*

Deathclaw snorted, but Justan did not sense the same derision in the raptoids thoughts that he had felt earlier. *I will think on this.*

Justan laid back down and looked up at the giant slab of the cliff face that hung out over him. Its position seemed so precarious. It was as if at any moment the cliff could finally let go and collapse, crushing him. He resisted the urge to run out from under it.

He wondered how long the cliff had been like this. Looking closer, he could see years of vine growth hanging from the top of the cliff face, just now sprouting with new spring leaves. There were trees up there way above, rooted to the top of the slab and they didn't stick straight out at an angle, like a tree would if it were fully grown when the slab tilted away from the cliff face. The trees had grown straight up, standing tall and reaching for the sun. That meant the slab had to have been hanging this way for decades. Still Justan knew the fall would come sooner or later. One small tremor of the earth or one torrential rainstorm, and the life of everything under the slab would be over.

In many ways it reminded him of the situation with those at the Battle Academy. Right now the forces were at a stalemate, but the end seemed inevitable. At any moment, Ewzad Vriil could give the command and his entire great army could descend. No matter how well prepared they were the numbers were just too overwhelming. Eventually they were going to be crushed.

He stood and walked out from under its hanging presence. The great need to act and act now rushed back over him. But how? What could they do? Master Coal was right. With their small group, they could never hope to break the siege.

Strike at their weak points, thought Deathclaw. The raptoid was still standing to the side and Justan hadn't realized he was listening. *That is how a pack brings down a large enemy. Weaken it until it can no longer stand, then go in for the kill.*

Yes, I have thought of that. But this enemy is far too large. A wise pack would not take such a beast on. Justan replied.

If an enemy is too large, a pack waits. Wait until the enemy is weaker or hide until it leaves your territory.

Waiting was Master Coal's preferred course of action. Wait and gather information. Wait until the army became hungry and fought amongst themselves. *I am tired of waiting.*

So am I. The wizard is still alive. Deathclaw said and Justan could feel his frustration.

What does a raptoid leader do when he is tired of waiting? Justan asked.

Deathclaw thought about it for a moment. *He may attack anyway but with such numbers, his pack would die. A good leader will be patient and keep his pack from attacking something they cannot defeat.*

This reminded Justan too much of his conversation with Master Coal the evening before. *And what if a raptoid disagrees with his leader?*

Deathclaw watched him with a calculating gaze. *The*

raptoid could challenge the leader for control of the pack. They would fight and the winner would become the pack leader.

This line of thought was getting him nowhere. Justan focused his mind back on the real problem; the army of thirty thousand goblinoids surrounding the Battle Academy. *Perhaps we have been looking at this wrong,* he sent. *We have talked about what a pack does when a large beast invades their territory. But what does a small pack do if a more numerous pack invades their territory?* He sent a vision of the size and scope of the enemy they were facing.

Deathclaw shook his head. *They must find a new territory or be destroyed.*

But what if the territory is too precious to give up?

Deathclaw had a hard time grasping that concept. *There is always another territory. A leader should keep the pack together and leave. Then he would seek out a territory owned by a weaker pack. He would attack and absorb the surviving members of the smaller pack, taking the territory for his own.*

Thus also increasing the size of his pack. Justan nodded, then a smile spilled across his face. *And if he continued to increase his pack, he could make it large enough that he could return and battle the enemy that invaded his territory!*

That would work . . . perhaps, Deathclaw agreed, though he still didn't seem to understand the importance of a single territory.

A plan began to gel in Justan's mind. "Thank you, Deathclaw. This time with you has really helped."

Helped? Deathclaw cocked his head again. *I defeated you and told you the enemy could not be beaten.*

"That's right," Justan said, feeling excited about their journey for the first time since the fight with Kenn. "You gave me exactly what I needed."

He called out to Gwyrtha through the bond. *Sweetie, I need a ride.*

Chapter Six

You are far, Gwyrtha sent with a reproachful tone. Justan had awakened her, but that wasn't what bothered the rogue horse. She did not like him to be far from her side. *I come.*

"Would you like to ride back to camp with me?" Justan asked Deathclaw.

Ride? Deathclaw snorted in derision. *I will not ride her. A raptoid does not need such things to travel.*

Justan's eyebrows rose. This was the first time he had felt such a distaste for Gwyrtha coming from Deathclaw. "Do you have a problem with Gwyrtha?"

She . . . is part of the pack. Deathclaw looked away, his emotions betraying nothing more. *I shall return on my own.*

Justan watched Deathclaw trot back through the trees and wondered what was bothering him. He felt that he had come to understand Deathclaw much better over the last few days, but the raptoid was still a mystery in many ways. What reason could Deathclaw possibly have for disliking Gwyrtha? She was the sweetest creature in the world. Perhaps he should link the two together through the bond so that they could get to know one another . . .

He pushed his worries away. There was plenty of time to work out their differences. For now he needed to focus on developing his new plan and figuring out how to get Master Coal to agree to it. The wizard was usually willing to listen, but Justan feared he had pushed things too far the previous night.

Gwyrtha appeared a short time later. She ran from the treeline and stopped in front of him. He walked towards her, but she backed away, her emotions chiding him through the bond.

You left.

Justan chuckled. "I'm sorry, Gwyrtha. I was just going for a run with Deathclaw."

Without me.

You were asleep. I didn't want to wake you. Justan sent. "And besides, you cheat when we run."

Gwyrtha had a nasty habit of trying to make everything into a game. Whenever she followed him on a run, she would try to trip him with her tail or sneak up from behind and pounce on him. While at Coal's keep, she had escalated her joke to the point where trying to run was useless and he had stopped even trying.

"Please, sweetheart. I'm tired," he complained.

She finally stopped and sidled up next to him so that he could climb up. *Take me next time,* she demanded.

Justan swung his leg over the saddle and sighed. "Fine."

She grunted in satisfaction and started back towards the camp. He wondered what this morning's contest would have been like with her around. He envisioned her racing back and forth between the both of them, alternating between tripping them up and pouncing on them. The thought of Deathclaw's possible reaction to being knocked on his face made Justan laugh out loud.

Funny? she asked.

I was just thinking, Justan responded and his smile faded a bit. *Gwyrtha, what do you think of Deathclaw?*

He is wild, she replied and her feelings seemed neutral on the subject.

Justan thought for a moment. It wasn't a bad way to describe him. Deathclaw was highly intelligent, but the way he acted around the others reminded him of the time his mother had tried to take in a feral cat as a pet. It would hide from them all the time and eventually ran away. He shook his head. That comparison was selling Deathclaw short. He wasn't an animal that ran only on instinct and he most definitely wasn't a pet. He was a full member of the group. *Is Deathclaw's wildness a bad thing?*

Gwyrtha gave a mental shrug. *He will change.*

What makes you so sure? He asked.

You are Justan, she sent simply, as if that conveyed everything he needed to know.

Justan held tight as she increased her speed, jumping over logs and bushes as she ran. He pondered what she said. Gwyrtha and Fist both had such faith in him. He wasn't sure why that was and he definitely wasn't sure he deserved it.

They arrived back at the camp shortly. Daylight had broken and everyone was up. Lenny had the remnants of last night's meal bubbling on the pot while a few bear meat steaks sizzled on a flat iron pan.

Coal and Samson were talking together to the side of the others. The wizard was rifling through one of the centaur's saddlebags, looking for something. Justan headed over to them, preparing his mind for the discussion that would ensue.

Samson saw his approach and must have said something to the wizard because without even turning around, Coal said, "Hello, Edge. Are you here to argue with me again?"

While Justan winced, Gwyrtha walked past him to nudge Samson. The centaur smiled and rubbed her beastly head in greeting. Samson had been enjoying their journey just as much as Gwyrtha had. It had been a long time since they had strayed this far from the farm. The only thing Coal and Justan had been able to agree on during the last few days was how annoying it was to be worried sick about something and have a bonded with such a cheerful mood in the back of your mind.

"No, sir. I don't want to argue with you," Justan said. "In fact, I owe you an apology."

"You do?" The wizard turned around and looked at him in surprise.

"Yes. I was out of line last night. I was putting my own need for action above what was best for everyone else."

Master Coal placed a hand on his shoulder. "It's okay, Edge. I understand. I have been struggling with the same emotions that you have. That's partially why I was so angry. It was like having my own arguments thrown back at me. But after Willum told me what Tad wanted, I had to agree that this was the best way we could help."

Justan nodded, but the urge to argue that point again rose within him. He forced the feeling down and said the words that he had prepared beforehand. "About our disagreement, Master. I have a proposal."

Coal's pulled his hand from Justan's shoulder and folded his arms. "I see."

"I think I have found a solution that answers both sides of our argument."

"Please tell me then, Edge," Coal said resignedly.

"Last night Fist said something that made me think," Justan said. "I was complaining and he said that the reason I was so frustrated was because I wasn't doing anything."

Master Coal blinked and a laugh escaped his lips. "This is true."

"Yes. He was completely right," Justan agreed. "Since Qyxal's death, I haven't trained. I haven't practiced. We haven't done any lessons. All I have been doing is pacing around and brooding and beating myself up."

"I have been trying to give you space to grieve," Coal said. "This is the first time you have had to deal with the death of a friend."

Justan looked down for a moment and stroked Gwyrtha's mane. "This morning I awoke early and ran. I challenged Deathclaw to a race."

"Ah, so that is what you were doing."

"It was good. It helped me clear my mind, and afterward, as I spoke with him, I thought of a way that we could gather information and at the same time do something active to help the academy," Justan said.

"Good," Master Coal said. "Then tell me. What is this idea of yours?"

"I think that we should build an army of our own."

Master Coal's eyes grew wary. "Build an army? How do you suggest going about this, Edge?"

Justan started in, excited to explain the plan, "We travel

east towards the Mage School. We stop at villages along the way and gather information like Tad wants. But we also find people willing to help and recruit them to help us break the siege."

Mater Coal frowned and opened his mouth, but Justan continued before the wizard could object, his words coming out in a rush. "We stop in Sampo and gather any men that will listen there. Then we go to the elves. Once we have brought Qyxal back to them and explain how Ewzad Vriil was behind his death, maybe we can convince them to help. Then we go to the Mage School. We can talk to the council and gather wizards and any of their guards that can be spared. Then we stop in Pinewood and on to Wobble. Lenny can help us drum up support there. By that time our army should be sizeable and with the might of the Mage School behind us, we break the siege."

Coal nodded thoughtfully, but his voice was hesitant. "It is an . . . ambitious idea."

Justan's heart sank a little.

"Ambitious? It's a good plan," Samson said with a smile. "An admirable plan. It makes far more sense than our current direction."

"But there are some issues," Coal added, giving Samson a reproachful nudge to the ribs. "We will have difficulty convincing anyone to follow a group like ours."

"You and I are named. That gives us credibility," Justan said.

"And what about the rest of our group? The people of Sampo aren't about to follow an ogre and a half-orc into battle against goblinoids. Not to mention our two rogue horses and Deathclaw."

Justan frowned. He had been so focused on the logistics of his plan that he had let a major flaw slip by. He came up with a quick alternative. "Then we go to the Mage School first. Our group won't be questioned by anyone if we have an official Mage School force accompanying us. Admittedly we will have some hurdles to deal with at the school too."

"Like our rogue horses," Coal said. "There are wizards at the school that will want to dissect them. My bond with Samson is what forced me to leave the school all those years ago."

"Yes, but if the council is on our side, the other wizards won't do anything. We will have Master Latva, Professor Valtrek, and Professor Beehn backing us at least. I know that much," Justan said. "Of course, we would have to explain our bonding magic."

Master Coal rubbed his face with his hands. "The school has actively been hiding the existence of bonding magic for centuries. Why would they reveal it now?"

"I think it's time they did," Samson said. "Valtrek knows already. So does Master Latva. And perhaps others we don't know about."

"But why do they hide it?" Justan asked. The situation had always bothered him. The Mage School prided itself on teaching all beneficial uses of magic. Why keep bonding magic a secret? "Every time I ask, you say, 'that is a topic for another lesson.'"

Coal pursed his lips, his brow furrowed thoughtfully. "The reason I have not discussed the matter with you thus far is that the why doesn't matter. It just jumbles up the issue and creates a mystery. I wanted you focused on learning how to use your magic, not worrying about side issues."

"And now?" Justan asked. "Evidently it matters now."

"The truth is that some of the reasons are lost to history. That's how well kept the secret is. I can only tell you what my master told me," Coal said. "The school hides the existence of spirit magic and thus bonding magic because the prophet asked them to."

Justan digested that information for a moment. The prophet seemed to have his hands in everything. Why wouldn't the prophet want people to know about spirit magic? Was it because that was the kind of magic the prophet himself used? But more importantly, "Why would the wizards agree to a request like that?"

"Perhaps I miss-phrased that," the wizard said. "It was most likely less of a request and more of a command."

"The prophet has that kind of pull with the Mage

School?" Justan thought back to the night the prophet had spoken to him under the fernwillow tree. That night Qyxal had told him that the prophet had caused a ruckus in the council room, berating the wizards about something.

"Surely if you paid attention in your history classes, you would know that the prophet was one of the co-founders of the Mage School. In some of the oldest histories, it is said that the school was his idea," Master Coal said.

"Well, sure. But that was thousands of years ago. Surely it isn't the same prophet." Justan knew that some scholars believed the prophet to be an immortal, but he had never believed it. He was of the opinion that being the prophet was more of a title passed down through the years.

Coal just shrugged. "Samson can tell you more than I. The prophet helped with the rogue horse migration hundreds of years ago."

"You have met the prophet?" Justan asked the centaur.

"I have met him many times over the years," Samson confirmed. "I can never seem to recall his face, but he has always been the same man as far as I could tell. The last time we met was the day he took me to the place where I met Coal. That was, what? Twenty years ago?"

"The same man? But how is that possible? Is he human?"

The wizard shrugged again. "Does it matter? Regardless of whether he is the same man or not, the prophet has ultimate authority. It was the prophet who gave the school the Bowl of Souls. It was the prophet who raised the wall around the school. He has a floor of the Mage Tower of his own that no one is allowed to enter. In the very bylaws of the school, it states that the wizards have to listen to his council. It is their choice whether or not to obey, but they must listen."

Justan tried to wrap his mind around the concept. "But why would the prophet want knowledge of bonding magic hidden?"

"My master didn't know," Coal said. "The prophet rarely gives his reasons. All I know is that they did obey. Any book on bonding or spirit magic in general was taken out of the library and hidden away. They stopped teaching it in class and began focusing solely on elemental magic."

"So what does this mean for us? Are we supposed to keep our bonding magic secret forever?" Justan asked, a sense of dread rising in his stomach. He tried to imagine how he could possibly keep his bonded a secret forever. No one would understand a group like his.

"No, Edge," Master Coal said firmly. "As far as I am concerned, the prophet's command was meant for the Mage School, not for us. My master urged me to keep it to myself while at the school to avoid too many questions, but in the world at large, I haven't bothered. I never hid anything from the people of Razbeck. They didn't completely understand my connection with my bonded, but they came to accept it."

"Yes, but you live in an isolated community. I want to go back to Reneul some day," Justan said.

"You worry too much," Samson said with a snort. "You are a named warrior and wizard. If we are able to help break the siege, you'll be a hero in Reneul. They will be more accepting than you think. I would be more worried about the Mage School."

Justan nodded. He wasn't so sure that Samson was right about Reneul, but the Mage School was the problem currently facing them. "Then what do you suggest, Master Coal? I don't know if we can gather the support we need without the Mage School's help."

Coal said nothing for a moment, frowning pensively. Finally, he said, "The only thing we can do is go to the Mage School and see what happens. Perhaps we can find a way to gather their help without revealing our magic."

"Maybe if we left them outside of the school . . ." said Justan thinking about the best way to hide them. Then a smile spread across his face as he realized what Master Coal was saying. "So we can do it?"

"It's a better plan then what we've been doing here. But," The wizard raised a finger. "Before we make this decision, we need to bring this discussion to the others. Everyone should have some input in our direction."

"Agreed!" Justan said with excitement.

They gathered everyone together and to Justan's happiness, the plan was met with a general feeling of relief. Most of them were just ready to get moving. Lenny was the only source of grumbles, but as soon as he heard that recruiting Wobble was part of the plan, he was on board with the rest of them.

Master Coal agreed to inform Tad the Cunning of their decision that night, but first they needed to head into town as planned. They now had even more reason to go, because not only did they need to gather information for Tad, they also needed to buy supplies. The Mage School was a two week journey away.

Out of their party, the only people that could travel into Filgren without raising alarm were Master Coal, Justan and Lenny. They saddled up Alfred and Stanza for the trip, but with the loss of Bettie's horse in the fight with Kenn, they were one horse short. Justan offered to let Lenny ride in front of him. Bettie laughed out loud at the idea, but the dwarf just scowled.

"I can walk, dag-gum it!"

"That would slow us down a great deal," Master Coal said. "We have a lot to do and I wish to be back by dark."

"You can ride Stanza, Lenny. I'll jog alongside you," Justan said. The morning run had left him tired, but the trip to town wasn't as long as that run had been. Besides, he could pull energy from Gwyrtha as he needed it. He looked to Coal. "Lenny can buy me a horse for the ride back."

"That's my gal-durn money!" the dwarf spat.

"We need another horse anyway. Especially if we are going to be making more trips into towns like this," Justan reasoned. "You can keep the horse after all this is over."

"Don't want no blasted horse," the dwarf grumbled, but didn't argue further.

They headed out and as Justan ran alongside them, something from his conversation with Coal bothered him. He reached out to Gwyrtha through the bond. She greeted him happily.

You need me? she asked and Justan knew she was already trotting out of camp.

No, Gwyrtha, sorry. Turn back around. You know you can't come. I have another question for you, he sent. *Do you know the prophet?*

John, she replied and he caught a brief glimpse of a man, average height, middle aged, with brown hair. His features were blurry, but he got the sense of a kind man. It certainly felt like it could have been the same man he had met.

He sent her his memories of the evening he had met the prophet. It had been dark that night and he could not recall every detail of the man's appearance, but their conversation and the feeling he had while the prophet spoke to him was still clear in his mind.

John, she agreed.

Can you show me more? Justan asked. There was a bit of hesitance at first as her desire to please him warred with her reluctance to relive the past, finally a flood of memories poured into his mind through the bond.

The oldest memories were blurry. She was in a room, hurt and confused, but a kind man was with her. A man she knew as Father. Then John barged in the room. He was enraged and yelled at Father before coming at her, his eyes blazing with the intent to destroy her . . .

Time passed. John stood by her and scratched behind her ears. Her brothers and sisters were with her, vague shapes in her memory. John visited with them all . . .

Time flew by. Father was gone now. Her herd was small and her herd was alone. They hid in the mountains, uncertain and scared. John came again and this time with sad eyes, led them away from the evil that hunted them . . .

Time flew again. The memories were a bit clearer now. John drew her away from her pack and rode with her for a while; months, maybe years; taking her all over the lands. Then he left her deep in a jungle, assuring her that she would be safe . . .

The last memories were much more recent and vivid in

their clarity. Gwyrtha was deep in a swamp-like jungle, crouched high up in a tree, looking down on a small village of humans. She looked down at them with yearning, knowing they feared her, knowing that she must stay away, but wanting their company. As she looked down, a man passed through the village. The people were in awe of him, bowing and reaching out to touch him. The man walked up to her tree and Gwyrtha smelled him. She pounced at once. People screamed and ran, but John laughed from his position in the mud under her feet. He rose and embraced her. They rode together for a time . . .

John brought her to another wood, a place both old and new. He introduced her to the elves and asked them to care for her. Then he left her once again . . .

The memories faded and Justan was left with a lingering sense of affection for the man Gwyrtha knew as John. She loved him and missed him still. Without a shadow of a doubt, the prophet was immortal as the scholars once said. He was the same, unchanging throughout Gwyrtha's memories.

Justan now knew he owed the man a great debt. The prophet's words as he visited him that night at the Mage School had helped him better understand himself and his powers, but more importantly, he had guided and protected Gwyrtha throughout the years.

"This'd better not be a dag-gum joke!"

A sharp pain in his side startled Justan to awareness. His face was in a pile of leaves.

"That ain't funny, you beet squisher!" A rough hand grabbed his shoulder and rolled him over. Lenny slapped his face. "Wake up, dag-blast it!"

"Ow," Justan sat up and winced, rubbing his side where Lenny had kicked him. Stanza was standing nearby. Master Coal had dismounted Albert and was running over towards him. Justan hadn't realized he had been so deep into the bond. He was fortunate he hadn't hit his head on a rock. "Sorry, Lenny."

"What the hell's wrong with you, Son?"

"It was the prophet, Lenny," Justan said. "He left her there with the elves."

"Huh?" The dwarf leaned in close looking into Justan's eyes, his one bushy eyebrow raised in concern. "You alright in there, son? What're you goin' on about?"

"He brought Gwyrtha there, Lenny. To the elves. All those years, he was saving her for me."

Chapter Seven

Willum stood at his post on the northwestern corner of the wall and watched the incident between the giants and goblins unfold.

It started when a hungry giantess walked into a goblin camp and stole a whole hog they had set roasting on a spit. The goblins gave chase and she trampled one of the goblin leaders in her haste to return to the giant army with her prize. Enraged, the goblins had chased her into the giant's territory and slew her.

The retaliation of the giants was brutal. A large group of them left their encampment and waded into the mass of goblins, smashing them with clubs, rocks, and fists. There was no way for Willum to know why they reacted so strongly. Perhaps they knew the female that had been killed. Perhaps they just didn't like the goblins invading their space. Either way, hundreds of goblins were killed before they were able to take down the invaders.

"Could this be it?" yelled a student from his post a couple of yards to Willum's left, his hands cupped on either side of his mouth so that he could be heard over the army's roar. "Could this be the start of the battle the council has been hoping for?"

"I don't know! Maybe," Willum yelled, but he didn't think so. Everyone hoped that the army would destroy itself from within, but though fighting broke out among the different factions of the besieging army quite often, it always died down. True, this fight was the largest so far, but the army was so numerous that even if thousands of goblins had died, the loss wouldn't matter. Maybe if they were lucky and the scuffle spilled over to the rest of the army, starting a chain reaction.

Maybe . . .

At any rate, both encampments were in an uproar and it seemed for a time that full out war just might erupt between them. Then one of the giant commanders appeared. He was a huge thing, at least half again as tall as most of the giants camped in the hills, and his skin was an odd bluish gray. Willum had manned the north wall many times before and knew most of the leaders by sight, but had definitely never seen this one before. He hadn't known giants like that existed. This new commander shouted down his people and forced them to withdraw from the goblin camp.

The goblins chose to see this action as a victory. They gathered at the dividing line between their army and the giants, taunting and brandishing their weapons. The giants looked back at them from their side of the line, most of them with a sense of bemusement, but there were a few that frowned and hefted large rocks in their fists.

"I'm a bit disappointed," came a voice behind Willum's shoulder. "I come up here to see the ruckus and find that it has calmed down already. I wonder if there is something we could do to get them fighting again."

Willum looked back, surprised to see Tad the Cunning standing right behind him. "Sir! What brings you up here?"

"I am inspecting the battlements, Willum," Tad said in amusement. "It is something everyone on the council does from time to time."

"Right. Of course, sir," Willum said, a bit awkwardly. His surprise had come from the fact that Tad was talking to him in public. Ever since Willum told him about Dann Doudy's past, Tad had made sure that no one ever saw them together. Lately they had only met in the dark of morning and Tad changed the location constantly.

"I am sorry I missed our meeting this morning," Tad said. "Doudy cornered me and wanted to talk."

"I understood, sir," Willum said. Tad was the council leader after all. "But is it okay for you to be seen talking to me now?"

"I can't always avoid you. That would be just as suspicious as being seen talking to you too much," Tad said. "This is a perfect time for our meeting, actually. I am here to investigate the skirmish amongst the enemy ranks and no one can hear what we are saying. So, let's dispense with official business first, shall we? Willum, what is the current status of the enemy?"

Willum smiled. When Tad was around, he always felt more confident in his abilities. "Since the giant commander arrived, both sides have backed down, sir."

"I see. Is that him?" Tad pointed down to the center of the camp, where the huge gray giant now stood. Several of the other giant leaders were gathered around him and one of the ogre chieftains was gesturing animatedly. The grey giant folded his enormous arms and nodded occasionally, but his eyes were focused up on the wall.

Willum nodded. "They are all bowing and scraping around him now. What kind of giant is he?"

Tad shook his head. "I have no idea. Giants vary in size, but that one's huge. His skin color is throwing me off too . . . maybe Stout Harley would know. He's from giant country." He looked over to the goblin side. "This appears to be over then. The goblins are putting on a show of aggression, but that's just to make themselves feel better. I am honestly quite surprised that they dared to chase the giantess down in the first place. Goblins would never hunt down a giant in the wilds. They are terrified of them."

"Maybe they are just getting too used to being around each other," Willum suggested.

"Fantastic observation, Willum. I wonder if we can use that fact to our advantage . . ." Tad rubbed his chin for a moment, then shrugged. "Now that we have that out of the way, what did your father tell you last night?"

"I told him your concerns about his plan of action, sir," Willum said. "He and Sir Edge are determined to move forward, though. They promise to continue to gather information for you as they go, but they feel that asking the Mage School for assistance is the best way they can help to break the siege."

Tad frowned. "I fear that it is a waste of time. We sent messengers out the moment we knew the army was descending on us, so they already know about the siege. They also know how well provisioned we are. They helped us stockpile our supplies after all. No, the wizards are secure behind their walls. I doubt that they will see an urgent need to march to our aid."

"My father has the same concerns." Willum said. "But he feels that if they can win even a few of the wizards over to our side, it would be a great help in giving them the legitimacy they need to raise an army."

"Maybe so," Tad sighed. "I suppose it gives us a distant chance of rescue if this siege doesn't break on its own soon."

"So you think that the enemy is going to break, sir?" Willum asked hopefully.

"I don't know. I have no idea what has kept them together so far. By all rights, this army shouldn't exist in the first place. They all hate each other as much as they hate humans."

"They believe that the Dark Prophet is leading them." Willum said.

"So we hear," Tad acknowledged. "But that can only go so far. Even when the Dark Prophet was actually alive, his armies constantly turned on each other. No matter how convincingly their leaders have deceived them, that belief won't be enough. Hunger should do it. Their supply trains have slowed down to a crawl recently and by all rights an army that size should have hunted down all edible animals in the area by now. As they run out of food, fights like today's will become more commonplace."

"Then why are you so worried, sir?" Willum asked. Tad's words were convincing, but his voice was full of doubt.

"Something's not right about this whole thing. There are so many aspects that remain a mystery."

"Then maybe it's a good thing that my father is raising an army to help," Willum suggested.

Tad gave him a half smile. "At the very least, with your father at the Mage School we will have a way to communicate with the wizards directly. Maybe we can convince them if your father can't. It will probably mean more concessions on our side of the school contract though." His smile faded at the thought. "At any rate, once we establish communication with them we won't be able to keep our meetings secret anymore. The council will need to know how we are able to get information to and from the Mage School."

"But what about the spy?" Willum's brow wrinkled in concern. "You said Doudy, er . . . Representative Doudy was asking questions?"

Tad snorted. "If he is a spy, as we suspect, he is a horrible one. If you hadn't told me about his connection with the Vriil family, I probably would have dismissed the possibility. Everyone has been suspicious of him from the moment he arrived and he hasn't even tried to get into our good graces since. He storms around asking odd questions, belittles everyone on the council that isn't noble born, and then complains about every positive decision made. The man is so obviously trying to undermine our efforts, it's laughable. No one takes his suggestions or demands seriously and any truly sensitive discussions are done away from the man. The only thing I can think of is that our security efforts have been successful and since he has no way to get a message out, he is just trying to sabotage us any way he can."

Willum frowned. "Maybe he's just acting like a fool to lull the council into dismissing him as a threat."

Tad gave him an appraising look. "That's some shrewd thinking, Willum. Have you been talking to Hugh the Shadow?"

Willum's eyes widened. "Why no, sir. I mean, I have taken his espionage classes, sir, but I haven't talked to him about anything else. I have done as you asked and spoke of my father's movements to no one . . . sir."

Tad laughed. "Don't worry, Willum. I wasn't accusing you of anything. I was just impressed is all. You are quite-." He paused and looked down at the giant army with interest. "What are they doing now, I wonder?"

The giant commander and his retinue of leaders were walking towards the wall, all of them talking to their commander at once. They stopped at the edge of the siege line. The gray giant said one word and pointed to the top of the wall, right at an academy graduate stationed only two spots down from Willum's. A hush went out over the giant ranks. The commander bent and punched into the rocky shale, breaking it up and pulling out a chunk that had to weigh as much as an average man. He tucked the chunk of rock under his arm like a great disc. He spun, gathering momentum.

"He's aiming for our man," Tad said.

"He'll never hit him. He's way too far away," Willum said, but Tad moved down to stand beside the graduate nonetheless.

"Stand firm, soldier," Tad said and the graduate nodded. "Show him we don't fear them."

The giant swung his arm in a wide arc as he released the rock. It hurtled towards the graduate's position with startling accuracy. Tad stood firm. He rested his hand on the graduate's shoulder and watched as the rock struck the wall just three feet below their position, shattering into a hail of tiny shards that fell back towards the ground below.

The graduate didn't flinch, but his face was pale and his breathing heavy.

"Good job, soldier," Tad said and walked back over to Willum's position. "Their new commander's showing off."

"The giants do this from time to time, sir," Willum said. "It's a game. They take turns throwing rocks to see if any of them can get them over the wall."

"I saw a report about that. But I was told they stopped this game a week ago."

"We started shooting them if they approached close enough to clear the top of the wall, sir. It stopped being fun for them after that." Willum explained. He looked down at the grey giant, who was shouting at the other giants around him, another hefty boulder clutched in one hand. "They must have told him about it. He's standing just out of range for most of our archers."

"Let's change that," Tad said. He walked a short distance along the wall to talk to one of the students at their post. The student nodded and rushed down the stairs. Tad arrived back at

Willum's post just as a commotion started below.

Two ogres came out from behind the hillside dragging a portly man behind them. He was bound hand and foot and seemed terrified, shouting and pleading as they dragged him to their leader.

The gray giant nodded in satisfaction and dropped the rock he was holding. He bent and grabbed the prisoner's feet instead, then lifted the man off the ground with one large hand and started to spin. The man let out a high pitched scream.

"By the gods!" Tad said.

With a mighty release, the giant sent the man through the air in a high arc, tumbling end-over-end, screaming all the way.

"He's going to clear the wall!" Willum gasped.

The man flew just over their heads and Willum caught a quick glimpse of his panicked face before the man fell into the school grounds. He crashed onto one of the rooftops with a thud, shattering tiles before rolling off and hitting the street below. A panicked crowd of refugees gathered around him.

Tad sent another of the students down to secure the body, telling him to take it to the infirmary immediately. There was no way the man had survived, but they needed to make sure that he hadn't been diseased. The last thing they needed was a plague behind their walls. The Dark Prophet's armies had used vile tactics like that in the past.

Willum felt sick. "I recognized that man, sir. He was a shopkeeper from Renuel. He was supposed to have escaped with the people that left before the army closed in."

Tad turned, his jaw clenched as he looked down upon the enemy commander. The giant pumped his fist and cheers erupted throughout the giant army. In their excitement, many of them broke out with a flurry of rock-throwing. These rocks didn't pose a threat though. None of them struck more than halfway up the wall. The giant commander laughed and motioned to the ogres that had brought the man. They nodded and ran back behind the hillside.

"I think he sent them to bring back more," Willum said.

"We can't allow this." Tad said grimly. "Emotions are

tense enough. If the bodies of friends and neighbors keep landing in academy grounds, there will be panic."

Willum shuddered at the thought of a constant barrage of Renuel's citizens hurled over the walls. He had read about such things and his teachers had spoken about the horrors of siege warfare, but nothing had prepared him for what he had just seen. He took a deep breath and forced the visage of the poor shopkeeper from his mind.

"What are they bringing now?" Tad wondered. The ogres had returned from behind the hill, but this time they were pulling a large boxed-in handcart. Willum hoped it didn't contain more prisoners.

A group of men rushed up the stairs to the battlements and Willum was glad to see Swen and Mad Jon among them. Swen carried Windy and Mad Jon carried a bow almost as big. They rushed over to confer with Tad and he updated them on the situation.

"Have there been any incidents anywhere else along the wall?" he asked.

"All is quiet, sir!" one of the men said.

"Good. All of you, find the other council members and tell them what is happening." The men nodded and rushed back down the stairs.

"Jon, Swen, do you think you can hit him?" Tad asked, pointing out the commander.

The two men looked over the side and nodded. They were the best archers in Dremaldria and quite possibly the only ones that could have made a shot at that distance.

"They're opening the cart!" Willum said.

One of the ogres opened the door in the side of the cart and out stepped a figure clad in bulky green platemail. The figure walked up to the gray giant and nodded in response to something that was said. Then one of the ogres handed it some kind of harness, which it proceeded to strap on.

"Ready your bows," Tad said.

The gray giant grabbed the back of the harness and lifted the armored figure off the ground. It pulled in its legs and curled up like a ball, wrapping its arms around its knees as if it had practiced this move before. The giant grunted in satisfaction and began his spin.

"Fire when you can!" Tad said. "Take that bastard down!"

Swen and Mad Jon fitted oversized arrows to their bows and pulled the arrows back. Wood creaked and muscles strained. They fired just as the commander released his throw. Both arrows found their mark, one arrow piercing his left eye, the other burying itself in his throat. The gray giant clutched its wounds in surprise and fell to the ground.

But the giant's throw had been just as accurate. The green armored figure hurtled right at them like a cannonball. As it neared their position it opened up, spreading its arms and legs wide. The figure looked intimidating up close, its armor covered in spikes and ridges, its head covered in a bony helmet with slits for its eyes. It landed nimbly on the top edge of the wall and reached for the short swords sheathed at its back.

Tad the Cunning was ready for it, waraxe in hand.

He swung before the armored figure could pull a sword, putting all his strength into the attack. The thick blade of his waraxe struck its armored chest with a sound like an enormous bell. The figure was blasted from the battlements, its armor rent in two. It rocketed towards the earth, trailing a red mist behind it, and struck the ground with an audible thump.

Willum saw smoke rising from the body below and looked back to Tad with wonderment. This was the first time he had seen Tad fight. Unlike the other instructors, Tad preferred to train away from the eyes of the students. Still, his prowess was legendary. Even Faldon the Fierce said he wouldn't want to risk fighting him. Now Willum understood why.

"You used your axe." Mad Jon said in surprise.

It was the first time Willum had seen the weapon unsheathed. It was about two feet long. The head had a wide flat blade on one side and a wicked spike on the other. The surface of the weapon was covered in runes, their impressions painted red.

"I had a bad feeling about that thing, Jon." Tad placed the

weapon back into the half-sheath at his waist. "There was something . . . unnatural about it."

"Well, it's definitely dead, sir," Willum said. From this height it looked like little more than a smoking green puddle. What did Tad's axe do to it?

"It had better be. I don't have many of those left." Tad turned back to the archers. "Jon, I want you to go get Bill the Fletch and tell him I want two ballistae brought up from storage. Have the engineers mount them at the corners of this wall."

"But the plan-," Mad Jon began.

"It is ahead of schedule, I know. But I want any giant that tries to throw anything at this wall put on a spit."

Mad Jon nodded and headed down the stairs. Swen went to follow him, but Tad laid a hand on his arm, "I'm sorry, Swen, but I need you to stay here and man this wall."

"Yes, sir." The large man nodded and though his tone was even, there was a hint of a smile around his lips.

Willum knew that there was no place Swen would rather be. Archery was the thing Swen cared about most. In fact, it was all Swen ever thought of. When he wasn't practicing, he was crafting arrows. He was quiet and people thought it was because he was shy and dull, but Willum was pretty sure that was just because Swen was thinking about shooting. The wall was the only place where he could actually put his skill to use. Swen had once told Willum that he liked being perched atop the highest structure around, looking at the army below, and knowing that he was the deadliest man on the wall.

Willum envied him that; being the best at something. Willum knew he was pretty good at a lot of things. He scored near the top of his class in several subjects, but was never quite good enough to stand out. He supposed that was one reason why he chose twin scythes as his weapon of choice. They were farmer's weapons, not commonly used by professional warriors. It wasn't until after he was accepted that he found out there were four other students using the same weapon.

He glanced back down at the giant army and started in surprise. The commander had shoved aside the giants that were dragging him away from the wall and was climbing back to his feet. He tore the arrow out of his throat and glared up at the wall with his one remaining eye. Ignoring the blood spurting from his wound, he barked out an order and the ogres rushed over to open the boxed cart again.

"Uh, sir? He's back up!" Willum said. Tad didn't hear him. He had moved further down the wall and was barking out instructions to the other soldiers at their posts. "Tad the Cunning, sir!"

Tad looked back at Willum, then down at the army below.

The ogres had dragged something out of the cart that looked like an enormous shaggy ball. They began rolling it across the ground toward the commander, but one of the ogres cried out and clutched his arm. Willum saw a gout of blood pour from its arm as both ogres backed away. Willum swallowed. This could be bad.

"Swen!" Tad shouted. "Don't let him throw that thing up here!"

"I see him, sir." The tall man said, an arrow already notched to the string. He began to draw it back towards his ear. "He just needs to come a little closer . . ."

The gray giant staggered over to the place where the ogres had left the ball, then stood in front of it and pointed to the top of the wall, his remaining eye glaring at Swen. He shouted something and the giant army roared in approval. Though he couldn't hear what was said, Willum knew it was a challenge.

Swen's voice was as monotone as ever. "Just come closer, Giant."

The giants began a rhythmic chant, punctuated by clapping and stomping. Their commander turned and reached down and gripped the ball's shaggy exterior with both hands. He lifted the ball and took several steps towards the wall before starting his spin.

"Stop him!" Tad shouted.

"Almost there . . ." said Swen, his bow drawn to its fullest extent, his arms quivering ever so slightly.

The chanting grew louder and the commander spun, picking up speed with every step.

"Now!" Tad shouted.

Swen shot. The arrow whistled as it arced towards his target.

The arrow destroyed the gray giant's remaining eye. Willum shouted in celebration, but the chanting didn't stop and neither did the blinded commander. He ended his final spin with a mighty heave and the ball left his hands, soaring through the air straight for his target.

Swen stared at the oncoming ball in disbelief and Tad had to pull the large man out of the way.

The large ball barely cleared the top edge. It struck the walkway right where Swen had been standing before rolling up to balance precariously on the edge of the inside wall. It stood still for a moment and Willum was able to see it clearly for the first time. The enormous ball was about the height of a man and was made of leafy tentacles. Willum's heart thumped in recognition.

"Whip beast!" he cried, drawing his scythes.

Tad moved Swen aside and raised his axe, but before he could strike, the ball shivered and began to open. The movement caused it to teeter and the weight of its unfurling pulled it off the wall. It tumbled into the academy proper, a writhing mass of tentacles.

The whip beast struck the ground not far from where the dead man had landed. A crowd of villagers that were still gathered together talking about it cried out and backed away as the whip beast spread out. Its thick roots dug into the hard packed gravel and its willowy fronds extended towards them. A single stalk rose from its tangled center, the tip opening to reveal a large eye.

"Get away from it!" Willum shouted.

It was too late. The beast's whip-like tentacles lashed out and people began to fall. Screams echoed from the streets below.

"Swen, you watch those giants!" Tad grabbed Willum and rushed for the stairs. "What do you know about that thing?"

Willum followed closely on his heels. "It's the same kind of beast that attacked my father by the Wide River! I recognized it from the memories he showed me. We need to keep people at a distance. It moves slowly but its attacks have a decent range!"

They reached the bottom of the stairs and ran down the path at the base of the wall. The area around the beast had been cleared of citizens and it was ringed by a group of wary guards with spears.

"Stay back!" Tad commanded. By the looks of it, they had already learned that lesson. Several of their spears were missing tips and two men had been wounded and pulled aside.

The scene around the whip beast was a massacre. It had cut down several citizens during the confusion and its willowy leaves rustled as its tentacles whipped about, slicing the bodies of its victims into smaller and smaller pieces. The white root-like vines at the beast's base slowly pulled it over their remains.

"Tell me more about it, Willum. What are its attacks?" Tad asked.

"Uh . . ." Willum tried to remember everything he had seen in Coal's memories. "It whips about with those tentacles, sir. They are very sharp and can take a man apart but shouldn't be able to cut through heavy armor."

Tad nodded and his shrewd eyes picked out two of the graduates that looked the most frightened. He called them by name. "Narl. Vaughn. Go and get some Defense Guild troops here, now."

"Shields too." Willum said.

"Tell them we need shields!" Tad added. The two men nodded and ran. "The rest of you, keep the citizens away from here."

One of the men raised a quivering arm to point at the base of the whip beast. It had moved its bristling bulk forward and settled back down on the bloody ground, its roots digging in. The beast was feasting. "But sir, it's . . ."

"Don't focus on that, graduate. Just watch its whips and stand clear, understood?" Tad turned back to Willum. "How did your father kill it?"

"Uh, he used magic to dry it out and they set it on fire," he said.

"Get me oil and torches!" Tad commanded. Two more men ran off. "Anything else?"

"Not as far as weaknesses, sir," Willum said. "But as far as father could tell, it absorbs the bodies of its kills to heal itself."

A guard in heavy armor ran up and Tad took his shield. He pulled his waraxe free of its sheath, the red runes along its length seeming to glow. He eyed the beast with a calculating gaze and stepped forward.

"Sir!" Willum said. "It's best to attack it from a distance. It will be difficult to avoid its tentacles up close."

"These men need to see it fought," Tad said quietly, his eyes not leaving the beast. "I will stall it until the fire arrives."

Tad took stepped towards the beast, but a man darted in ahead of him. Willum's eyes widened in surprise.

Dann Doudy ran at the beast, his gaudy jeweled sword swinging. The whip beast lashed out at him, but Dann was quicker than he looked. He dodged the attacks, his stocky body always seeming to move aside just enough. His sword arm was just as fast. He severed each tentacle that came at him and the beast shuddered. More tentacles grew to replace the ones lost, but Dann moved in close, cutting wide swathes of leafy fronds. Wherever his blade touched, the leaves shriveled and browned.

The whip beast shook, its roots digging deeper into the ground. Tad ran up to help him, but tentacles lashed out at him and he had to raise his shield to block the attacks. The stocky man kept dodging attacks and swinging his sword, hacking and slicing, the ground around him littered with shriveling plant matter.

The beast flailed at him in a panic, but Dann upped his speed, dancing about nimbly as if he knew where each attack would land ahead of time. He severed tentacles quicker than it could replace them. Great patches of the beast turned a sickly yellow and the beast shuddered and contracted, pulling its leaves in, but Dann's attack was unrelenting.

He lopped off its eye stalk just as the two men returned with a bucket of oil and torches. Dann saw them coming and smiled. He strolled over and grabbed the bucket from the surprised graduate's hands, then doused the beast as Tad stared in stunned silence.

"Torch it, lads!" Dann Doudy said with a grin.

The graduates tossed the torches onto the beast and it went up in flame. Dann laughed and turned towards the people watching. He raised his sword in triumph and cheers erupted from the crowd. He sheathed his sword and walked towards them, shaking hands and accepting pats on the back.

Willum looked at the burning beast and the bloody remains of its victims and he didn't feel like cheering. He looked around and saw others with similar somber expressions. It would be difficult to identify the bodies from what was left of them. They would need to question the people who escaped. There were families that needed to know. Funerals to be held . . . He glanced over to Tad the Cunning and he could see that the instructor was thinking the same thing.

Tad walked over to Dann who was chatting with the crowd gathered around him. He had unsheathed his sword again and was pointing out the runes that snaked around the jewels on its hilt. "It's called Wither. It's been in the Doudy family for generations. My father slew-."

"Dann," Tad interrupted. "You shouldn't have run in there. That was very dangerous."

The nobleman smirked. "Come now, Tad. It was just a hedge that needed trimming." He walked off, laughing and talking to the people that followed in his wake.

Tad's eyes narrowed, but he busied himself organizing the soldiers. He assigned men to keep the fire under control and set others to cleaning up and finding people that might be able to help determine who had died. The grounds were as crowded as ever and people called out, asking questions about what happened. He handled the citizens remarkably well considering the circumstances, assuring them that an investigation was underway.

Willum thought back to the fight, frowning. Something about it just wasn't right. Doudy's skill and dexterity, the ease with which he battled the beast had all been a surprise, but it was more than that. There was something else . . .

He was still worrying it over in his mind as Tad walked by, headed in the direction of the infirmary.

"Sir!" Willum said, jogging to his side. "About that fight-."

"You should return to the wall with Swen, Willum. Make sure that the giants aren't causing more problems," Tad said, his eyes lost in thought. "I need to go check on the body the giant threw over."

"Sir, the whip beast! What was it doing here among the enemy army? Not only that, but my father spoke of a green armored figure like the one you struck down that attacked his friends. Both of them were constructs made by Ewzad Vriil."

"Interesting," Tad said, still walking forward.

"Interesting?" Willum said in exasperation.

"This information doesn't change anything. You convinced me that Ewzad Vriil was behind this long ago. It's the rest of the council we have to prove it to and unfortunately, it still just comes down to your father's word against his."

"But sir! There was something else I realized. Something that was bothering me about the way Representative Doudy fought that beast."

"You mean besides the way he stepped in and made me look a fool?" Tad asked with a weary smile.

Willum shook his head. "Not possible. He didn't do that, sir. No, its . . . well, first of all, you saw the way he moved."

"I was just as surprised as you, but you can't judge a man's skill by his appearance."

Then it came to him. "His appearance! Sir, you've watched him during council meetings. How does Representative Doudy react to the slightest bit of stress?"

Tad shrugged. "He turns purple as a grape."

"Exactly," Willum said. "And he acts as if he can barely restrain his anger. But during that fight . . ?"

116

Tad stopped walking and turned to face him. "His face didn't darken a shade."

"You couldn't get close to the beast, but he wasn't stressed at all. I would swear he knew exactly what the beast was going to do, before it did it," Willum said.

Tad stood in silence for a moment, stroking his chin thoughtfully, a deep frown on his face. "My intellectual side says we're being ridiculous, but my warrior instincts disagree. I have been rewatching that battle in my head and I find myself taking your theory one step further. I think he was controlling it."

Chapter Eight

Talon flitted through the leaves as happy as she had been in a long time. She was outside. Outside and running free, feeling new and different, thanks to Ewwie. Her sweet master had improved her body in so many ways. The changes had been painful, but it was a sweet pain, a pain she craved, and nearly every change was for the better.

She inhaled deeply, thrilling in the interesting and luxurious scents of early spring. It was so different from the way she had used to taste the air. Her master had torn the scent receptors from a prized bloodhound and placed them deep within her nasal slits. There was food everywhere and her nose told her where to find it far better than her forked tongue had.

The smell of fresh prey caused her stomach to rumble and Talon began to jump as she ran, hoping to better hone in on the scent of the birds that nested high in the trees. Ewwie had changed the structure of her legs, making the muscle more densely corded and powerful. The improved strength allowed her to leap with great bounds, reaching twice as high as before.

Talon latched onto the trunk of a tree that she knew was occupied. Her claws dug into the bark and she climbed it with practiced dexterity knowing that the prey would not be caught unawares. With a startled squawk, a fat bird flew from its perch. Talon did not let it get far. She sprung from the tree and snatched the bird out of the air.

She hit the ground with a roll and continued to run. Talon would have enjoyed killing the thing slowly, but she did not have the time to stop. Instead, she let the bird's panicked strugglings amuse her for a few brief moments before tearing its head off with her teeth. She wolfed it down and savored the various textures and flavors of her meal.

Talon's new tongue didn't work like it used to. She couldn't taste the fear of her prey or the tiny particles of blood in the air. But it was thick and dexterous and sensitive to different kinds of sensations. There was a depth of flavor to the flesh of her kills that she had been missing before.

"*You are fooling yourself,*" said the moonrat mother. "*Your body was perfect before he touched you. Ewzad Vriil mutilated and enslaved you.*"

I am free, Talon thought.

"*You are only let out of your cage because he needs you to do his bidding. He'll throw you back in as soon as you are done,*" the voice snorted. "*This is not freedom.*"

The moonrat mother liked to play this game, trying to see if she could get Talon to run off on her own. Talon had done so before, thinking that escaping her master would bring her happiness. But now she understood that true freedom was only given her when she obeyed her master's commands. When she did as he asked, Ewwie let her stay near him as he worked and sometimes let her run free and hurt things and eat things. Refusal to obey only resulted in confinement and loneliness. If there was one thing Talon hated, it was loneliness.

She lifted her arm and kissed the shriveled eye imbedded on the inside of her forearm. At first she had seen the moonrat mother as an intruder, but she had come to understand that the eye was a precious gift. Her beloved Ewwie had given her a constant companion. There would be no loneliness on this journey. This time she would make sure to do just as Ewwie asked.

"*By the gods! Must you think of him that way?*" the voice complained.

Talon gurgled in happiness at her irritation. The moonrat mother hated it when she called the master Ewwie and when the moonrat mother was angry the moonrat mother talked to her. Talon liked to talk.

"Why you hatess Ewwie, female?" she asked, enjoying

the feel of the human language on her lips and tongue. Of all the changes to her body, her favorite new feature was her lips. Talon spent much of the journey experimenting with them. She puckered and popped and blew as she ran, enjoying the variety of new sounds she could make. This annoyed the female voice to no end.

"He's foolish and insufferable and ignores my council," replied the female with a mental glower. *"And you shall call me mistress."*

Talon knew there was more to it than the female admitted. She had been thinking on it as she ran. "You hate that Ewwie ruless you. You hate that Ewwie can hurtss you."

"Be silent, you foul creature," the female hissed.

"Will you hurtss me now, female?" Talon asked hopefully.

"You don't think I can hurt you, you insignificant thing?"

"You can not hurtss me like Ewwie," she teased, hoping to enrage her companion. The moonrat mother was good at causing pain. It wasn't quite as delicious as the pain Ewwie could give out, but she found it stimulating nonetheless.

"Oh can't I?" Talon could feel the rage burning inside the mother. *"You tempt me, but it is best I don't punish you now. We are getting too close to your goal and in my present frame of mind, I might kill you."*

"Death? From pain?" Talon shivered with anticipation. "Thiss you sshould try, female. I do not believess you."

The moonrat mother snorted. *"Run faster. Your master is impatient. He keeps asking if we have found them yet."*

Talon smiled. This was a thing her new lips did when she was happy and any way she could please Ewwie made her happy. She increased her speed as much as her body would allow. It wasn't a lot because she had already been at her limit, but the bird she had eaten would give her body the extra energy it needed to go a little bit faster for a time. She had been running for several days, stopping only a few short hours each night to sleep. All of her meals had been eaten on the run.

It grew dark, but that didn't slow her stride. Not anymore.

Ewwie had torn her new eyes from the skull of a mountain cat and now even starlight shone bright as noon day. In the past darkness had been a useful tool but it had also meant isolation. With her new eyes, the darkness was her friend.

She headed into an open field and was just getting into the flow of the new speed when something caused her to stop as abruptly as if she had hit a boulder. At the edge of the field, standing right in front of her was a thick forest line. She felt a shiver deep within her. The bark of each tree had been carved with an x.

"What is this, creature? Why have you stopped?"

Talon reached out and traced the x with one claw. She had not felt this way in years. A memory came fresh to her mind. She could almost feel the heat on her scales and feel the sand between her toes as Deathclaw stopped and tasted the air before turning the pack around to find easier prey. The memory vanished as quickly as it appeared, but Talon understood. She was standing at the edge of another creature's territory. Her lips pulled away from her razor teeth in another wicked smile. This was the territory of something powerful.

She let out a hissing chuckle. What a battle this would be.

"No, Talon!" The female voice had heard her thoughts. *"The thing that lives here is none of your concern. Go around this territory. The place Ewzad wants you to find is very near."*

"Ssilence, female." Talon whispered and took a step forward, entering the beast's territory.

"He has a reward waiting for you when you return," the female urged. *"But you cannot have it if you fail him now."*

Talon paused, frozen with indecision. Ewwie wanted her to obey, but something that powerful so close . . . she hissed, itching to destroy it.

"Ewzad says for you to obey him now, or-or . . ." The voice grew harder now. *"He shall lock you away again."*

Talon's heart sank. She whimpered but finally, reluctantly, pulled her foot back out of the territory. She slunk along the edge of the treeline, grumbling. The urge to kill lingered. She glanced around, sniffed and listened, but there was nothing living nearby but the plants and insects. Why was it so quiet?

A minute later her nose caught a scent that sent a shiver down her scales. There was power in the air. She stopped and scanned the forest edge. There it was.

He was standing so still that despite her new eyes, it took a moment for her to pick him out among the trees. He was huge. Standing at twice Talon's height, he looked like he was carved out of rock. She would have thought him a statue, if not for the slight rise and fall of his chest. His skin was the color of granite and his only clothing was a pair of bedraggled breeches. Around his neck hung a thick chain of black iron with a crystal shard pendant.

"*Be still,*" the female said. "*Wait until he moves on.*"

The giant stood at the very edge of his territory looking out, a pensive look on his chiseled face. Slowly he looked down at the territory line marked by the trees and then turned and looked back over his shoulder at the forest's center. He let out a sigh. In this moment of unease he looked vulnerable. Now could be the perfect time to attack.

A chirpy giggle escaped from her throat.

"*By the gods, be silent you stupid creature!*"

The giant turned his rocky head and looked right at her. "Who is it?"

"*Run around him!*" the female encouraged. "*You are faster than he is.*"

"Have you come for my treasure?" His voice was deep and throaty. "Well whoever you are, I don't care. You can have it."

The giant turned away from her and took a deep breath, then stepped out of his territory. He walked away from the forest, heading east with a sure and steady purpose. Talon found this unacceptable. She crept after him, her fingers trembling with anticipation.

"*Stay back,*" the moonrat mother warned.

Talon snuck up behind the giant without making a sound, following close behind him for a few moments, listening to him mumble to himself. Her tail twitched as she thought of the battle that would ensue and of the misery and helplessness she would make him feel before he died.

"*He will kill you,*" the voice promised.

That made him all the more irresistible. Talon took two running steps and jumped to his back. She clawed and scratched at him, but could not pierce his stony skin.

The giant swore and reached back for her. He was amazingly quick for a beast his size, but she was quicker and scrambled to the other side of his back, evading his fingers. She continued to claw and stab with her tail, looking for a weak point.

"You little!" the giant snapped, contorting and twisting in an attempt to grab her.

Talon knew how the battle would go, having fought many large creatures before. She continued to dodge, waiting for the moment when he would give up his reaching and try to roll on the ground and crush her. She would leap away just in time and then while he was on his back, she would have him.

Her plans were disrupted when one of his hands seized her leg. He ripped Talon from his back and slammed her to the ground before pinning her with his other hand. His wrapped his thumb and forefinger tightly around her neck and lifted her with one arm. He held her out in front of him, a scowl on his face.

"What are you?" He asked, looking her over with curiosity. "I haven't seen a lizard woman like you before."

She hissed at him in defiance, clawing at his fingers.

He rolled his eyes. "Look, I don't care really. Just leave me be. You can't hurt me and besides, I don't want to fight right now." He tossed her to the side and started to walk away.

"*Good,*" the voice said. "*Now get out of here before he changes his mind. Our goal is very close.*"

Talon pushed the voice away and sprang at him again. She wrapped an arm around his neck and strained, digging in her claws, trying to tear out his throat. To her satisfaction, she felt his skin give. Then he grabbed her and tore her free once again.

The giant held her at arms length once more and this time

his scowl was replaced by a glare. She saw the red gouges in his neck where she had scratched him. She could smell his blood. There was power in that blood. Talon licked her lips.

"Just . . . leave me alone!" he said.

Talon smiled at him, then puckered her lips and made kissing sounds. She chirped at him and cooed suggestively. She waited for the giant's eyes to widen in confusion, then she bit into his finger as hard as she could. Three of her teeth shattered, but she broke through his skin. The taste of his blood was intoxicating.

Power coursed through the giant's veins and though the flavor was somewhat different, she knew that his body had been transformed by magic just as she and her brother had been. The difference was that where Ewwie's transformations were rushed and slip-shod, the flavor of this giant's transformation was orderly and perfect in its execution. That was something she couldn't abide.

The giant's glare deepened and he pulled her closer. "Are you crazy, lizard woman?"

She thrust out her tail, sending the barbed tip up his nose. To her satisfaction, the flesh inside was as soft and yielding as any creatures.

"*Idiot,*" said the female voice.

The giant roared and drew his arm back, yanking her tail barb out of his nose with a gush of blood. He took a step and threw her as hard as he could. Talon had never been hurled at such a velocity before. The ground streaked past her and she knew the landing was going to hurt. Talon savored the anticipation.

She struck a tree, snapping several small branches before slamming into the trunk. Three of her ribs broke on impact. Then she fell and cracked another when she hit the ground. Talon lay there among the tree's roots for a few moments unable to breathe, watching the tree branches spinning above her. It was a new feeling. She smiled.

"*Have you learned your lesson yet, you foolish thing?*" the moonrat mother chided. "*Stay where you are. Luckily he hasn't come to finish you. For some reason, he doesn't seem in the mood to fight tonight. He is still standing there watching you, though. Lie still until he walks away."*

Talon took a deep breath. Her ribs cried out, but the pain was muted. They were already healing. Ewwie had made her body heal far too fast. She giggled and climbed to her feet.

"Stop!"

Talon walked towards the giant. She ached to kill it. She wouldn't be satisfied until she had torn its rocky skin off and rolled around in its eviscerated remains.

"You will obey," the female said.

Talon felt the moonrat mother moving around in the back of her mind and knew what was coming. She ran towards the giant, getting two full steps in before the pain hit. Every nerve ending along her legs burst into flame. Talon could feel her flesh searing, felt flames licking up her back. It was ecstasy.

Talon kept running, screeching in agony and pleasure, enjoying the increased efforts of the female to ratchet up the pain. Her stomach cramped. She was hit by a wave of nausea. Her teeth exploded. Her lungs filled with glass. Her eyes boiled in their sockets. Yet they didn't, not really. She was aware that blood leaked from her nostrils and ears, that much was true, but the rest of it wasn't real. Ewwie liked to hurt the body physically, but the female could only cause pain in the mind.

The giant crouched and watched her manic approach. His eyes were wary, but his body ready, arms extended in front of him ready to grab her. The scratch on his neck was gone and the bite marks on his hand were healed. The dried blood around his nose was the only sign she had hurt him at all. This both disappointed her and excited her all the same. This giant was a challenge.

"Fine," the female said. *"I leave you to your death. Ewzad will be so disappointed."*

Talon watched the giant's stance and prepared to leap over his outstretched arms. A single tail thrust would put out one of his eyes. Then she would start the slow dance of death, staying just out of his reach while sending her attacks into his every oriface. He would slow down once he could no longer see or hear.

The female cut off the pain so abruptly that Talon stumbled. She leapt, but the giant snatched her out of the air. He gripped her around the torso with both hands, pinning her arms to her sides.

"Did someone send you here to attack me?" he asked, his eyes intense.

She cocked her head and chirped questioningly.

"No? Then why are you here? What do you want?"

"To killss you," she said and licked her lips.

"Is that all?" he asked in amusement. "So you talk. That's good. Tell me what you really want."

"To tearss you," she hissed, her eyes wild and menacing. "To open your skin and eatss your meat."

His amusement faded. "Is that so?"

"Eatss you. Bleedss you. Hurtss you. Killss you!"

These were the things that Ewwie had taught her to say. These were the things that she knew would bring fear to her prey. It had always worked before, but the giant's reaction was disappointing. All she saw was sadness in his eyes.

"I wasn't that much different than you once," he said, then looked away. "Well, I hope I wasn't quite so . . . broken as you."

Talon didn't like his tone. She put on her most hideous smile. "I will killss you! Eatss you!"

The giant sighed. "I suppose I can't put you down and let you go. You'd probably go kill some farm family."

Now she saw a hint of fear. Talon pressed the advantage. "Yess! Make them cry. Eatss the babies! Make them ssee the blood."

"I will try to make this quick, then," he said with a sad shake of his head. "I wish my master had been brave enough to do this for me long ago."

"Eatss your masster-!"

The giant slammed his forehead into hers with a thud.

Talon's neck bones compacted. Her skull fractured in several places. The pain was so sharp and quick that she wasn't able to enjoy it. Her limbs spasmed. He squeezed her with his powerful hands. She felt bones break and organs rupture. Her vision dimmed. Blood poured from her open mouth and the giant threw her on the ground. The last thing she saw was tears on his face as his enormous foot descended on her again and again.

Then there was only darkness. Even her new eyes couldn't see. There was . . . nothing.

"Wake, foolish one . . ."

Talon's eyes fluttered open. The sudden light was overpowering and she winced. The sun was shining directly overhead.

"You are amazing. You really are. I see now why he favors you so much."

She sat up and looked around. She was sitting in the impression the giant had stomped her into. Her body ached and tingled, but it was the familiar ache of newly healed flesh. Her bones were unbroken. Her organs tender but whole.

"That attack would have killed most of us. Even your master would have died, crushed faster than Stardeon's rings could have saved him." Her voice grew thoughtful. *"This explains why he is so fixated on bringing in your brother. It is hard to imagine there being two beings like you."*

Talon struggled to stand and barely made it to her feet. Swaying weakly, she looked down at herself. She was emaciated to the extreme, her muscle all but gone. Her skin left looking as if it were plastered on her bones. Her body's healing ability had taken over again it seemed, using up all her stores in order to heal the damage.

"How long hass I-?"

"A day and a half. And Ewzad is very angry. He is throwing a tantrum about it right now," the moonrat mother said casually.

"Ewwie iss mad?" she asked with a shudder.

"I think I shall take you for myself when we return. Oh

the things we could do together. If only he hadn't used such a pitiful eye when joining you to me. If I had known, what he was up to, I would have sacrificed one of my most special children for you. I bet he will put an orange one in you for me when we return. I shall have to be sweet to him for awhile . . ."

Talon ignored her, placing one thin hand against her shriveled stomach. Why wasn't she hungry? Whenever her healing magic had to repair heavy damage, it made her ravenous.

"I have taken your hunger away for now. It was too overpowering and I need you to focus on the reason Ewzad sent you here. The site of the bandham's demise is very close by. You can eat after we get there."

"Yess. I eatss later," Talon agreed. She crouched low to the ground and sniffed at the impressions left by the giant's feet. With his scent firmly in mind, she began to follow his trail. The taste of his blood still lingered on her tongue and she wanted more.

"*No,*" said the moonrat mother.

"Will you hurtss me again?" Talon said, with a smile.

"*I will do worse,*" she said and Talon sensed the female moving around in side her mind again. Talon opened her mind in anticipation of the pain, but she felt nothing.

Talon blinked. She felt nothing. She could see, but she couldn't hear. She couldn't feel the air on her skin or the ground under her feet. Panic rose within her. She raised her bony arm and bit into it, but there was no pain, not even the sensation of tearing. She couldn't smell or taste the blood, though she saw it flowing from her arm. She screeched and threw herself on the ground, but there was no sound, no sensation. Just complete numbness.

"*You disobeyed me, dear Talon. This is your punishment.*"

Talon raised her right arm in front of her face and looked at the shriveled eye that bulged from her scrawny forearm. It would be so easy to tear it out and be rid of the female.

"*You do that and you will lose your senses forever.*"

Ewwie would not let you, she thought desperately.

"As if he could stop it."

"Why you do thiss?" she said aloud, though she could not feel her lips and could not hear the sound.

"Because you disobeyed me," she said. *"And because I know you now."*

You know me? Talon thought.

"It took me a while to realize why my efforts at punishing you were worthless. But I have been around a long time. I have been in the minds of countless beings and though it has been a very long time since I encountered someone like you, the giant said something that jogged my memory. And he was right. You, my dear, are broken. Ewzad broke you long ago."

Talon lay still, not even sure if she was breathing. Not that it mattered. Without sensation she would rather die. *I am . . . broken?*

"I have seen it before. Indeed, I have been the cause of it before. The pain your master put you through would have killed most beings. But not you, Talon. No, you are a survivor. You would not die and that allowed Ewzad to do things to you that he could not do to others." She chuckled. *"There was a point some time along the way where his experiments went too far. You had a choice. Either die, or embrace the pain. You went a step further. You chose to love it."*

In a brief moment of clarity Talon saw that she was right. She could dimly remember that for most of her life, she had seen pain as something to be avoided. Deathclaw spent decades trying to save the pack from pain. Deathclaw tried to save her from it again when he freed her from the wizard's castle. Talon realized that he had still been trying to save her from it one last time the day he tried to kill her. Was he right to do so? Was she truly that broken?

C-can you fix me . . . Mistress?

The moonrat mother let out a gloating laugh. *"Oh I could, dear. But why would I? I know what your weakness is and now . . . I control you."*

You control me?

"Do you wish to feel again?"

Yes, Mistress.

"Then you shall do as I command."

Talon would have grit her teeth if she could feel them. *Yes, Mistress.*

The world of sensation came back in a rush. She gasped in the sweet air, absorbing the scents around her. She felt the pain of her arm knitting itself together and her fleshy tongue hurt. She had bitten it several times without knowing.

She stood, enjoying the feel of the earth beneath her feet. "Where sshall I go, Mistress?"

"Follow the forest edge towards the river."

Talon walked south along the treeline until she came upon the grassy slope leading down to the shore. She smelled faint traces of smoke in the air and saw a burnt patch of ground. A small trace of Ewwie's power clung to the area and she knew that one of his creatures had died there.

"There. Ahead."

She ran down the slope and across the graveled riverbank and came upon the scene of the battle. The earth was blackened and in places had turned to glass. Sheets of rock had turned molten and fused together. And at the center of it were the remains of Ewwie's pet bandham. Her mouth watered as the stench of decay filled her nose.

Talon sniffed at the gelatinous chunks of its flesh that still rotted on the ground. The remains were unrecognizable as the creature that had battled her for days before dragging her back to Ewwie's side. Talon only knew what they were because of the tiny shreds of her master's power that still clung to them.

The mother of the moonrat released her hold on Talon's hunger. *"Now you can feast."*

Talon had no choice but to obey. Her body cried out for sustenance, and it did not matter that the bandham's remains were devoid of texture and repulsive in taste and smell. She was consumed by the need to fill her belly. Her body demanded the building blocks it needed to replace the tissues that it had broken down to heal her.

She gobbled it down by the fistful, unaware of anything

but the sensation of swallowing. Her body took care of the rest, breaking the material down and redistributing it as fast as she could eat. The remnants of her master's power combined with her own, speeding up the process. Finally she slumped to her side, the hunger sated. Her body had already begun to fill out nicely.

"Now," said the moonrat mother. "Find the trail of the bandham's killers."

"Yess, Misstress," Talon said and obeyed.

Chapter Nine

Justan released the arrow and smiled as it struck the stump, proud to see it quivering precisely in the center of the rest of the arrows he had fired. He could feel Ma'am's pleasure at finally being put to use. Justan slid the bow across his back and went to retrieve the arrows.

The further east they traveled, the more it seemed that spring was setting in. The forest in this area had already budded with new leaves and he could hear birds chirping in the trees.

"Good shot, son," Lenny said and Bettie, who was standing beside him, added an impressed nod. It had been the dwarf's idea to get in some practice with the bow. The other members of the group were setting up camp for the night. Justan had been reluctant to leave the work to everyone else, but they hadn't seemed to mind and shooting was a welcome diversion after the daily ride.

They were only a week out of Sampo and the Mage School was only a half day's ride from there. The only thing slowing them down was stopping in the towns and so far, their excursions hadn't provided much information they didn't already have. The townsfolk knew of the siege and most of them seemed to be of the opinion that Dremald should send its garrison to help. However there were others who believed Ewzad Vriil's claim that a foreign army was approaching and the garrison was needed to protect the city.

Meanwhile, the entire Dremald army was huddled around the city. About the only useful rumor was that the army had been slowly reducing in numbers. They had heard some say that a disease was killing the men. Others said that a group of soldiers had deserted in order to help the academy on their own.

Justan wrenched the arrows from the stump, surprised to see that all but one of them were still useable. He placed them back in his quiver, glad he had decided not to use the dragonhair string. It tended to blast the arrows to pieces and though Bettie had told him she didn't mind making more along the journey, it seemed a waste.

"Alright. Your turn, Bettie," Justan said as he started back towards them, making sure to step out of the line of fire.

"Yeah-yeah. You know it ain't fair you got that Jharro bow while I got this dumpy one." The half-orc lifted a wooden bow that she had carved and runed the day before. Master Coal had magicked the wood for her and she said that the runes would keep the wood supple and protect it from the elements better than any seasoning.

"Come on, woman. Both of us know you did a dag-gum fine job with that bow," Lenny said. "'Sides, I told you this weren't a competition. It's just practice."

"Yeah-yeah," she said, and pulled an arrow out of the quiver on her back. It was made of scotch bark and leather. Bettie had Lenny make it while she worked on the bow. She loved to ridicule him about his leatherwork.

Justan had been impressed at how excellent an archer Bettie was. She had always seemed like more of a short range fighter, but after him, she was probably the next best shot in their group. He walked over and stood by the dwarf.

"Thanks for suggesting this, Lenny. It feels good to get some practice in."

"Sure, son," the dwarf said, scratching his upper lip. His mustache was growing in nicely, though Bettie still gave him grief about it. She thought it looked like a furry red caterpillar perched under his nose. "I done seen you runnin' in the mornin and practicin' yer magic at night. You aughtta be trainin' with yer weapons too. It's dag-gum easy to go rusty on the trail."

Bettie fired off two shots, both of them striking right next to the knot Justan had aimed for. "Ha! Nearly as good and I ain't no named warrior!"

133

"Nice, Bettie!" Justan said with a smile. He felt a sense of approval coming through the bond and he looked up in the branches of a nearby tree. *I am surprised you took an interest in this, Deathclaw.*

It is good that you are not the only one who can attack from far away. This adds depth to the pack, Deathclaw sent.

Deathclaw seemed to divide his time either scouting ahead as they traveled or staring at the various members of their party from some hidden vantage point. He was constantly evaluating them and even though Justan explained to the others what he was up to, it still made them nervous. *Would you like to come down and try your hand at the bow?*

Deathclaw sent a mental snort. *Raptoids do not shoot arrows.*

And why not? You just mentioned how useful they are. Justan sent.

The raptoid's only answer was another snort before he slid down the tree and slunk away. *I go hunt now.* Justan wanted to press him on the issue, but he was interrupted by an elbow from Lenny.

"So listen son, there's somthin' I wanted to talk to you about," the dwarf said.

"You see that?" Bettie shouted, pointing towards her target. "Right on the center! Beat that, Lenui!"

Justan applauded. "Bettie, I have to tell you. I've seen you run, I've seen you spar, and I've seen you shoot. I have no doubt that you could easily pass the entrance exams to the Battle Academy."

"Ha! Ain't you sweet," Bettie said with a grin. "But I'm a smith first, warrior second."

"The academy needs smiths too," Justan said. "You would be a highly prized edition to the school. Your work is far superior to most of what I have seen out of the academy forges."

"Yer dag-gum right, son. At the least, she's better at leatherworkin' than Forgemaster Stanley and he's a gall-durned legend!" Lenny said with a gruff nod.

"You think so?" Bettie mused.

Lenny looked startled by the speculative look or her face. He hastened to add, "But she don't want to join the dag-burned academy anyway."

"Oh, I don't know about that, Lenui. I've thought about it before," Bettie said. "But there's two reasons it'd never happen. One, I'm a woman. Two, I ain't human."

"That shouldn't matter." Justan replied. "Women may not be as common as men at the academy, but they're there. Remember, I was trained by one. As far as being human is concerned. I've never heard of anyone being turned away. There are at least three dwarves at the school last I heard. And the bowmanship instructor Bill the Fletch is half-elf."

Bettie folded her well-muscled arms and frowned. "We both know that being half-orc is different. Most of the students would turn blue in the face if I was let in the academy."

"Yeah-," Lenny started.

"It wouldn't be that way," Justan assured, though he knew she had a valid concern. Half-orcs were the result of orc raids on human villages, which pretty much made them universally despised by both races. "Once they got to know you, they would have to be impressed. I could talk to my father and introduce him to you. No one would give you a hard time if Faldon the Fierce was on your side."

Betty's brow furrowed as she considered it for a moment, but she shook her head. "Naw. Thanks for offering, but it ain't worth talking about anyway. Home's back in Razbeck and I'm going to be needed back at the farm after all this is over."

Lenny's shoulders slumped in relief.

"Well, okay," Justan said. "But if you change you mind, let me know."

"Sure, I'll keep it in mind." Bettie said and went to retrieve her arrows.

Lenny elbowed him again and whispered, "Would'ja stop messin' with the woman and listen to what I wanted to say?"

Justan winced and rubbed his side where Lenny's elbows had hit. The dwarf was strong. He was pretty sure he was going to have a bruise there in the morning. "Why don't you want her to consider the academy?"

"This ain't about that, dag-blast it!" Lenny swore. "It's about the dag-burned reason I wanted to talk to you away from ever'body. It's about your dag-gum swords."

"What about them?"

"I done been watchin' you, son, and I ain't seen you even touch the gall-durn things in days. You ain't practiced with 'em once since yer fight with the dag-blamed bandham."

"I know," Justan said. "You're right. I need to work with them."

"Then why don't you?"

"I . . . don't know what to do with them, Lenny," he confessed. The swords sat in their sheathes on his back all day, but he avoided touching them.

"They're dag-gum swords. You know what to do with 'em," Lenny said. "They're gall-durn awkward, but that was yer design I used."

"No, it's not that. I mean, I definitely need to practice fighting with them. I have been planning out swordforms to use them most effectively, but . . . It's their powers," Justan said with a wince. It was embarrassing to admit. "The left one sucks my emotions away, which is taking some getting used to, and the right one . . ."

"What's the problem with your swords?" Bettie asked, just rejoining them.

"The right one is still full of the energy, it absorbed from Qyxal's pain," Justan said. "It's just sitting there begging to be used."

"Wait a dag-burned minute," Lenny said. "You never done told me 'bout this. What does yer right sword do?"

Justan sighed. "The right sword gathers and stores the emotions that the left one takes in. Then it somehow converts the emotions into an energy that can be released. I only used it once. It was when I was fighting Kenn. It caused the explosion that shattered him."

"I'll be dag-gummed," Lenny said. "All that time makin' the gall-durn things and I never knew. So right now yer right sword is-."

"Full of Qyxal's pain, shouting to be released. I feel it every time I touch it."

"That's a tough one," Lenny said with a frown.

"If it burns you that much, why don't you just get rid of it?" Bettie suggested. "Just take that energy and blast a rock with it or something,"

"Because it's Qyxal!" Justan said. "The pain of his death is in that sword. To just use that pain without a purpose seems like it would be . . . wasting his final moments."

Lenny places a hand on Justan's arm. "I'm sorry, son. That's a crab-kicker. I can't say as I know how to handle that one."

"I'll tell you what to do. You deal with it!" Bettie snapped. "If you're so determined to take responsibility for the elf's death, then stop being such a gall-durn baby about it. If you don't want to use the elf's pain, then learn to live with the fact that it's there. Don't hamstring yourself and maybe hurt your ability to protect your bonded. A real man isn't afraid to use his sword!"

"I-I . . ." Justan stammered. When she said it that way, it made him seem incredibly juvenile. "I hadn't thought about it like that. You're right. I can't avoid it. I just need to learn to handle it."

"Actually, you might be able to do better than that," Lenny said, his brow furrowed in thought. "Them swords are special. They're namin' swords. They don't act like reg'lar magic swords."

"What do you mean?"

"Well, son, let me tell you somethin' 'bout enchantin' weapons," Lenny said. "When yer shapin' the weapon, you got to keep in mind what you want it to do. That way yer tellin' it what to be from the start. Now the raw elemental magic's already inside it. It's different with every chunk of magic ore, dependin' on what kind of magic the wizard put into it."

Bettie rolled her eyes. "This is why it takes your apprentices so long to figure out how to make things right. What he's trying to say, Edge, is that before you start making the weapon, you need to find out what kind of magic is in the metal. That way you can decide what you can get the weapon to do."

"Dag-blast it, woman! That's 'zactly what I gall-durn said!"

Justan nodded. "It's okay, Bettie. I've been around him a long time. I speak Lenny."

The half-orc shrugged. "Sorry then. I used to have to explain everything he said to Benjo."

Lenny fumed a moment longer, then continued, "Anyways, there's only so many options dependin' on the metal."

"So it's like working a spell. If there's fire magic in the metal, you can make it into a hammer that sets your enemies on fire," Justan said.

"Like Bertha, that's right. But once you finish the weapon and you've shaped the magic with yer runes, the magic is set. It ain't changin' after that," Lenny said. "What I'm gettin' around to sayin' is that most magic weapons act the same way every time. Buster always hits twice as hard as I swing, whether I swing fast or slow. Bertha's going to heat things up to the same temperature every time."

"I understand," Justan replied. "But how is that supposed to help me?"

"It's not," Bettie said with a glare. "Thanks for wasting our time, you stupid dag-gum dwarf!"

"Would'ja let me friggin' finish! Blast it Bettie, if you wasn't a woman, I'd smash you right upside your dag-blamed head!"

She stormed up to him and bent over, glaring into his eyes. "Try it, dwarf! You couldn't even reach my dag-gum face!"

"If you two want to start kissing now, I am more than happy to leave," Justan said. They both turned their glares on him and Justan was sure that if eyes could burn, he would be a pile of ashes. He didn't back down, but just stared back at them calmly. Their anger faded to embarrassment.

Bettie straightened and cleared her throat. "That can wait for later."

Lenny looked down in shock and rubbed the back of his neck. "Can't believe you just said that, girl."

"Well everybody knows it!" She folded her arms and scowled. "No sense pretending otherwise. Coal's been telling me so for weeks."

"It's been pretty obvious," Justan said. "And I'm happy for both of you. Now that we have that out of the way, Lenny can you get to the point?"

"Er, right," the dwarf said, his cheeks red. "What I was sayin', dag-nab it, was that namin' weapons are different. They're bonded to you, so youc'n tell 'em what you want 'em to do.

"Fer instance, when I made yer friend Sir Hilt's swords, I made 'em with air magic. When he cut with his swords, it would cause a sharp blade of air to stick out past the edge. But I done heard that after he came back from the Bowl of Souls, he learnt to control what they did. He can make the blade of air longer or shorter, or even just make a big gall-durn gust of wind."

"So I can learn to control their magic?" Justan asked in surprise.

"Dunno why not," said Lenny. "Not quite sure how it'll work, but then again yer swords was strange from the beginnin'. The magic in the metal came from them broken weapons we found in the giant's cave. When I tested the magic, I was thinkin' of makin' one a fire sword and the other'n an ice sword, but when I put yer namin' blades in, they pretty much runed themselves. Dunno how they ended up doin' what they do. They don't follow the usual rules."

"Thanks, Lenny, I'll think on that," Justan said. He placed a hand on the dwarf's shoulder. "Both of you were right. I'm going to head back to the campsite. I'll talk with Master Coal about naming weapons during our lesson later."

Lenny nodded and Justan left the dwarf and half-orc standing there, eyeing each other.

He walked back towards the campsite and thought on

what they had said. The swords were part of his bond now. Preferably he needed to learn how to control them, and if not, he needed to at least get used to them.

Justan reached up and grasped the hilt of the left sword first. All his emotions slipped away until only his thoughts remained. It wasn't an uncomfortable sensation at all. It was quite freeing. In truth, he had been avoiding using the sword for just that reason. He was afraid that he would start using it as a crutch, clutching the sword any time he felt anxiety. Justan refused to get out of it that easy. He needed to feel the pain of his mistakes. Otherwise how would he figure out how to stop making them?

He let go of that sword and grabbed the hilt of the right one. He immediately felt its power buzzing in the back of his mind. It was eager to release Qyxal's pain. It was an uncomfortable sensation, similar to the feeling of a full bladder. He ached to find a way to release all that energy.

He gripped the other sword again and the urgency faded. As long as he held both of them the sensation was manageable. When he really focused on it, the power in the second sword didn't feel like pain. It was just pure energy. It was his knowledge of where the energy came from that made it uncomfortable.

Justan released both hilts as the camp came into view through the trees. The ground had been cleared and the warhorses' saddles had been removed. A fire crackled and Justan sensed that Fist had left to go hunting with Deathclaw.

Master Coal sat cross legged on the ground not far from the campfire as had become his custom. It still struck Justan as odd to see a named wizard wearing simple pants and a work shirt sitting in the dirt. He didn't look like a wizard at all, just a farmer. But then again, that was probably what he wanted.

"I hope you weren't waiting too long, Master Coal," Justan said.

"No, we just got the fire started before you arrived. Please, sit down."

Justan joined him, sitting and crossing his legs with a

grunt. He had never been a big fan of sitting on the ground, especially after a long day of riding. But Master Coal preferred it, so he bore with it, hoping his legs didn't cramp up.

"So, Edge," Coal began. "How did your practicing go today?"

He wasn't talking about the archery. Since resuming their lessons, Master Coal had given Justan a list of things to work on while they traveled. Right now it was sharing information under stress. Transferring memories through the bond was complex work and had even become quite dangerous.

"I-I am doing better, sir," he said. "It is still difficult at times. I have done as you asked and I think I have learned to keep my body in riding position as I work through the bond. It's just that I become so engrossed in what I'm doing-."

"And how many times did you fall off of Gwyrtha today?"

Justan winced. "Twice. But that was at the beginning of the day. I think I have it down much better now."

"Good," Coal nodded. "It is something that will come easier with practice, and eventually it will become second nature to you, but you need to learn quickly. What happens when you need to use the bond during battle? You can't be falling over while you try to heal one of your bonded."

"Yes, Master. I know," Justan said.

"And Fist?"

"I have passed our lessons along to him. He has been practicing with Squirrel as he walks," Justan said.

"And how is he doing?"

Justan's shoulders slumped a little. Fist hadn't even stumbled. "He does great. For some reason, the exercises come easy to him."

Coal chuckled at his embarrassment. "Don't let yourself get too discouraged, Edge. Each of us has areas we excel in and areas we find hard. You do most things better than any student I've taught."

"I will try to take that to heart."

"Good! So as usual, before we get started, I must ask

you," Coal leaned forward. "Do you have any questions for me?"

"Yes. It's about naming weapons," Justan said. He related the discussion he had with Lenny earlier. "Is he right? Do you know of a way I can learn to control the power of my swords?"

"Hmm," Coal stroked his chin. "First of all, you need to stop thinking of them as just swords. They are bonded to you just as Fist or Gwyrtha or Deathclaw are. You need to communicate with them. Get to understand them."

"Get to know my swords?"

"Yes," The wizard nodded. "And it might not hurt to give them names of their own, so they're easier to relate to. My naming dagger's name is Jewel. She may not have the kind of special powers that yours do, but that rune on her blade makes her a part of me. Through our bond she is an extension of my body and mind. Jewel allows me to enact spells in ways I could not otherwise. But it took me a while to learn how to use her.

"In the beginning, I was like you. I didn't know what to do with her, so I let her sit ignored on my belt. But my master took me aside and encouraged me to spend time communing with my dagger through the bond. He made me practice sending spells through her until I got it down."

"I see. I will think on giving them names," Justan thought of the hunger of his left sword and the impatience of his right sword. In a way they did have personalities of their own. "I suppose this is just another thing I have to practice."

"And I am going to give you more. We don't have much time before we reach the Mage School. You need to take advantage of every moment you have so that you will be ready to use your powers when the time comes," Coal said.

"Yes, sir," Justan said. The immense number of things he needed to work on was daunting.

"Now to start our lesson for this evening," Coal said and climbed to his feet.

Samson walked over to join them, Gwyrtha by his side. The centaur had shrunk down from his usual size to that of a small pony, making his torso the size of an average man. It was the first time Justan had seen Samson do that on this journey. He had only seen him do it while walking around Coal's keep.

"You ready, Coal?" Samson asked.

Justan stood. "Are we going for a ride somewhere?"

Ride! Gwyrtha agreed, as excited as ever even though they had been riding all day.

"No, but considering the subject matter of today's lesson, I thought it would be better if they were with us."

"What are we doing?" Justan asked, intrigued.

"Well, Edge, I think it's about time you learned about rogue horses."

Chapter Ten

Justan grinned in excitement.

"Samson has been pressing me to teach you this for quite a while, but I wanted to make sure you had more experience using the bond before bringing up these particular applications," Coal said. "There are many ways you could end up hurting Gwyrtha or yourself if you are not careful."

"What do you mean?" Justan asked. "What applications?"

"Manipulating body structure."

When Justan didn't immediately respond, Samson placed a hand over his face. "See, Coal? He has no idea."

Coal raised his eyebrows. "Why surely you've noticed the way I'm able to change Samson's size?"

Justan's eyes widened in understanding.

"You were doing that? All this time I thought that was just a unique ability Samson had. " He looked at Gwyrtha and she stared back at him quizzically. "So I can learn to do that? With Gwyrtha, I mean?"

"Yes or so Samson assures me," the wizard said. "I have only ever been bonded to one rogue horse, but he says it is an ability that Stardeon built onto all of them."

"Incredible." *Did you know?* He asked Gwyrtha. She didn't seem to understand the question so he pushed an explanation through the bond.

I can grow big like Samson? She asked in surprise.

"Why doesn't Gwyrtha know about this?" he asked Master Coal.

Coal looked to Samson who scratched his head. "Well . . . Gwyrtha was one of the first of Stardeon's successes, if not really his first successful template for the rest of us. She was not made with the mind to . . ." he winced. "Sorry, Gwyrtha."

Gwyrtha cocked her head at him, not understanding the need for an apology.

"Let's just say that she has become a lot smarter since bonding with you," Samson said. "She didn't understand a lot of things that Stardeon intended at the time."

"Not many of the rogue horses were particularly smart," Coal added. "I don't think Stardeon thought intelligence was an important factor in what he was trying to build."

"That's because Stardeon had planed on being around to distribute them," Samson said. "He would have been able to explain their uses to anyone."

"I'm sorry," Justan said. "I'm really not following you. What do you mean by distributing them?"

Samson scratched his head again and Coal stepped in. "Perhaps we should start from the beginning? It's what I was planning to do before we were sidetracked."

"Good." Justan put his arm around Gwyrtha's shaggy neck. "Please continue, Master."

"The Mage School records say that Stardeon was named at the Bowl of Souls and was even on the High Council at one point," Coal said. "He was one of the foremost experts in making magical constructs."

Justan's brow furrowed. He had learned about magic constructs at the Mage School. It was a means by which wizards could animate non-living things. The golem that Arcon, Pympol, and Piledon had created was a magical construct. They were difficult to make and not many wizards currently alive could manage them.

"What the records don't say was that Stardeon was also a powerful bonding wizard and an expert in spirit magic," Coal said. "He was a resident professor at the Mage School for several decades before he left and went into seclusion."

"We're not sure why he left but it was several years later

that he created his rings," Samson said. "He was quite proud of them and used to tell me about them all the time. He had come up with the concept of a spirit magic amplifier during his studies at the Mage School. He had never quite figured out how to make it work, but during his seclusion he had a breakthrough. He took his bonded and defeated a creature known as the Great Wyrm."

"One of the ten monsters of legend!" Justan said with a grin. He had read books about them as a child. His mother had told him the stories were nonsense, but he had been fascinated. The Great Wyrm was a snakelike dragon that lived in caves deep underground. It was said that it could control a person's body with its eyes and force them to do its bidding.

"Yes," Coal said. "A rare beast. Stardeon was able to take the spirit of this Great Wyrm and split it into ten parts which he imprisoned in his rings. Somehow this gave him the ability to temporarily bond with the body of another living creature and change the characteristics of its flesh."

"So that's how Ewzad Vriil changes his creatures," Justan surmised.

"It does explain his ability, yes," Master Coal said. "And that was how Stardeon made the rogue horses."

"But in making the rings, he made a great sacrifice," Samson said. "In order to keep the Great Wyrm bound to the rings, he had to tear away part of his bonding magic and leave it in the rings. Two of his bonded died from the shock of it. Only his first bonded, his closest and dearest friend survived. He was never able to bond in the traditional manner again."

"But why?" Justan asked Samson, "Why would he do that? What could possibly be worth losing his bonded?"

"He didn't know that the creation of the rings would kill his bonded. It was a tragedy that haunted him the rest of his life and was most likely the reason for his demise. As for why he wanted to make the rogue horses, all I know is that Stardeon had some bad experiences with his bonded in the past," Samson said. "He had become obsessed with creating the perfect creature to bond with."

Master Coal nodded. "He thought of every trait that could

be useful to a bonding wizard and began collecting creatures that had them. Eventually he had his own menagerie of beasts. He then began to take aspects from each creature and bind them together to form the one perfect bonded."

"The perfect bonded . . . It sounds like a gruesome process." Justan said, frowning as he ran a hand down Gwyrtha's flank. Her body was a hideous patchwork of different creature types, mainly lizard and horse, but he knew there were more. Some of her skin patches were the tawny color of a great cat. Some were slick and shiny like lake beasts. Others were unidentifiable. She had one small patch on the left side of her neck that was covered in scales that were pearlescent white. *What did he do to you, sweetie?*

To me? Gwyrtha asked in confusion. *Father?*

"She doesn't remember," Samson said. "None of us do. Stardeon wasn't cruel. He wasn't unfeeling either. He felt a genuine affection for all of us, I believe. When he created a rogue horse, he would sedate the animals with magic before taking them apart."

Justan winced.

"Besides he needed the animals to be comfortable," Samson continued. "Otherwise their spirits wouldn't have cooperated."

"Their spirits?"

Master Coal explained, "Bonding is only one form of spirit magic. Just like elemental magic has four aspects, earth, fire, air, and water, spirit magic has four aspects. They are bonding, binding, blessing, and bewitching.

"Back in those days, the most common form of spirit magic was binding. It was a process by which a person killed an animal and bound its spirit to an object, thus giving it various magic properties. For instance, one could bind the spirit of a bird to an arrow to make it fly true or bind the spirit of a horse to his boots to give him more stamina."

"How horrible," Justan said. The thought of killing a creature and enslaving its soul seemed evil to him.

The wizard shrugged. "It was a temporary magic. If the

item ever broke, the spirit was released. Many people came to see it the way you do, though. It was one of the oldest forms of magic, but binding came to be looked down upon by most of society. Eventually its practitioners were hounded until it was mostly eradicated. Now it is only practiced in more . . . savage cultures.

"At any rate, in Stardeon's time, binding was the preferred method used by wizards to create a magical construct. But Stardeon tried something new. Instead of binding the spirits of the animals to an object, he bound the spirits of each beast to each other. What he learned was that when multiple spirits were bound to each other, they lost their individuality and melded into something new. They became a single being with a very complex spirit. A being that was so full of spiritual energy it would attract the magic of the first bonding wizard it came across."

"And a being that was very unstable," Samson said. "Which is why he had to bring internal magic in to stabilize his creation."

"Internal magic like elves have?" Justan asked.

Coal nodded. "Yes. Elves, dwarves, gnomes, and dragons."

"The heart of a dragon, of course." Justan said. It was the reason why the rogue horses stayed together despite the immense energy that flowed within them. It was also the reason why Deathclaw hadn't melted into a pool of goo after Ewzad Vriil had left him behind.

"Correct," Master Coal said. "So now you know how rogue horses came to be. Now let's talk about the attributes that Stardeon built into them."

"How many rogue horses did Stardeon make?" Justan asked.

"There were just over two hundred of us at the end," Samson said sadly.

"We will get to the rest of the story soon," said Coal. "We need to keep this discussion within a certain framework or you'll end up missing something."

"Yes, sir," Justan said.

"So, back on topic then. Edge, what are the attributes that Stardeon built into the rogue horses?"

"Well, each one was different, right?" Justan said. "Samson said before that the only thing they all have in common was the dragon heart."

"Physically, yes," Samson said. "Stardeon was fond of dogs and horses, so he used them when creating most of us, but I believe Coal is talking about other similarities. There are certain things that all of us have in common."

"Oh, uh, they live long lives. They produce a seemingly endless amount of energy. Um . . . and you just said earlier that all of them have the ability to change size," Justan said.

"Well, it's more like a capability than an ability, but we'll get to that soon. Good," Coal said. "But there is something else and it was probably the most single important thing in his mind. Stardeon built a trigger into each of the rogue horses that happened as soon as they bonded. He made them unable to disobey."

"More than that," Samson said. "He made them eager to serve."

Justan looked at Gwyrtha in surprise. Now that he thought about it, she readily agreed to his every request, no matter how tired she was, or no matter how uncomfortable it might make her. The only time she disobeyed was when she was being playful, but even then she acquiesced as soon as he got serious.

"Samson, I noticed you said 'them'," Coal said with amusement. "Are you saying that you're not affected by the same compulsion the others have?"

"The difference is that I was the only rogue horse created with a human mind and therefore I have more willpower," Samson said. "It was difficult when we were first bonded, but I hardly feel the compulsion to serve anymore."

"Oh, really?" Coal said with a twinkle in his eye. He looked right at the centaur. "Samson, would you please dance for me? I am asking with all seriousness. Will you dance? Right here, right now?"

Anger flashed across Samson's face. Then he grimaced and squeezed his eyes shut. His body quivered and he began to sweat. "Damn . . . you . . . Coal!"

"Hmm, I was wrong," Coal said, looking impressed. "Even though I asked you to dance and still want you to dance, you sit there completely unaffected. You truly are over that compulsion. How about if I were to whistle a tune right now? Would that make it more difficult?"

"P-please don't."

Justan was torn between laughing out loud and feeling sorry for the centaur. He swallowed his mirth. "Good for you, Samson," he said in support. "Don't you listen to him."

"I hate it, but I so want to dance right now," Samson said, his jaw clenched. His rear legs twitched. "I mean, I don't, but . . . I really do. My mind says not to, but I really want to." He grimaced.

Master Coal's mirth faded replaced by a look of concern.

"You can do it, Samson," Justan said. "You're better than the spell Stardeon cast."

The centaur opened his eyes and looked at Justan pleadingly. "I-I-. Tell me, Sir Edge. I can't quite remember. Why shouldn't I dance?" Tears began to fall from his face.

Coal reached for his bonded. "Samson, it's ok. You don't have to. I don't really want you to." The centaur stopped quivering and took a deep breath. Coal patted Samson's back, looking mortified. "I'm sorry. I'm so sorry. I was simply trying to prove a point and I didn't realize-."

"Let's never try to prove that point again, Coal," Samson said darkly. "Never."

Coal swallowed and turned back to Justan. "I-I make it a point to be very careful what I ask him to do and how I ask it. Quite honestly I had forgotten how much he hated that feeling."

Justan blinked and realized that he was hugging Gwyrtha's head tightly to him. "W-why did Stardeon do such a thing?"

"As we said, Stardeon had some issues with his bonded in the past. In his mind, the perfect bonded would adore their bonding wizard and do anything he or she asked without question," Coal said.

"But that isn't a bonded. That's a slave," Justan said. In his mind, a bonded was meant to be a companion, someone that was a part of you. His bonded were family to him as much as his own parents were. Even Deathclaw, whom he didn't understand and who wasn't exactly friendly, was someone he valued. "What good is a bonded that won't tell you when you are wrong? Both Fist and Deathclaw have given me fantastic advice recently and the things they had to say weren't things I wanted to hear."

"I agree with you," Coal said. "Stardeon's reasoning was wrong. And perhaps that can help you understand his character better."

"Stardeon wasn't evil, Sir Edge," Samson said. "He didn't take pleasure in subjugation or administering pain. He suffered from the same problem that many wizards have. He thought only about the logic of things. It never occurred to him that he was creating a race of slaves for bonding wizards. It never occurred to him that killing thousands of beasts and destroying their souls was wrong. He simply saw a problem and came up with a way to fix it."

Justan shook his head, "Somehow that almost seems worse."

"You aren't the only one to think so," Coal said. "Stardeon did all of his work in secret, but somehow the prophet caught wind of what was going on."

"And he was furious," Justan said, the vision of the angry prophet from Gwyrtha's memories flashing through his mind.

Coal nodded. "John came to Stardeon's secluded laboratory with the intention of destroying the rogue horses. He considered them to be abominations."

"What prevented him?"

"I asked John that question the day he left me to wait for Coal," Samson said. "He said that his hand was stayed because however vile the process was that made us, the rogue horses were innocent. Instead of destroying them, he told Stardeon to stop his experiments. He said that if Stardeon continued to create rogue horses, he would end up crossing a line so vile that John would have to return and strip away his bonding magic."

"But Stardeon wouldn't stop," Justan guessed.

"Oh, he was good for a while," Samson said. "Several years went by where he didn't make any new ones. He began reaching out to the other bonding wizards, inviting them to his hideaway. Each one walked away bonded to a rogue horse. Soon word got out about their amazing properties and he began receiving letters from bonding wizards everywhere, even in far kingdoms. They wanted rogue horses of their own and some began making requests.

"They wanted theirs custom built. Wizards began to bring him exotic creatures with special properties that they wanted in their own mounts. He turned them away at first, but their suggestions got his mind thinking again and some of their ideas were too hard to resist. He eventually started making rogue horses again."

"What finally stopped him?" Justan asked.

Coal glanced at Samson and cleared his throat. "His last remaining bonded was attacked by one of the creatures as he brought it to the laboratory. The wound was so severe that Stardeon couldn't repair his body. All he could do was keep him clinging to life. Finally in desperation, Stardeon decided that there was only one way he could save him."

"He made him into a rogue horse," Justan said in understanding. He looked at Samson. "I'm so sorry."

Samson smiled sadly. "It's Stardeon you should feel sorry for. His bonded's name was Sam and they were friends since childhood. On the day Stardeon's mother died, he was in so much pain that his magic exploded. He ended up bonding to three birds, the family dog, and his friend, who was sitting next to him at the time. Their bond was a fluke. There was no mutual need involved. It was just an awakening.

"It was a strange bond. Stardeon had all the power. Stardeon had the intelligence. Sam was just an average man. He wasn't even a very good fighter. The only thing he brought to the bond was his friendship. Throughout all the years, throughout all the mistakes Stardeon made, Sam stayed loyal to him. So at the end, Stardeon refused to let his friend die.

"He tried to give Sam all the attributes he lacked in life; strength, speed, stamina, agility . . . he took the spirits of seven beasts and tied them all together with the heart of a dragon. Stardeon thought that by leaving the upper half of his friend's body intact and letting him keep his brain, Sam's soul would be dominant and absorb the energy of the others. Unfortunately, he was wrong.

"As with all the other rogue horses, the process blended all the spirits together, destroying their individuality and creating something completely new. Sadly, by trying to save his friend, he destroyed him completely."

Justan swallowed. "S-so you don't remember anything about Sam's life?"

The centaur shook his head sadly. "All his memories and everything that made him who he was were erased. Sam's soul couldn't leave this existence to continue on wherever it is that spirits go. Sam was gone and I . . . was created in his place. Stardeon had committed the greatest of sins. He destroyed a man's soul."

Samson looked down and Coal took up the tale, "With Sam gone, Stardeon's last bond was severed. He was alone for the first time since his childhood. The only thing he had left was the temporary bond that came when he used his rings on another creature's body. And he knew that the prophet would soon come to take that away as well."

"It's okay, Coal, I can finish the story," Samson said, his voice thick with emotion. "My memories of that day are kind of hazy. I was new then. Fully grown, but completely unaware of what was going on. Rogue horses . . ."

The centaur frowned, trying to put the words together. "We awaken from our creation without any memories, but somehow we retain a basic understanding and awareness from the spirits that were fused together to form us. E-even though my body was much different from the creatures that it was made up of, I-I knew how to walk. I knew how to run. I was basically a child.

"I didn't know how to speak, but somehow I understood what Stardeon wanted of me. He knew that the prophet was coming for him. The sky darkened and there was this heavy feeling in the air. Stardeon climbed on my back and told me to run. Thunder roared in the sky and lightning crashed all around us. Stardeon's hideaway was destroyed."

Father, Gwyrtha whimpered softly. A tear ran down her face and Justan knew that was the last time she had seen Stardeon. Her memories whizzed by in his mind too fast for him to fully grasp. He saw fires raging while rogue horses ran around, terrified. Some fled, while others gathered together and huddled in the pasture.

Justan stroked her head, *It's okay, sweetheart. It's okay.*

"Stardeon fled with me, running from place to place for many years. He stayed in the wilderness, keeping away from people in fear that we would be seen and somehow the prophet would know where to find us.

"I was a a a reminder of his guilt and he found it difficult to speak with me at first, especially since I had Sam's face. Then one day he gave me my name and somehow that seemed to help him feel better. He started teaching me how to read and write and told me about magic and the way things worked. In many ways he was a father to me. But he never talked about the past.

"Then Stardeon began to age. It happened rapidly. He seemed to age five years for every year that passed. He told me that it was because he had broken the bonds that gave him a long life. Then one night, he broke down and told me everything that had happened. Once he had confessed what he had done, I was shocked. I told him that we had to return and care for the other rogue horses."

"But what happened to them while you were gone?" Justan asked. Gwyrtha had cut off her memories but he thought he had an idea.

"The rogue horses were found by brigands and smugglers," Coal said. "By then they had become highly sought after for their attributes and the majority of them were rounded up and sold off to wizards and wealthy nobles."

"I've heard it said that rogue horses died in captivity." Justan said. "But that never made sense to me. Why would that be?"

"That tale started because the majority of them were accidentally destroyed by wizards who tried to discover how they were made. Unfortunately, the benefits of having a rogue horse mean nothing if you aren't a bonding wizard and this frustrated the people who wanted to use them. They were fine until their captors tried to tamper with the magic that held them together." Coal sighed. "Continue on please, Samson."

The centaur nodded. "Stardeon and I discovered what had happened when we arrived back at his hideaway. The rogue horses were gone and most of the buildings had been destroyed. The only place that hadn't been looted was Stardeon's laboratory and that was because the entrance had been well hidden. But when we entered, we found John waiting for us. He didn't look angry. Just sad.

"Stardeon fell to his knees, begging him to tell us where the rogue horses were. John said, 'I was only able to save a small number of them. I have them hidden in a safe place.' Stardeon wept and said, 'Are you here to take my bonding magic away?' John shook his head and replied, 'You tore away most of it yourself the day you made those rings of yours. The rest of it left you the moment you destroyed your friend.'

"Then John called me by name, climbed on my back, and took me to join my brothers and sisters. He had them hidden in a small mountain valley. There weren't very many, just a small herd of thirty. He put me in charge and left me instructions that I was to make sure we stayed in the valley and approached no one unless they were with him.

"We stayed in that valley over the centuries, running and playing. John was our only visitor. A few times, he brought in stragglers, members of the herd that he had found and saved. Then one day he began to take them away. Gwyrtha was one of the first to go. One by one, the prophet came and took the rest. There were only five of us left the day he came for me."

"And what happened to Stardeon?" Justan asked.

"We don't know," Coal said. "But over the years his

rings reappeared from time to time, always in the hands of some foul wizard doing the dark prophet's bidding."

"What a sad story," Justan said.

"It's a story I wish more wizards knew," Coal said. "The mentality that led Stardeon to do the things he did still thrives at the Mage School."

"How long ago did this happen?" Justan asked.

"The records of those days are a bit disjointed since the prophet's ban on spirit magic caused many of the relevant histories to be expunged from the library. The only mention of Stardeon that I was able to find was just over a thousand years ago."

"A thousand years . . ."

Justan stewed over the lesson all evening. Stardeon's tragic story was hard for him to stomach. What the man had done was so evil and yet the result of his mistakes had been the rogue horses, a race of beasts that were pure and innocent. It didn't seem right that something so good could come out of something so wrong. Justan was still churning the story over in his mind as he recounted the lesson to Fist later that night.

"Gwyrtha is a thousand years old?" Fist said.

Shh! The others may be sleeping, Justan sent. They had bedded down for the night an hour prior and Gwyrtha lay right behind him, snoring lightly.

But . . . All those years and there were so few of them. Fist thought. *What about their babies?*

I wondered the same thing, Justan responded. *Rogue horses can't breed. Stardeon felt that having children was a distraction that his 'perfect bonded' didn't need. He didn't make them with . . . the necessary parts.*

Ohhhh. That explains it, Fist sent. *I wondered why Samson was . . .* He made a cutting motion with his fingers.

The term is gelded, Justan said. *But no, he was just created that way.*

Oh. Fist settled back onto his pillow. *So when do you start learning how to make Gwyrtha grow?*

Tomorrow, Justan said. *But I feel uneasy about it. I'll be using the bond to go inside her body and change her basic structure.*

Coal will help you. You will do good.

Yeah, but what if I mess up? I mean, you are right that Master Coal will be guiding me, but at the very least, it could be uncomfortable or even painful for Gwyrtha.

She won't mind, Fist said. *She likes to help you learn.*

"But that's the thing, Fist. She has no choice." *I learned that tonight, remember? Stardeon made rogue horses to be willing slaves. Gwyrtha was created to be eager to do what I ask of her.*

"You don't treat Gwyrtha like a slave," Fist said aloud.

"Well, I definitely don't try to." *But now I have to question myself every time I ask her for something. And then when she does what I ask her to, I have to wonder if she is doing what I asked because she really wants to or because she is forced to want to by the compulsion that Stardeon built into her*, Justan sent, his mind awash with worry.

Fist scratched his head as he processed Justan's rambling thoughts. *But she does not always obey you. What about when she buries Lenny?*

Well, I tell her not to, but I think she knows that I actually find it kind of funny, Justan admitted. *Even Lenny, as loud as he gets about it isn't seriously angry. I think he kind of likes having something to bluster about.*

"And when she plays that game where she tries to buck you off?" Fist asked.

Justan shook his head. *I thought about that, and you're right, I do get frustrated with her when she does that and I tell her to stop, but I know she's being playful, and she can sense that. She always stops when she knows I am really upset about it.*

"Hmm . . ." *What about the time when you were at the Mage School and she left the elves to come see you?*

Well, she . . . Justan thought about it and a slow smile began to spread across his face. He had been completely serious about wanting her to stay away then. He told her not to come and she came anyway. "I think you are right, Fist. Thank you."

You think about these things very hard, Justan. Fist smiled. *That is because you are a good man and that is what makes you a good leader.*

Justan blinked. He felt a surge of affection coming through the bond from the ogre.

"I am proud to be your bonded," Fist said aloud.

"Th-thank you," Justan said in surprise. He returned the ogre's affection. "I am glad to have you with me, Fist."

Me too, said Gwyrtha. Evidently she was not as asleep as Justan had thought.

Deathclaw sat in the trees above and listened through the bond, his mind full of confusion.

Chapter Eleven

"Very good, now delve deeper into the bond," Coal said from his perch on Samson's back. The wizard had stepped up Justan's training during the day as they traveled. For several days in a row he had been following right behind Justan shouting out encouragement, making sure that he didn't fall off. "Just don't lose hold of your tether. Make sure that you keep the sense of what your body is doing."

Justan heard Coal's instructions through Gwyrtha's ears. He had extended his mind as far into his bond with her as he had ever let himself go. The last time he had been this deep within her mind, he had almost abandoned his body altogether. It didn't take long for him to remember why.

Even after getting used to the enhanced senses his bond with Deathclaw gave him, Justan found the depth of Gwyrtha's senses overwhelming. While his nose recognized the complex smell of the grassy plain they traveled through, her nose picked out each individual element; the damp earth, the freshness of newly growing grass, the smell of Alfred and Stanza in the lead, and the pungent tang left by the wolves that had marked their territory the night before. Where his ears caught the sound of each horse's hoof-falls, she could differentiate between them by their heaviness and rhythm.

Justan did his best to fight through the sensations and remain aware of his body as it lay forward in the saddle, his hands gripping Gwyrtha's mane and his feet in the stirrups. Gwyrtha could feel his weight on her back, but even added with the weight of her saddlebags and Qyxal's body, it wasn't much of a burden. The thought of Qyxal sobered his mind and he refocused on the task at hand.

"Are you to the point where you are at one with her senses?" Coal asked.

Justan made his head nod.

"Now, switch to your mage sight."

Justan's mind was ablaze with color. He almost lost track of his body again, but somehow retained enough focus to grip her mane more tightly. Gwyrtha's every cell was ablaze with elemental magic strung together in a complex and chaotic looking pattern.

"And now spirit sight."

Justan pulled the wispy shroud of the bond around his mind and saw the spirit magic that tied her body together. He could now see how all of it moved in rhythm with the beat of her dragon heart.

"Now focus on her right ear."

Justan guided his senses though her body to focus on her ear. They had agreed beforehand that it was the most unobtrusive part of the body to manipulate while she was on the move. *Now please bear with me, sweetheart*, he sent.

Are you tickling me now? Gwyrtha asked.

I'm not sure how it will feel. Samson says it doesn't hurt though. Just let me know if it gets too uncomfortable. Justan reached out with his magic as he would if he were healing her ear, but this time he used his spirit magic instead of elemental magic. He willed the ear to grow.

"Go slowly, now," Coal said.

Her horse-like right ear shot up four inches.

"Slowly!" Coal said. "Too fast and you could burst some blood vessels. You can go faster once you get the hang of it, but you need to give her body time to adjust to the change."

Justan heard the wizard's warning, but couldn't help exulting in his success. This was the third day of trying and finally a result! He checked her ear and it seemed to be fine. *How did that feel?*

My ear is big, she replied.

Yes, but was it uncomfortable?

I felt it get big, she said and Justan could tell that though she didn't necessarily like it, it hadn't been painful.

"Now the other one. See if you can make it grow to match." Coal said. "That will be key, especially when we get around to making her whole body grow."

Now that Justan had done it once, he had a better idea of how to approach it. Her left ear grew, this time more slowly. When he stopped, it was very close to the same size.

"Good, now it's time to bring them back to normal. Her body will know automatically when it is back in the proper form. You'll know what I mean when you get there. It will just feel right."

Justan was dubious, but the wizard was right. When he had shrunk her ears back to their correct size, they seemed to want to stop. It would take extra effort to get them to shrink further.

"Good. Again!"

This went on through much of the morning, Justan making Gwyrtha's ears grow and shrink, alternating back and forth, then making them grow together. Gwyrtha was a remarkably good sport about it. Even though she wanted to please him, it was a constant irritation. Justan could tell she was relieved when they stopped for midday break. He was going to have to make it up to her later which, he noted ruefully, probably meant letting her play that game where she tried to buck him off.

They dismounted and Lenny passed out dried meat and hard rolls. It was a meager meal for someone that had been using magic all day, but it was what they had. Justan was half way through his roll, when Deathclaw interrupted.

There is an encampment ahead.

Justan paused mid-bite. He scanned the horizon, but the ground ahead was hilly. He didn't see anything at first, but then his eyes caught the faint smudge that could only be smoke from a campfire. *How many?*

Deathclaw thought a moment, still working on translating his way of thinking about numbers to Justan's. They had been working on it together bit by bit, but the raptoid had little patience for training through the bond. *Six*, he said finally. *And they are short ones . . . like Lenui.*

Dwarves? Justan asked in surprise.

Yes.

"Lenny!" Justan said.

"Huh?" The dwarf was sitting next to Bettie, talking quietly. Since deciding to be open about their relationship, the two bickered quite a bit less. They were even affectionate from time to time. Justan had seen them holding hands the night before.

"Deathclaw says there's an encampment of dwarves ahead," Justan said. "Six of them. And by the smell Deathclaw sent, they have been on the road a while."

Do I attack? One is making waste in the bushes. I could tear its throat without a sound.

No, Deathclaw. Dwarves aren't likely to be enemies. Just watch them.

Lenny approached him, worry on his face. "What'd they look like? Was they ridin' horses?"

Justan asked Deathclaw quickly. "No, but they have a horse-drawn wagon. Does that count?"

"What's got you worried, Lenui?" Bettie asked.

The dwarf ignored her question. "What 'bout their faces?"

Justan frowned. What was Deathclaw supposed to do with that question? "What is it exactly you're looking for, Lenny?"

"Their gall-durned face hair, dag-nab it! Beards or 'staches?"

Deathclaw sent Justan a vision of what they looked like.

"Full thick beards," Justan said. "Also, they are wearing mismatched sets of armor."

"Is there any reason we shouldn't simply travel around to avoid them, Lenny?" Coal asked.

Lenny scowled in thought for a moment. "Nah, I'd better

talk to 'em. Dwarves ain't usually out in these parts. Maybe they know somethin' we can use. Edge and I'll go."

"Just the two of you?" Coal asked.

"Less questions. Edge'll call over and let Fist know if we need you," Lenny said.

Master Coal looked a bit surprised to see Lenny take control like this, but he didn't question him. "Of course, Lenny. If that's what you feel is best."

One of them sleeps, Deathclaw sent. *I could take him and one other, then draw them towards you.*

Don't attack, Justan sent. *Lenny and I are going to talk to them.*

I will stay ready, Deathclaw replied, though Justan could tell he questioned the wisdom of conversing with a potential threat. *Tell me when to strike.*

Justan shook his head and led Lenny in the direction of the dwarven camp. Even with spring just begun, the grass was as high as the dwarf's chest. Justan waited until they were out of earshot of the others before speaking. "What was that about back there?"

The dwarf raised his one remaining bushy eyebrow. "Whaddya mean, son?"

"Why were you so concerned about what the other dwarves looked like?"

"Look, there's certain kinds of dwarves it'd be best fer us to avoid is all. Just wanted to be sure."

"Why should we be worried about dwarves?" Justan asked. He had never heard of dwarves being anything but hard working industrial folk. Dwarven bandits would be an oddity for sure. "And why did you ask about their facial hair? The only dwarf I've seen wear just a moustache is you."

"Look, son. It ain't somethin' I talk 'bout and now ain't the time."

Justan wanted to press him on the issue, but he could smell the smoke of the campfire wafting up from over the next hill. He could also smell something cooking. Some kind of meat covered in spices? He could almost pick out what kind of meat.

Maybe . . .

Rabbit, Deathclaw answered with distaste. He felt that cooking wasted the meat. Justan hadn't been able to talk him into trying it yet. *They have them cooking on sticks.*

Thanks, Justan sent a bit dubiously. Deathclaw had become quite adept at monitoring his thoughts through the bond. He listened so quietly that Justan couldn't tell when the raptoid was doing it. On some level it was concerning, but Deathclaw had so much to learn about humanity that Justan had decided it was best to let him observe.

They walked around the edge of the hillside until the dwarven camp came into view. Five dwarves sat in a semicircle around the fire laughing and talking while one of them snored away on the ground not far away. None of them noticed the two approaching.

Two horses stood to the side with feedbags attached to their heads. They were hitched to a long red wagon. With a start, Justan noticed the words, "Firegobbler : Weaponsmith" painted along the side in bright yellow letters.

Before Justan could stop him, Lenny cried out in outrage. He pulled Buster from the straps on his back, started towards the dwarves, and yelled, "What the dag-blamed, horn-chewin', hell are you doin' with my wagon?"

The dwarves scrambled to their feet, drawing finely polished steel weapons. One of them kicked the sleeping dwarf awake. Justan swore. What was Lenny thinking? He drew his swords and sent a mental command, telling Deathclaw to ready himself.

Then the dwarves saw their attacker. All at once, they backed away, holding their weapons behind their backs. One of them, an older dwarf with a heavy mat of graying hair forced a smile and said, "Lenui! Sorry, couldn't tell it was you at first. Uh . . . what happened to yer face?"

"What're you doin' with my wagon, Pall?" Lenny scowled, drawing close. Justan noted that Lenny was at least a good inch and a half taller than the others. He swung Buster menacingly. "And my dag-blamed weapons? Never took you fer the stealin' type."

"Stealin'?" The older dwarf paled. He was wearing a chainmail shirt and shiny plate boots. "Well, uh, we're just traveling with Nhed like you wanted."

"That was over a blasted month ago! Y'all should be in Wobble settin' up my shop right now! Not lollygaggin' in the plains wearin' my gall-durn armor!"

"Uh, well, we weren't able to get . . . there . . . yet," Pall said.

"What's going on, Lenny?" Justan asked.

"'Fore I left Dremald, I told Nhed to close up shop and head fer Wobble," he explained, then returned his glare to the dwarves. "Where is my stupid nephew anyway?"

Pall grimaced and stepped back behind the others. They all glanced away, refusing to look Lenny in the eyes.

"Someone durn well better speak!" Lenny growled. They stared at the ground and began nudging each other. Finally, he pointed a finger at one of them. "Rahbbie! Spit it out 'fore I grab you by yer dag-burned head and stuff yer mouth full of road apples!"

"Uh, well . . ." Rahbbie was balding badly, and wore a shining breastplate over leather armor. "He's been nabbed."

"Nabbed?" Lenny shouted. "Dag-blast it, by who?"

No one spoke up. Lenny stomped forward and swung a fist into Pall's face. The older dwarf's head whipped back and he fell in the dirt.

Lenny stomped on Rahbbie's foot. "By who, I said?"

He swung Buster low as one of them tried to get away, sending the dwarf sprawling in the dirt. "By who, you garl-friggin' sons of goblins?"

He wasn't getting anywhere. Justan spoke up. "Lenny!"

The dwarf rounded on him. "What?"

"Can I ask them a question?"

"When I'm finished bashin' heads, maybe!"

Justan kept his voice even. "That's fine. I just want to ask them something first. Can I do that? Please."

Lenny's scowl softened slightly. "Ask somethin' then."

"Okay," Justan said. He looked them over. "Which one's the most trustworthy?"

"Well 'fore today, I'd've said all of 'em!" Lenny replied. "Well, maybe 'cept fer Derk."

One of the dwarves whose face was covered by a platemail helmet looked down in shame.

Justan shook his head. "Okay, so which one's the best talker?"

Lenny frowned and pointed to a dwarf with a deep black beard and a pointy nose. "That'd be Kile."

Kile's eyes widened and Justan beckoned him forward. "Why don't you tell us what happened, Kyle? And from the beginning, please."

Kile frowned slightly at the pronunciation of his name. "And who are you?"

Lenny lifted Justan's right hand and shook it at them. "He's Sir Edge, named at the Bowl of Souls, you pie-pinchers! Give some respect!"

"Named? I guess you're okay then," Kile said. In truth, the dwarf, who wore chainmail headgear and shiny plate greaves, looked glad to be talking to anyone besides Lenny. "So, uh, right after Lenui left Dremald, Nhed started asking around seeing if there was any dwarves that'd come to Wobble with him. A lot of us wasn't happy with the way things was going in Dremald. He had ten of us getting ready to go when a big order came in at the shop. There was a noble that wanted a set of ten daggers made and he was offering a lot of coin."

"That crab-snatcher! I told him to leave right away!" Lenny snapped. His brow furrowed. "How much coin we talkin'?"

"Three gold apiece!" piped Rahbbie.

"Yeah," Kile agreed. "But that's 'cause he wanted the hilts jeweled and stuff so Nhed charged him extra."

"Dag-nab it! Nhed still should'a turned him down," Lenny grumped, though he didn't seem quite as angry as before.

"Anyways, so he made the order and that took some

time," Kile said. "And then just when he was done, the king got killed and we heard the place was under lockdown. Then word got out that Duke Vriil had saved the princess and was being made Lord Protector and Nhed panicked. He got us all gathered together and packed up, but by the time he was ready to leave there was twenty more dwarves wanting to go."

"Twenty!" Lenny said.

"That made thirty of us all together," Rahbbie added.

"What'd he promise to pay you?" Lenny said darkly.

"Well the ten of us he started with was going to be able to pick out the weapons we wanted when we got out on the road, but the others just wanted out of the city," Kile said.

"Yeah? And he gave you the last suit of armor I made too?" Lenny asked suspiciously.

"We was just gonna wear it till we got Nhed back," spouted the dwarf wearing the helmet.

"Shut up, Derk!" Rahbbie yelled.

"Did you have a hard time getting out of Dremald?" Justan asked Kile.

"Yeah, the guards didn't like the look of thirty dwarves leaving Dremald so soon after the king was killed-."

"Wait! That's thirty one counting Nhed," Rahbbie said.

"So Nhed had to pay 'em off," Kile finished.

"How much did he pay?" Lenny asked with a glare.

"A sword for the guard captain, a dagger for the sergeant . . ." He swallowed. "And ten golds to keep the rest of the men quiet."

"Dag-blamed son of a hoop-skirtin' frog-licker!"

Kile winced, "He said you'd be mad."

"If'n he'd only left when I told him to! Wait 'till I get him in front of me."

"Lenny, ten gold isn't going to break you," Justan said, knowing the dwarf still had a nice little stash left over from his raid on the rock giant's cave. "So what happened after you left Dremald, Kyle?"

"Well we tried to keep as quiet as possible, which was

kinda hard with thirty dwarves and two wagons. Soldiers was riding back and forth on the road a lot, but nobody bothered us till we got to Sampo. There was a big ruckus going on when we got there. A bunch'a scruffy soldiers wearing Duke Vriil's colors was roughing up some of the townsfolk.

"They was saying that Lord Protector Vriil had sent them to come and guard the town since the Dremald garrison had been recalled. They had a whole list of new rules and the local folks didn't like it."

"The mayor of Sampo was telling 'em all to cooperate," Rahbbie said.

Lenny snorted. "'Course he did. Mayor Hoofer's always been in cahoots with them Dremald nobles."

"Well Nhed told us to stay out of things and had us set up the wagons near the edge of town, selling weapons out the back. He wanted to take in some extra cash before heading to Wobble. We was doing pretty good too, 'till Vriil's men surrounded us. They said the Lord Protector has suspended all weapon sales in Sampo until after the Queen was safe."

"Of course he did," Justan said with a frown. "Sampo is the most well armed city in Dremaldria and next to Dremald, the one best able to send help to the academy."

"Nhed had us pack things away and we was going to leave town, but more of Vriil's men came. They wouldn't let us leave with the weapons."

"They was gonna take all of it," Rahbbie said.

"Those hog-lickers!" Lenny swore.

Kile nodded. "Well, Nhed wouldn't stand for it either. A scuffle broke out and Nhed broke their captain's arm. Then it became a big fight and the Duke's men hauled Nhed and the other boys off. We was the only ones that got away."

"Dag-blast it! Where're they keepin' 'em?" Lenny asked.

"In their camp just outside town," Rahbbie said.

"How many of them are there?" Justan asked.

"There was maybe two hundred of 'em at the time," Kile said. "There wasn't nothing we could do."

"Why didn't you head to Wobble fer help?" Lenny asked.

"We couldn't cross the bridge. They had it guarded," Kile said. "That night we was gonna try crossing the river ourselves but there must've been a thousand moonrats on the other side. It was lit up like a carnival, all of their glowing eyes just pacing back and forth while they made those terrible moans."

Justan shivered. He wasn't looking forward to traveling through the Tinny Woods again. Hopefully when it came time to cross the bridge, they would be doing it with the might of the Mage School behind them.

"How long has it been?" he asked.

"A week," Kile said. "We didn't know where to go. Couldn't go back to Dremald. To be honest, some of us was figuring on leaving Dremaldria altogether. Maybe go to one of the dwarf towns in Razbeck. I've got kin there. So does Rahbbie and Derk."

"You'd just leave Nhed and the others to stew with Vriil's men?" Lenny said.

"I wouldn't have let 'em do it," said Pall. The old dwarf was still sitting on the ground where he had fallen after Lenny punched him. He was holding his nose and glowering. "I've been sayin' go around the mountains and take the back pass to Wobble. We could get men together there and come back fer Nhed."

"But that way's-," complained Rahbbie.

"Nhed would've done it fer us," Pall snapped.

Lenny's eyes softened a little. "C'mon, Pall! Get yer butt up off the ground."

The dwarf grunted and climbed to his feet. "You know I hate it when you break my durn nose, Lenui!"

"It'll heal. But yer right, Pall. That was uncalled for," Lenny said. To Justan's surprise, he looked a bit ashamed. Lenny wasn't one to apologize. "Just wanted some answers is all." Lenny stuck out his chin. "C'mon. You owe me one from last time anyway."

"Durn right I do," Pall said. He took a step forward and swung, putting his weight into it. His fist caught Lenny's nose at an angle, knocking his head back and staggering him to the side.

"Hah! Feel that one, Lenui?"

"Dag –burn it!" Lenny said. He swayed and squatted to gather his balance, then stood. "Kept my feet." He reached up to feel his face. Blood streamed from both nostrils, but Justan was just glad to see that he still had a nose after such a brutal punch. "Hah! Still not broke!"

"Blast!" Pall shouted. "Next time fer sure."

Lenny tossed an arm around the other dwarf's shoulders. "I gotta admit, though. My dag-gum eyes are a spinnin'." Both dwarves laughed and Justan thought they had to be crazy.

"Seriously, Lenui," Pall said. "What happened to yer face? Why'd you trim your 'stache?"

Lenny ran his fingers over what Justan felt looked like a respectable moustache now and frowned. "Done got it burnt off fightin' a bandham. It's takin' its gall-durn sweet time growin' back."

"A bandham!" Pall's eyes nearly fell out of his head. "You don't friggin' say! How come yer alive?"

"Edge killed it," Lenny replied. "Now show me what you got in my wagon."

Pall stared at Justan in awe as he led them over. "M-most of the weapons and good eats was in the other wagon that Vriil's boys took. All we got here is a few crates of weapons and some sacks of dry goods."

"Dog-gone it, what was Nhed thinkin'?" He hopped up and pulled himself up over the top lip of the wagon. Lenny rustled around, cursing, and Justan peered over the edge to see what he was up to. "Where's my pepperbean wine at?"

"We been on the road fer weeks. It's gone, of course. There was two cases left, but they was Hubert's brand and Nhed made us keep 'em in the other wagon," Pall said.

"Alright," Lenny announced, hopping back down. "The good news is I still got most'a what I need. My tools're there and all the good weapons. Always told Nhed to keep the good stuff in the family wagon. Looks like he listened to that much anyway."

"So what are we going to do about your nephew,

Lenny?" Justan asked.

"We're gonna go get him," Lenny replied. "Him and the other dwarves them corn-chuckers took."

"I-I dunno, Lenui," said Rahbbie. "There was two hunnderd of 'em before, but more and more keep coming up the road from Dremald since we been here."

"Don't matter," Lenny said.

"But it ain't just men," Kile said. "There's . . . things with 'em too."

"Ain't gonna stop us!" Lenny said, yanking a thumb in Justan's direction. Justan stood tall and folded his arms, trying his best to look imposing.

The others seemed to relax a little, but Pall shook his head, "Yeah, Lenui, you got a named warrior with you, but Kile's right. You ain't seen what we saw during that fight with Vriil's men. They got some durn scary things fighting for 'em."

Lenny snorted. "You ain't seen the rest of our party yet. We done fought what Vriil's got on his side and it don't scare us."

"Lenny's right," Justan said. He called out through the bond and Deathclaw stepped out of the grass, his magic sword in hand. The dwarves took one look at the raptoid and stumbled backwards, clutching their weapons. "You see? We have scarier things on our side."

Chapter Twelve

I have found the short ones, Deathclaw sent.

They're called dwarves, remember? Justan replied and sighed at the mental shrug the raptoid sent in response. *How many of Vriil's men are watching them?*

Deathclaw thought for a moment. *Ten and two more.*

Twelve, Justan said. *You really should let me teach you numbers through the bond. As our scout, we will need you to make these kinds of calculations all the time.*

Deathclaw ignored his suggestion. *The short . . . dwarves are stacked in boxes. Not many are needed to watch them.*

How close are they being held to the rest of the men?

Close.

Let me see, Justan said and Deathclaw fed him a steady stream of memories. The raptoid didn't usually like to share his thoughts, but Justan found him to be quite good at it.

Vriil's men had stuffed the prisoners in small individual cages stacked three high and two deep. Justan calculated that there were sixty in all stacked in one long line and a group of guards were stationed on either side. The rest of Vriil's troops were camped a few hundred yards upwind and Justan could see why. They didn't bother to let the prisoners out of their cages for any reason and the resulting smell was atrocious.

Justan reported Deathclaw's findings to the others.

"Sixty cages, and most of them full?" Pall said. "Looks like they're keepin' more than just dwarves in there."

"Got 'em stacked like chickens!" Lenny said with a scowl. "That just ain't right."

"At least they're alive," Bettie said. She stood behind him, one arm around his shoulder. The other dwarves watched her with a dubious eye, but said nothing. They had learned their lesson when Lenny punched out Derk for asking why he let the half-orc touch him.

"This news is both a good thing and a bad thing," Justan said. "The fact that they've been isolated means a small number of us could possibly go in and take out the guards to free the prisoners. However, after being cramped in those cages this long, they aren't going to be in good shape for an escape."

"Bah!" said Rahbbie. "They're dwarves. A week of sittin' ain't gonna stop 'em."

"Yeah, they're tough," Lenny said. "But we don't know 'bout the human folk they locked up. Maybe Coal should come with us to heal some of 'em if'n we need to."

"Stealth isn't a strength of mine, I'm afraid," Coal said apologetically. "Besides, if what our good friend Kile tells us is true, I am needed elsewhere."

The dwarves had seen a large contingent of armed people from Sampo camped out on the plains. Evidently there was a segment of the population that chafed under Lord Protector Vriil's new rules and Master Coal wanted to talk to them. The hope was that he could convince them to join in on an assault of Vriil's men. If they could free Sampo, they might be able to get a head start in recruiting their army to help the academy.

"'Course it's true. We saw 'em out on the plain the other day," Kile said with a frown.

"Then I am glad you will be there to guide me," Coal replied with a good-natured smile and the dwarf relaxed. Having the named wizard along had helped to put the dwarves at ease. They acted tough, but by the way they kept their hands on the pommels of their weapons it was obvious they were nervous around the bonded.

"Then we'll need the wagon with us when we rescue the prisoners," Justan said. "We won't be able to fit all of them inside, but we can load up the ones in the worst shape."

Justan laid out a plan. While there was still daylight left,

Bettie would take the wagon and drop off Master Coal and five of the dwarves at the camp of the estranged people of Sampo. Then she would return to join the rest of them in the rescue attempt that night.

"How come Pall's the only one who gets to help free the boys?" Rahbbie asked. "They're our friends too."

"'Cause Y'all are noisier than a bucket of empty bottles dropped down the stairs," Lenny said. "We're only takin' Pall 'cause we need one dwarf that knows the others and he's the least likely to do somethin' stupid."

"Rahbbie, the people of Sampo have already seen you fighting Vriil's men," Justan added. "Having you with Master Coal will help lend him credibility. Other members of our group can't go because . . ." He gestured at Fist and Samson who stood a short distance away talking. "We don't want to scare them off."

Rahbbie nodded reluctantly.

Coal smiled. "Come on, then. It's time we set out to meet them. It will only be light for a few hours yet and if we leave now, Bettie can return for the others by dark."

The five dwarves climbed into the back of the wagon and Coal sat next to Bettie on the driver's bench. She would have to drop them off a short distance from the Sampo refugees to make sure that no one noticed she was half-orc.

Lenny watched them drive away. "I'll tell you right now, Bettie's gall-durn pissed 'bout bein' the driver tonight. She wants to be fightin' along side us."

Samson chuckled. "She is seething. Coal's trying his best to calm her down."

"Someone needs to wait at the road with the wagon while we free the prisoners," Justan said. The wagon was too noisy to bring all the way to the enemy encampment undetected, so it would have to wait a short distance away ready to pick up the others when things got hairy. "She's the only one that makes sense."

While they waited for her to return, Lenny and Pall reminisced about old times and Justan spent the time teaching Fist through the bond. It was nearly dark when the wagon came rolling back up the road. Bettie was still fuming.

"This sits about as well with me as a stomach full of rocks," she said as she pulled up.

"How'd it go, darlin'?" Lenny asked.

"He's talking to them now. There are a lot more people down there than we expected. Maybe two thousand people. All of them left their homes rather than give up their weapons to Vriil's men. Even if he can convince them to join us, I don't know what we're gonna do with them. More than half of them are women and children. They're families, not soldiers."

"We'll worry about that when we get back with the prisoners," Justan decided. "Let's go."

Justan rode Stanza and Lenny took Alfred, leaving Fist and Pall to sit in the wagon while Gwyrtha and Samson ran alongside. Justan checked in with Deathclaw along the way. The raptoid had been spending the time scouting out the rest of Ewzad Vriil's forces and he had some unwelcome news.

There are many more humans camped on the far side of Sampo.

How many? Justan asked in concern.

Many many. More than I know to count.

Show me. Justan wasn't as used to Stanza's movements as Gwyrtha's. He held tight to the reins, trusting Stanza to follow the wagon as he absorbed Deathclaw's memories.

The encampment was enormous. It blocked off the road from Sampo to the Mage School, stretching from the river Sandine to the ravine on the far side of the road. There were thousands of troops, all flying the banner of House Vriil.

All those soldiers the dwarves saw on the road. Justan sighed. *So that's where they were going.*

They stink of the wizard, Deathclaw said.

This will impede our plans, Justan thought. Every new development made things worse. How were they to get to the Mage School now? *What have you seen of the city?*

The raptoid did not know much of human cities. *It is the largest I have seen. But it seems . . . quiet. The streets are empty. I saw only a few of the wizard's men.*

Alright, what about the encampment near the prisoners?

Nothing has changed. The other men camp away from the cages. Only the twelve men guard the prisoners.

Are there any scouts we need to worry about? Justan asked.

None, Deathclaw replied, his thoughts laced with ridicule. *What a lazy human pack. No-one takes watch. They all huddle together laughing. They see nothing to fear. I could kill many before they even noticed.*

I am glad you are in my pack, Deathclaw, Justan said, thinking of the many times he had been guilty of the same lack of discipline as Vriil's men. He had come to rely on Gwyrtha's sharp senses and Deathclaw's vigilance to warn him of danger. *What of the guards around the prisoners?*

Some play at . . . Deathclaw sent Justan an image of what the men were doing.

Cards.

They play 'cards' while others drink. But I have gone closer and there are two of them that taste . . . dangerous. I smell the wizard's taint on them.

Justan nodded grimly. He rode up next to the wagon. "Stop here, Bettie. Any closer and they might hear us coming."

Justan hopped down from Stanza's saddle. He opened up pathways between all of his bonded so that they could stay in communication with each other. *It is time to set up our attack. Gwyrtha, go ahead of us and help Deathclaw keep an eye on the men guarding the prisoners. Watch for weaknesses. Fist stay with me for now. We'll fine tune our plan as we get closer.*

I hunt! Gwyrtha said as she slid into the grass, eager for the chance to hunt with Deathclaw.

She may get in the way, Deathclaw said.

Gwyrtha can be just as silent as you when she wants to be, Justan said. *And her senses are more keen. She will be valuable. Just tell her what you wish her to do.*

Very well, the raptoid replied, his thoughts thick with irritation.

He will learn her value, Fist assured him.

If he doesn't learn quickly, I may just tie them together until he does.

Samson trotted up to them and Justan saw that he had changed. The centaur was slightly smaller in size and Coal had thickened and solidified his skin, making it hard and segmented, giving his upper half an almost insectile appearance. The hair along his equine half looked coarse and slightly shiny as if made of wire and he carried a heavily runed spear.

Samson saw Justan's stare and his stiff face formed a slight smile. "Coal prepared me for battle. He thought that now would be a good time to show you what can be done."

Justan wished he had started learning to transform Gwyrtha sooner.

Lenny hopped down from Albert's saddle. He walked by the wagon towards Justan, but Bettie reached down and grabbed the back of his collar. Lenny's eyes widened in alarm and her muscular arm flexed. She yanked him up off of the ground and slammed him down on the seat next to her.

"I don't like sitting here waiting with the blasted horses while you run off and fight, Lenui!" she growled.

"I don't friggin' blame you, darlin'," Lenny said with a tender look. He gently pulled her hand from the back of his collar and kissed it. Justan nearly fell over. Pall let out an audible gasp. Lenny ignored them. "You know I'd rather have yer arms swingin' a hammer right beside me. But there ain't nothin' we'cn do about it. Yer the only one can do this. Edge is our best fighter and the boys need to see me and Pall. No one else can drive the wagon. We need you to be ready to come save our arses if'n it gets too heavy out there."

"Still don't mean I have to like it," she grumped. A slight smile touched her lips. "And don't go sweet talking me around other folk. You almost gave poor Pall a heart attack."

"He'll live, dog-gone it," the dwarf said and pulled her in to kiss her full on the lips. Her hands gripped his hair and drew him in closer for a moment. Then he dropped down from the wagon to join the others. She watched him walk away, her eyes still angry, but the slight smile never left her lips.

"You will not be alone. Squirrel will stay here with you, Bettie," Fist said and extended his hand. Squirrel darted up his hand and leapt to the wagon bench. Bettie's eyes widened in surprise as he scurried up to sit on her shoulder.

"Uh, thanks, Fist," she said.

The ogre nodded and left to join Justan and they headed through the grass towards the distant campfires.

They hadn't traveled fifty yards from the wagon before Lenny shot Justan a glare. "What're you smilin' at?"

"Nothing. I was just surprised to see you kiss her like that in front of everyone. I thought she was going to smack you."

Lenny rolled his eyes "Son, you know nothin' 'bout women. Sometimes they need to be hollered at, sometimes they need to be ignored, and sometimes they need kissin' on. This was one of them kissin' on times."

Justan blinked. "I'm pretty sure that's just dwarven women . . . and Bettie, I guess."

"Nope. Lenui's right," Pall said with a nod, though from his face Justan could tell he was still shocked to see his friend with a half-orc.

Lenny noticed it too. "You got somethin' to say, Pall?"

"Nah," Pall said.

"Keep your voices down," Justan said. They were still a fair distance from the prisoners, but this late at night, sound traveled differently. Justan could faintly hear men laughing.

Lenny grabbed Pall's shoulder. He turned the older dwarf to face him and said in a voice which for him was an intense whisper, "You done think it's her fault her ma got raped by an orc?"

"No!" Pall whispered back, though he wouldn't meet Lenny's eyes.

Lenny grabbed the older dwarf's face and pulled him in close so he couldn't look away. "You think her ma should'a strangled her at birth? Fed her to the dogs?"

"'Course not! Nobody thinks like that," Pall said.

"'Cept you do. That's the kind'a thing good folks only

think down deep and only say out loud when they're nice and drunk. I've heard it in taverns all my life. So've you," Lenny said and Justan saw shame in Pall's eyes.

"Quietly," Justan reminded and Lenny's voice lowered a little, though it remained just as fierce.

"Think what you want 'bout her daddy. She'd right kill him herself if she knew where he was. But that's where you stop. Her ma raised her good, but she died when Bettie was young. She done been mistreated all her life fer just bein' born and I ain't gonna stand fer it no more. Bettie's a fine woman. Finest woman I seen in two hunnerd years."

Pall met Lenny's eyes glare for glare and he pried Lenny's fingers from his face. "I believe you, dag-gum it! If you say so, Lenui, that's good enough fer me. I'll treat her like she was my own daughter."

"Good. You watch her and you'll see what I see," Lenny said with a curt nod. "And better tell the others to respect her like they'd respect me. If'n I see even a hint of disgust in their garl-friggin faces, so help me, I'll plant Buster right between their goat-lickin' eyes!"

"I'll tell 'em." Pall said. "You know they'll come to accept her eventually. Just . . . gimme a chance to talk to 'em before you start killin' folks, okay?"

"Are you two done?" Justan asked. They both turned their glares on him. He pointed to the flicker of the enemy camp fires. "The real enemy is over there and we need to get moving if we are going to save your friends."

"Right, let's go then," Lenny said and marched ahead through the grass.

He needed to say it, Fist sent as they followed behind him.

I agree, Justan said. *He just could've used better timing.*

I could hear the short dwarves talking from here, Deathclaw said. *But these humans are too stupid to listen. They will be easy prey.*

I heard too, said Gwyrtha.

Justan turned to the task at hand, focusing in on the

enemy position through his bonded's eyes. Deathclaw had situated himself in the grass between where the prisoners were being held and the rest of the camp. He could see five guards sitting around a fire and drinking while one more was in a tent snoring away. Gwyrtha was on the far side of the cages, watching six more guards playing cards.

Which men are the ones you said were dangerous? Justan asked Deathclaw.

One sleeps in the tent. The other plays the game on Gwyrtha's side. It is hard to tell which man. Their scents are mingled with the prisoners.

Can you pick it out? Justan asked Gwyrtha.

The one with the red hat or the one with the blue hat, she replied and Justan could see why it was difficult. They were sitting right next to each other.

Justan pulled the rest of the group together. "Lenny, Pall, and Samson, join Gwyrtha on the side of the cages facing away from the rest of Vriil's men. There are six guards playing cards. Take them out as quickly as you can. The quieter the better. Fist and I will join Deathclaw and take out the guards on the other side."

"How can you see all that from here?" whispered Pall.

"He's named, you idjit," Lenny replied with a sharp elbow to the dwarf's side.

"Just be careful," Justan added. "One of the men on your side has been modified by Vriil's power in some way. Gwyrtha will try to smell him out. Watch her and attack when she does. I will signal her when it's time. The moment the guards are down, open the cages as fast as you can. If we're lucky, we will be on our way before the rest of Ewzad's men know we attacked."

They split up and Justan and Fist circled around towards Deathclaw's position. They crouched in the grass, doing their best to remain unseen. Justan's bond with Deathclaw allowed him to see much better at night and it was hard for him to gauge how bright it would be for the guards. Luckily they kept the camp lit with fires and torches, so their ability to watch the darkness would be impaired.

Are you okay with this? Fist asked. *Killing other humans?*

Justan frowned. It had indeed been bothering him. *We have no choice. My father taught me that killing men was only okay if they were attempting to harm me or people I cared for.* He clenched his fists. *Ewzad Vriil declared war on people I care for, Fist. These are his men. They have chosen the side of monsters.*

Yes, but what if they have families at their homes? Fist asked. *Small children of their own to care for?*

We can't think about those things. If we hesitate it could get us killed. Don't forget, I have been around Vriil's men before. They are the worst kind of men. Right now I can hear the screams of women in their main camp. They were probably dragged from Sampo. Justan grit his teeth and tried to ignore the sounds. *If I had the power to do so, I would destroy them all right now.*

Fist's large hand patted his back. *It is okay, Justan. I just wanted to be sure.*

Justan felt Deathclaw's confusion through the bond. *Do you understand why I would be hesitant to kill my own kind?*

Killing without reason is waste, Deathclaw replied. *Raptoids kill for food or in defense of the pack.*

Then why are you confused?

I cannot decide if you are a good leader, Deathclaw said. *Sometimes you are weak. Sometimes you are strong. You keep surprising me.*

You do not know tact, do you, Deathclaw? Fist asked. He was proud of using his word of the day.

Tact?

We can explain it later, Justan sent. He and Fist had crept within a few yards of where Deathclaw was hidden. The grass seemed undisturbed. He would never have known where the raptoid was if not for the bond.

He could see the stacked cages, only four-foot square, and the dark forms of the prisoners inside. The smell turned his stomach.

Why keep them? Fist asked. Ogre tribes did not keep

enemy prisoners. *What good are the dwarves to these men?*

Yes, why not just kill them? Deathclaw asked in disgust.

Killing is a waste, remember? Justan replied. *Keeping them like this is a deterrent to others in Sampo that might want to revolt. Besides, slaughtering them would only cause Ewzad Vriil to look worse and possibly make the people want to revolt even more.*

We are ready, Gwyrtha sent.

Wait for my signal. Justan pulled Ma'am from his back. He wished he could just run in with his swords and finally put Qyxal's pain to use, but stealth was more important.

He considered stringing her with his dragon hair string, but decided against it. The shots fired would be too loud and destructive. Besides, they could possibly pass through Vriil's men and hurt the prisoners. He strung her with a regular string instead.

I can slip inside the tent and kill the one with the wizard's taint without being seen, Deathclaw sent.

Justan thought about it for a moment, then nodded. *Do it. I will fire when you are finished.*

As Deathclaw approached the tents, Justan looked at the five men drinking around the fire. He tried to determine which were the bigger threats, knowing that he could take out one or maybe two before they knew they were under attack. He shifted to mage sight. None of them seemed to have magic weapons, but two of the men had bows across their backs. Justan nodded grimly and cocked an arrow. Oz the Dagger had taught him a firm rule. When in doubt, always take out the archers first. He focused on Deathclaw's thoughts, waiting for the proper moment.

Fist pulled the enormous shield from his back and slid forward through the grass. He got as close to the camp as he dared and stopped, planting the shield in the grass in front of him. He hovered one hand over the handle of his mace, ready to pull it the moment Justan fired his first shot.

Justan sensed Deathclaw sneak up behind the tent. The raptoid could hear snoring issuing from within and he smelled the wizard's stench very strongly. Justan saw the glint of Deathclaw's eye peering around the edge of the tent as he waited for the right moment. Then when all the men were looking away from the tent entrance, Justan saw his body slide into the firelight for a brief moment before slipping inside the tent.

The raptoid paused. *There is a problem. There are two sleeping here. One is a female.*

She is probably a girl taken from Sampo. Just kill the man, Justan replied.

But the stink of the wizard is too strong. I cannot tell which one it is. I should kill both just to be sure.

Just the man, Justan repeated.

Very well.

As Deathclaw tore out the sleeping man's throat, Justan fired and Fist and Gwyrtha darted from the grass.

The arrow pierced the first archer's temple with a faint popping sound, stopping him mid-laugh. The other men stared with mouths open for the few seconds it took Justan to have another arrow ready.

The first swordsman to stand caught the spiked end of Fist's mace in his face and Justan's second arrow caught the other archer in the throat before he could reach for his bow.

Shouts rang out from the other side of the cages, joined by the thudding sound of Buster pounding away. Justan drew another arrow as Deathclaw leapt from the tent opening to take down the fourth man at the campfire. The fifth man shouted for help and he had just drawn his sword when Fist reached out and caught him by the throat. The ogre lifted the man up off the ground and swung him around his head, breaking the man's neck.

Why not use your weapon? Deathclaw asked the ogre.

"It is stuck," Fist said, straining on the handle before finally ripping it free of the first man's skull.

Just then the tent behind them swelled and tore open as a misshapen beast burst from within.

It was the female, Deathclaw said sourly.

Chapter Thirteen

Lenui crouched in the tall grass and looked at the stack of cages. They looked to be made of steel. It was the only way they could've kept a determined dwarf from breaking free. Soft moans issued from the cages above, while the occasional curse came from below. The light from the fire kept him from making out any faces in the cages, but from the size and shape of the shadows inside, it looked like the dwarves were being kept on the bottom two rows.

The guards probably thought it was funny, leaving the dwarves to be crapped and pissed on. Of course, the dwarves' constitutions could take it. It was humiliating, but if the human prisoners had been left on the bottom, they'd likely get sick and die.

He clenched his fists around Buster's handle. He couldn't stand just watching the prisoners in misery while the guards sat there, laughing and playing cards. Edge needed to give the dagblamed signal already so he could bust some heads.

The six men sat around a wide table and played from a universal card deck. Such a stout oak table was an odd thing to be sitting in a camp of men out on the plains. Lenui understood when he saw the house crest of Sampo's mayor on the side, engraved in fancy gold filigree. One of the men wiped his snot on the underside and laughed.

There was a sudden movement behind him and Lenui was nearly bowled over as Gwyrtha streaked out of the grass, heading right for the card players. Was that her idea of a galldurn signal? He stumbled a few steps before charging after her, Buster at the ready.

Gwyrtha had a specific target in mind. She made a beeline for a man wearing a red hat sitting on the far side of the table. The guard saw her coming at the last second, but only had time to widen his eyes before she pounced. Her leap cleared two men sitting with their backs to her and, stout oak or not, the table was smashed to kindling by the weight of her body as she caught the man's head in her jaws.

The guards cried out in shock and fear. Cards fluttered through the air as Lenui swung Buster into the back of one man with a booming thud. Lenui spun, satisfied that the man's insides were turned to jelly and swung at the man beside him, a balding fellow with a yellow-dyed goatee. He threw up his hands, but Buster smashed them aside and crashed through his lower jaw before shattering his ribcage.

Gwyrtha wrenched her head back and forth, her claws tearing into the man beneath her. He screamed and began to change, his limbs growing and turning black, his hands sprouting long glistening claws. Gwyrtha jerked her head one last time and there was a crack. The man shuddered and his body started to smoke and deflate.

One man managed to unsheathe his sword before being impaled by Samson's spear. Pall had his sword in another's gut. The remaining man, a wiry and sickly looking fellow wearing a blue cap backed towards the cages, his brow sweating profusely. His face contorted in fear as he begged, "Please! Please! Don't kill me!"

The dwarves in the cages yelled, some calling out to him. Lenny saw Nhed in a cage at the bottom of the stack. His nephew, his eyes haunted, pointed at the man. "Don't listen to him, uncle! That's Bouto the Jailer!"

The wiry man smiled and his body exploded outwards in sudden transformation. His arms and legs extended and hardened, while a long tail sprouted from his back. His head bloated and swelled before shooting upwards on a long snakelike neck. Rams horns sprouted from his swollen temples.

Gwyrtha turned from the melting mess of the thing underneath her and leapt at the creature. It swung an arm in a backhanded blow that caught her in the side and tossed her heavy body into the cages, causing the stack to teeter. One cage at the top fell and crashed to the ground, the man inside crying out in pain.

Dag-gum thing was stronger than it looked, Lenui thought. He ran towards it, his hammer pulled back. Bouto swung its long neck and its misshapen head caught Lenui's midsection before he had the chance to bring Buster around. The air blasted from his lungs and he was knocked high in the air.

Lenui crashed into the grass and quickly regained his feet. His chest ached, but once again, he was glad to be a dwarf. A human would have busted his dag-burned ribs. Still, his vision swam as he watched Samson and Pall attack the thing.

The centaur dodged one swing of Bouto's ugly head, and jabbed out with his spear, piercing its neck. Bouto reared its head back, blood spurting from the wound. Pall slashed with his sword and cut a shallow wound in its side before its tail whipped out, knocking him to the ground.

Samson charged and the creature spun. His spear plunged into Bouto's back, but it swung its tail low, sweeping the centaur's legs out from under him. Samson crashed hard to the ground and struggled to stand.

Lenny started forward, but realized his hands were empty. He frantically searched the grass around him for Buster. Where was the blasted thing? He looked back to see Gwyrtha grapple with the beast.

It tried to hold her at bay with one arm. Her jaws snapped at it and one of her front legs tore at the arm, but her other front leg hung limply and Lenui knew it was broken. With a mighty shove, it tossed her into the cages again.

Pall ran forward and stabbed his sword deeply into its side. Bouto screeched and drew back its long neck, then launched its head forward and smashed the dwarf like a battering ram, driving him into the ground.

Samson had regained his feet, but Lenui watched in misery as Bouto jumped forward and crashed into the centaur, knocking him down again. Lenui swore. He was just going to have to do this without his hammer.

"Hey, Bouto!" He shouted, stepping out of the grass. "I think yer head's a dag-gum joke!"

Justan shook his head as the creature rose out of the remains of the tent, roaring in anger.

"You killed him!" it cried, its black lips parting to reveal a fang filled mouth and white tongue. She had swelled to just over ten feet tall, a wide fleshy giant with skin as black as coal. "You killed my David!"

Justan drew another arrow. He heard some startled cries over the laughter in the camp behind him. So much for the idea of stealth. They really needed to hurry or they would be dealing with a much larger force.

A crash resounded from the far side of the cages. The stack swayed and Justan could feel Gwyrtha's pain through the bond. One of her front legs was broken. She had killed one man with Vriil's taint, but evidently he hadn't been the only one.

You said there were two! he sent at Deathclaw as he fired. The arrow pierced the she-beast's chest and disappeared within. It howled but didn't seem to slow.

You said, kill only the man! the raptoid replied, using his claws to climb up the beast's fleshy back. When he reached its head it grimaced and flexed. White spikes twelve-inches-long sprang out all over its body. Deathclaw was thrown away and the white spikes detached and came with him, jutting from his skin in multiple places.

Fist held his heavy shield in front of him and swung his mace. The spiked end caught the beast in the face, knocking her head to the side and tearing black skin away, revealing white flesh and blood underneath.

She staggered to the side, then swung a fist in retaliation. Fist caught her punch on his shield. The white spikes protruding from her knuckles shattered, but the force of the impact threw him to the ground. He rolled to his knees and held up the shield again as she swung down with her other fist.

Gwyrtha cried out in pain again and Justan knew time

was running short. He slung his bow across his back and drew his swords. Immediately, he felt the calmness of his left sword overtake him. His right sword raged to release its power and he ran towards the beast.

Deathclaw arrived first, ignoring the painful white barbs that protruded from his body. He spun and lashed out with his tail barb, avoiding more of the beast's spikes and slashed the back of her leg. The she-beast cried out and fell to one knee.

Justan rushed forward and stabbed her foot with his left sword. She froze in confusion as all her rage and pain was sucked away. She looked at Justan in wonder as he brought his right sword around. The moment the tip of his sword touched her chest he released the energy pent up within.

The impact of the energy was devastating. The beast's chest caved in and her back exploded. Debris sprayed into the night beyond and she crumpled to the ground, smoking as she melted.

Justan said goodbye to Qyxal's pain and turned to check on his bonded. Fist stood, a bit bruised, but otherwise okay, while the spikes in Deathclaw's flesh had fallen out upon the beast's demise. Both of them stared at him in surprise at the ferocity of his attack.

Justan pulled his left blade out of the creatures melting foot. *Deathclaw, go and slow down any men approaching from the camp*, Justan sent. *Fist, start opening cages. I need to go around and help the others.*

Deathclaw blinked, then nodded and disappeared into the grass. Fist and Justan didn't take two steps before the stack of cages bowed out again from an unseen blow. This time the stack crashed to the ground all around them.

Lenui readied himself as Bouto's head streaked towards him, propelled on its snakelike neck. He clenched all the muscles in his chest and abdomen, bracing for the impact, holding his arms at the ready.

It hit harder than he expected.

He was smashed to the ground, throwing up a plume of

dust. Luckily his dwarven muscles, hardened by centuries at the forge, absorbed most of the impact. Even so, he barely remembered to reach over the creatures head and wrap his arms around its neck.

Bouto reared back, withdrawing its head and taking Lenui along with it, his legs draped over its eyes. It lifted him into the air, its neck quivering and straining with his weight. Lenui clenched his arms as hard as he could, pinching off the blood supply to its misshapen head.

It swung him around wildly, crashing into the cages and slamming him into the ground. Lenui held tight, his eyes squeezed shut, ignoring the pain from the repeated beating his body was taking. He concentrated on one thing only and that was killing the dag-blasted thing. It seemed like he was bashed about forever. Then he felt something give within its neck.

Bouto collapsed. Its body began to smoke and its neck turned slick and rubbery in his arms. Lenui tried to let go, but his muscles were clenched so tight, he couldn't release his arms. Finally, its head popped free and he rolled to the side.

Voices shouted out all around him.

"Lenui!"

"Lenui Firegobbler!"

"By the da-gum gods, its the hero of Thunder Gap!"

"Shut yer face," he mumbled. "You know I hate bein' called that."

Strong hands grabbed him and lifted him to his feet. He opened his eyes to find himself surrounded by dwarves, some of them old friends, some of them only acquaintances, all of them stinking like the gall-durn Dremald sewer. Then someone thrust Buster's handle in his hands and the cobwebs cleared from his mind.

"Let go of me, you stinkin' hog-lickers!" he shouted and they backed away long enough for him to draw a breath. He glanced over to see that the stack of cages had crashed to the ground. Half of them still looked unopened. "What're you doin' standin' around me? Break everyone loose so we can hightail it out of here!"

"Uncle Lenui," said a voice behind him.

"Nhed," said Lenui, and he turned to find that his nephew wasn't as chubby as usual and his curly red beard had been stained a filthy brown. He smiled anyway. "Glad to see yer alive. I'd hug you, but dag-nab it, you smell like a fresh turd."

"Yes, uncle. Uh . . . thanks fer-."

"You done busted yer arm?" Lenui asked. Nhed's arm hung limp at his side and he could see it was swollen and purple.

"Bashed it when the cages fell, but it ain't broke," Nhed said,

"Then go grab Pall and get out of here, dag-blast it! We'll talk 'bout how much you owe me later."

Nhed nodded and went to help Pall open cages.

"Lenny!" Edge said, running to his side. "Sorry it took so long for me to get to you. We had problems on our side."

"Yeah, how much time we got?"

"The men in the camp heard us and some of them are coming this way, but I sent Deathclaw and Gwyrtha out to slow them down."

"But Gwyrtha's hurt, son," Lenui said.

"I healed her. She's fine," Edge said. "Come on, let's get your men moving."

"Right," Lenui said and started shouting out orders.

They had the cages cleared out in short order. There had been forty eight prisoners all together. All the dwarves had survived, but two of the humans were dead in their cages.

"Bettie is on the way with the wagon," Samson said. The centaur was a bit battered, but Coal must have been paying attention because his wounds were closing fast.

"I hope the durn thing holds together," Lenui replied. "It's well-made, but its made fer ridin' on roads."

They ran into the grass, those too wounded to run helped along by the others. Fist carried two men over his broad shoulders, while Samson had three awkwardly clinging to his back. Bettie rumbled up with the wagon a short time later and they loaded up all the wounded and any other escapees they could fit inside, Fist tossing them in as fast as he could. Edge and one of the strongest humans climbed up on the warhorses.

Lenui ran by the wagon and yelped as Bettie jerked him off his feet and dropped him down on the seat next to her.

"I'cn run, gall-durn it!"

"No way, you're the one driving now, Lenui!" she said and tossed him the reigns. She pulled her bow off her shoulder and pulled an arrow. "It's my turn to fight!"

Lenui looked back. Several of Vriil's men ran around the empty cages towards them. "Hyah!" he cried and the horses churned forward through the grass, the wagon jolting about awkwardly. "Where we goin?"

"Once we hit the road, go left!" she replied over the uncomfortable shouts of the wounded in the back. She fired and one of the Vriil's men fell, clutching his leg. "We're heading to the Sampo refugee camp. We'll drop these folks off in a hurry and come back for the rest!"

Justan stood up in the stirrups and pulled back an arrow. He felt Ma'am's eagerness mixed with the familiar hum of the golden string and smiled, glad that he had taken the opportunity to switch out strings. Stanza, well trained, stood perfectly still as he released.

The arrow jerked the lead rider from his saddle, tearing him away so suddenly that he left a boot behind in the stirrup. Justan saw Gwyrtha run up behind one of the other horses and latch onto its rear end with her claws, pulling it to the ground.

Onto the next one, Gwyrtha, Justan sent as he fired again, this arrow taking the head off of a helmeted rider.

Yes! she replied, running for another target.

He hated that she had to hurt the horses, but the enemy pursuit was scattered and undisciplined. If they could strike enough fear into the enemy, they might decide the chase wasn't worth it.

Another mounted rider went down with an arrow from Bettie's bow just before the wagon reached the road. That made three riders the half-orc had taken down from the bench of the

191

jostling wagon, a feat that Justan found quite impressive. Somehow he had to talk her into joining the academy when this was all over.

Until the wagon could drop off the others and return for the rest of them, the remaining prisoners were on foot and vulnerable. It was up to Justan and his bonded to protect them while they ran. While Justan and Gwyrtha took out the mounted men, Fist and Deathclaw stayed afoot.

The raptoid weaved through the grasses, sowing chaos where he went. Vriil's men went down in a seemingly random pattern, some screaming in pain from a sliced hamstring, others falling in silence with a sliced neck.

Fist trotted alongside the escapees in case some of the pursuers caught up to them. One man stepped in a hole and wrenched his ankle. The ogre placed his shield on his back and tossed the man over his shoulder, never letting go of his mace.

Lenny's nephew Nhed led the prisoners on foot. His arm was in a sling, but he had insisted on staying with the others. Justan figured he still felt guilty about getting his men captured in the first place.

A roar erupted among the enemy on foot as one of them turned into a raving beast as large as a horse. It ran on all fours, its skin a mottled blue and brown, its head a spiky maw with three bulbous eyes. Justan planted an arrow in the center eye, blowing the top of its head off and sending it tumbling through the grass, bowling over two of its own men before collapsing in a smoldering heap.

Justan forced away a shudder, wondering how many of his men the wizard had transformed. If he had done this among this small army, what kind of creatures were among the thousands besieging the academy? They would have to be prepared when they arrived, and Justan already had a plan forming in his mind on how to do it.

The pursuers were either stubborn or crazy. Justan and Gwyrtha had to take down twenty riders and Deathclaw had to disable over thirty men on foot before the enemy gave up. The men finally turned and ran back to their encampment, glancing back over their shoulders in fear, most of them not even bothering to help their wounded comrades.

They retreat, Deathclaw said in satisfaction. He was eager to get the stink of their human blood off him.

Yes, Justan agreed. *Still, would you mind watching to make sure they don't try to follow us again?*

The raptoid hissed. *Yes.*

You too, Gwyrtha?

I would go with you, she grumbled.

And you will soon, sweetheart. But for now I need you to help Deathclaw make sure we are safe. Will you do it? Justan asked, feeling just a bit guilty knowing the compulsion she felt to please him.

Okay, she responded gloomily.

I don't need her, Deathclaw said in irritation.

You have her nonetheless, Justan replied and he left their communications tied open. Deathclaw would come to respect her sooner or later. Maybe this would be the time.

Justan turned Stanza towards the road and soon caught up with Fist and the escapees. They had slowed to a trot once Fist had told them they were no longer being chased. All but one of them were dwarves, and though they were breathing heavily and stank to high heaven, they were in good spirits. The way they shoved each other and laughed, they looked like they could keep running for miles.

The one remaining human stumbled and wheezed, looking as if he might fall down any minute. Justan drew up next to him. "Hey, can you ride?"

"I can," The man looked up at him and though his body was in ragged condition, his eyes were strong and steady. "But since these good dwarves are walking, I don't see why I can't as well."

"Go on, Aldie," Nhed said with a laugh. "We don't expect you to keep up with us."

Justan smiled and climbed down from the warhorse. "I'll take your place and walk alongside them, then."

"Who are you?" the man asked.

"I'm Edge," Justan said and stuck out his hand.

Aldie reached out to shake it and his eyes widened when his fingers felt the thicker skin on the back of Justan's right hand. He turned it over and saw the naming rune and a smile lit up his face. "Nice to meet you, Sir Edge. I'm Aldie and I believe I know a man you saved at Castle Vriil. He'll be excited to see you!"

The man climbed into Stanza's saddle and asked Fist to set the wounded man he was carrying up there with him. Then he galloped down the road towards the camp.

"That man is very brave," Fist said. "He helped me load the wounded into the wagon and refused to ride when he saw the dwarves walking."

"Yeah, Aldie's a good one," Nhed said. "He only got locked up 'cause he protested when Vriil's men started dragging us away."

"Do you know how yer wizard and the boys did with the Sampo folk?" asked Pall. The old dwarf's face looked like one solid bruise.

"No, but the fact that Bettie told us to head to their camp is a good sign," Justan replied.

Bettie brought the wagon back for them a few minutes later, turning it around and shouting at them to get inside. The wagon wasn't meant to hold ten people, much less twenty, but somehow they all wedged in and kept each other from falling out while it bumped down the road.

Justan and Fist crowded up on the driver's bench next to Bettie and Justan took the chance to ask her how Coal was doing with the Sampo people.

"They're still talking," she said. "They've been pretty determined to stay put, but one of the men you rescued seems to be convincing them otherwise. Evidently things are much worse than we realized."

"In what way?"

"Coal didn't say, but you should find out here pretty soon," she said.

The Sampo encampment soon appeared in front of them

and by Justan's count, two thousand seemed like a cautious estimate. Campfires dotted the landscape, surrounding a slow moving river inlet.

They came to a stop and the dwarves ran for the water, eager to wash. Justan didn't blame them. A good bathing sounded nice to him as well, and he hadn't been sitting in filth for a week. But it would have to wait until later.

"Can I?" Fist asked, eyeing the water wistfully. Justan was surprised. The ogre didn't usually look forward to bathing. Then he realized that Fist had been carrying the filthy and wounded men around.

"Please do," he said. Fist smiled and ran after the dwarves.

Bettie pointed him towards the center of the camp where a large group was gathered around a wide tent. The crowd moved aside as he approached. Justan could hear them whisper to each other as they stared at the odd swords on his back and the rune on his hand. Evidently word had already gotten around about the named warrior that helped free the prisoners.

He ducked his head into the tent and saw Master Coal, Lenny, and Rahbbie sitting on benches across from two grizzled warriors. The man that had rode Stanza back earlier stood behind them.

"Ah, Sir Edge," Coal said, standing and extending his arm towards the men in front of them. "Might I introduce Aldie, son of Lance."

"We've met," Aldie said with a smile. Somehow he had found the chance to bathe before they arrived.

"This is Lieutenant Jack, formerly of the Dremald guard," Coal said.

There was something slightly familiar about the old man. "Lieutenant Jack . . . I believe you were with us during the escape from Vriil's dungeon?"

"Yes," the man said, smiling and shaking his hand. "I am so glad to see you again, Sir Edge. Evidently freeing prisoners has gotten in your blood?"

"I hope not to run into the situation often, Lieutenant,"

Justan replied.

"And this," Master Coal said, gesturing to the remaining man on the bench. "Is Sir Lance. He is the one in charge of this camp."

Justan's eyes moved to the warrior's hands and saw the naming rune. "So good to meet you, Sir Lance." He held out his hand, but the man did not shake it.

"You done, Coal?" Sir Lance said. "I told you, I ain't the leader here because I want to be. I'm just the one they elected to come talk to you. Sit down, Edge." He gestured to an empty space on the bench next to Lenny.

"I apologize for my father's directness," said Aldie. "He's been through a lot and has little patience for forma-."

"That's enough, Aldie! If he gets his feelings hurt this easy, he's got lots to learn about being named," Lance said. He directed his glare to Justan. "Let me see your hands."

Justan was surprised by the man's rudeness, but stuck out his hands anyway and turned them over, showing the warrior the runes on the palm of his left hand and the back of his right. Looking at the man's hard gaze, he started to sweat and wondered if he would ever stop feeling unworthy of his name.

"Hmph! Don't know why the bowl done it, but them runes are genuine." His eyes moved up to meet Justan's. "Alright, Edge. Coal's been talking all afternoon. Tell me why you think we should uproot all these families and rush to the academy's aid."

Justan blinked. He had several reasons, but the man's attitude had put him on edge and he hadn't expected to be put on the spot like this. He struggled to force his thoughts to his lips. "I-uh, Sir Lance, the Battle Academy needs all the help it can get right now. Dremald has been taken over and-."

"I know all that," Lance said with a slight roll of his eyes. "But this ain't an army. We have probably a thousand good sword arms, but the rest are just families. We ain't going to leave 'em here by themselves while we go off to fight."

"Okay. That is completely understandable," Justan said. It felt like he had lost the argument before even knowing it started. "Now I just walked in and I am unaware of what's been discussed, so you have me at a disadvantage. Perhaps if you fill in the details, I can better give my opinion?"

The named warrior sighed, but Coal took the opportunity to lay it out for him. "We are not the only ones here trying to raise help for the academy. Lieutenant Jack is here representing Captain Demetrius."

"Really?" Justan said with a smile. "I was worried for him when I heard that Ewzad Vriil took over."

Jack nodded. "The Captain wisely left before Vriil knew of his presence. He has been gathering a force of like minded individuals, mainly deserters from Dremald's garrison that wish to help the academy. I was sent here ahead of time to see if I might recruit the people of Sampo only to find that Ewzad Vrill had beat us here. The mayor has agreed to his terms. These good people are the only dissenters."

"Those were our plans as well," Justan said. "Though we had hoped to get the Mage School's support first."

"I am afraid that will no longer be possible," Coal said.

"I know," Justan replied. "Deathclaw showed me the large army blockading the road to the Mage School."

"At least eight thousand men so far," Lieutenant Jack said. "And more arrive every day."

"That's another reason we can't stay here," Aldie said. "While they had me caged up, I heard the guards talking. They said that the Lord Protector sent a new leader to command the blockade. He knows we're here and he doesn't like it. The guards said he was planning on sending soldiers to force us back to Sampo."

"Then we may have no choice but to go with 'em," said Sir Lance, stone-faced. "Doesn't make sense to get ourselves killed fighting that kind of force."

"But father," Aldie said. "I have been around those men for over a week. They're animals. Even though the people that remain in Sampo are cooperating, the men already rape and steal from them. If they drag us back, we will be little more than slaves."

"Alive slaves," Lance said, unmoved. "Slaves can become free again. You don't come back from being dead."

"Then come with us," Justan said. "Help us free the academy and then we can return to free the rest of Sampo."

"And just how're we supposed to get there?" Lance asked.

"We take the protected road through the Tinny Woods," Justan said.

"That way is closed," Master Coal said with a sad shake of his head. "The wards are down and from their description, the woods are flooded with more moonrats than I ever thought possible. We would have to fight every step of the way and it would mean passing through the darkest part of the woods."

"See?" said Lance. "Your way is even worse than Demetrius'. He would have us stay mobile, traveling the plains and hills until a way to help the school presented itself. Imagine that. A thousand women and children roaming about, out in the elements, hoping that Ewzad Vriil doesn't find 'em. I'm telling you. There is no way for us to help the academy and no place fer us to go, but back to Sampo."

"Out in the elements is better than holing up in our homes, leaving ourselves to the whims of those men," Aldie said.

Justan thought furiously, but he couldn't come up with an answer. The only other way he knew to get there would be to climb through the mountains and he didn't see how they could get these people through safely.

"Yer wrong!" Lenny said. "There's both a way fer you to help the academy and a place for yer people to stay. Come with us and we'll take the back way to Wobble."

"But Lenui," said Rahbbie.

"Aw shut-up 'bout that, con-found it. We ain't got no choice. The secret ain't been well kept anyway. Every drunk dwarf in the kingdom's blabbed 'bout it once or twice. Only reason no one else tries goin' through there, is it's a dag-gum pain to find."

"What are you talking about, Lenny?" Justan asked.

Lenny ignored Rahbbie's scowl and said, "Look, on the

west side of the mountains, 'bout fifty miles east of Dremald's a narrow passage right through a crevasse that takes you right to Wobble. Dwarves use it sometimes 'cause it's a lot faster than goin' the long way around. Anyways, there's a set of caves 'bout half way to the town. It's big enough to hold all Sampo's families while we're off fightin'.

"The dwarves've piled enough stores there over the years to last a durn long time. Old Stangrove Leatherbend planned out the place well. He meant it to be a refuge in case Wobble ever got attacked. Thing is, the town never grew as big as he thought it would. Now them caves're only used as a place to stop fer the night on the way through."

"The narrow paths make it easy to defend too," Rahbbie admitted.

"I've been thinking for awhile that Wobble would be a great area for us to stay in while we staged raids on the army," Justan said. "This makes it even better."

Coal nodded and looked at the named warrior. "It sounds like we know where we are going, Sir Lance. The question is, will your people come with us?"

"We have to do it, father," said Aldie.

The grizzled warrior frowned. "Very well. I suppose this is the plan that makes the most sense. I'll take it to the others and have you an answer by morning." He stood with a scowl and left the tent.

Aldie sighed. "It may not look like it, but I can tell by the look on his face that father is going to push for your plan. The people here respect him. They will follow."

Lieutenant Jack stood. "Sir Edge, this back way to Wobble may very well be the path Captain Demetrius has been looking for. I will go and report back to him. If all goes well, we may just join you along the way."

Chapter Fourteen

"You are marked for death, Jhonate Bin Leeths."

Jhonate spun, her staff forming a razor edge, and took the troll's arm off at the elbow. The thing barely noticed in its hungry rage, swinging its other muscular arm at her. She leaned back to dodge, but not far enough. Its filthy claws dug at the skin of her face. The ring's enchantment held, deflecting the blow. If not for Justan's gift, she would have earned some disfiguring scars.

"You are marked."

Jhonate swung her staff again, this time making it hard as steel. The blow barely moved the troll, but she was able to use the impact to push her body out of the way of its next lunge. She rolled to the side and up to her feet, backing up a bit, hoping to give herself a little fighting room.

This was the third modified troll they had come across in the last week. The mother of the moonrats knew they were somewhere nearby and she had started laying traps. Faldon kept them on the move so that she wouldn't find their main camp, but every caravan they attacked now carried a few nasty surprises.

To Jhonate's left she could hear Tamboor's Howlers screaming as they dealt with the witch's latest trick. Several of the orcs in this particular caravan had looked ill and when the howlers cut them down, their bodies had burst open to release a swarm of stinging spiders.

She would have to go and help them once she had dispatched the troll. She didn't think it would take long. It just hadn't given her enough room to use her own trick yet.

The troll swung around and screeched at her, ravenous

hunger blazing in its beady eyes. The stubby fingers of a new hand had already begun to grow from its elbow stump and as it charged her again, she saw black claws sprouting from the fingertips. It truly was unfair how quickly these things regenerated. Locksher said it went against the laws of nature and energy. She just thought it immensely inconvenient.

"*Death, Jhonate Bin Leeths,*" the voice said again.

"Enough, witch!" she spat. Jhonate glanced behind her to make sure she had plenty of room and waited for the troll to come. The thing most difficult with these modified trolls was their sheer size and weight. Try to hold your ground and they would bowl you over. It had forced her to change her fighting style.

The troll lurched towards her and Jhonate formed the tip of her staff to a fine point. One advantage she had was that even modified trolls were predictable when hungry. It charged, arms straight out, mouth agape.

Jhonate ran backwards. It was a form of training she had forced upon herself years ago in order to train her agility and balance. Now it came in handy as she was able to match the troll's pace. Unfortunately, it was also very dangerous. One trip and the troll would be on her.

She needed to time her attack just right. She slowed down to let it get just close enough that it could almost reach her, then she thrust her staff forward and up. The point jabbed through its open mouth, piercing its tender soft palate. Once it started to spasm, she knew she had hit the right place.

Jhonate opened a small hole in the tip of the staff, and injected pepper directly into the base of the troll's brain.

The trick had been her idea. Her people often stored water inside their Jharro weapons. There were many places within the jungles and swamps where clean water was hard to find and having a few swallows of water in a hollowed section of your weapon could keep you alive. Wizard Locksher had prepared a liquid pepper solution at her request and this had been her first chance to use it.

Stabbing the troll anywhere would have allowed her to

poison it and stop its regeneration. But these modified trolls were slow to go down, peppered or not. Locksher had suggested a dose directly to the heart or brain could stop it quicker. She hoped he was right.

The troll's teeth clamped down on the staff and it lunged for her. She backpedaled, but her heel caught on a rock.

"*You are marked,*" the voice said. She fell backwards, the troll looming over her.

"*Death.*" Her back struck the ground. The troll descended on her.

"*Death!*" Jhonate wedged the butt of the staff into the ground next to her head and ordered it to harden and lengthen. The staff's pointed tip jammed up against the inside of its skull.

"*Death!*"

The troll jerked to a stop, its arms dangling just above her, its weight suspended by the length of the staff. The troll hung there for a moment, unmoving and she wondered if it was dead. Then its lower body sagged and the tip of her staff popped through the back of its head.

The troll slid down the shaft of her staff and collapsed on top of her. She swelled the staff within its head, stopping its descent at the last possible second to keep its face from resting against her. Its eyes twitched and its jaws worked soundlessly, but she knew it to be from reflex only. She had injured its brain and with the pepper inside it, the damage would not heal.

"*You are-!*"

"Silence!" Jhonate yelled in disgust and the voice quieted. The troll was abominably heavy, the weight of its lower body pinning her legs. She tried to push it off of her but it was slippery with slime and she could not find any leverage.

Jhonate pushed and shoved at the troll, trying to work herself free. She could still hear the howlers running about and some of them were pretty close. Hopefully they hadn't brought the stinging spiders with them.

She had finally worked one of her legs out from under the thing when she saw movement out of the corner of her eye. Jhonate turned her head and scowled. How had she forgotten the arm she chopped off?

A miniature version of the troll, maybe one-foot-high, was coming at her with hunger in it eyes. Its approach was slowed by the enormous forearm and hand it dragged behind it.

The little thing got closer and her struggles to free herself produced little progress. Finally, she thinned the staff within the poisoned troll's head, letting its drooling face fall against her shoulder. Ignoring the way its tongue slithered against her skin and the way its teeth grazed her, she reached around and pulled the length of the staff from the back of its head.

The miniature troll let out a tiny screech as it neared her side. She was barely able to shape the butt end of the staff in time to jab it into the troll's tiny chest. She pumped the last of the pepper into its body and it fell to the ground, twitching.

With a sigh, she wedged the staff next to her and tried to use it as leverage to pry the thing off. She had nearly freed herself of the thing when Jobar and Faldon appeared to help her.

"Are you alright, Daughter of Xedrion?" Jobar asked as she stood and wiped the slime from her arms. His face looked truly concerned.

"I am unharmed," she replied. "Though my tactics were successful, the beast's weight worked against me."

"*You are marked for death . . .*"

"I wish Tamboor's men could say the same," Faldon said. "Many of them were stung badly before crushing the last of the witch's little surprises." Faldon, like most of the men, had followed her lead and now referred to the mother of the moonrats as simply, 'The witch'. "They're making brave faces, and none of them act like they're poisoned, but I want all of them checked out as soon as we get back to camp. Somehow I doubt she left those spiders there simply to provide an inconvenience."

"The worst part is that the wagons contained nothing useful," Jobar said. "Just junk and empty crates."

"I am afraid we are wasting our time hiding out in the mountains," Jhonate said. "We have done little to help the academy lately. The last two caravans we have hit were nothing but traps."

"You're right," Faldon said, his face darkened with a deep frown. "It's time we changed our tactics. I will think on it tonight."

Later that evening she sat cross-legged outside of Locksher's tent. She closed her eyes and rested her staff across her knees as she tried to calm the nervous energies that tussled inside her. Justan's ring had protected her from injury twice that day. She needed to train more.

Jhonate opened her eyes briefly and focused on turning on her mage sight. As Faldon had hoped, nearly one out of every ten men in their force had just enough magic ability to use it. Locksher had them practice every night, though he felt guilty for doing it.

Her vision flickered a little bit before finally shifting. Locksher's tent glowed in a myriad of colors with all the magic at use inside. She turned her gaze to her hands and sighed at the soft blue glow that outlined her skin. The sight both comforted and confused her. She thought on it time and time again but still could not understand why, which was one of the reasons she needed to talk to the wizard.

It was nearly another hour before he showed up, his arms folded, his brow furrowed in thought. He was so distracted, he walked right by her. He would have entered the tent and not even known she was there if she had not spoken.

"Wizard Locksher," she said and the wizard jumped in surprise.

"Jhonate! So sorry I didn't see you there," he said with a smile. "Are you wanting more of that pepper mixture? I am glad it worked for you."

"No, it is not that," she said. "Though I would like you to make more."

"Of course," he said.

"My question is of an . . . uncomfortable nature. I hesitate to discuss it with anyone, but I thought perhaps you-."

"Wait," he said, holding up one hand. "Is this a . . . womanly concern?"

She frowned. "I do not know what you mean."

"Evidently not." He looked relieved. "Why don't you come on in so that we can discuss it, then?"

She followed him inside his tent and was instantly surprised by how cluttered it was. Books were piled haphazardly, many of them spilling over his rumpled bedroll. Several stacks of loose parchment stood at the rear of the tent and his overlarge pack lay tipped over on the other end, its contents scattered about haphazardly. Many of the items looked innocuous, but they radiated a sense of danger. Likely it was these things that made the tent glow to her mage sight earlier.

"How did you acquire all these books?" she asked.

"I picked up most of them in Jack's Rest. One of the retirees that died in the raids was a wizard. Let me tell you, old Vincent will be quite happy when I return these to the library," he said with a laugh. "Please sit down."

Jhonate pursed her lips. "And where would you like me to sit, sir?"

"Oh!" Locksher shoved a few of the items aside to clear a space for them to sit. Once they had done so, he pulled a small pot from the pack.

He yawned and poured some water into the pot and reached into his robes to pull out a thin leather case. He opened it and pulled out two small pouches full of greenish powder, then took a pinch from each and added it to the pot.

"Sorry, I have been far too busy to rest lately and-." Locksher yawned again. "I need something hot to keep my mind going."

He held the pot between his hands and the water began to boil. A slight minty aroma began to fill the tent. He flashed her a smile. "So! Were you waiting for me long?"

"Just a few hours, sir."

"I'm sorry about that. Vannya needed my help at the infirmary. Those spider bites Tamboor's men had were nasty." He shook his head. "It ends up they were bitten by redhost spiders. They're parasites. When they sting you, they pump eggs into your body. If untreated, the eggs hatch into larvae that burrow to your bloodstream where they feed off of you and multiply until you die and they find their next host. Terrible little things."

"Will the men be okay?"

"Yes. Vannya and I had to burn out all the little wounds. It is a painful process, but Vannya has a way about her that seems to distract the men from their pain."

"I am not surprised," Jhonate said.

"At any rate, what do you need to talk about?" Locksher asked.

"It is . . . about the ring I wear. It confuses me and I fear there may be something wrong with it."

"Oh? How so?"

She frowned. "I am reluctant to remove it. I find this disturbing because . . . Among my people, magic is a tool, but we are taught not to depend on it. When the ring was given to me, I was not told its properties and unknowingly I allowed it to protect me during battle."

"So you feel it to be dishonorable to use the ring to protect you in battle?" he asked.

"Well, no. But . . . I fear that relying upon such protection could make me lose my edge in battle. Then one day, if the protection was not available, I would no longer have the conditioning needed to survive," she said. It was the same argument she used against herself, but it seemed even more hollow spoken aloud.

"If you are concerned, why don't you simply take it off?"

"I have tried," she said, leaning forward. "This is why I have come to you. For the last two weeks I have tried to remove it multiple times, but when I do and I see the blue glow flicker and go out, I feel. . ." she lowered her eyes in shame. "I feel such a panic well up inside me that I have no choice but to put it back on."

Locksher raised one eyebrow and gave her a thoughtful look. "That does seem a bit unlike you. And you feel that this compulsion is something coming from the ring itself?"

"It is the only answer I can think of," she replied.

"May I see it for a moment?"

He sat the pot of boiling liquid to the side and held out his hand. Jhonate slid the ring off her finger and winced only slightly as she placed it on his palm. He rolled it over in his fingers. "Do you feel any panic now?"

"I . . . no." She didn't like it being off her hand but there was no sense of panic.

"Hmmm. Can you switch to mage sight?" He waited for her to do so. "Good. Now let's look at it together, shall we? What do you see?"

"It is dark blue."

"Good, let's look closer." An image appeared above his hand, a hazy vision of the ring but much larger in size. The vision zoomed in much closer. "Now what do you see?"

Her brow furrowed. "Blue and black strands sort of . . . woven together."

"Yes, the earth and water magic are what forms the barrier. But what's fascinating to me is that I can't quite make out how it knows what to . . . Oh! Oh my!" He grinned and pulled out his smoking pipe. He picked through his packets of herbs until he found what he was looking for and stuffed the pipe. "This is great. Wow, Jhonate, you have no idea how fantastic this is! This is old magic. Ancient stuff!"

Jhonate looked at him curiously. When Locksher became excited, he stopped sounding like a wizard. He sounded more like an average man.

Locksher reached into his robes and handed her a pair of glasses. She put them on as he lit the herbs and smoke began billowing from the pipe.

Jhonate saw a smoky white nimbus surrounding her staff. "This is the same smoke you used when we examined the troll."

"Yes indeed. Now look at that! Interwoven between the strands of earth and water, do you see it?" Locksher laughed.

"Do I see it?" How could she miss it? Something shining a hot white, underneath those blue and black strands. "What is it?"

"This is binding magic!" he said. "Somehow a wizard

long-long ago, bound the spirit of some kind of animal or creature to this ring. It is the energy of that spirit that makes it so powerful and the intelligence of that spirit that tells the ring how to distribute its protection about your body."

"I see," she said in sudden understanding. "There are those among my people that can do that. Yntri Yni, the weaponmaster of my people, is a master at spirit binding. This is the first time I have been able to see what the magic looks like though."

"Truly?" His grin was positively childlike. "I must go visit your people some time. From everything you have told me it seems that they know more about spirit magic than I have been able to find out in the deep histories of the Mage School."

"Perhaps," she said. "Lately I hear that my people have been letting more and more visitors into our land. They might let you in as long as you don't tell them you are a wizard." Jhonate returned her focus to the vision of the ring that floated above Locksher's hand. "So this spirit . . . Is it the reason I am having this difficulty?"

"I doubt it. Do you feel any panic right now while I hold it?" She shook her head and Locksher nodded. "As I thought. The magic doesn't seem to be interacting with you in any way right now. Still, perhaps I should have Vannya wear it for a few weeks and perform some tests, make sure that there are no ill effects-."

"No! That will not be neccesary." she said, reaching for the ring.

He smiled and pulled it back. "Did you see that? Just there?"

She blinked. "No, sir. What did I miss?"

"Nothing," he said and tossed the ring to her. "The ring did nothing to cause that reaction."

She frowned, "Then what is it?"

"Oh, you don't really want to hear this from me. It would be much better for everyone involved if you just figured it out for yourself." He poured some of the steaming liquid from the pot next to him in a small tin mug.

"What do you mean?" Jhonate asked. She hadn't liked the weary look in his eyes while he said it.

Locksher sighed and took a sip from the mug. "This ring is not a danger to you. The reason you want to keep it on has nothing to do with its powers or any magic influences. So, you tell me. What is left?"

"Are you saying that there is something wrong inside my mind?"

"Ah! You girls! At least Vannya admits it to herself," he said with a shake of his head.

Jhonate's eyes narrowed in anger and she gripped her staff. "You will tell me what I need to know right now, Wizard. Remember, you are not my superior. I am not above beating the answer out of you."

Locksher nearly choked on the liquid in his mouth. Anger crossed his face. "Fine, if this is the way you wish to learn. The reason you feel this way about the ring is because of who gave it to you. You are infatuated with the boy. You and Vannya both, which is why you keep fighting with each other."

Jhonate's jaw dropped.

"Quite frankly, I have known it for some time and I am pretty sure Faldon sees it too. At least, I think he hopes its so, because he would truly like to see the two of you together and-." the wizard winced. "Sorry. I went too far there, didn't I? I must blame it on lack of sleep. Ohh . . . Faldon won't be happy with me for this."

She looked down at the ring in her hand, her heart aflutter. With trembling fingers, she placed the ring back on her finger and watched the blue glow flicker back on. She repressed a shiver. Was it truly that simple?

She would ponder it later. Jhonate took a deep breath and composed herself, then gave the wizard a brief nod. "Thank you, sir. I apologize for my threats of violence."

"Oh, um-." He lifted the cup back to his lips and peered at her suspiciously. "I am glad to have been of service. Uh, is there anything else?"

She looked down for a moment. "There is one more

thing. It is perhaps of more importance than the ring, but I have more difficulty speaking of it. I . . . Normally I would not come to a man of your age and experience with these kinds of concerns, but as you seem highly competent and you are the only expert in magic here, I-."

"Jhonate," Locksher said, stopping her. "Just how old do you think I am?"

She blinked, "I would say no more than thirty, sir. I hope you did not take offense. It is just that usually I would go to someone more experienced with this kind of matter."

"Thirty?" He laughed and shook his head. "The kind of magic that I work with tends to slow down the aging a bit. Actually I turned forty-four last week. That still may be younger than you would like, but surely you have seen that I have more experience than my years would suggest?"

Jhonate could see that she had offended the man. "I am sorry, sir. I did not mean to question your abilities."

"It's fine. Please, go on. I will answer to the best of my ability and we can both get some rest, hmm?"

She swallowed and nodded, then said matter of factly, "My problem is that I have been hearing the voice of the mother of the moonrats in my head."

Chapter Fifteen

To Jhonate's relief, he did not scoff or laugh at her.

Locksher stopped sipping his drink and set it down on the floor next to him. He leaned forward, resting his elbows on his knees. "Would you care to elaborate, Jhonate?"

"I think something may have happened to me when I battled the witch. Ever since that day, I hear her voice from time to time. It happens most often during battle, as if she is taunting me."

His brow furrowed in thought. "And what does it say?"

"It says, 'Jhonate Bin Leeths, you have been marked for death.'"

"Always the same phrase?" he asked.

"Yes," she replied. "It is the phrase she said to me the first time I faced her."

"I see . . . are there any other effects?"

"I have . . . dreams. Dreams of a horrible nature where I am not myself and I am using my mind to control people and make them . . ." Her bottom lip trembled. "And make them do cruel things."

Locksher nodded. "I was afraid of this type of reaction when you told us about your encounter. Then you acted so composed, I figured there was no need to worry."

"How can I get her voice out of my head?" she asked. "Do you have a spell that will help?"

He shook his head. "You are being attacked by spirit magic, and I don't have a spell to counteract that. I can, however, perhaps guide you to a way to fix the problem yourself."

"I would be grateful, sir," she said, twisting the ring on her finger. "Can we do it now?"

He blinked and a sudden weariness passed over his face for a brief second, but he forced it away, replacing it with a smile. "Of course. So what we will be looking for is some part of the mother of the moonrat, a small trace that was left within your mind. You will need to locate it and then find a way to destroy it."

She clenched her jaw and nodded. "I am prepared to do so."

"Very well. First," He snatched another tin cup out of this oversized pack, then filled it with the steaming liquid from the pot. "Drink this."

He held the cup out to her and she took it hesitantly. The cup was hot, but not uncomfortably so. She leaned down and sniffed the liquid. Its minty aroma filled her sinuses and she felt a clearing sensation within her mind. "What is in it, sir?"

"It is a special brew I discovered when studying with the Lisenti. It clears and focuses the mind. It is a common ritual there for students to drink a cup before beginning class." She hesitated and he assured her, "Don't be concerned. I give it to you because it is late and you have been through a very tiring day. What you are about to undertake will require great focus and concentration. You will need all the help you can get."

Jhonate nodded and sipped the liquid, expecting a bitter medicinal flavor. Instead, she was quite pleased to find that it tasted much like it smelled; minty and slightly sweet. She felt the warmth of it settle in her stomach and the tiredness faded from her muscles.

"Now I want you to close your eyes and fall into meditation like you did the day you held the eye. Don't completely close off the outside world, though. I need you to be able to hear me and respond."

Jhonate nodded and did as he asked, bringing up the soft whiteness that was her innermost mind. She built the figure within that represented herself; a woman, lightly armored holding a staff. "I am there, sir."

"Good. Now the most likely place for this piece of the witch to be hiding is within your memories." The small figure within her could hear his voice as a soft echo coming from the white emptiness around her. "What you need to do is pull up the thoughts that you sifted from the mother of the moonrat's mind that day. Perhaps you pulled more than just memories back with you."

Locksher spoke about memories in intangible terms, but Jhonate was a physical thinker. Her teachers had recognized this when she was a child and taught her to deal with her mental world in the same way she would deal with the physical.

The figure that represented her walked forward into the whiteness until she stood before an iron door. It opened into a wide room with walls, floor and ceiling of the same white mist as the rest of her mind, but around the edges there were tall bookshelves made of Jharro wood that held volumes upon volumes of memories.

She walked past them all, heading to a section of the library that contained all her memories of battle. There, in the corner, sat a locked chest. There was a black glow radiating from it, and she knew she had found the source.

"I found the memories," she said, knowing that her body was repeating her words aloud.

"Y-you found them?" he asked, sounding confused. "Alright, have you sifted through them for her contamination?"

"I will start going through them now." She reached for the chest and the locks fell away. The lid sprung open. Inside was stored all the memories of her encounters with the witch in the form of letters and books.

First, she removed several stacks of loose pages. These were the facts pulled from that witch's mind that she had found most relevant the day of her attack. Jhonate flipped through them quickly, her mind instantly processing each page as she touched it. They were troop locations and movements, orders and processes. Now that they were weeks old, the information was basically useless. She found no traces of maliciousness in them.

She set the pages aside and picked up the book that

contained her memories of her first encounter with the witch. This was where she had first heard the phrase that kept repeating in her mind. The event flashed through her mind again, but the thoughts within that memory were untainted. She lifted out the rest of the books, all containing her own thoughts and ponderings regarding the witch.

"Have you found the contamination?" Locksher asked, his voice sounding impatient.

"No. And I have sifted through everything," she said in irritation. There was nothing left in the bottom but tiny tatters of parchment. These scraps were all that remained of the big secret she had stolen from the witch's mind. Jhonate had escaped with it, bringing it all the way back with her, just to have the witch tear it away. "Well . . . perhaps not . . ."

Darkness still radiated from within the chest. She reached in and lifted out the parchment pieces, tiny flashes of half memories and thoughts. These were ancient thoughts, and she recognized them as the thoughts that had invaded her dreams. Thoughts of someone hungry for power, ecstatic about domination, enraged by disobedience. Still, they were not the source of the darkness. She sat them aside. The chest was empty, yet it still burned black with malice.

"There is something else here, but I cannot see it," she said.

"This is your mind," said Locksher's voice. "Focus. She cannot hide anything from you there."

Jhonate gripped her staff and with a mental command caused white flame to burst from the end. She dipped the flame down inside the chest, illuminating the bottom. There, in the corner, she saw something, a tiny notch. She reached in and pried at it with her fingernails. It resisted, but then, with a creak, the bottom opened on concealed hinges.

"There! Memories hidden from me until now!" A series of black scrolls were lined up snug in the secret compartment. The smell of rot wafted up from them and they glistened dark and wet in the light of her staff as if covered in a filthy residue.

"Fascinating. Now be careful. If she was able to keep

them hidden even within your mind, they may be protected."

"Of course they are." Jhonate smiled. The witch hadn't taken everything important after all. "But that means they are valuable."

She touched the burning end of the staff to her left hand, transferring the flame to her fingers. She reached her burning hand into the bottom of the chest.

"Careful now," Locksher said.

"Of course. I am always careful," she said. The blackness recoiled from the flames that enveloped her had as she grasped the first scroll. "I'm-."

Her eyes fluttered open but there was no light, just dirt. Dirt! It scratched at her eyeballs! She tried to blink it away, but more came in until it became caked under her eyelids. She opened her mouth to scream, but there was no air. Nothing but dirt. It filled her throat, covered her skin.

She struggled, trying to breathe, but finally realized it didn't matter. Breathing was no longer a necessity for her. It was a pleasant sensation and allowed her to speak, but she had discarded the need some time ago, just as she had discarded the need to eat or drink. No, there was no need to panic. She would not die. But no matter how she strained, she could not move.

Trapped! Of course. They couldn't kill her so they sealed her away. Her, the most powerful wizardess in the known lands, no, a goddess! Trapped under a tree. She would have laughed were her lungs not filled with earth.

Her enemies had chosen well. The tree was strong, and the weight of it along with the earth around her body held her still. The insult of her imprisonment ignited a fire within her. Rage burned like coals in her mind. She reached out with her powers, looking to seize the closest creature. Anything would do. Anything that could dig her out.

But nothing happened! Her magic traveled only inches from her body before dissipating. Somehow it was the tree's roots. They surrounded her like a cage. She switched to mage sight, then spirit sight, then blood sight. Were it possible, she would have howled. It was one of the sacred trees; one of the immortals. Its roots were made of a wire framework of elemental magic, powered by the brilliant white of spirit magic, and pulsed with the neon rush of blood magic. She despaired.

Then she heard it, faint, a whisper. *Time*, it said and she recognized the voice of the Dark Prophet. *You have time. Fight. Weaken this prison. I will come for you.*

Jhonate gasped. The scroll in her hand pulsed, its blackness over taking her hand and climbing up her wrist.

"*Jhonate Bin Leeths. You are marked.*"

She frowned. *Not here, witch.* She flexed her mind and white flame burst from the skin of her arm, burning the blackness away until her hand was whole again. Then she turned the flame on the scroll, searing it until all the blackness was gone. The witch's memory was hers now. She sat the scroll down beside the other memories.

"Jhonate! Are you okay?"

"I am fine," she said, and white flames continued to blaze from her hand as she reached for the next scroll. She was eager to learn more, but more wary now that she knew what to expect. She focused on maintaining her sense of self despite the nature of the memories.

Much time has passed. She has moved beyond the pains of her body now. She feels the pain only if she wants to. Instead, she focuses solely on breaking free. The tree's power is strong, but she has weakened it ever so slightly. She has learned how to tap into its strength to sustain herself.

More time passes. She has slipped some tiny portion of her presence past its roots. The tree still holds her in place but she feels a sense of triumph, knowing that rot slowly extends in the soil around the tree. She can sense the decaying leaves of the forests, the worms of the ground, and the insects that live in the leaves.

The dark voice can still only reach her in whispers, but they have grown fainter rather than stronger. She cannot make out what he is saying. She realizes that the Dark Prophet himself is now confined.

Jhonate burned the last vestiges of darkness from the scroll and set it aside with the other one. How long had the witch been trapped? Who was she really?

"Jhonate!"

She ignored Locksher's voice and reached for the next scroll.

Centuries have passed. Her persistence has paid off. The tree sags and rots. Its branches are dying, but that core of spirit magic that powers it still holds her captive. Unfortunately, her body has also weakened. It is now but a withered husk, barely living at all and she knows her mind will soon fade. Her presence now clings mainly to the talisman they buried with her; her token; her link to the dark voice.

She comes up with a desperate solution. She seizes control of the insects within her limited but growing range and begins the process of transferring her mind, her very thoughts and memories to their tiny and primitive brains. Unfortunately, their minds are so small, so ineffective that her powers remain limited. She continues to spread her rot, calling in more insects, inviting them to feast on the decay, transferring more and more of herself before her body fails completely.

Jhonate placed the scroll down with the others. The white fire blazed bright in her hands. She reached for more, ignoring Locksher's concerned voice.

Time has passed once more. One day the dark voice speaks to her again.

"*I have slipped my confinement, dear one. The tribes of the mountains worship me once again. I gather them together now.*" She wanted to reply to him but her thoughts were too scattered now. Only the strength of the talisman allowed her to keep her mind from simply blowing apart. "*I know you have been weakened, but fear not, I still have use for you. You will be freed.*"

This emboldens her. She sends out her swarms to search her limited range for the mind of a superior creature. They come upon a tree rat. She attacks and seizes its mind. Its brain is small, only capable of shallow thoughts and instincts, but far superior to the insects nonetheless. She has the rat return to its hole where it has suckling young. She seizes their tiny minds as well, planting bits of herself within them. They grow swiftly, as does her control over them.

She overpowers more rats and breeds them together. Their gestation period is brief, which she uses to her advantage, discarding those that are weak, and focusing on those with favorable traits. She learns to take control of them early, while still in the womb so that she can use the small traces of her old power that remain to make changes to their bodies as they develop.

The more minds she controls, the more her thoughts expand and the more her abilities grow. Her mind becomes vast, spread out within hundreds of the beasts. Their eyes are weak, but their other senses are acute and she can now process incoming information from all the creatures simultaneously.

She uses them with efficiency, breeding them while they are young. When they reach their prime, she uses them as soldiers to drive away predators from her land. If they live long enough to become old or feeble, she simply feeds them to the others or lets them fall where they are and rot, adding to the decay of the forest.

"Jhonate!"

"Just a moment! I am nearly finished!" There were only two scrolls left. The flames in her hand didn't burn quite as brightly as before, but she reached for the next one anyway.

The Dark Prophet doesn't come to save her. His body is destroyed, his voice extinguished. She does not mourn him. She sees little use in it. Instead, she increases her work.

She continues to breed certain traits within her children, for that is what they are to her now. She makes them bigger, stronger, smarter. She grows their eyes, hoping to make them better able to see in the dark, but instead of enhancing their sight, these changes have an unforeseen effect. Some of her children are born with eyes that glow a dull yellow in the dark. She finds that she can reach out through the eyes of these children and touch other minds. The signal is weak but true and she is spurred to breed them faster.

Time passes. Traces of her old magic have begun to reappear. It is evident in the voice of her children. They know her pain. They know her loneliness. They know her hunger. It is in their very genes and it can be heard in their chittering moan. The locals begin calling her children moonrats. The world can hear her sorrow through her children and it makes them shudder in fear. This brings her great pleasure.

The tree is all but dead. The tiny core of power within it can no longer constrain her. Unfortunately she has no physical body to inhabit. It rotted away decades ago. Her spirit stays near the tree, bound to her talisman, yet her mind is free; free to roam as she spreads her children's territory further into the forest.

She has a new breed of children now. Their eyes are green and they can control lesser minds. She comes up with a new goal. She will continue to breed her children until their eyes become powerful enough to control the minds of humanoids. Then she will spread her rot throughout the land. Then she will dominate the world.

Jhonate placed the purified scroll down beside her. There was only one left. She noticed that the nails on the fingers of her hand had turned black. She quickly regained her focus, burning the black away.

She peered back into the chest and saw that the last of the darkness had pooled around the final scroll.

"*You are marked*!" the voice cried in protest. "*Death*! *Death*! *Death*!"

"This is the last time you speak to me," she snarled.

Flames roared from her fingers, filling the interior of the chest with white hot energy. As she grasped the last scroll, the chest itself burned away.

Elves have moved into her forest. Elves! Their minds are large and their blood is full of magic. How she craves them. Oh the things she could do with them under her power. But they are stubborn and cruel. They combat her rot with their blood magic and kill her children. That is unacceptable. She strikes back and there is war.

Time passes. The war is at a stalemate. Her children die as fast as she can breed them and the elves' magic grows at the same pace as her rot.

Then one day she becomes aware of a presence in her section of the forest. It is a man. Young, weary, and vulnerable. She sends her children to surround him. One of her favorites, a member of her new breed goes with them. As she is about to command the man's destruction, she hears a voice at the back of her mind for the first time in two hundred years.

"*Do not kill him*," the dark voice says. "*He is important. He is worth a sacrifice*."

She obeys, taking her precious child and pushing all of its thoughts and abilities into its eyes. Its life is extinguished. When it falls from the trees and lands before the man, an eye pops free and rolls to his feet. The young man is startled, but bursts into laughter. She reaches through the eye, sending every amount of power she can at him.

Pick it up, she commands.

The man cocks his head, his eyes burning with curiosity. He slowly reaches towards the eye, fingers trembling softly. As he grasps the eye, she sends her thoughts through his, grasping his nature. She sees at once what the dark voice likes in this one.

He has a raw talent, though relatively untrained and he has noble blood, which gives him connections. Even better, his soul has already been twisted. He is fertile ground.

He nearly drops the eye when she speaks to him, putting all the sultry seduction she can manage into her words.

"Hello, Ewzad Vriil."

"I did it!" Jhonate opened her eyes in excitement, only to find a set of blue eyes glaring right back at her. "What do you want . . . Mage Vannya?"

"Sometimes I wonder about you," Vannya said.

Jhonate glanced around. She was still in Locksher's tent, but sunlight was streaming in from the tent flap. "How long have I been here?"

Vannya snorted. "I wondered where you had gone last night. This morning I woke and saw that you never came to bed. When I headed to the infirmary, I heard rumors of moans coming from Professor Locksher's tent."

"Moans?" Jhonate frowned and noticed that for some reason her face hurt. "Ridiculous, I never moan." Vannya's eyebrows rose and Jhonate added, "I came to Wizard Locksher for advice. . . who is this person spreading rumors?"

The mage shrugged. "Who can blame the women for talking? If I didn't know the professor better, I might have believed them myself. Some might think you were out to take all the good men."

Jhonate's frown turned to a glower. Why did her face hurt? She reached up to find her cheeks flushed and tender.

"At any rate, the professor found me and said that you were in a deep trance. He asked me to watch over you and make sure that you didn't get worse."

"Have you been slapping me?" Jhonate asked.

Vannya's face reddened, but she didn't shy away. "I tried many things to wake you, as is my duty as a healer."

But how could the mage's blows have hurt her unless . . . Jhonate looked down at her hand and gasped. "Where is my ring?"

"Oh," Vannya said. She reached into her pocket and held it out to her. "When my attempts to wake you failed, I removed it to see if that would help."

Jhonate calmly took the ring from the mage's dainty white hand. She suppressed a sigh as the ring nestled back in its rightful place on her index finger. Then her hand shot out and delivered an ear-ringing slap to the mage's face.

Vannya cried out in surprise and pain, her hand shooting to her face. "Why, how dare yo-!"

Jhonate's other hand whipped out, slapping the woman's other cheek so hard that it stung her palm. Her voice was deadly serious. "You had no right to remove that ring, Mage Vannya. If you handle my possessions again without my permission, your next punishment will be much worse!

"Now tell me, girl. Where are Locksher and Faldon the Fierce? I have urgent information to give them." She stood and winced as her legs cried out in protest, stiff from the way she had been sitting all night. They were also partially numb, which was why she didn't dive out of the way in time.

Vannya's air blast spell caught Jhonate square in the chest, hurling her out the open tent flap. She landed on her back in the wet leaves of the forest floor and tumbled a couple times, barely avoiding a tree trunk. She rolled to her feet and turned, her staff at the ready as the mage exited the tent after her.

Vannya's teeth were clenched in fury and two welts in the shape of hand prints stood out angrily on her fair face. Her robe flapped as wind gusted around her. Tiny arcs of electricity crackled around her fists.

Jhonate gathered every bit of information she had on how to battle a magic user. She spun her staff. This would have to be quick, before Vannya was able to summon a more powerful spell. She started towards the mage, trying to make sure a tree trunk was between them at all times. It would be difficult to knock the woman unconscious without doing permanent damage, but perhaps a disfiguring blow to the face would teach her some humility.

"Stop it, you two!" shouted Faldon the Fierce as he and Locksher ran towards them.

"She slapped me!" Vannya shouted indignantly.

"Sir!" Jhonate said, standing at attention. "She slapped me first."

"You let her slap you?" Faldon said in amusement.

"I was meditating at the time," she explained.

"She wouldn't wake up!" Vannya exclaimed.

"Enough, Mage Vannya," Locksher commanded, his face uncharacteristically stern. "Return to the infirmary. You and I will discuss this later."

Vannya glowered and stormed away. With a shake of his head, Locksher turned his gaze on Jhonate. "Since you have awoken, I assume you fixed your little problem?"

"Yes, sir," she said, regaining her composure. "I have retrieved vital information that was hidden to me before."

She related what she had learned from the witch's hidden memories.

"This is fascinating! But what is she? Who was she?" Locksher wondered. "Someone so powerful that they required a binding of that magnitude should be well known. Why haven't I heard of her before?"

"All I know is that she must be destroyed," Jhonate said.

"You are right. If it is possible it must be done," Faldon said thoughtfully.

"We should seek the advice of the High Council before attempting anything," Locksher said. "We need to find out more about her."

"One thing for sure," said Faldon the Fierce. "This information does no one any good if we continue to hide in the mountains. It is time we took a more direct approach."

Chapter Sixteen

"There are so many, Mistresss," Talon said. Her quarry had joined up with a large number of humans traveling along the riverbank.

"*How many?*" her mistress asked absently. The female's voice had seemed preoccupied lately, dealing with her army's problems. Talon didn't like being ignored, but she also didn't like being punished so she said nothing.

"It'ss . . ." She hissed in uncertainty. Numbers were hard for Talon to express. Ewwie had taught her how to speak and how to kill, but how to count had not been a priority for him. Instead, she sent the female a vague image of wagons and carts and horses and fire sites where the humans had stopped to cook. This seemed to get the female's attention.

"*How long ago were they here?*"

"A day or lesss," Talon hissed.

"*Find them.*"

Talon trotted along the tracks left by the humans, absorbing the smells and flavors of their passing. They were a diverse group, both old and young. They were so numerous that they overpowered the scent she found most interesting.

As she had followed the trail of the bandham killers, she had been surprised to discover Deathclaw's scent and tracks all around, mainly in the trees around their camping places. She wondered why he was watching them. What was it about these creatures he found so interesting?

"*Why do you move so slowly?*" the female said and the right half of Talon's face went numb. "*Faster. Now!*"

Talon ran. Her new mistress was far more cruel and randomly tempered than sweet Ewwie. The moonrat mother prodded Talon's every move, numbing portions of her body as punishments. Talon had learned to obey her without hesitation, her mind fueled by fear and hatred and yearning, hoping the moonrat mother would offer pain or pleasure as a reward.

She ran throughout the day and into the night and soon began to grow frustrated with the lack of food. The humans had been efficient in their advance, stripping the land of all edible game along the way, leaving behind only discarded bones and scraps of fur and skin. These did little to satiate her hunger and finally Talon was forced to stop and dig up the grave of one of the human elderly that had died on the way. It had taken Talon a while to develop a taste for the flesh of humans, but Ewwie had fed her on it enough that she had come to like it. Unfortunately this one was old and stringy.

Her feast ended when the moonrat mother noticed her lack of movement. Talon ran forward again, this time with a numbed tail. It was a greatly disturbing sensation and Talon would have cried if she had the capability.

She caught up with the tail end of the human group before morning. There, bedrolls tightly grouped with the river at their backs, were human men huddled around a central fire. Two more stood watch, pacing the edges of the camp with wary eyes.

"I have found them, Mistress," she said quietly.

"*Good girl*," the female said and Talon was rewarded by a return of sensation to her tail and face along with a pleasant tingling sensation that ran up her back and along her scalp.

"Sshall I killss them?" she asked, suppressing a gurgle of pleasure. She could take the watchful ones and half the sleepers before any of them noticed.

"*They are nothing*," the female said. "*Just hurry and find those that killed Ewzad's bandham so that I can stop wasting my attention with you.*"

"Yess, Mistress," Talon replied in disappointment. She had not been allowed to kill in such a long time.

She traveled down the length of the human encampment.

These were not just soldiers. There were women and children as well. Their numbers were too many for her mind to process, but she did realize something important. The humans were all armed. Even the children had weapons at their side. Talon smiled. She liked it when her prey fought back.

The sky had started to lighten when she heard the chase. By the sounds, there were two runners breathing heavily. The moonrat mother was not watching, so Talon let her curiosity guide her. She followed.

The two scents caused her heart to race. One of them was her Deathclaw and the other one smelled of the magic that destroyed Ewwie's Kenn. They ran so fast that she could not tell who was chasing whom. Perhaps her Deathclaw was chasing the man. What if she could arrive and help him kill it and then they could kill the rest together? Ewwie would be so happy.

She followed behind them for over a mile before they stopped near a small stand of trees. She hid behind a large rock and peered around the edge, watching them. The human laid on the ground laughing while Deathclaw stood over him. She waited for her brother to attack, but he didn't. He and the human just looked at each other as if carrying on a conversation in silence.

Finally the man stood and drew two strange weapons from sheaths on his back. Deathclaw nodded and pulled his own sword. Talon hissed. It was the sword that had burned her the night Kenn took her away. The wounds that sword made had not healed on their own. Only Ewwie had made her whole again.

She smiled when they finally attacked each other. Both struck out with swords dancing, clanging out with the sharp ring of metal when they met. Deathclaw's movements were fluid and graceful, but his swordwork was clumsy. The human disarmed him quickly and laid the tip of one sword at Deathclaw's throat.

Talon snuck out from behind her rock and slid towards them, readying herself to strike the man. But the man simply smiled and stepped away, allowing Deathclaw to retrieve his weapon.

She flattened herself to the ground and watched as they circled each other again. Why was Deathclaw allowing the man to toy with him so?

"*What are you doing?*" the female demanded.

I have found Deathclaw and the one who killed Ewwie'ss Kenn. They fightss. This perked the female's interest and Talon felt her presence watching the scene through her eyes.

The moonrat mother gasped. "*I know this man! He is older now, larger, but it is him nonetheless. He slaughtered my children in the forest. He destroyed my golem in the Mage School. Arcon calls him Justan, son of Faldon the Fierce. He is marked for death!*"

Deathclaw struck out in earnest this time, determined to strike a blow, but the human's swordplay was pure and refined. He deflected Deathclaw's attacks with ease before disarming him again. This time he didn't even bother to place the blade at Deathclaw's throat, he just stood and laughed.

"See, Deathclaw, you may be faster than me but you aren't better in everything," the man said. Deathclaw cocked his head in response and the man replied. "As I said before, we all have our strengths. You are getting better. Come again."

As Deathclaw picked up his sword, the female gasped again. "*No, it can't be!*" Talon felt the female messing around inside her head and she felt a definite pressure just between her eyes. Her vision shifted.

"*It is! That man is a bonding wizard!*" Talon saw tentacles of white cloud sprouting from the man's body. They danced around him, two of the lines attached to his swords. "*And he is a powerful one.*"

What is thiss? Talon asked, eyeing one thick cord that connected the man's chest with Deathclaw's.

"*He is bonded to your brother,*" the female growled. When Talon didn't understand, she added, "*Deathclaw has joined this man.*"

Joined? she asked, the concept unfamiliar to her.

"*They are linked together, much like you and I.*"

Talon hissed inwardly. So that was it. Deathclaw was doing the man's bidding now.

I sshall kills him, Talon said, eyeing Deathclaw's captor with hatred.

"*Yes you shall, but not yet,*" the female said. "*Follow them. I wish to see the rest of their group.*"

She stayed low in the grass and observed as they fought several more times, each bout resulting in Deathclaw being disarmed. She watched her brother intently, looking for signs of distress. Oddly, she saw no anger towards the human, just frustration. Then they headed back the way they came.

He will ssmells me, she thought as she followed. She had not bothered to hide her tracks or scent during the chase. But Deathclaw ran alongside the human without a sign that he had noticed her. Perhaps he was distracted or perhaps he was no longer as good as she remembered.

"*Or perhaps his bonding wizard has a tight leash on him and he cannot give away that he knows you are here,*" The moonrat mother intoned.

Yes that was it. Deathclaw was waiting. Waiting for her to make a move. Waiting for her to free him. Then she could bring him to Ewwie and they would be a pack again.

Still, just in case, she activated her musk glands, surrounding herself in a pheromone cloud. This was Ewwie's newest gift. Perhaps of all the changes he had made for her, this one was the most useful. This was the one that Ewwie said proved his faith in her loyalty.

Talon had seen Ewwie cut the glands from a rare python before inserting them at the base of her tail. He told her that they helped that python find mates, but they also confused the senses of other predators, letting it hang in the trees unnoticed by the sensitive noses of the jungle beasts. Now they would hide her scent from pursuers or prey.

She had made a wise choice for soon after dispersing the cloud, she saw a large creature bound into view. It darted from the trees and bowled Deathclaw over, planting him on his back. Talon recognized the beast. It had tracked her around the farmland quite effectively. The moonrat mother gasped again.

"*The rogue horse that hounded my children! I wondered where it had gone.*"

Another thick white cord connected the human to this

beast. As it moved off of Deathclaw with a chuckling snort, she saw that a thin wispy line connected her brother to it as well.

Her brother stood and gave the beast an irritated hiss. The human chastised the beast for its unprovoked attack and they moved on. Talon shadowed them to the front of the human line. There they joined up with an ogre carrying a large shield and spiked mace. He was linked to them as well.

"*That Justan has a powerful group of bonded,*" the female said with concern.

The four of them stood, looking at each other, nodding silently, and Talon realized that they were communicating with their minds. Something else bothered her. The human was not raging at them or punishing them. Then Deathclaw let out a chirp of acquiescence and she understood. Her brother had found a new pack.

She let out a low growling hiss. The rogue horse perked up her ears and Talon had to force herself to stop. The human led them to a campsite that was being dismantled for travel. They stopped to talk to an older human male and to Talon's surprise, they were joined by an enormous man with the lower body of a horse.

"*Two bonding wizards! Two rogue horses!*" the female spat. "*Where are they headed?*"

I will kills them now? Talon asked.

"*No, you fool! Not yet. We find out who they are and where they are headed. Follow them. Show me every detail!*"

*   *   *

Ewzad Vriil peered down his nose at the dwarf. "And what of my special request? Hmm?"

The dwarf scowled right back at him, his handlebar mustache curling up so high it nearly touched the edges of his bushy eyebrows. "That'll take a while, dag-gum it. We done sent a whole posse, but that's a long friggin' trip."

"My-my." Ewzad's lip curled. "I paid you for quickness. Didn't I? Yes-yes I did."

The dwarf shrugged. "We're cuttin' the dag-burned time in half. That's what you done paid extry fer."

The vein in Ewzad's forehead throbbed. His fingers writhed and he nearly lost control of his arm. These dwarves didn't fear him. They specialized in retrieval of rare animals and had centuries of experience dealing with dark wizards. The dwarves all had protective trinkets stashed all over their bodies. That, along with their innate resistance to magic made intimidating them problematic. Money was the only thing that motivated them; money and assets they could turn into profits.

"If you don't have what I asked you for, what do you have for me, smuggler?" he asked, his jaw clenched.

"It's ringmaster, dag-blast it!" the dwarf said. "C'mon and I'll show you."

The dwarf led Ewzad towards the back of the menagerie. The place was crawling with dwarves. Performers practiced their acts while others lugged things about or prodded animals in their cages. Hamford and Arcon followed behind Ewzad obediently, keeping an eye out for treachery. These dwarves had dealt with other bearers of the Rings of Stardeon in the past. No doubt they had considered the price they could get for the artifact if Ewzad were dead.

The dwarf stopped before a series of cages covered with silk tarps. He put two fingers in his mouth and let out a piercing whistle. Dwarves standing by the cages whipped off the tarps, revealing their catch. The night air was filled with growls and hisses.

"We done brought you four giant red spiders. Three dag-gum snake runners, and four bog tortoises. Blasted things're heavy. That'll cost you extry."

Perfect! Ewzad forced away a giggle, putting a frown on his face. "Oh my, is this all? That won't do, will it? No-no it won't!"

The dwarf rolled his eyes. "Dag-nab it, it ain't worth hagglin' over. Just pay up, yer lordship so's we'cn take the durn beasts down to yer dungeons. We'll bring more next week."

"*Ewzad*," said Mellinda.

Ewzad considered turning his magic on the dwarf. Just what could he do with one? Would the rings be powerful enough to burn through their blood magic? He itched to try it.

"*Master, I have news.*"

"Silence, you terrible hag!" he spat.

"What'd you say?" The burly dwarf turned a glower Ewzad's way, murder in his eyes.

Ewzad wondered how large he could make the dwarf's head swell before bursting.

"We apologize. He wasn't talking to you, Ringmaster." Arcon said, bowing deferentially. "He was talking to the demon in his head."

"You yankin' my leg?" said the dwarf with suspicion.

"*Talon found the men that killed your bandham,*" Mellinda purred.

"Oh really?" Ewzad said with a smile. "This is excellent, yes?"

"As you can see, our master is busy." Arcon said. "Hamford, would you pay the good dwarf?" The large guard didn't like the scrawny mage ordering him around, but he tossed the Ringmaster a sack of gold.

"Oh," said the dwarf, weighing the sack in one hand as he watched Ewzad speaking to himself. Obviously he had seen stranger things because he shrugged and started directing his men to move the cages.

Ewzad ignored them. "Has my sweet Talon killed them yet?"

"*There are . . . complications.*"

"Well? Come-come. Tell me quickly!" Mellinda filled him in on the details. He was aware of bonding wizards. The dark bowl had forced that information into his mind. "Ah, powerful foes, yes? But two? Insignificant against our numbers, don't you think?"

"*But they do have that army with them.*"

"What? Two thousand armed women and children? Those are merely the missing people of Sampo. Yes-yes. Rabble with cheap weapons." Ewzad laughed.

"*But-!*"

"Where are they headed, you wretched thing? Hmm?" he asked.

"*Today they left the banks of the Fandine River and traveled along the foothills of the mountains heading west.*"

"Oh my! Towards Dremald? And me with the might of the Dremaldrian garrison to protect me? Oh dear, I should be so frightened."

"*I doubt they intend to attack directly,*" she said in irritation.

He waved a hand. "Yes-yes, have sweet Talon kill the wizards, hmm? We'll see what those weaklings do then."

"*And if they join up with your deserters?*"

Ewzad frowned momentarily. There were a few thousand missing soldiers on the move. So far they had evaded him, but . . . He smiled again. "No, that would be a shame, yes? Captain Demetrius slowed down by two thousand on foot? Oh my, that would be horrible indeed. I can only hope that happens."

"*I see,*" she said.

"Now leave me, witch. Yes, I have work to do." He pushed her presence from his mind and walked towards the dwarf ringmaster, wondering if he could convince him to leave one of his fellow dwarves behind for experimentation.

*   *   *

Talon sat in the tree watching as the humans set up their camp at the mountain's edge. It amused her that her brother sat in a tree not far away watching them too, her pheromone cloud keeping him completely unaware of her presence.

"*Your master agrees. They must be killed,*" the female said, her attention finally returning.

"Yess!" Talon whispered. She wanted to kill the beast that had pounced on Deathclaw first. Its tracking skills would make it a nuisance otherwise.

"*No*," the female said. "*When fighting a bonding wizard, never kill one of the bonded first. It just enrages the others and makes them focus on killing you. Kill the wizard. If he is dead, the others will fall helpless to the ground and you can kill them at your leisure.*"

Talon liked the other way better. To fight the human and ogre while they wept for their lost creature would be very interesting.

"*Nevertheless, you will obey*," the moonrat mother reminded.

Yess, Mistresss, she thought. *But what of Deathclaw?*

"*He will fall too when the wizard dies, but worry not. I have ways to revive him.*"

The female sent a vision to Talon's mind. A moonrat with orange eyes dropped dead at her feet. She took its eye to an unconscious Deathclaw, then cut open his chest and placed it inside and then . . .

He will be partss of my pack again, she thought with a smile.

"*Yes*," agreed the mother of the moonrat. "*First we must find a way to separate the wizard from his bonded and then-.*" the voice paused. "*What's that? Something feels . . .*"

The wizard Justan was untying a bulging pack from the saddle of the rogue horse. He placed the pack on the ground and the moonrat mother twisted something behind Talon's eyes. She again saw the white ropes of the wizard's magic but there was something else. Something deep within that pack radiated a burning darkness.

The moonrat mother screeched. "*How did he get that?*"

What iss it, Mistresss?

"*Only one of the Dark Prophet's great talismans would glow like that!*" she spat, enraged. "*You must retrieve it! Retrieve the talisman, then kill the wizard!*"

Talon watched the wizard named Justan and smiled, anticipating how good it would feel to kill him. She would first disable his arms, then play with him a little before removing his head. When the other humans reached the scene, his head would greet them with a smile, impaled on the tips of his two strange swords.

Chapter Seventeen

What's the matter, Deathclaw? Justan asked. He could feel the raptoid's agitation through the bond.

I smell something, Deathclaw replied. *Something on the wind . . . it's her!*

Gwyrtha, who had been laying on her side, sat up suddenly and sniffed the air. She growled and jumped to her feet, her hackles raised. *I smell it too!*

She lives. Talon is here! Deathclaw leapt down from the tree.

"Squirrel smells it!" Fist said. Squirrel stood atop the ogre's head, sniffing the air.

Justan stood and drew his swords, feeling the calmness and eagerness of both simultaneously. They had wondered about Deathclaw's sister. She had been gravely wounded when Kenn had taken her away and Deathclaw had assumed her dead. But after their fight with Kenn, Justan had thought it unlikely that Ewzad Vriil would kill his prized possession. "Nearby?"

Deathclaw rushed across the camp and scrambled up another tree. *She was here! Not long ago. I must track her down.*

"No! This could be a trap. If Talon is here, Ewzad Vriil may have sent others. Take Gwyrtha with you."

I would do this alone, Deathclaw said. Despite the respect the raptoid had gained for the rogue horse over the last week, there was still something about her that bothered him.

You will take her, Justan said, his tone firm. It was the most direct order he had ever given Deathclaw and Justan could tell that it chafed the raptoid. He opened up the link between the two bonded as wide as he could. *She is the only one better at tracking than you. If you work together, Talon will not be able to evade you.*

Gwyrtha ran and skidded to a stop at Deathclaw's side. She nudged him. *Ride.*

To Justan's surprise, Deathclaw gave a stiff nod and leapt on her back. His clawed feet gripped her saddle and he crouched, grabbing two fistfuls of her mane. With complete focus they melted into the night.

"Deathclaw riding Gwyrtha," Fist said. "Is scary."

Master Coal ran over, Samson at his side. "What is it, Edge?"

"Deathclaw's sister is somewhere nearby. I just sent him and Gwyrtha to find her," Justan said.

"I feared this might happen eventually," Coal said. "If Ewzad Vriil has sent her after us, she could be accompanied by a much larger force."

"That's what I'm afraid of," Justan said. In truth, Talon alone was scary enough. If she was able to evade them, she could terrorize their whole party, killing off individuals one by one.

"She will attack the women and childrens!" Fist said in sudden realization and Justan swore. He was right. That's exactly what she would do.

"Fist, head down and watch over them. Let me know the minute you or Squirrel sense anything!" Fist nodded and ran towards the center of the encampment where most of the women and children slept.

"Bettie is headed there as well," Coal said. "She's dragging Lenny and his dwarf friends with her."

Shouts rang out somewhere in the distance.

"Are we under attack?" Coal wondered.

"I don't think so. Deathclaw and Gwyrtha are out tracking Talon's scent and they didn't sense any other threats nearby." Talon's trail had meandered about. They were currently somewhere just east of the camp in the foothills.

"I don't smell anything either," Samson said.

"We should tell Sir Lance what's going on," Justan said. He didn't relish the thought. Sir Lance was difficult to deal with. Any issue that came up, be it their speed of pace or their food reserves or whatever else, the old warrior seemed to place the blame on the shoulders of Justan and Coal. This particular problem actually was something they had brought with them which would make it worse.

They headed towards Lance's tent at the center of the refugee encampment, but before they reached it Aldie intercepted them. The man was pale and sweating, but his eyes and voice were firm as he spoke.

"We are under attack! At the rear there are reports of packhorses with their bellies torn open. Several men on watch are injured. One of them had half his face ripped off! He says it was some kind of snake woman. As I ran up here there was more yelling coming from the west side of the camp!"

Coal jumped up on Samson's back. "I'll go see if I can treat any wounded. Edge, coordinate our defenses with Lance."

Justan nodded and the wizard galloped off. It was so strange. How could Talon pull off so many attacks so quickly? And all over the camp? It spoke of multiple attackers, but his bonded had only sensed her.

"Tell me again, Aldie, where did these things happen and in what order?" Justan asked.

"Uh . . . first there were the watchmen, I guess," Aldie said.

"Where were they?"

"On the east side, watching the foothills."

Justan nodded. "Alright, and then the packhorses at the south end, right? Then you just heard commotion to the west so . . . she's running. Making a loop around the perimeter of the camp. Attacking as quickly as she can and moving on."

Deathclaw, how old is that trail? Justan asked

Fresh! No more than fifteen minutes.

Get back here. That trail's too old! She's here attacking right now and she's headed . . . back towards our camp!

Justan ran back the way he had come, Aldie running at

his heels. What was Talon doing? She must have first set off into the foothills to give Deathclaw and Gwyrtha something to chase, then returned back to reveal her scent to the camp. Then as soon as Deathclaw left, she ran around the encampment, causing commotions all for what? Just to draw them away from their camp? But what was she going to do there?

He thought of Alfred and Stanza left alone by the tents, but would she go through all that trouble just to kill their horses? What else was there she could possibly want? Then it came to him. Qyxal's body. They had left a preserved elven corpse sitting there with the rest of the saddlebags. How could he have been so stupid? A few elven herbs had helped power the golem. What could Ewzad Vriil do with an entire elf body?

The startled whinny of the warhorses told him he had been right. He ran into their campsite and there she was. Talon heard his footsteps and froze, hunched over his pack. She had torn it open and half its contents were scattered in the dirt.

She's here! Justan sent. He pulled his swords and heard Aldie gasp as he saw her. "Aldie, get out of here."

"But I can help. I-."

Talon looked over her shoulder at them and Justan could tell that Ewzad had made some changes. Her eyes were different, more cat-like and her mouth . . . Her lips pulled back in a smile, revealing a mouth full of curved teeth.

"No. Sstay, human," she said, her voice a throaty hiss. Justan was glad his swords absorbed his fear. He hadn't expected her to speak. She stood and turned to face them and Justan saw that even more changes had been made. Why had Ewzad done that? Why had he made her look even more womanlike? She stepped towards them, clicking her long claws together and giving her hips a sultry sway. "I can eatss both of you."

"Run, Aldie," Justan said, stepping towards her, his swords at the ready.

If his sword had not been siphoning his emotions away, he would have been terrified. Instead he was able to carefully analyze her movements. He noticed that she carefully kept her tail out of his line of sight and how she walked slowly so that his guard would be down when she struck.

"Why are you here, Talon?"

Her eyes grew wide, her voice high pitched. "To killss you, Jusstan, sson of Faldon the Fierce. You have been marked for death!"

It was as if time slowed down for him. He saw her begin to roll forward, launching her tail barb towards his throat. He dodged right, sending his left sword in a sweeping slice. The razor edge caught her tail just below the barb and sheared through.

In the precise moment his sword touched her, time stood still for both of them. Talon felt all her excitement, anticipation, and fear vanish. The slice of the sword caused no pain, yet she felt it split her flesh. The lack of emotion sent a numb shock through her brain.

Justan felt Talon's emotions sucked away by his left sword and in that brief instant he understood something about her. Something important. Then the sword cleared her flesh, sending the barb spinning off into the dirt.

All of the emotion and shock rushed back in for Talon. She completed her forward roll and sprang to her feet, letting out a bloodcurdling screech.

Justan stepped back and moved his swords into defensive position. His blow had struck fear into her. He had stolen her emotions away for only an instant, but for a creature like Talon, that was a grievous wound.

"No, Misstress. No! He takess!" She backed away from him, hands out, pleading and for the first time Justan noticed the shriveled sphere embedded in her arm. There was something strange about it. Something . . . He switched to mage sight, then spirit sight.

Talon paused, her head cocked, pure agony twisting her nightmarish features. Then she crouched down to gather her strength and launched her body towards him, her claws swiping.

Justan dodged to the side, having anticipated her attack, but she was too fast. Her claws tore through his jacket and sliced into his skin, leaving three furrows along his chest just under the frost rune. Justan felt the damage, but his sword drained the pain and he had the clarity of mind to swing his right sword in a downward slash. The blade struck her forearm right above the embedded sphere.

In that moment, he released all the energy pent up in his sword in a concussive blast. Talon's arm blew apart and the force of the blast sent her sprawling into the fire.

Burning tinder scattered. She arched her back in the coals, squirming, then rolled to her feet. She screeched and ran into the trees, her scales smoking, blood spurting from the shreds of flesh that hung ragged where her elbow should have been.

Justan watched her disappear into the darkness and sheathed his swords. Immediately he felt the burning pain of the deep scratches on his chest. He turned and looked behind him to see Aldie standing there, jaw dropped in wonder.

"Go. Tell everyone that the beast will not bother them again tonight," he said. Aldie nodded and ran towards his father's tent.

Deathclaw and Gwyrtha appeared a moment later and Justan pointed in the direction Talon had gone. Gwyrtha stopped briefly to give him an apologetic look and then took off, Deathclaw still clinging to her back.

It's okay, Gwyrtha. Just track her down.

What happened? Deathclaw asked, and Justan sent a compressed version of his memory to all three of them. He sent it a bit too fast and Gwyrtha stumbled. Fist almost fell. Then, for the first time, Deathclaw sent Justan something that felt like approval through the bond. *You did well.*

Justan searched around with his spirit sight until he saw a faint glow at the base of one of the trees. There lay the end of Talon's arm, a thin white nimbus surrounding the shriveled orb that still clung to the shreds of muscle at the edge of the stump.

He picked it up by the wrist and stared at the orb. Somehow, Talon's master must have been speaking to her through it. But why did it look familiar to him? It didn't matter. He had a message to deliver. "We are coming for you, Ewzad Vriil," he said and tossed it into the remnants of the fire.

Justan walked around the fire, kicking back in the live coals that Talon had scattered and tossing some fresh wood on the top. Let the wizard think on that for a while. Meanwhile, they would get the Sampo refugees safely to the caverns behind Wobble and start waging war on his siege.

The flesh of Talon's arm smoked and blackened. The orb swelled a bit, then burst open with a sound that sounded eerily like the cry of an infant. Justan shivered and resisted the urge to grasp the handle of his sword.

He felt Fist walking up behind him before the ogre laid his hand on his shoulder. Justan didn't, however, expect Fist to spin him around and lift him in a huge hug. Justan grunted and patted him awkwardly on the back.

The ogre placed him back on the ground. "When I knew you were fighting her I was scared."

Justan smiled. "I was the one scared. If not for my swords, she would have killed me."

"Why was she here?" Fist asked.

"I don't know." He walked over to the saddlebags and crouched by his torn and scattered pack. "I thought she came for Qyxal's body, but she didn't even touch him. She went for this."

He picked up the few shirts and pairs of pants that Talon had thrown out. What was she looking for? He started pulling things out and setting them aside until his fingers brushed something cold. He jerked his arm out, feeling ill. "What was that?"

"What is it, Justan?" Fist asked, peering over his shoulder.

Justan moved a few things away carefully until a cloth wrapped bundle was all that remained. He reached for it, but just before his hand touched the metal, he remembered. "The dagger. How did I forget the dagger?"

Coal stared at the dark dagger over steepled fingers. No one had wanted to touch the thing until finally Lenny had retrieved it and unwrapped it with a pair of tongs. Now it lay in the dirt a few feet from the fire, the rubies in its hilt gleaming in the firelight. Its blade was stained brown, caked with dried blood.

"This is it. It's the one. The proof we need," Coal said.

"How can you be sure?" Justan asked. He ran his fingers through the tears in his ruined shirt and ran them over his skin where Talon had cut him. Coal had healed the wounds but his skin tingled as if they were still there.

"The Dark Prophet had just six of these daggers made; one for each of his high priests. Each one was set with different gems. This ruby dagger was the one Dann Doudy presented to the king and court as evidence that Willum's parents sacrificed his grandfather to the Dark Prophet."

"But what're we provin'?" asked Lenny. "So Vriil had the dagger that killed his daddy. That don't prove he was usin' it."

"Ah, but this dagger was supposed to be taken away and destroyed. The king ordered Dann Doudy to take care of it personally." Coal said. "At the very least, rescuing such an evil thing from destruction is a crime vile enough to have Doudy stripped of rank and title. As for Ewzad? We have two highly accountable men in our own party that saw the dagger used in Ewzad's throneroom. Not to mention any others that survived the ordeal. Elise herself said that she found it in Ewzad's study."

"Well, Queen Elise isn't likely to remember it that way anymore," Justan said. "By all reports, she is with him now. All she would have to do is say it didn't happen. The nobles wouldn't take our word over hers."

"You're right," Coal said. "Unless we had the academy and Mage School councils at our side. Then the nobles would hand him over without a fight."

"So," Justan said. "What we need to do is break the siege, convince the academy that Ewzad was behind it, then fight our way to the Mage School and convince them as well."

They all stared blankly into the fire for a few moments.

"It is a difficult challenge," Coal said finally. "But we have the evidence we need and that's a start."

"So what do we do with that thing in the meantime?"

Bettie asked, nodding towards the dagger.

"I don't like being around it," Justan said. "I still have no idea why I kept forgetting I had the thing. There must have been half a dozen times since taking it from Ewzad's castle that I meant to tell you about it."

"The dagger is directly linked to the Dark Prophet," Coal said. "Look at it with your spirit sight and you will see. It actively uses spirit magic to influence those around it. I wouldn't be surprised if your foul moods were partially the fault of sitting near that dagger all day."

Justan saw a smoky cloud-like haze around the dagger, but where other spirit magic was white, this was black as soot.

"But what if we just all forget it is there?" Fist asked.

"I don't think that's possible," Master Coal said. "It has too great an importance to our mission now. Most likely Edge would not have forgotten it if he had known. It's a lot easier to influence someone when they are unaware."

"Have Lenui carry it," Bettie decided.

"What the? I don't want the dag-blasted thing!" Lenny protested.

"Dwarfs are resistant to magic, right?" she said. "Just wrap it in leather and put it in your pack. You'll be fine."

"She's right," Coal said. "I should have thought of that."

"You shoud've?" Lenny grumped, eyeing the dagger with disgust. "Confound it all, don't I get a say in this?"

"No you don't!" Bettie said.

"Lenny, if you don't want to carry it, we won't make you," Justan said. "I carried it this far, I can carry it again. Just . . . keep reminding me that I have it this time."

"Alright, you squirmy manipulatin' son of a weasel! I'll carry the stupid dagger!" Lenny snapped. He walked over and picked it up with his tongs, then stormed over to his pack.

"What about Talon?" Samson asked. "Have they found her yet?"

Justan sighed. "Deathclaw and Gwyrtha are still searching. They followed her blood trail for a while but each time they were sure they had caught up to her, she somehow evaded them. Then she stopped bleeding and now the only evidence they can find is the odd track. Deathclaw thinks that she has somehow found a way to turn her scent on and off when she wants to."

Me too!

"Gwyrtha agrees," he added.

"That is bad," Fist said. "She could come back."

"We will have to be prepared," Coal said. "There are simple wards that I could place that would warn us if she came near the camp. If I make them powerful enough, they might even injure her. You would have to show Deathclaw where they were, though. And we'd have to warn everyone else in the camp."

"Definitely," Samson said, "We don't want any women running to Sir Lance because her baby walked into one."

"And what if Talon returns to Ewzad and he sends an army after us?" Bettie asked.

"Wouldn't worry yer head 'bout that," Lenny said. He had pulled a mirror out of his pack and was examining the length of his still-growing mustache. "In just a couple day's ride, we're gonna disappear."

"You keep saying that," Justan said. "But I really don't see how we're going to take two thousand people into that crevasse without leaving any evidence of where we went."

"Dwarf ingenuity!" Bettie said. "That's what he'll say. And I don't believe it either."

"Gall-durn it, woman, I done told you already! Trust me!"

"Trust your loud mouth?" Bette yelled.

Coal shook his head and looked at Justan. "Well, its time I spoke with Willum. When Tad the Cunning hears about the dagger, he'll have just what he needs to take Dann Doudy down."

Chapter Eighteen

Willum hid in the darkened alcove, his back pressed against the stone wall as the guard walked past. He caught a quick glimpse of the guard's face and winced. Willum knew him from archery class his first year and felt stupid hiding from a fellow student. He wasn't doing anything wrong after all.

He peeked out of the alcove and waited until the guard turned the corner, then walked down the corridor as quietly as he could, remembering everything he could about his stealth training. It hadn't been his best subject.

He stopped in front of the door and looked down the corridor again before giving a quiet knock. The seconds ticked by and Willum began to worry that another guard would come. He knocked again, a little harder this time.

He heard a latch being moved and the door opened inward. Tad the Cunning stood there blinking at the torchlight streaming in from the corridor, hair mussed, one arm behind his back scratching. He wore a chainmail shirt over a cloth tunic, but no pants.

When Tad saw who it was, he frowned and yanked Willum into the room, then closed the door and latched it behind him. Willum stood in the dark and waited while Tad tapped something against the wall. Light burned to life from within a glowing orb that Tad placed in a sconce on the wall. He moved his other hand out from behind his back and Willum saw that he hadn't been scratching after all, but holding his wicked axe.

"What are you doing here, Willum?" Tad asked. "Didn't I say to be careful?"

"I was as stealthy as possible. No one saw me," he said.

Tad gave him a dull look.

Willum sighed. The academy was so crowded it was impossible to truly go unseen anymore. "At least no one saw me after I went behind the council building."

"Well then what was so important that you broke protocol?" Tad asked.

"It's about Representative Doudy, sir. My father has uncovered evidence that proves he and Ewzad Vriil are involved in dark magic."

"Hmm, have a seat." Tad yawned and gestured to a chair beside a small table in the corner of the room. He grabbed a pitcher from a small desk near the door and sat it on the table, then walked over to a cabinet to get some goblets.

Willum sat and took a look around. He had been in Tad's quarters before, but he was still shocked by how sparsely furnished the place was. There was just the bed and desk, a small table, a cabinet, and a few wardrobes. And it was quite tidy. If not for the pants and boots strewn on the floor by the bed, he would have thought the quarters unoccupied.

"Do you always answer the door like that, sir?" Willum asked.

"I've got my smallclothes on." Tad said lifting his shirt. Willum pointed at his other hand which still held his axe. "Oh, that." He laid it gingerly on the bed and picked his pants up off the floor. Tad yawned again. "Bad dreams lately, Willum. Strange dreams."

"It hardly seems like I dream anymore," Willum said, stifling a yawn of his own. "I am up late talking to father every night and then I am off at whatever hour to meet with you. I think I'm too tired to dream."

Tad belted his pants on and plopped down in the chair across from Willum. He started tugging on his boots. "Not me. It seems the more I think and the more I worry, the more convoluted my dreams get."

"What do you dream about?

"Oh, death, destruction, the kinds of things you shouldn't tell your students you dream about," Tad chuckled. "But that's what you get for barging in my room at unholy hours when I'm not on my guard."

"Is it because of the siege?" Willum asked. "Your dreams I mean."

Tad's eyes moved to the bed where the runes on his axe gleamed a dull red in the light of the orb. "No, it's that axe of mine. It's a mischievous, mean thing and I have played with it far too little lately."

"What does it do?" Willum said. He had been wondering about it ever since he saw Tad use the axe for the first time.

Tad took his eyes off the axe and sighed, shaking his head. He lifted the pitcher and poured water into the two goblets, then slid one over to Willum. "Let's talk about why you're here, Willum. Tell me about this evidence your father found."

"Actually, it was Sir Edge that found it." Willum told Tad everything his father had told him regarding the dagger. Tad listened intently, rubbing his jaw, and Willum could almost see the plan forming in his mind. When he finished, Tad stood.

"This is definitely helpful," he said with a pleased grin.

"So what is your plan then? What are you thinking?" Willum asked.

"Well, the dagger isn't definitive proof against your uncle. The same men who saw it at his castle are the same men claiming to be witness to his atrocities and the queen is not likely to back them up. We need more." He raised a finger. "But what this dagger does give us is significant leverage against our dear friend Representative Doudy. If he is in this as deep as we think, I may be able to convince him to deliver us the evidence we need to overthrow our Lord Protector."

Willum smiled, "You mean like proof that Ewzad Vriil framed my parents for my grandfather's murder?"

"That is the kind of proof we're looking for," Tad agreed.

"So what do we do?" Willum asked.

"Oh, there are so many factors to consider. So many ways this could go." He paused and rubbed his chin some more. "First of all, you are going back to your bunk and get some sleep. You have watch in the morning, don't you?"

"Yes, sir." Willum frowned.

"Well I have some preparations to make and then I shall go have a chat with Dann Doudy." Tad said. He walked to his bed and strapped his axe sheathe to his hip, then slipped the waraxe away. "While he is trapped here with us in the academy, there is no where for him to run. I rather think I can get him talking soon enough."

Tad walked to the small desk and pulled out some sheets of parchment. He grabbed a quill and started writing furiously.

"Are you sure there is nothing I can do to help?" Willum asked hesitantly. When Tad didn't immediately respond, he shook his head and grit his teeth in determination. "Sir, I . . . I spent my childhood dreaming of ways to clear my parents' name. I want to be a part of this."

Tad paused his writing and looked at him for a moment. "Of course you do." He took another piece of parchment and wrote a detailed note. He slid it into an envelope. Then he dropped something small and metallic inside with it, sealed it with wax and handed it to Willum. "I am reassigning you. Take this letter to your new commander in the morning."

Willum's heart sank. "But sir, I like my assignment."

"You just said you wanted to be part of this, didn't you?" Tad said. "This will take you off the wall for awhile, but believe me, you won't miss any action."

Willum took the envelope. It was just addressed with the letter 'D'. "So who is my new commanding officer?"

Tad smiled. "Only the fiercest commander here."

Willum frowned. "But-."

"Just report to the assignment desk in the morning. I'll have it all set up in the meantime."

"Okay, sir," he said and reached for the door.

"And Willum?"

"Yes, sir?"

"Please try to be as stealthy on the way out as you were on the way in. If all goes to plan, we won't have to keep our meetings secret any longer, but if Representative Doudy proves difficult to break . . ."

"Yes, sir."

Willum snuck down the corridors and out of the rear door of the Council Hall without incident, both excited and nervous about Tad's plans. As the door shut behind him, the dull roar of the enemy camp jolted him back to reality. Here he was worried about intrigues while thirty thousand enemies surrounded them all.

"Willum!"

A large rough hand shook him by the shoulder and Willum turned in his bunk to see Swen's stony face staring back at him. He blinked the sleep from his eyes. The morning sun had risen outside. He hoped he wasn't going to be late reporting to his new assignment. "What time is it, Swen?"

"Get up," Swen said and his eyes looked genuinely disturbed.

"What's wrong?" he asked.

"It's . . . bad."

That woke him up. Willum jumped down and saw that he had been the only one in the room asleep. All the other bunks were empty, which was rare since some of them had night shift on the wall. A chill went up his back. "Has it started? Are they attacking?"

Swen gave a slight shake to his head, but that somehow didn't make Willum feel any better. The large man's eyes welled up. "It's . . . Tad the Cunning is dead."

Willum stared back at him in shock. A wave of numbness crawled up his body. If it had been anyone but Swen talking, he would have thought it a cruel joke. "How . . ?"

"I don't know. It was in the council building in one of the back meeting rooms. They found Tad the Cunning and Demon Jenn, both of them dead."

Willum sat on the lower bunk and ran his hand through his hair. Even his scalp felt numb. Surely it wasn't true. "But I-I just saw him last night."

"He asked me to make him some arrows," Swen said, looking down. "Long ones. I didn't have the chance to give them to him."

"No-no," Willum said. He stood and started throwing on his clothes. "I spoke to him last night. Just a few hours ago." He buckled on his scythes and dagger, then pulled on his boots. "He had a plan, Swen. Somehow . . .."

Swen looked puzzled as Willum backed away then ran out of the door. He left the dorms and headed into the crowded walkways. All the noise roared in his ears, but he caught snatches of conversation, ". . . All that blood . . . infiltrated, I tell ya . . . some kind of monster . . . this is it, the attack is coming, you watch!"

He closed his ears to the talk. No, Tad had a plan. This was a feint, a dodge. Tad was famous for them. So something must have gone wrong when he confronted Doudy and he had been forced to fake his death or something. Tad had helped certain nobles fake their deaths before. He had said so in class. The academy could be asked to perform any number of favors for a client, he had said.

But why hadn't Tad told him of the possibility? Willum realized that he was walking, but he had no idea where he was going. He stepped off of the walkway and pressed himself up against the side of a class building so that people could pass by. What should he do? Tad had told him to speak to no one. He couldn't even talk to Coal until nightfall.

He thought of the letter Tad had given him. That's right, he was supposed to report to the assignment desk. His hand went to his jacket pocket and he felt the crinkle of the paper within. But what if that was before? Was that still the plan? Had Tad even made the arrangements? If not he was going to be in trouble for not being on his post at the wall.

Willum pushed away from the building and stepped back into the crowded walkway. He pressed forward until he came to the Council Building, then started down the narrow path to the rear entrance. If he could get into Tad's room, maybe there was something, a note left behind that could tell him Tad's plan.

He walked around the back of the building and swore to himself. There was a guard posted outside the door.

"Hey, Zhed," Willum said and tried to edge by.

"Wait! Wait, Willum," Zhed said. "I can't let you in. Nobody but council members are supposed to come in this door right now."

"Why? I go in this way all the time," Willum said.

"Not after what happened last night."

"What are you talking about?" Willum said.

"Y-you didn't hear?" Zhed looked around, then motioned Willum closer. "Tad the Cunning's dead."

"No," Willum said, raising one hand to his temple.

"Yeah, him and Demon Jenn both. They found 'em this morning. Torn to pieces! They still don't know what happened. Hugh the Shadow has all his men looking into it."

"Torn to pieces?" He didn't have to feign shock anymore. His belief that Tad had faked his death was shaken a bit. But wait. If Hugh the Shadow was investigating, maybe he was helping Tad somehow.

"Yeah, like some kind of troll or something went crazy in there. The thing is, the monster left no tracks. It's like it just disappeared."

"This is horrible. I just talked to Tad the Cunning yesterday. I-I've got to go talk to them. Are they in there investigating now?" Willum asked

"Uh, yeah. I think so, but-." Zhed said.

"Thanks, Zhed. You've been a great help," Willum said and pushed his way inside. As the door fell shut behind him, he realized he had made an error. He had just told Zhed that he had spoken to Tad. Now word would get around. What if they decided to question him? He pounded his fist against his leg. Still, all he could do was move forward.

Willum slid down the corridor quietly, hoping that no one would barge around the corner. He could hear voices coming from one of the corridors, but couldn't tell which one. He came to the intersection and peered down to the left where Tad's room was located. The door was open and it sounded like voices were coming from within.

Willum leaned against the wall. What now? He should

probably turn back the way he came and come back later. But he heard the latch on the door to the rear entrance. Someone was coming in behind him.

He hurriedly ducked around the corner and headed towards Tad's room. The voices were getting louder and one of Hugh's men could come out the door at any moment.

Halfway there, he ducked into the alcove he had hidden in the night before. It was a small area, just big enough to perhaps squeeze two people into. He wasn't quite sure what the alcove was supposed to be used for, but he was glad it was there. It gave him just enough shadow to hide in as footsteps came up the corridor.

The person that had entered behind him walked into view. It was Dann Doudy. He had gained some reputation after his fight with the whip beast and had made the most of it. He had lost some weight and changed his style. His clothes looked less foppish and more swarthy now, still expensive, but made for free movement. He also walked with more confidence, his hand resting on his sword hilt.

Doudy paused just outside the alcove where Willum hid and listened to the conversation going on in Tad's room. Willum's fingers itched and he wished more than anything that he could unsheathe his scythes and attack the man then and there. But he forced himself to stay perfectly still. Tad had a plan. He had to wait. Doudy lifted his foot as if deciding to move on, but paused instead and turned to look right at Willum.

"Well, hello there," the man said and then stepped into the alcove with him. Doudy slid in close until their chests were almost touching. His face tightened into a glare, his nose darkening. "Willum, son of Coal."

Willum's heart pounded. He was six inches taller than Doudy, but somehow the man didn't look so unimpressive up close. In the shadow, Doudy's eyes were so full of menace that it seemed as if the man towered over him. Willum squeezed against the wall as tightly as he could, wanting nothing more than to run, but he was trapped. A voice inside him shouted to fight or at least push past the man, but he couldn't move.

"What are you doing here, hmm? Coming to look through

Tad's things like a stinking thief, I bet."

"Tad is my teacher," Willum said.

"Was your teacher," Doudy said with a sneer. Somehow the whites of his eyes melted away as if they had gone completely black. "He died this morning." The man put his hand on the wall by Willum's head. His breath smelled like rot. "How about you? Where were you this morning?"

"Get away from me," Willum said, some of his strength returning. "Or I'll-."

"You'll what?" Doudy said, pressing up against him. His nose touched Willum's chin. It was cold and mushy. "You'll fight me? Huh? You academy boys are all the same. I catch you here, hiding in a place you're not supposed to be and you think, 'I can take that guy'?"

Willum couldn't speak. His mouth felt as if it were glued shut. Somehow he forced words past his teeth. "I c-could."

"Oh, you think so?" The man pulled his head back a bit and smiled up at him and Willum swore for a moment that the man's teeth were sharp as knives. Doudy grabbed Willum's wrist and stepped back out of the alcove. As the torchlight hit his face, it looked normal once more, though his nose was still a throbbing purple. "Come on, then. Let's go somewhere where you can show me your skills."

"Let go," Willum said. Though Doudy looked like a man again, his grip was like iron.

"Ah! Representative Doudy," said a woman's voice.

Doudy turned his head to look at the speaker, but he didn't let go. "Huh?"

"Hello, so good to see you. I was wondering-."

Doudy snorted. "Yeah-yeah. If you'll excuse me, miss, I have a little disciplinary issue I'm dealing with." He yanked Willum into the light.

The woman stood just outside the doorway to Tad's quarters, a sheathe of papers tucked under one arm. She was beautiful and looked to be perhaps in her early forties, with deep brown eyes and a charming smile.

"Ah! Good! I see you've found my guard." A stern look

replaced her smile. "Willum, where have you been all morning?"

Willum felt as confused as Dann Doudy looked. "I-I was looking for you."

"Excuse me. Who are you again?" Doudy asked the woman.

"I'm Darlan Begazzi, provisional mayor of Reneul. I was voted in last night, remember?" she said, bringing on her smile again. "I'll tell you what. I'm sure that we will get the chance to speak again in the council meeting later. As for now, if you'll excuse Willum and I, I am quite busy, what with all the things to arrange after Jenn's death."

She stepped forward and when he didn't immediately let go of Willum's wrist, she laid one finger on Doudy's hand. He blinked and let go. "Thank you," she said and walked down the corridor. Willum followed after her, taking one glance back to see Doudy glaring after them, his face red as a cherry.

Willum didn't say anything until they exited the rear door of the Council Building. "Thank you, uh, miss Darlan, I-."

"Shut up, Willum," she said the smile gone from her face once more. "Just follow me."

Willum closed his mouth and followed the woman, confused. Why had she saved him back there and why was she so angry? There was something familiar about her name. What was it? He brushed the thoughts aside and wondered how he was going to get back in the council building.

She led him to the assignment office and tapped her foot while he checked in. The student on duty looked through a stack of papers until he found one for Willum, then handed it to him. Willum turned it over in his hands. The word 'reassignment' was written on the front.

"Willum, son of Coal, reassigned to the position of personal guard and assistant to Darlan Begazzi, provisional mayor, the City of Reneul?" Willum said in shock. The student on duty snickered, Willum turned to Darlan. "I thought that was just a ploy."

"A ploy? Follow me and don't you make me twist your ear the whole way," she snapped, but as she walked down the crowded pathway, the smile reappeared on her face as she greeted everyone she passed. They all seemed to know her and smiled back, most calling her by name.

Willum still could not figure out why her name sounded so familiar. It wasn't until he heard someone jokingly call her 'Darlan the Fierce' that he understood. This was Sir Edge's mother, the wife of Faldon the Fierce. Sir Edge had asked after her at the beginning of the siege, but once Tad had told him she was safe, Willum hadn't thought about her since.

She led him to the far side of the grounds and to a set of stairs leading down into the bowels of the academy. The academy was actually several levels deep, full of storage and training areas along with extra barrack space and kitchens. This was also where most of the City of Reneul and the Training School students were now housed. Families took up most of the barracks and unused storage rooms, while trainees took up the old training areas in the lowest level.

Darlan walked through the press of people and though she moved quickly, she also took the time to smile or say a few words to people along the way. Several times he saw her pull sweets from a pocket in her dress to hand to a crying child. Finally she arrived at the entrance to one of the medium sized storage rooms that had been converted into the Reneul Mayor's office.

The right side of the room was still piled high with barrels of stored goods, but the rest of the room had been cleared. A wide table stood in the middle with several medium sized barrels around it to be used as chairs. People stood around inside arguing with one another and when Darlan walked in, everyone began speaking at once.

She immediately took charge. While Willum watched in stunned silence, she lined up everyone in order and began hearing their issues. They ranged from squabbles over sleeping arrangements, to disagreements over rations.

As Darlan handled each separate issue with quick efficiency, Willum wondered what in the world he was doing there? Why had Tad placed him here with Sir Edge's mother? How did this help him expose Dann Doudy and clear his parent's name?

It was an hour before she heard the last complaint. She then turned the rest of the business over to the other city officials and ushered Willum through a door in the back of the office.

Beyond the door stood yet another storage room, this one much smaller. It smelled of spices. All along the back wall were shelves of small tins. Again, barrels had been cleared away and stacked. In one corner was a makeshift bed. A straw mattress on top of some barrels covered by a quilt and with a small embroidered pillow. Somehow to Willum it felt like a tiny slice of home in the middle of all this chaos.

"Sit down, Willum," Darlan said, pointing to a barrel a few feet away. Then she sat on the bed and put her face in her hands.

She stayed that way for a while, her shoulders shaking silently and Willum realized she was crying.

Willum glanced around uncomfortably, not knowing what to do. She had obviously been through a lot already today. He felt like he should comfort her somehow. He walked over to her and patted her shoulder. "Ma'am I'm so sorry-."

"Sit down, Willum," she said and he rushed back to the barrel.

She looked up at him, her eyes red-rimmed and full of grief and he felt a lump rise in his own throat. He forced it away. Tad was alive somehow and this was part of a plan.

"What a blasted horrible day," she said. "Tad was an old friend. A dear friend. Jenn too."

"Yes, Ma'am." Willum said, looking down.

"You don't believe it?" she said. Willum continued to look down. "Look at me. You think this is one of Tad's plots, don't you? Well listen to me now. When I awoke this morning there were two letters here from Tad that made me so angry I went to the council hall first thing to talk to him. I barged in just after they found their bodies. I forced my way through. I saw them."

"Whatever you saw, it wasn't him," Willum said, his voice shaking now.

"The room was covered in blood. His head and Jenn's were both sitting on the table." Her voice shook and tears streamed down her face as she spoke. "He did not fake that. He is gone and we need to figure out what we are going to do."

"W-what do you mean?" the lump in his throat had returned and he wasn't able to swallow it away this time. It just sat there thick and painful.

"You are not alone, Willum. We are in this together." she said and stood. She wiped the tears off of her face with the back of her hand. "Tad told me what you two were up to. What he thought you were up against. He told me that he was going to need my help at some point. Damn him, I told him I didn't want to do this. 'A time of war,' he said."

Darlan's lip quivered, her sadness giving way to anger. She raised a fist in front of her eyes and to Willum's surprise, flames sprouted from her knuckles. Her face glowed in the light of them and Willum could feel the hairs on his arms stand on end. "Tad is forcing me to become something I haven't been in a long time. Something I wanted to give up forever."

She shook her hand and the flames went away. "Tell me, Willum. Tad has always been too secretive for his own good. How much has he told you?"

Willum blinked, unsure what he should tell her. "Tad told me not to speak about it with anyone."

"Of course he did." She sighed. "I shall start then. For a while before the siege began Tad had been convinced that one of the members of the Academy Council was passing on academy secrets to someone outside the school.

"Every time the academy made a move against the goblinoid forces, the enemy seemed to know about it ahead of time. They moved their troops around the academy's patrol routes no matter how often they changed them. When the council would try to clean out a certain area of goblinoids, they would have already fled. It was giving the enemy growing confidence."

"But the council members are his friends. They have all been comrades for years," Willum said. "Why would it have to be someone on the council? Couldn't it have been one of the sergeants or field commanders? Even one of the Dremald captains?"

"I argued the same points, but Tad said that the enemy's knowledge was too pervasive. They knew things that only the council members knew," Darlan said. "Then the siege hit and Dann Doudy showed up on our doorstep. Tad was convinced that our enemy now had two spies on the council. With two members, they might be able to flip a vote one way or another.

"So he hatched a plan to get another member on the council that he could trust. That's where I came in. Tad knew about my past and what I'm capable of and since the new War Council included the Mayor of Reneul, he tried to find a way to have me take Demon Jenn's place."

"B-but why not just confide in Demon Jenn? She wasn't part of the council before the siege. She couldn't be the one," Willum asked.

"Because he had uncovered other things about Jenn." Darlan shook her head. "Tad discovered that Jenn had been siphoning funds away from city coffers for a few years. She was planning on retiring and living out the rest of her days in some mansion in Razbeck. I was able to confirm his findings and he confronted Jenn and threatened to turn her in. At the council meeting yesterday afternoon, she resigned as mayor and Tad nominated me to be the provisional mayor until the siege was over. Everyone on the council knows me, so they voted me in."

"So that's why he had me reassigned to be your guard," Willum said.

"In one of the letters he left for me during the night he said that you had brought him new evidence and that he was going to confront Dann Doudy. If it worked, he might be able to get Doudy to tell him the identity of the other spy. If it didn't, he feared for your safety. Since he couldn't watch over you day and night, he had assigned you to be my personal guard so that I could watch over you."

"Why my safety?" Willum wondered.

"I'm not sure. What was this evidence you found?" she asked.

Willum told her about the dagger.

"I see. So that's the leverage he was going to bring against Doudy," she said, frowning. "Well since he failed, we can only assume that Dann Doudy knows your father is coming with the dagger and since you know about it, he is going to want you dead. And I don't know Jenn was doing there, but since she was found with him . . ."

"We have to assume that he learned about your part in it too," Willum finished. He swallowed. His first guard duty assignment and it was protecting the mayor of Reneul and the wife of Faldon the Fierce against something so strong it tore Tad the Cunning apart. How was he going to watch after her and at the same time keep an eye out for the dagger in his own back?

Darlan cocked her head at him, "You're doubting my ability to protect you, aren't you?"

Willum's eyes widened. "I-I, well no, of course not."

She pulled a silver coin out of her pocket and set it on the open palm of her left hand. Waves of distortion rolled up from her skin and the coin began to glow red. Willum could feel the heat of it from where he sat. The coin melted to a puddle in her hand, then floated up above it to form a perfect sphere. She gripped the sphere between her thumb and forefinger and blew on it, then tossed it to him. He reached out and caught it by reflex. It was cold in his hand.

"Willum, if I wanted to, I could broil every man alive within two hundred paces of where we stand," she said. "Believe me, I can watch your back."

"Yes, Ma'am," he said, feeling a chill run up the back of his neck. "What are you, anyway?"

"Never mind that. But I can't protect both of us. That's why Tad sent you here to watch over me too. Without my husband here, I need someone as skilled with physical weapons as everyone says you are." She held out her hand, "So, Willum, since it is the two of us in this alone for now, will you protect me in turn?"

He clasped her hand. "I will."

"Good. Now we have about twenty minutes before the

next council meeting. We need to plan out how we're going to figure out who the traitor is."

"Yes, Ma'am," Willum said.

"Good," Darlan smiled. "And once we get back from that meeting, you are going to tell me the truth about how you communicate with your father. Then you are going to tell me every single thing that Tad has left out about my son. Understood?"

Willum hesitated, but she was Sir Edge's mother. She was going to learn about bonding magic soon enough anyway. "Yes, Ma'am."

"Alright then," she said. "So on to our plans . . . If only we knew what Tad's next move was going to be."

"Oh!" Willum's hand flew to his pocket as he remembered the letter. He handed it to Darlan. "He said to give it to my new commander."

She broke the seal and opened the letter. Her eyes scanned the message. "He says to have you watch the council member's assistants . . ."

"That makes sense! Whatever the council members speak about in meetings is usually passed on to their assistants. The spy could be one of them," Willum said with a smile. The thought of one of his teachers being a traitor had been weighing on him.

Darlan hadn't stopped reading. A frown grew across her face. She tipped the envelope and a small silver key fell out into her palm.

"What is it?" Willum asked.

"He said that there was a small chance he was making a grave miscalculation. If at any time between now and the end of the siege, he should lose his life, he wanted me to give you this and . . ." She looked up, her eyes flaring with disapproval. "The blasted fool planned to give you his cursed axe."

Chapter Nineteen

I'm big!

Gwyrtha had in fact doubled in size, and though Justan felt a sense of triumph, he checked to make sure that his body still clung to her back. Thankfully, he was still there and the saddle still held. Justan was grateful that Coal had the foresight to have Benjo rune the leather to stretch under these conditions.

I'm big, Fist! Gwyrtha ran forward and pranced around the ogre, her hind quarters now at Fist's shoulders. *Want to ride*?

"Yes!" Fist said. Squirrel ran and jumped from his shoulder to Gwyrtha's back.

Not now, please, Justan sent. *I'm not fully in control at the moment.*

Samson trotted up to them. The centaur laughed. "You look good, Gwyrtha!"

I'm big! she said and ran up to nudge him. She pushed a little hard and Samson had to canter to the side to avoid being knocked over. Master Coal was nearly jostled out of his saddle.

"Woah, woah!" the wizard said. "Good, Edge! Fantastic work. Now if you'll notice, the larger you make her, the smaller her core of energy will be. Can you see?"

Justan looked to the core of her through his spirit sight and saw that the wizard was right. The amount of energy she produced was lesser than before, perhaps by a fourth. He told his body to nod.

"That is the trade off with making changes to your rogue horse," Coal said. "It takes a lot of energy for her to maintain the changes. If you continued to make her larger the energy would continue to shrink until she eventually had the energy levels of a normal creature. This would mean that she would tire quicker and you won't be able to siphon her energy if you need it."

Justan nodded again.

"Alright, now shrink her back down and we'll practice again," Coal said.

No! Gwyrtha replied and took off at a run. She veered off of the narrow trail and plunged down a steep incline heading towards the flat grassland below.

Justan felt his body being jostled around and worried it would slide off. He hurried and rushed back through the bond just in time to right himself. The wind rustled his hair and the scent of the verdant spring filled his nose as she hit the grassland and plowed along, startling tiny grasshoppers and butterflies into the air.

Riding a large Gwyrtha was a new sensation. The ground sped by faster than normal and yet the ride wasn't as rough. He felt Gwyrtha's joy and a smile spread across his face.

Justan noticed a weight on his shoulder and turned his head to see Squirrel sitting there. It was calmly shelling a seed. Justan's eyebrows rose in surprise. Squirrel normally ignored him. "Uh, hey, Squirrel."

Squirrel cocked its head and handed the seed out to him. Justan tried to say no thanks, but Squirrel just placed the seed in his open mouth. Justan repressed a grimace and watched as Squirrel pulled another seed out of its cheek to work on. He forced himself to chew and swallow, then returned his attention to the ride, trying not to think about it.

Justan, Deathclaw sent. *I see riders.*

I'm big, Deathclaw! Gwyrtha sent in excitement.

That is . . . good, Gwyrtha, Deathclaw replied.

The two of them had returned from their fruitless search for Talon a day before. The raptoid was frustrated that Talon had evaded them, but the two of them had grown much closer. Deathclaw seemed to have gotten over whatever it was about her that had bothered him before. When Justan had asked him about it all he had said was she wasn't so different from him after all.

Come ride!

Not now. Deathclaw said patiently. *Justan, they will cross our path.*

What kind of riders? Justan asked.

Ten men on horses, Deathclaw replied, proud of his count.

Show them to me.

Deathclaw sent an image of the men he saw.

The men were far away, but Justan's heart lurched. It couldn't be. *Can you get a better view?*

Yes. The raptoid darted from behind the boulder where he was hiding and scampered up the short cliff face next to the trail. He moved a bit further down before laying flat against the ground and peering over the side. Now Justan could see the riders clearly.

Justan smiled, his heart pounding in excitement. *Go, Gwyrtha, let's greet them!* The men would get an awful fright, but why not give them a great entrance? *Fist, tell everyone that we have friends ahead.*

Who is it? The ogre asked.

"My father!" Justan said and laughed out loud as tears of happiness began to stream from his eyes. He soon spotted the men traveling along the trail up above and Gwyrtha angled towards them. He could already see Faldon sitting high in his saddle, the pommel of The Monarch jutting up from his back.

The men saw them coming and shouted out in alarm. Two of them drew back arrows, and Justan tensed up, but a third man yelled something and they put their bows down. Faldon had one hand on his sword pommel but when he realized who it was, raised both fists into the air and laughed.

Gwyrtha pounded up the incline, her claws digging into the loose dirt as Justan was already mid-dismount. He leapt off before she had come to a complete stop and crashed into his father's open arms. The two men wrapped each other in a crushing embrace.

"It's so good to see you, son!" Faldon said.

"Father! My gosh, what are you doing here?" He held

him back at arms length. "I mean I knew you weren't at the academy, but-!"

"Look at you!" Faldon exclaimed, his eyes shining. "By the gods, son. You have grown!"

Justan realized that Faldon was right. His eyes met Faldon's on nearly equal terms and their musculature looked almost the same. For the first time in his life they looked like father and son. "I-I've been through a lot, father."

"When I saw you riding up on that-that-."

"Her name's Gwyrtha," Justan said. "And she's a sweetheart. Come say hello to my father." Gwyrtha came up and nuzzled her huge head against him.

Faldon hesitantly patted her head.

"Scratch behind her ears. She loves that."

Faldon shook his head as he did so. "It's a good thing Captain Demetrius told us what to expect or we might have fired on you."

"Captain Demetrius?" Justan looked over at the other men and smiled as the captain dismounted and walked over. He clasped hands with the man. The captain wore his full Dremald Guard armor. "So good to see you, sir. Lieutenant Jack said you were out there gathering support. I was afraid Ewzad Vriil might have caught you."

"I was able to sneak out in the confusion following the king's death," The captain said. The man looked much healthier than when Justan had last seen him after weeks stuck in Vriil's filthy dungeon. "I have gathered over three thousand men who want to fight against the dark wizard's forces. Jack says that you are bringing the refugees from Sampo?"

"We have just under a thousand fighting men and women with us, Captain. The rest are families and children. Has my father been with you this whole time?"

"No son," Faldon said. He had grown a bit flustered under Gwyrtha's constant attention and shared a bewildered look with Squirrel who was sitting on Gwyrtha's saddle. "We were uh, in the mountains on a mission when the siege started. We've been gathering an army of our own. We are nearly three thousand strong ourselves, mostly academy retirees and hardy mountainfolk."

Justan was thrilled with the news even though, with their forces combined, they were still outnumbered five to one. "Amazing. So where is everyone else?"

"We're camped just a few miles to the north. The captain and his men just joined us a day ago. We've been looking for the rear entrance to Wobble, but our dwarven guides can't quite remember where it is. Lieutenant Jack told us you were coming so we decided to see if we could meet you."

"I'm glad you did," Justan said.

"Let me see those runes of yours," Faldon said and Justan held out his hands. Faldon turned them over, inspecting the runes and smiled into his son's eyes. "Son, I . . . I'm so proud of you."

"Father . . . The naming thing just sort of happened," Justan began.

"It's not that," Faldon said. "The bowl chooses who it's going to name. I'm talking about the tales I hear of my son freeing a dungeon full of prisoners and fighting against Ewzad Vrill. I'm talking about my son who freed the men of Sampo and brought the refugees over to our cause."

Justan felt a lump in his throat. "Thank you, father."

Faldon clapped him on the back, then was nearly knocked over by Gwyrtha, who had nudged him just a bit too enthusiastically. "Whoa, this um, rogue horse of yours is quite affectionate."

"She's happy to see you. Gwyrtha has seen you so many times in my thoughts, it's like she knows you," Justan explained.

"Now . . . can you explain how that works for me? Your friend Zambon was a little hazy on the details."

"Zambon's here with you?" Justan asked.

"Yes. And Tamboor." He smiled and added, "Jhonate is here with us as well."

Justan's heart thumped. Jhonate was there, just a few miles away. He could feel his face flush. He was excited and terrified at the same time.

"Uh, well uh, the way the magic works is, um." His

mouth seemed dry all the sudden. "My magic makes a permanent bond between me and someone else. It . . . connects our minds together so that we know each other's thoughts and feelings."

"So, you are 'bonded' with Gwyrtha here and also that ogre Zambon and Tamboor know?"

"Yes. His name is Fist. I'm eager for you to meet him. I think you will hit it off. And . . ." Deathclaw slid down from the cliff ledge above them and turned to face Faldon. Several of the men gasped. "This is Deathclaw. My newest bonded."

The raptoid cocked his head and chirped as he and Faldon measured each other up. *He is . . . dangerous.* Deathclaw sent.

Faldon stuck out his hand and to Justan's surprise, Deathclaw reached out and shook it. The raptoid stepped back and gave a short bow. "Sir." Then he scampered back up the cliff face and disappeared.

"He's . . . our scout. He was a raptoid until Ewzad Vriil used his magic to change him into what he is now," Justan said. "He's not very comfortable around humans yet."

"Scout?" Faldon rubbed his chin thoughtfully. "He has more of the feel of an assassin to me."

"That too," Justan agreed.

"You say this bond is permanent?" Faldon asked. Justan nodded and Faldon shrugged. "At least he's on our side. Shall we head on and meet the others?"

He returned to his horse.

Justan hesitated. "Wait, uh, father. I-I don't know how to tell you this, but . . . Tad the Cunning is dead."

Faldon paused mid-mount. He took his foot out of the stirrup and turned back to face Justan, his face grim. "How do you know this?"

"We learned two days ago," Justan said. He explained how Tad was found murdered and that Darlan was now mayor. "Right now mother is working with Willum to find out who the traitor is."

"Blast it, Tad!" Faldon slammed his fist into his palm, his face twisted with rage and grief. "He told me about his suspicions before I left. I told him he was being ridiculous. Why did he have to go and get Darlan involved?"

One of the other riders dismounted and ran over to join them. Justan was surprised he had not noticed him before. "Qenzic! Good to see you!"

Qenzic, son of Sabre Vlad nodded at him. "Ju-, uh Sir Edge." He looked to Faldon. "Sir, if Tad the Cunning is dead, my father could have had no part in it."

"I know, Qenzic. I trust your father. I trust all those men. There has to be something else going on." Faldon frowned. "Listen, I want you to take the men back and let the others know we found the refugees. Have everyone begin clearing a place for them to camp until we can find the entrance."

Captain Demetrius told his own men to follow. "I'll head on back with them. We'll all meet back together later tonight."

"Of course, Captain," Faldon turned to Justan. "Come on, son. Let's mount up and go talk to your Master Coal. I have information that you are missing and it could change everything."

Justan climbed on Gwyrtha's back and trotted alongside his father. At Gwyrtha's current height, she was taller than Faldon's horse by a good six inches. The horse was frightened to be this close to the rogue horse, but it was well trained and Faldon led it with a steady hand.

"Father, tell me. Why has mother become part of this? Coal knows something, but he won't say. He just says that she can take care of herself."

"That's probably because Darlan warned him not to tell you." Faldon's brow furrowed in thought. "Son, your mother has a history that she isn't proud of. I have wanted her to discuss it with you many times over the years, but she was always determined to wait until you were older. I . . . I see no reason to keep it from you now."

"Then what is it?"

Faldon paused. "Your mother is a wizardess."

"But . . ." Justan stared at his father for several seconds while he processed the information. How could it be? She was a mother. She cleaned. She made pies. She. . . Finally he nodded.

"You know, for some reason it kind of makes sense. I mean, I should be more surprised, but it just explains so much. So many times over the years, mom just seemed to know what I was doing. Like with grandpa's box. She always knew when I found it."

"Wards," Faldon said with a shake of his head. "She's an expert at them. Darlan wanted to put her past behind and stop using magic, but she couldn't help herself. The woman had wards strung all over the house. She had the place warded for prowlers. She had wards over your bedroom in case you got up in the night. She would even put wards on her pies so she would know if someone stole them off the windowsill."

"But why did she want to hide her magic?" Justan asked.

"Because she was powerful. Your mother's magic was strong in fire and earth and she had destructive spells you cannot imagine. She was a war-wizard and she was so good at it that the Mage School turned her into a dark wizard hunter. They used to send her in when a bad wizard needed to be quelled or destroyed. But she was too powerful. Sometimes she got carried away and bystanders were hurt by her magic.

"Finally she tired of it. She sat on the council for a while and even took on an apprentice, but she was always fighting with the other council members about laws and regulations at the school she disagreed with. Finally, there was an . . . incident where the council punished her apprentice and your mother quit."

Justan's mind reeled with the information. His mother a High Council member? "Was that before you met?"

"Well, we told you part of that story. Your mother and I met when I was out on an academy mission fighting some bandits that were harassing a small town. What you weren't told was that your mother was with us because these bandits were run by a wizardess that had gone rogue." Faldon said. "Your mother and I really hit it off and after she left the Mage School she came through Reneul. I met with her and after a time, I was able to convince her that a life with me meant she didn't have to use her magic anymore. I could be the protector in the family and she could be . . . whatever she wanted. We married. Then she got pregnant with you and . . . the rest is happiness."

"But Tad knew about her. Didn't he?" Justan said in sudden understanding.

"Tad knew. He was part of that same academy operation. It's one of the reasons we were all so close. But he was the only one. No one else at the academy knows and the only one at the Mage School who knows who your mother's true identity is Valtrek. Unless he told someone, but I don't think so."

"So that's why he was watching me in Reneul," Justan said. "He was waiting to see if I had inherited her magic."

"Yes. Darlan caught him watching you and they had words. But Valtrek was persistent and she knew that if you did have magic, you would have to go to the school anyway."

Justan frowned. "But why didn't anyone at the Mage School figure out who my mother was? I mean, I must have mentioned her name several times while I was there and no one batted an eye."

"She only became Darlan Begazzi after she left the school. At the Mage School she went by Darlan Sherl, which means that most of them just knew her as Wizardess Sherl," Faldon said. "Begazzi was her grandmother's name."

Justan felt a chill. He had heard the name Sherl before. One of his teachers had spoken of a spell designed by Wizardess Sherl wherein a single wizard could stand in the middle of an army and release a wave of fire and molten earth, incinerating all combatants in a hundred yards from their position. His mind went back to the night when Valtrek first showed him the potential of magic power. Valtrek had showed Justan a vision of himself using his mother's spell. What had been the point of that?

"You should have told me," Justan said, frowning.

"I know. It was-."

"I went to the Mage School so angry. Father, if I had known that mother had magic, I would have understood. I would have acted so differently!"

"I'm sorry, son. You're right. I told Darlan that you should know. I think she was just scared of how you would take it," Faldon said.

They rode in silence for a while, both deep in thought. Then Justan sensed that they were nearly there.

"Oh, Father, you should know some things about my travel companions." Justan told Faldon what to expect and the refugees soon came into view, following the trail that wove through the foothills. Their travel line snaked off into the distance. Master Coal rode at the head, Fist walking beside him.

Faldon whistled. "You weren't kidding. A centaur."

"And that's Fist walking beside him," Justan said.

"He has to be one of the biggest ogres I've ever seen and the way he stands up straight, why he walks like a man."

"I've had him working on his posture," Justan explained. "He's had back troubles in the past and I wanted to make sure he put less stress on it."

"Amazing," Faldon rode up and held out his hand. "Fist, good to meet you. I'm Faldon."

Fist reached out and shook his hand. "I am glad to meet you, Justan's father. He has shown me so much about you. I hope to spar with you some time."

"That would be a pleasure, Fist. Zambon told me how you tried to help Tamboor's family. They will both be happy to see you again."

Fist beamed. "I want to see them too. Is Tamboor . . . better?"

Faldon shook his head. "It's hard to say. He doesn't speak. But he survives. We have hope that he will return to himself some day."

Fist nodded. "I see." Squirrel took that moment to leap from Gwyrtha's back to land on Fist's shoulders and the ogre scratched behind its ears. "This is Squirrel."

"We've met," Faldon said. He turned to the centaur. "You must be Samson."

"Yes, sir," Samson said in surprise, not expecting to be directly addressed.

"And Master Coal," Faldon said. "I met you briefly once;

long ago when I was at the Mage School. It is good to see you again."

Coal smiled. "I must say it is a great relief to know that you are here. Fist was telling us about the number of men you have gathered."

Faldon looked back at Justan and Justan nodded back at him. "I see. It's that bonding magic. My son was explaining it to me earlier. Listen, while we are on the subject, I understand that you have a bonded in the academy right now working with my wife."

"Yes, Willum is there with her," Coal said.

"Okay, listen, this is very important. The next time you speak with him, tell him not to tell anyone other than Darlan that we are coming. Whoever the spy or spies in the school are, they have the means to communicate with the mastermind behind this siege."

"They have been operating under that assumption already," Coal replied.

"Good, tell them that what they are looking for are moonrat eyes," Faldon explained. "The mother of the moonrats uses them to communicate with members of her army."

"Father, what are you talking about? That's Ewzad Vriil's army," Justan said.

Faldon explained how they had discovered the role of the moonrats in Ewzad's army. Justan listened mouth open as Faldon described Jhonate's battle with the witch and their subsequent encounters with her traps.

"So this witch is coordinating everything," Justan said in understanding.

"That's what keeps the army from falling apart," Coal said.

"Exactly," Faldon said. "Let's hurry on and meet up with the others. Between our two groups and Captain Demetrius, we may have all the information we need to understand this puzzle."

"Indeed," Coal said. "I'll ride back and let Sir Lance know what the plan is."

"Did you say Sir Lance?" Faldon asked.

"Yes," Justan said.

"That old terror is still alive?" Faldon laughed. "He was one of my teachers when I went through the academy. Tough as nails and a pain in the butt."

"Well, he hasn't changed," Coal said. "But the Sampo people asked him to be their representative so we have to deal with him."

Faldon sighed. "I'm not looking forward to dealing with him again, but I guess it can't be helped."

Master Coal turned Samson around to leave. "Edge, you may want to return Gwyrtha to her proper size. This is her first time being that large. With practice, she can hold it indefinitely, but until that time if she maintains the changes too long, she will tire out."

I like being big, Gwyrtha protested, but as Samson ran back towards the center of the refugees, Justan did what Coal asked.

"Amazing," Faldon said in surprise as she shrank to her regular size. "No one told me anything about that."

"It's something new," Justan said. "I just recently learned about it myself."

They started down the trail, Fist walking right behind them.

"Tell me more, son," Faldon said. "I want to hear everything you've been up to."

"Well, alright." Justan started from the beginning and told him everything that had happened; from his ride to the Mage School and bonding with Gwyrtha, to his naming, to the fight with Kenn and the way the Scralag came out of his chest to freeze the bandham. Faldon listened in rapt attention, exclaiming appreciatively at times.

Seeing his father's reaction to the story surprised him. Looking back, he was really quite proud of what he had accomplished. But while everything was going on, he had just been reacting the way he felt best at the time.

"So how much further is it?" Justan asked once he had finished his story.

"Not much further. Just around the next hill I think."

"So, uh, father," Justan cleared his throat. "How is Jhonate?"

Faldon smiled. "She is doing quite well. Partially in thanks to the ring you gave her."

"It works?" Justan asked, though he immediately felt stupid for asking after what he had learned about his mother. "Of course it works."

"It's been protecting her in battle this whole time," Faldon said. "She was quite perplexed when she learned that it was magic."

Justan raised a hand to his forehead. "Oh . . . she's going to kill me."

Faldon laughed and gave him a calculating look. "Actually I think she'll be quite happy to see you. She asks about you often."

"Really?" Justan said with a smile.

"Yes. She keeps asking even though I haven't had any new information since the siege began. She-." He shut his mouth as if reconsidering what he had been about to say. "I just think she'll be glad to see you is all."

The haze of camp fires appeared on the horizon and soon Justan heard the sounds of men. As they rounded the corner of the hill, the sprawling camps came into view. The two armies were camped close together, but Justan could see a clear delineation between the two.

Both camps were orderly, but Captain Demetrius' men wore uniforms and their tents were standard Dremald garrison issue. Faldon's soldiers wore mostly farming clothes and their tents were a mis-mash of old academy tents and shelters the people had cobbled together on their own.

They rode through the camp, Faldon introducing Justan to various people as they passed by. Everyone gave Gwyrtha a wide berth, many of them looking quite frightened. Justan saw a few faces that were vaguely familiar, mainly old colleagues of his fathers, but it wasn't until they neared the command tent that Justan saw the person he was looking for.

Jhonate watched him approach, her Jharro staff clutched in one hand. She looked much like she had on the day they met. She wore her leather breastplate and her black hair was interwoven with those green ribbons that matched the color of her piercing eyes.

Justan dismounted and walked towards her. All peripheral sights and sounds faded. He saw only Jhonate. The expression on her face was hard to translate. He couldn't tell if she was truly happy to see him or if there was a hint of fear. But as he approached, he saw the beautiful smile from his memories begin to form on her lips and his heart hammered in his chest.

Somewhere to his left came a squeal that jolted his attention away for just a brief moment. He turned just in time to see a flash of blond hair and blue eyes speeding towards him. Then soft curves slammed against his body and a pair of arms were thrown around his chest. Justan's nose was filled with the scent of flowers as Vannya's plump lips wrapped around his in a deep kiss.

Chapter Twenty

Justan froze, his arms held to the side, helpless against Vannya's ardent attack. His brain screamed at him that something was wrong, but his body wouldn't move. The sensation was so nice and his enhanced senses made it even more intoxicating. It was all he had dreamed a kiss with Vannya might be, all softness and sweetness. But Jhonate-

Justan's hands finally found Vannya's shoulders and pushed her back. Her lips left his and his eyes darted around but Jhonate had disappeared. All around him people were staring, the men jealous, the women amused.

He held the mage at arm's length. "V-vannya! Wh . . . what was that?"

Her cheeks were flushed, her lips slightly parted. She was breathing heavy and her eyes looked slightly confused. It was unfair how gorgeous she was. "I saw you and I didn't know-. I didn't expect you to be here and I-I was just so happy that I . . . overreacted."

"Y-you think?" Justan said in frustration. She bit her lip and tears began to well up in her eyes. He could have punched himself. He didn't want to hurt her again. This wasn't a dream. This was a nightmare. He hugged her. "Vannya, I'm sorry. I am happy to see you too, I just . . . didn't expect you to kiss me."

It didn't help. She pushed back from him and ran off between the tents, her shoulders trembling. The stares around him turned into head shaking.

"I can't believe she did that. I don't envy you one bit, Sir Edge," said a man standing next to him.

Justan turned in surprise. "Professor Locksher! You're

here too? Is anyone else from the Mage School with you?"

The wizard shook his head. "No. Vannya and I came up to Reneul on our own to investigate your frost rune and we got caught up in everything else."

Justan's hand went to his chest. "About my frost rune, it's-." He looked around, uncomfortable with so many people around. "I would like to talk to you about that later in private."

Faldon walked up to them. "Son, what was that about?"

"I don't know, father. That was . . . out of nowhere," Justan said, his face red, "And now Jhonate is gone. Do you know where she went?"

The two older men looked at each other and Faldon said, "She may have gone back to the student tents that way. Um . . . good luck with those two."

"What do you mean?" Justan asked.

Justan these people fear me. Gwyrtha came up and shoved her head between Justan and Faldon.

Locksher jumped, then a smile spread across his face and he raised one eyebrow in interest. "Amazing! This is your rogue horse, isn't it? Valtrek told me about your bond."

"Uh, yes. Her name is Gwyrtha," Justan said, rubbing her head comfortingly. *It's okay sweetie.* "And she is a bit uncomfortable with all the looks she's getting."

Some commotion broke out behind them and Justan felt Fist's distress. He looked back to see the ogre standing with his arms raised defensively as a group of angry men wearing forest garb surrounded him. They were shouting and cursing, telling him to pull his mace and fight. One man drew his sword. Another poked at him with a spear.

"Hey! Stop!" Faldon shouted and he and Justan rushed towards them. The spearman's jab had caused a small wound on Fist's chest and he began to bleed, but the ogre refused to pull his weapon. The swordsman drew back his sword.

Tamboor arrived before they did.

The silent warrior felled the swordsman with one swift elbow to the temple. The man lay still on the ground and Tamboor grabbed the spearman by the hair. He yanked the man's head down to meet his upthrust knee. There was a loud crack and the spearman collapsed motionless at the other man's side.

The other men backed away, babbling, "Tamboor the Fearless, Sir!" "We were just-!" "We saw the ogre and-!" Tamboor silenced them with a piercing glare.

"Tamboor!" Fist said, his arms opened wide, and the warrior walked in for a fierce hug.

The men looked at each other with shocked expressions. Faldon walked up to them, his face twisted with anger.

"Listen up! Take those two to the infirmary tent and wake them up. Then I want you to spread the word. That ogre is a family friend. He is on our side in this war. I don't care what you think of him or any of our new allies. I want them treated with respect."

The men nodded and fell over each other in their haste to drag the two unconscious men away.

Faldon turned to Justan with an apologetic look. "I'm sorry, son. These men have been fighting the goblinoid army for weeks. Some of them have seen family members killed by ogres."

"I know, father. It will be a tough adjustment for some people," Justan said. "But I am sure that when they get to know him, they won't be able to help but like him. Just . . . Can you give me just a minute?"

He closed his eyes and checked out Fist's wound. It wasn't too bad, but the spear had pierced about a half inch into his muscle. Justan quickly closed the wound.

Fist barely reacted other than to send a quick thank you through the bond. He was busy chatting away at Tamboor, telling him of their journey. Tamboor stood with arms folded, nodding occasionally, but not once did a smile touch his lips.

"That's the closest thing to a regular conversation I have seen him have with anyone but his son," Faldon said. "What were you doing just now?"

"Oh, I was healing Fist," Justan said. "Where is Zambon by the way?"

"He's out with our dwarf 'guides' trying to find the

entrance to the crevasse. Did you say healing?"

"Yes, but I can only heal my bonded. It's kind of complicated."

"Huh," Faldon said. "What you really should be doing is looking for Jhonate."

Justan winced. "I know. I'm afraid to talk to her after what Vannya did."

"I should warn you right now. Those girls haven't been getting along."

Justan moaned. "Considering what just happened, maybe I should stay here with Fist and Gwyrtha."

"I'll keep them with me, don't worry. Go. See her," Faldon said sternly.

"Yes, sir," Justan headed in the direction his father pointed.

"Oh, uh, what about your . . . uh, Deathclaw?"

Justan looked up at the cliff face high above them. "He'll take care of himself."

Justan made his way past multiple rows of tents looking for a group that were standard academy issue. The problem was that a lot of them were. When people retired from the academy they were allowed to take their things with them and it looked like a lot of them had taken good care of their old equipment. He stopped and scratched his head, looking around.

"This camp is huge," he grumped. "Yeah father, point a finger. That really helps."

Finally, he stopped and spoke to a short, but powerfully built man that was hunched over, pounding in a tent stake. "Excuse me. Do you know where the tents of Faldon the Fierce's academy students are?"

"You're kidding, right?" said the man and as he turned to face him, Justan recognized him at once.

"Jobar da Org!" Justan said with a smile. "Good to see you."

Jobar stood and faced him but he didn't smile. "Oh. There you are. Faldon the Fierce said they were going to see if they could track you down."

"Yeah, well we just arrived. I'm looking for Jhonate. Have you seen her?"

"She lets you call her that?" Jobar asked in surprise.

"Yes," Justan said his smile fading. There was something about Jobar's attitude he didn't like. "Can you tell me where she is?"

"Maybe." Jobar looked him up and down. "You've, uh, grown since the last time I saw you."

"It's been nearly two years since our arena fight," Justan said.

"Huh. Well I'll tell you what. If I know her, and I think I know her pretty well. There's only a couple places she'd be in the camp this time of day. Come on, I'll take you to her," Jobar said and walked towards the center of their spread out camp.

Justan wondered what Jobar meant by knowing her 'pretty well'. Was he trying to say that they were in some sort of relationship? Surely not. Jhonate wouldn't take up with the likes of Jobar da Org, would she? Then again it had been a long time and Justan really had no idea what kind of man Jobar was. They had only had that one fight after all.

Justan soon knew where it was Jobar was leading him. An area of the camp had been cleared off for sparring and weapons practice. Jhonate was in one corner of the area squaring off against a young man with red hair and a freckled face.

The man carried a wooded practice sword and shield and he was quite skilled. He was holding his own against her pretty well, but Jhonate was attacking with such ferocity that he could do nothing but block and back away. Justan had a sinking feeling that her anger was directed at him.

"Hey, they could be a while," Jobar said. "What do you say we have a sparring match of our own? Hand-to-hand. Like last time."

"Not right now, Jobar, thanks. I just want to talk with Jhonate. I can wait."

Jobar grabbed his shoulder. "Hey, come on, kid. It'll be fun. Let's see how much you've improved."

Justan reached back and grabbed Jobar's wrist with his right hand. Slowly he turned to face him and lifted the man's hand off his shoulder. "You can call me Sir Edge, Jobar. And I might take you up on that offer some time. But not now. Thank you for helping me find her."

He dropped Jobar's hand and left the man standing there with a mixed look of anger and shame. Justan strode across the practice area towards a piece of canvas that had been laid out and covered with a bunch of wooden practice weapons. He picked through them until he found two swords that were of a similar weight and balance, then watched Jhonate's fight. It took a few minutes, but her exhausted opponent finally made a mistake.

The red haired man brought his shield up a little too high. She swung the end of her staff up under it knocking the shield even higher, then lashed out with her foot, kicking him in the abdomen. He hunched over and she whacked him on the head with a solid blow that certainly looked more harsh than necessary.

""You did well, Poz," she said as he crouched and groaned rubbing the top of his head. "Though you were a bit careless at the end. Get up. We shall try again."

"Wait, Jhonate!" Justan said, and she whipped around to face him, an angry retort already forming on her lips. But when she saw who it was, her eyes widened in surprise and she took a step backwards. He walked towards her. "Sorry to interrupt your training. It's just that when I came to greet you earlier I was, um, interrupted."

"Yes you were," she said, her voice cool.

"I'm sorry about that. I was wondering if you might give Poz over there a break and knock me around for a while. Like you used to," Justan smiled, holding up the two practice swords. Poz grinned thankfully from behind Jhonate's back and snuck away to stand by Jobar.

She blinked at him. "I . . ."

"I'll even call you Ma'am again if you like," he offered.

"Yeah! Make him grovel!" cried Jobar.

She darted an irritated glance at the man that made Justan

feel a bit better. "That will not be necessary."

"So you'll spar with me?" he asked hopefully.

She shifted her stance and any hesitation vanished from her face. "Have you continued your training?"

"Yes," he said.

"Have you improved?" she asked, one eyebrow raised.

"Somewhat, I believe," Justan said. "Though I was hoping you could tell me just how much."

"Be aware that I will do my best to defeat you," she warned.

Justan chuckled. "You wouldn't be Jhonate if you didn't."

"Very well, Sir Edge," she said and a slight smile touched the corners of her lips. She twirled her staff. "Have you stretched?"

"That would be a good idea. I've been riding all day."

Justan took his Jharro bow off his shoulder and unbuckled his sword sheaths, then set them gently to the side. As he stretched out his muscles, a crowd began to gather. Justan looked over to see Jobar smiling and knew that the man had taken the time to spread the word.

People say that you are going to battle with the staff girl, Daughter of Xedrion, Fist sent. The ogre seemed amused. *We are coming to see.*

Me too! Gwyrtha agreed.

A leader should not lose in front of other packs, Deathclaw sent and Justan knew that the raptoid had found a way to get a view. Justan glanced around, picking out one particularly robust tree not far away. He peered up into its branches and Deathclaw added, *I was not seen.*

Justan sighed. This could be humiliating. He had never defeated Jhonate before and she seemed particularly motivated. He finished his stretching and walked up to her.

"What are the rules?"

She gave him a puzzled look. "We fight until I say we are finished. If you drop a sword, you must fight on with the other. If you drop both swords I may decide to let you pick them up again."

Justan shook his head and rotated his shoulders, getting in a defensive stance. "I really have missed you."

"Hmph!" she said and came at him.

Her staff whirred and the familiar sound reminded Justan of their days facing off in the dirt of the training grounds. There was a full year of memories; the early ones filled with frustration and anger; the later ones filled with determination, but all of them were fond to him now. But this time there was a difference. Justan was good.

As her staff swept in, his heightened awareness made it seem as if time had slowed. He brought his left sword up to block, his right arm already moving to the place he knew she would strike next.

She worked her staff carefully at first, measuring his reaction and skill, then gradually sped up, sending her staff in at varying angles. "You are much better," she said.

"I had a good trainer," he grunted, barely dodging a determined jab.

She began to pace around him, forcing him to keep turning and watching for new angles. She struck a glancing blow to his forearm that would have knocked the sword from his hands in his training days, but now he had the strength to hold on.

"That stung," he remarked.

"You did not drop it," she replied as she brought the staff down in a vicious overhand swing.

Justan had to bring up both swords to block the attack and saw her kick coming in at the last moment. He brought up his knee to absorb the blow. "You taught me not to drop my sword."

She ducked down and swung her staff low at the back of his leg and Justan jumped, bringing both legs high to avoid it. It was a move he wouldn't have been able to do with out Gwyrtha's agility.

"You are not attacking," she observed, sending in a

double flurry of blows.

"Oh. I can attack, then?" Justan said through gritted teeth as he barely blocked a strike to his knee.

Jhonate stopped and stepped back. The assembled crowd erupted in applause. Justan glanced around and saw that they were surrounded.

Your father is betting against you, Fist sent.

I don't blame him. Justan replied.

"I did not tell you not to attack," Jhonate said with a frown.

"Oh, I guess I was just going by the old rules. You always started out with me on defense," Justan said.

"That is because defense is the first thing a student should learn," she replied, then got in ready stance. "Come at me then."

Justan went at her with a series of alternating jabs and slashes, impressed by her anticipation. He started in on the sword forms Sir Hilt had taught him, going from the simple ones to the more complex. She picked off every stroke. He picked up speed.

"I'm sorry about what happened earlier," he said, jabbing forward with a double thrust.

She spun her staff, deflecting both attacks simultaneously. "I know."

"I mean, it's never been that way between Vannya and I," he said and jumped back to avoid a sweeping counterattack. "I don't know why she kissed me."

"I know," she said and Jhonate went on the offensive again, raining in blows.

Justan was struck in the shoulder and thigh, but he managed not to lose his composure. "If you know, then why were you so angry?"

His left sword smacked the knuckles of her left hand. She winced and jumped back, shaking her hand before shifting her grip as he came on again. "Why should it matter to me if that girl threw herself on you?"

Justan didn't know how to answer that one. It was pretty presumptuous of him to assume she would feel scorned. After all, they hadn't seen each other in a long time and even before that, they had only been friends.

Faldon says she likes you, Fist sent.

Justan faltered and Jhonate's staff caught him across the face at an angle in a wicked blow, smashing his nose and right eye at the same time. The crowd gasped. As he stumbled backwards trying to blink away blurred vision, he realized that she hadn't softened her staff at all.

He kept working his swords defensively, remembering how these things usually went. She would knock the swords out of his hands while he was dazed and sweep his legs out from under him and then he would lay in the dirt hoping his head would stop spinning before she made him get up again.

She knocked his swords aside and he waited for the inevitable match ending blow, but instead he felt her hands on either side of his face.

"Are you okay, Justan? Why did you not block that blow?" Jhonate spread his eyelids open to inspect the damage.

It hurt but he didn't mind. "Fist said something."

Sorry.

"I forgot to pad the staff." She pressed his nose with both thumbs, shifting the cartilage and he let out a yelp of pain. "It is broken. Come, Justan, we should . . ." She paused. "What are you doing?"

Justan realized that he had wrapped his arms around her. He squeezed her close. "Greeting you properly. I-I missed you. I really did."

"I . . ." She hugged him back, pressing her head to the side of his, then froze as she realized the eyes of everyone on them. She withdrew her arms. "Let me go, Sir Edge. People are staring." When he didn't let go immediately, she whispered, "I am not brave enough to kiss you."

Justan let his arms fall from her shoulders, his heart pounding, and smiled despite the way it stretched his swelling face. "That was worth a broken nose."

She picked up her staff and grabbed him by the wrist. "Come, let us get your wound tended to."

"You alright, son?" Faldon called out.

"Oh, I'll be fine," he replied. *Fist, will you grab my swords and bow?*

Okay, Fist replied.

"I am taking him to the infirmary, sir." Jhonate announced.

"Just have him back for the meeting after dinner," Faldon said.

"Yes, sir," she said and pulled him away from the crowd.

An embarrassing loss, Deathclaw said.

Why? Justan replied. *I won.*

Chapter Twenty One

Jhonate dragged Justan past several rows of tents, saying nothing. Justan's vision finally cleared enough to see that her face was red, though whether from exertion or embarrassment he could not tell. Her lips were pursed, her face unreadable.

"Jhonate, I-."

"Just do not say anything right now, Sir Edge," she said. "I must apologize. My conduct back there was inexcusable."

"What do you mean?" Justan asked.

"I did not call you by your proper name and I . . . said something inappropriate."

Now Justan was sure why her face was red. "It's okay. I don't mind at all. I felt the same way. The reason I hugged you so tight back there is because I was afraid to ki-."

She stopped him by placing a rigid forefinger to his lips. It pressed against his nose and he winced. She was breathing heavy and Justan had never seen her look so anxious. "I asked you not to speak, Sir Edge. Before we discuss the proper penance for my behavior, there is something that must be settled."

Justan did not see the need for penance. He wanted her to call him by his real name. There was so much he wanted to say to her, but he kept his mouth shut and let her lead him past more tents.

They came to the large white infirmary tent and Jhonate dragged Justan inside. Multiple rows of cots were lined up but there were only two men in them. Justan was surprised that the infirmary tent was so empty with an army this large. Surely there would be more injuries, even just in the day to day business of traveling. Then he saw Vannya sitting in the corner. The mage was sitting there with her face in her hands and hadn't seen them come in. He looked at Jhonate in surprise, but she just pulled him right towards her.

"Mage Vannya," Jhonate said. "I need you to heal this man."

Vannya looked back at them in irritation but her eyes flew wide when she saw Justan standing there. She ran up to him. "Sir Edge, what happened to your face?"

"Oh, well-."

"She did it to you, didn't she?" Vannya narrowed her eyes at Jhonate. "What did he do, call you by your real name?"

"Sir Edge is allowed to call me by my name," Jhonate replied coolly.

"Oh, I'll bet he is," Vannya said with a glare. "Just hold still, Sir Edge," She placed her hands on either side of Justan's head and pulled his face towards her.

Justan tensed, unsure of what she was going to do, but then her healing spells went to work and he felt that familiar tingling sensation in his nose and eye. His swollen nose opened up and became filled with her flowery scent again.

Justan's mind wandered back to the kiss. He forced the thought away. Jhonate was standing right behind him. Was he crazy?

"There," Vannya said, smiling at him. She released his head and let her hands slide down to rest on his chest. He could feel their warmth through the fabric of his shirt. "You had a broken nose and a burst blood vessel in your eye. I repaired the cartilage and healed the capillaries. You should be fine."

"Thanks, Vannya," Justan said, swallowing.

"You're welcome," she breathed. Even her breath smelled sweet.

Justan felt Jhonate's hand grip the collar of his shirt. She jerked him back and the back of his knees struck the side of the cot behind him. Justan sat clumsily, nearly falling over backwards. He saw the two women exchange scowls and knew he was in big trouble.

"What did you do that for?" Vannya asked.

"Sit down, girl. It is time we discussed our problem," Jhonate said and both of their eyes darted at him. Justan's insides squirmed.

"Alright. Fine then," Vannya said, then she gave Justan an uneasy look. "But do we need to do it right here and now?"

"We do not have time for you to do your hair and bathe again," Jhonate said. "Sir Edge will need to eat before our meeting tonight."

"That's not what I was thinking," Vannya retorted. "Why do you always focus on my hair?"

"I'm not really hungry," Justan said. Food was the last thing on his mind. They ignored him.

"What exactly do you want me to do, Daughter of Xedrion?" Vannya asked.

"Tell Sir Edge why you kissed him," she commanded.

Vannya blushed. "I already tried to explain earlier. I was just happy to see him and I-."

"You did it because I was standing there," Jhonate said.

"I did not!" Vannya protested, but Justan could tell in the way she averted her eyes as she said it that there was at least a little truth in Jhonate's accusation. "I just hoped that he would be just as happy to see me."

When the womens are fighting over you, it is best to leave and let them do it, Fist advised.

He was beginning to regret leaving the bond open all the time. Just how much did they monitor him? *They're not fighting over me.*

Yes they are, said Gwyrtha.

Can you two please not listen to this part? Justan asked. *Besides, I have a feeling Jhonate wouldn't let me leave anyway.* He looked up and realized that Jhonate was staring at him.

"Yes?" he said.

"Go ahead, tell her," Jhonate said, tapping her foot expectantly.

"I'm sorry?"

"Tell her what you told me earlier," Jhonate said.

He looked at Vannya, trying to figure out what it was that Jhonate wanted him to ask. Finally he said, "Vannya, back at the Mage School, we were friends, but we were never . . . involved in that way."

"But," Vannya reached in her robes and pulled out a folded piece of parchment. "In your letter . . ."

Justan frowned, trying to remember what he had written that night as he left the Mage School. Surely he hadn't said anything to suggest he wanted to kiss her. "Well, I was apologizing for being mean. I still feel truly sorry for that, by the way. But that was all there was to it."

Vannya's jaw dropped. "That is not true!" She thrust the letter into Jhonate's hand. "Look, you'll see!"

Jhonate unfolded the parchment and began to read. Her brow furrowed. Then she looked up at Justan and glowered.

"What did I say?" he asked.

"You don't know?" they both asked in unison. Vannya took the letter from Jhonate and handed it to him.

Justan read:

> *Vannya,*
>
> *I owe you an apology and I'm sorry that I cannot tell you in person. Through no fault of yours, I misunderstood the relationship between you and your father. I felt betrayed and as a result I treated you horribly.*
>
> *Tonight I discovered that we are far more alike than I thought. Both of us live our lives in our father's shadow. I feel terrible about the way that I treated you. Please know that I value our friendship. You went out of your way to be kind to me when I had very few friends. You are wonderful and beautiful and precious to me and I hope to make it up to you when I see you again. Please can you forgive me?*
>
> *Justan*

He began to sweat. "I was apologizing."

"But you said that I was precious to you," Vannya said.

"Well, yes, but I didn't mean it like that. I mean there were times that I thought that there could be something between us, but the reason I never did anything about it was Jhonate. I-I . . . she was always in my mind," he said and looked to Jhonate in hopes that she would understand. But the glower hadn't left her face.

"So you liked me, but you liked her more?" Vannya said.

"Then why did you say these things to her, if you were thinking of me?" Jhonate asked.

"Well, she was my friend and I was leaving," Justan said to Jhonate. He looked back at Vannya. "I was in a hurry and . . . I wanted to make you feel better."

"If all you wanted was to make me feel better, why not stop at the apology? Why did you add that line about me being 'wonderful and beautiful and-'?" Vannya's hand flew to her mouth. "You were leaving the possibility open, weren't you? That way if she rejected you, you could come back and try with me."

Justan winced at the hint of truth in her accusation. He shook his head at both of them. "No, it wasn't like that."

Jhonate pursed her lips and threw an arm around Vannya's shoulder. "Come, Vannya. Let us go eat." The mage nodded and with one parting glare, they walked out of the infirmary tent.

Justan stood and went after them. "Come on, you two."

"You can eat with your other friends, Sir Edge," Jhonate said.

Justan watched them walk away, his mind numb.

I told you to leave, Fist said.

Justan sighed.

"What on earth did you say to get those two to act so friendly?"

Justan turned, surprised to find Professor Locksher standing behind him. "I . . . suppose I gave them both something to be mad at."

"Ah, that can happen when dealing with women," Locksher said sagely.

"I woke up this morning wondering if I would see either one of them again and now it feels like I could lose them both," Justan said, reaching up and gripping his hair. "What should I do, professor? Vannya is my friend and I don't want to lose her, but Jhonate . . . she is the one I have feelings for."

"That is a tough one," Locksher agreed. Then when he noticed Justan's expectant look, jumped and said, "Oh! I apologize! I didn't mean to give the impression that I had experience dealing with this kind of situation. Romance is a distraction I have been fortunate enough to avoid."

"Oh," Justan said in disappointment. He watched them round the corner in the distance.

"However I do have that information I found about your frost rune if you have a few moments," Locksher said.

"Of course, professor," Justan said, glad for something to distract him from his other troubles. Maybe he could finally learn why the Scralag was living in his chest.

"Please follow me to my tent and I will show you what I found," the wizard said, leading the way.

Locksher's tent was only a short distance away. Justan noted that it was situated apart from the others as if everyone else gave it a wide berth. The moment the wizard opened his tent flap, Justan understood why.

An unpleasant stench wafted out. It smelled like burnt leaves and spoiled meat. Justan covered his nose as he followed the wizard in. The tent was just as messy as the wizard's apartment in the Mage Tower, but Locksher cleared away a place for Justan to sit.

Justan switched to mage sight and sat down carefully, making sure that he wasn't touching anything. The floor of the tent was littered with magic items. Next to him was a soiled piece of blue cloth that had been draped over a large object on a platter. Justan saw slight movement from the object and felt a little queasy.

Locksher noticed his expression. "Please forgive the

smell. Faldon won't let me keep my experiments in the command tent anymore."

"I can't imagine why," Justan said.

"Well, the search for knowledge isn't always pleasant," Locksher said. The wizard dragged over an oversized pack that was mostly empty and rummaged around inside. He pulled out a ragged-looking book and handed it to Justan.

"The Scralag's book," Justan said. The book was old, its leather binding faded and cracked. The front cover was torn in half. The only words he could make out were the letters 'BO' on one line and what looked like the letter 'A' further down. "Were you able to decipher it?"

"Unfortunately, no," Locksher said. "I took it to the Mage School in Alberri to Wizard Flenn, the foremost expert in Magical Encryption. He studied the book for some time. The kenetosia spell on it was particularly nasty, but he eventually found a way around it. That didn't help much, though. Even when he wasn't vomiting, it was unreadable. The letters just shifted around.

"Flenn is convinced that this book was enchanted by a wizard that wasn't trained in magic ciphers at all. He must have used some sort of personal formula because the book uses a very unique set of spells that don't follow the usual patterns. Flenn thinks it was likely either a private diary or spell book."

"So the entire trip was a dead end?" Justan asked, disappointed.

"Perhaps not. Flenn said that there was likely a key to the book that one had to be in possession of to read it. If we could find the key, we could disable the spells."

"Oh. Well the Scralag didn't give me any key," Justan said. "I don't even remember it giving me the book, really. I just found it shoved down the back of my pants when I finished running away."

"Are you sure?" Locksher asked. "The object wouldn't necessarily look like a key. It could be anything really. Most likely small, something that could be carried around easily and used when reading the book."

Justan shook his head.

Locksher raised a finger. "There is something that might help. The morning we left Reneul, your father took Vannya and I into the Scralag Hills and we were able to find the spot where you described meeting the elemental. Now you said that it stood by a large boulder and pulled something out from under it?"

"I assumed that that was the book," Justan said.

"Well, we found that cluster of boulders you spoke of and under one of them we discovered what I believe to be the remains of the wizard that eventually became the elemental you call the Scralag. It was a crushed skeleton that had been there for decades. It was wearing what was, as close as we could tell in its deteriorated condition, once a blue wizard's robe. In what was left of a pocket we found these."

Locksher reached into his robes and pulled out a small pair of wire spectacles. "The lenses were cracked, but I was able to repair them."

Justan picked up the spectacles and examined them. The frames were square and the lenses themselves fairly thin. The right one had a round hole carved out of the center of it large enough to poke a finger through. Justan looked at them with his mage sight.

"There's barely any magic to them at all," Justan said. "Did you try to read the book with them?"

"Of course. That was the first thing I tried, but there is no effect. I have examined the magic in them as well, but there is no rhyme or reason to it, almost as if they were part of an unfinished spell. This made me think that perhaps the key we are looking for would be small and round, maybe the missing piece of that lens. Perhaps if it were put together, we could read your book. Does that jog your memory?" Locksher asked hopefully.

"No. I'm sorry. There wasn't anything else that it gave me, not-." Justan grimaced. "Not unless it did give me something and I dropped it in my hurry to get away."

Locksher's face sank. "Well that is unfortunate, because I searched the place for magic and there wasn't any trace of it other than what's in these spectacles."

"Well in regards to the Scralag itself, the reason you weren't able to find a trace of it is because it isn't there any longer," Justan said. He pulled up his shirt and tapped his fingers on the rune. "It's here inside my chest. Master Coal says it's bonded to me just as much as Fist or Gwyrtha."

Locksher's eyebrow rose. "I must know more."

Justan told him about the fight with the bandham and how the Scralag had appeared and defeated it.

"You know, this information may have helped earlier in the conversation, Sir Edge," Locksher said. "The elemental itself would likely have the answers you seek. Have you tried to communicate with it since it re-entered your chest?"

Justan sighed. "Yes, but the barrier across our bond has reformed. I can't get through it unless I try to unravel the spell again and the last time I did that, I watched it eat Kenn's frozen heart in front of me."

"Well, you may have no choice if you want the answers to the questions you seek. I would go ahead and have you do it now, but you make a good point. We can't have a frost elemental roaming around the camp freezing people." Locksher frowned thoughtfully. "How about this? When this battle is over, come to the Mage School and you and I will go to the Magic Testing Center together and unleash the thing in a safe environment. Perhaps then, we'll solve your mystery."

Justan smiled with relief. "Thank you, Professor Locksher. That would be a great help."

"Very good," the wizard said. "Now we only have a short time until Faldon's meeting. We should head over there."

"Okay, but before we go, I must ask you." Justan pointed to the soiled blue cloth. "What on earth is under that? There has been movement under there ever since we've been talking."

"Ah, now that is an interesting thing," Locksher said and lifted the cloth away.

Underneath was the rotting head of a monster. It was emaciated, its greenish skin barely stretched across the bones of its skull. Yet it still seemed alive. Its beady eyes, shriveled and half decayed, rotated in its sockets and its large toothy mouth hung open, the jaws moving slowly back and forth while a long withered tongue lolled around on the platter beneath it, trailing a thick slime.

"What is that?" Justan asked in disgust.

"Ah, fascinating, isn't it?" Locksher said with a grin. "That is the head of a modified troll."

"Modified?" Justan asked, grimacing at the grisly trophy.

"Yes, the mother of the moonrats began throwing these creatures at us when we were harrying her caravans in the mountains. Nasty things. Completely inflammable. Not only that, but they are resistant to the effects of pepper."

"Pepper, sir?"

"Oh, that's right, you wouldn't have heard. The pepper discovery is a recent one. Pepper is poisonous to trolls. It halts their ability to regenerate and kills them if you give them a large enough dose. However to these modified trolls, pepper only stops their regeneration. It doesn't deteriorate their cell structure at all."

"But that thing is barely alive at all. It's rotting," Justan said.

"Ah yes, well that's because it's starving," Locksher said. "Right now as it is just a head, it has no means by which to digest any food. That's why I'm keeping it here, you see, to see how long it continues to live without sustenance. It is quite amazing, really. Speeding up the regeneration rate of the troll should have also rapidly increased its metabolism. It should have wasted away long ago."

"How long have you had it?" Justan asked.

"Oh, several weeks. It is quite fascinating how efficient it is. A normal troll has a metabolism so high it will die of starvation in a single week without food. It's the only reason that the whole land hasn't been overrun with them."

Justan looked at it more closely and switched to his mage sight, then spirit sight. "Professor, this troll was transformed by Ewzad Vriil."

"By Ewzad Vriil, you say?" Locker raised an eyebrow. "And how do you know this?"

Justan told Locksher of the Rings of Stardeon and how Ewzad Vriil used them to transform creatures. "But what worries me with this one is that it isn't acting like the rest of his creations. They usually melt away once slain."

"Ah, I see," Locksher said. "As their spirit leaves the body, the transformations have nothing left to power them and the whole process unravels. Fascinating!"

"Master Coal also says that a creature transformed by the Rings of Stardeon will eventually die unless the magic is constantly charged by the power of the rings," Justan said.

"Very strange. I wonder why they are holding together."

Justan began to worry. If Ewzad Vriil had figured out the secret to keeping his beasts alive, he had become far more dangerous. "Did this troll by any chance have the heart of a dragon?"

Locksher gave him a quizzical look. "No, I examined it thoroughly. Its cell structure was changed to make it larger and faster, but its heart was still a troll heart."

"Do trolls have blood magic?" Justan asked.

"Not in the traditional sense, though I can see how blood magic could be a catalyst to help stabilize magic changes. A very astute question, I'm impressed, Sir Edge," Locksher said. "But no, the only beings with blood magic are Elves, Dwarves, Gnomes, and Dragons. However, a troll's sheer regenerative ability and metabolism may act as a substitute, keeping the changes from weakening."

"I just had a frightening thought, professor," Justan said.

"Oh?"

"How many of these creatures have you fought?" he asked.

"Jhonate defeated four of them herself. We had to completely incinerate their bodies to kill them," Locksher replied.

"What would have happened if instead of killing it, she had cut it up in tiny pieces?"

"Each piece would eventually grow into another troll as long as it had enough food to sustain its growth," Locksher said.

"But would the new trolls be regular trolls or modified trolls?" Justan asked.

"I don't know." Locksher said, then swallowed, "I see your concern, but that shouldn't be possible. By the very laws of magic, there has to be a give and take. In order to both increase the regeneration rate for these trolls and at the same time decrease their metabolism, it would take a fantastic amount of energy. That may be supplied by Stardeon's rings, but I don't see how that could be maintained through multiple generations of trolls."

Justan shrugged grimly. "Nevertheless, we need to consider the possibility that Ewzad Vriil is growing an army of modified trolls out there somewhere."

Chapter Twenty Two

"First I must say how pleasing it is to see the sheer number of people we have gathered together," Faldon said, his gaze sweeping across the representatives of each group that stood in the command tent. "I believe that with the force assembled here, we have enough manpower to disrupt the besieging army and scatter them back into the mountains."

There were mixed grunts around the room, some in agreement, others with apprehension.

Jhonate stole a glance at Justan. Her heart thumped and she quickly turned her eyes away. He was still watching her. He had been doing so ever since they entered the command tent.

When she had seen him ride into camp earlier that day on his monster mount, her heart had nearly stopped altogether. He looked so different from the boy that had left her standing at the southern entrance to Reneul. He was taller and more muscular and his face had filled out some. She had been worried that perhaps he had changed too much. But then he had walked towards her, the look in his eyes had reminded her so much of the old Justan. Then that girl had kissed him.

She looked at Vannya and noticed that the mage was still steadfastly resisting the urge to look at him. It bothered Jhonate that the girl had a stronger willpower than she did. They had promised each other earlier that they would ignore him for a while.

Vannya had assured her that silence was the best way to punish a boy that misbehaved. Jhonate didn't completely understand but she knew it would be torture if Justan refused to speak with her, so she had agreed. They had waited until the others had entered the tent and then Jhonate had gone to stand with the other students while Vannya stood by Locksher. Neither of them acknowledged Justan, who stood by Master Coal and their bonded.

"Right now it may seem like we know little of what we are facing," Faldon said. "But gaining that knowledge is the purpose of our meeting tonight. I want to go around to each group and share what we know about the enemy. I believe that divided amongst our separate groups are all the pieces of the puzzle we need."

The meeting lasted into the night. Faldon started things off, telling the others of their discoveries in the mountains and Jhonate's revelations regarding the mother of the moonrats. He then asked Captain Demetrius to speak.

The captain told them about the state of affairs in Dremald. The city had been locked down, only merchants being allowed to come and go. The nobles were restless, upset at being kept in their estates, and the people were frightened and angry. Queen Elise was the only thing keeping the city together, making constant appearances and giving speeches regarding the enemy threat that could fall upon them at any moment.

Then there was Lord Protector Vriil, secretive and dangerous, quick to accuse people of treason. His men walked the streets doing as they wished, sometimes ripping men or women from their families, arresting them without giving reasons.

The garrison was held close, camped around the city, told only that they were there to protect Dremald from an unknown foreign menace. Everyone had heard of the academy's predicament but most were unable to help since any soldier that left would be charged with treason.

The soldiers that had been willing to risk it had already left to join Demetrius' force, but it was unlikely that they would see any more. Most of the men in the garrison had family in Dremald and the word had been passed around that the families of the deserters were gathered up and held in the dungeons.

Master Coal then spoke of their journey from Razbeck and what they had learned about Ewzad Vriil and his magic rings. Jhonate was impressed with Justan's accomplishments and everything he had overcome. It took enormous effort on her part not to stare at him. Master Coal then spoke of the army blocking the way to the Mage School and the deterioration of the protected road through the Tinny Woods.

Faldon spoke of the need for solidarity and outlined the plan he had been working on with Captain Demetrius. They would pass through the back entrance to Wobble and stage their army in the caverns while they launched a series of raids and disrupted the besieging army. With Master Coal's bonded inside the school, they could coordinate attacks with the academy and eventually drive the goblinoids back into the mountains.

Once the academy was free, they could head back to Dremald. Captain Demetrius assured them that the garrison would change to their side as soon as they knew they would be able to keep their families safe. The city would fall easily at that point and once they had deposed the queen and gotten rid of Ewzad Vriil, they would be able to help the Mage School.

This was where the disagreement began. Sir Lance argued that they should go and free Sampo first and clear the path to the Mage School. Once that was accomplished they could return to Dremald with the might of the wizards behind them. Master Coal was in agreement with that plan.

Captain Demetrius objected and finally Faldon tabled the discussion. They would meet again and decide their final course of action once the Battle Academy had been freed. Their one remaining problem was finding the entrance to the back way to Wobble. So far their dwarven helpers had been unable to find it.

"I know where the dag-gum entrance is," said Justan's dwarf friend from the back of the tent. "Whoever yer dwarves are, they probly ain't been there in years. Old Stangrove was clever when he hid it. I'll tell you what. Pack up in the mornin' and I'll lead you through to the caves."

"Thank you, Lenui," Faldon said. "That is exactly what we'll do. Gentlemen, let your people know to pack up their tents first thing in the morning. We'll travel to the caves and meet once again to discuss tactics once our scouts have had time to look at the enemy positions."

Everyone began talking amongst each other. Jhonate glanced over and saw that Justan was talking with Master Coal. She took the opportunity to sneak out of the tent, staying behind some of the others so that he would not see her leave. Once she had reached the safety of the night, Jhonate jogged towards the training area, constantly checking behind her to make sure Justan hadn't followed.

She stood underneath the large tree on the edge of the training area and paced, unsure what to do next. She and Vannya had not gotten very far in their plan. How long was she supposed to ignore Justan before he learned his lesson and then how was she supposed to make sure that Vannya didn't try to take him for herself?

Jhonate finally turned and began to climb the tree, searching for a thick branch that she could sit on and still have a clear view of the ground below while she meditated. She saw an ideal branch but when she climbed towards it, her hands closed on something warm and scaled.

She drew her hand back in alarm and looked up into the face of a reptilian man. It had been sitting so still, she hadn't noticed it before. Its eyes were large and round in the darkness, his mouth lined with razor sharp teeth. It hissed and climbed further up the tree.

Jhonate focused the tip of her staff to a spear-like point and jabbed up at it, certain that it was a spy for the witch. It deftly dodged her attacks, using the trunk and other branches to its advantage.

Jhonate snorted. The creature was nimble, but she was born in a forest. Even with her staff in one hand, she was confident that she would corner it soon.

"Jhonate wait!" came a deep bass voice from below.

She glanced down to see a large ogre standing below the tree, breathing heavily peering up at her. It was Justan's bonded, Fist.

"Oh, sorry, I meant Ma'am," he said. "That is Deathclaw in the tree above you. He is one of us, Justan's bonded."

She looked back up at the reptilian creature. Justan had

bonded with such strange things. She removed her staff and said, "I am sorry for attacking you."

It chirped back at her.

"Deathclaw does not talk very often," Fist explained. "That's why he asked me to come and talk to you. He doesn't have lips and his tongue is different. Justan has been practicing with him, but it is not easy."

Jhonate climbed down to the lowest branch and hopped down to stand in front of the ogre. His movements were quite humanlike. "You speak very well, Fist."

The ogre's face split into a wide grin. "I have been practicing. Justan teaches me new words every day and I can even read and write."

"I am impressed," she said.

"Thank you, Ma'am," he said.

"You can call me Daughter of Xedrion," she said.

"Oh," Fist said. "But can I call you Ma'am anyway? Justan remembers calling you that."

"If you wish," she said. This ogre was quite interesting. "So why are you here?"

"Deathclaw called out to me through the bond," Fist explained. "He was worried that he would have to hurt you and Justan would be very mad at him if he did that."

"You two can speak together through this bond as well?" she asked. Locksher had told her about the bonding magic Justan had, but he knew very little about how it worked.

"Justan can make it so we can talk to each other," Fist says. "He leaves it open most of the time now."

"So you can speak with him too? Just with your thoughts?"

"Yes and we can see each others memories and feel each others feelings," Fist explained.

Jhonate blinked. Such fascinating magic. It seemed similar to her bond with her staff. "What is Ju-, Sir Edge doing now?"

"He was coming this way but the girl Vannya has stopped

him."

"She has?" Jhonate said. She gripped her staff tightly.

"Yes. Vannya is talking to Justan right now." Fist said.

"That liar," Jhonate said under her breath. She should have known Vannya would betray her. "What is she saying?"

"She is asking him if he really meant what he said in his letter," Fist said.

Jhonate frowned. "And what did he say in reply?"

"He did," Deathclaw remarked from the branches above. The beast's voice was strained and whispery.

Fist frowned up at the creature. "What Justan said was that he meant every word he wrote. Their friendship is very important to him," Fist clarified. "She then asked him if he really thought she was beautiful."

"I will smack her if she does not back off," Jhonate said.

"She gets closer. He likes her scent," Deathclaw remarked.

"He does?" That Vannya with all her primping. Jhonate began to feel sick to her stomach.

"Yes," said Fist shooting a glower into the trees. "But there is one scent he likes more."

"There is?" Jhonate sat down at the base of the tree and drew up her legs, wrapping her arms around her knees. She twisted the ring on her finger once more, feeling the urge to hurl it away into the darkness.

"He carries a letter with him always," Fist said. "Inside there are green ribbons. Some times at night he cups them in his hands and presses them to his nose. The scent is faint but it is his favorite scent in the world."

She clutched her hand to her chest, tears forming in her eyes. He had kept the ribbons. When she had sent the letter, she had debated against such a personal and bold message. She hadn't understood why she had wanted to do it. It had been so important to her at the time.

Why was the man able to both infuriate her and endear himself to her so easily?

"It is a warrior's scent," Deathclaw said from above. "Your scent."

"She knows that," Fist remarked in irritation.

"What is Mage Vannya doing now?" Jhonate asked.

Fist looked hesitant.

"Tell me," she said.

Fist winced and said, "She says that she enjoyed their kiss."

"I will kill her," Jhonate growled, jumping to her feet.

"But Justan says that she must stop what she is trying to do. He wants to be her friend, but it cannot be if she continues to act this way." Fist said. "He is angry because it was his first kiss and she had not given him a choice."

"Why didn't he slap her?" Jhonate asked. "Tell him to slap her."

"He says no," Deathclaw said from above, sounding disappointed.

"Deathclaw! Now he is angry with us," Fist said.

"What did he say?" she asked.

"Deathclaw told him that you wanted him to slap her and he closed off the bond so I can't hear," Fist said. The ogre grimaced. "Now he is coming this way."

"I see," Jhonate backed up until she felt the wood of the tree trunk against her back. "Goodnight, Fist. Goodnight, Deathclaw."

"Wait, Ma'am," the ogre said, but Jhonate did not stay.

She ran to her tent and slipped inside. She laid on her bedroll fully clothed, her heart racing. Jhonate bit her lip and waited, worried that Justan would follow and ask her to come out and speak with him,

Jhonate was afraid to face him at that moment. She knew that she would be unable to control herself. There were certain proprieties to be observed, certain rules to be obeyed. If he spoke to her again that night, she might kiss him herself just as Vannya had and if she did that, she would lose all discipline. That was unacceptable.

A half hour passed and he did not come. Part of her was relieved, but part of her was disappointed. Then Vannya didn't arrive and she began to worry. What if Vannya was with Justan? What if he had changed his mind? Perhaps she should go and find him herself.

Jhonate sat up and crossed her legs, forcing her mind into a meditative state. She forced the fears and worries away and relaxed in the calm whiteness. She walked into her mind's library and looked up the memories of her time training Justan, remembering what it was that had so endeared him to her back then.

Slowly she drifted off to sleep and dreamt and in her dreams Justan kissed her over and over again, but her father found out and came after them, sending an army to track them down.

Chapter Twenty Three

Justan awoke that morning sore and exhausted. He couldn't remember his dreams, but they left him feeling uneasy. He had spent the night tossing and turning, wondering what he should say to Jhonate in the morning. He was still angry with Fist and Deathclaw for butting in and telling Jhonate about his conversation with Vannya, but he was relieved that he had said the right things to the mage. She had laid the charm on really thick and it had been very tempting.

His first instinct when he had arrived at the tree had been to chase after Jhonate but after Fist showed him how their conversation had gone, he had decided against it. She didn't want to talk to him right then and though that was painful, he was pretty sure Jhonate was angry with Vannya, not him and that had to be enough.

He reached for Gwyrtha through the bond and asked for some extra energy. She gave it to him and greeted him with her mental version of sloppy good morning kisses. When he still didn't jump up right away, she appeared at his side and nudged him, rolling him off of his bedroll.

Up! Up!

Justan laughed out loud and that uneasy feeling left him. He scratched Gwyrtha behind the ears and got dressed. He and his bonded had camped with Coal's just a short distance from Faldon's army. People were up and walking around and he could hear the sounds of tents being taken down.

He prodded Fist. "Time to wake up."

Fist groaned and Squirrel, who had been curled up in a ball on the ogre's chest, sat up and shook an angry fist at him.

Justan passed some of Gwyrtha's energy on to the ogre for good measure, and Gwyrtha gave a great lick to the side of the ogre's head that left all the hair on that side sticking straight up.

Up, Fist!

"Okay, Gwyrtha. I'm up!" Fist said in irritation, frowning as he wiped her slobber off his large face.

"We need to get our things together," Justan said as he quickly rolled up his bedroll and put his belongings away. "Lenny is leading us into the crevasse this morning and I want to be there to see how the dwarves hid it."

Gwyrtha let out a mental shout of excitement and Justan turned to see her rush over and nudge a familiar figure.

"Hi, Gwyrtha, good to see you," said Zambon with a smile as he rubbed her mane. "Good morning, Edge!"

Justan clasped arms with the man. "When did you get back? I had hoped to see you last night."

"Yeah, we got back late," Zambon explained. "We still didn't find the stupid pass. Those dwarves I was with had heard of the back way to Wobble, but none of them had used it themselves. I didn't find out you were here until this morning."

Fist walked up and patted the guard on the back. "Hello, Tamboor's son!"

"Hello, Fist. Glad to see you're looking well." The guard gave his weapon an admiring glance. "That is one wicked looking mace."

"I know! Lenny made it for me. It's magic!" Fist said. "You are wearing Tamboor's sword?"

Justan noticed the hilt of Tamboor's legendary sword Meredith protruding from Zambon's back. He had seen his father spar against that sword many times as a child. "Didn't Lenny make you a sword?" Justan asked.

"I carry Meredith for my father when he isn't heading into battle. Her magic increases emotion and toughness, which is perfect for a berserker, but he is already too full of anger," Zambon said candidly. "I try not to speak of it to others, but . . . it was hard for him to function when he carried her in his hands. My sword Elise on the other hand heals and seems to make him feel better. Carrying it helps him control himself."

"Do you think he's getting better, Zambon?" Justan asked.

"Maybe," Zambon replied. "But it's hard to tell. He still hasn't said more than three words to me since we left Vriil's castle."

"I'm sorry to hear that," Justan said. "Maybe when this war is over he'll be able to heal."

"I hope so," Zambon said, though he didn't look very confident in his father's chances. The guard changed the subject. "So are Lenny and Qyxal around? I have something for them."

Justan swallowed. "That's right. You wouldn't have heard. I . . . I'm sorry. Qyxal was killed in a fight with one of Ewzad's monsters. We're bringing his remains back to his people."

"Oh . . . that's horrible," Zambon said, his eyes downcast. "He was a good friend."

"Ah! No! I forgot to tell Vannya!" Justan said, bringing one hand to his mouth. "Oh, that's going to be bad. They were close. She'll need me to hug her."

Zambon gave him a puzzled look. "I can think of worse things."

"You don't know what I've been going through with her since we've arrived," Justan said.

Zambon nodded in understanding. "Let me guess. It has to do with the Daughter of Xedrion, right?"

"Yes!" Justan said.

"I was going to warn you about those two. They questioned me about you several times and I knew you were heading for trouble."

"Vannya kissed him," Fist said.

"No way," Zambon said with a laugh.

"Yeah. First thing when I walked into camp," Justan said.

"What did the Daughter of Xedrion do?"

"She broke his nose with her staff," Fist said and laughed along with Zambon.

"It wasn't quite that simple," Justan said. He saw Master Coal walking towards the camp and called out, "Master Coal!"

The wizard turned and approached them with a tired smile. "Good morning, Edge."

"Good morning, Master," Justan said. "Um, do you know where Lenny is?"

"He and Bettie left with the other dwarves a little while ago to speak with your father," the wizard said.

"Oh, we're running late," Justan said. "Did you hear anything new from Willum last night?"

"Well, your mother is very happy that you are back together with your father," Coal said. "Willum says that she wants me to tell you all the regular mother to son things again, and I have a slightly inappropriate message she wants delivered to your father."

"You don't need to tell me that part," Justan said.

Coal chuckled. "Yes, well she and Willum have made little progress tracking down the traitor. Willum is keeping an eye on the council assistants while your mother has been watching the Council members themselves for any odd behavior. I did give them the information about the moonrat eyes and they have a better idea of what to look out for now so maybe they'll find out something soon."

"Are we close enough yet that you can link with Willum without waiting until night time?" Justan asked.

"Almost. I should be able to stay in constant contact with him once we reach Wobble," Coal said.

"Having a bonded inside the academy is going to be really useful when the fighting begins," Zambon said.

"Master Coal," Justan said. "This is my friend Zambon. I've told you about him before. He's Tamboor the Fearless' son."

"Ah, yes," Coal said and shook Zambon's hand. "Well shall we go? Bettie says that they are already heading to the secret entrance."

They rushed up the path Lenny and Faldon had taken. The trail ran right up to a sheer cliff wall, then meandered along the base of it. The ground around them was littered with boulders and Justan found it hard not to stare up the whole time looking for falling rocks. When they caught up with the others, Lenny was leading the way, talking to Faldon and Locksher as he walked. Justan looked around, but Jhonate was nowhere in sight.

"Now," Lenny was saying. "Once we get inside a couple miles, the path narrows up to 'bout seven foot. Too tight fer some wagons, so we're gonna have to leave the wider ones behind. There's a dag-gum big cave just inside the entrance that's been hollowed out so's you can leave 'em there, but I can't guarantee they'll still be there if y'all want to come back fer 'em later. Us dwarves usually just take 'em or leave 'em as we come through."

"Some of the families won't like that," said Sir Lance, who was walking closely behind them. "Many of them brought precious belongings they didn't want to leave behind."

"Well ain't durn much we can do 'bout that," Lenny said. "Some things could be okay. Hand carts and the like, but just remember the seven foot rule. We got too many folks comin' through to have to stop'n turn everybody 'round cuz some stubborn folks want to bring gall-durn heirlooms."

"How much further is it?" Faldon asked.

"Perty close. We're almost there."

"I don't see how it could be," Zambon said. "We were all over this area yesterday. It's just a solid cliff wall the whole way."

"You'll see why," Lenny said with a grin. "It's somethin' special."

Lenny stopped a short time later and turned to look at the base of the cliff.

"Why are we stopped here?" Faldon asked.

"This here's the entrance," Lenny said, kicking some rocks away from the wall.

"What are we supposed to do," grumbled Sir Lance. "Climb it?"

"Just watch, you gall-durn ornery cuss!" The dwarf got down low to the ground, planted his shoulder against the rock, and gave it a shove. There was a groaning noise from inside the rock and a section of the cliff face about ten-feet-wide and eight-feet-tall swung inward and upward. "See!" he said, his voice echoing into the tunnel beyond. "Old Stangrove Leatherbend was a genius!"

"You must me kidding me," Justan said, his mouth hanging open. Inside the opening was a dark tunnel about twenty feet deep but he could see light and open space on the other side.

Locksher laughed out loud and darted inside, casting a light spell so that he could see the mechanism behind the door. "As I thought! It's done with counterweights. Your Stangrove was a genius indeed."

"That's right," Lenny said. "That rock slab's gall-durn heavy, but it opens so easy a single dwarf could open it by himself. And yet if'n you needed to, you could disable the weights and a hunnerd men couldn't move it."

"Amazing," Justan said as he walked into the tunnel. He ran his hand along the rock and felt the tiny ridges left behind by what ever tool the dwarves had used to carve the walls. He couldn't tell how it had been done. "Sandstone. This area sure has a strange mix of rock."

"Alright!" Lenny shouted. "Come on through. Pall and Rahbbie're bringin' up the rear so's they'cn shut the door once everybody's in!"

The word went out and the long procession started. The plan was for Faldon's troops to head in first, followed by the people of Sampo. Captain Demetrius' cavalry would ride in last.

Justan walked out of the tunnel and stared up in amazement. The passage Lenny had called a crevasse was a narrow canyon that ran like a long crack through the plateau high above. The floor of the canyon was flat and slightly sandy but well cleared of debris, perfect to travel down.

Fist and Gwyrtha entered right behind him, the ogre staring up with a wide grin, just as amazed as he was. Deathclaw on the other hand, had a different route in mind. As people began pouring through the tunnel into the passage beyond, Justan sensed that the raptoid had just finished climbing the cliff face. Justan looked up and caught just a brief glimpse of Deathclaw's head peering down from the top of the plateau high above.

Lenny and Faldon led the way and Justan told Fist and Gwyrtha to go on ahead with them. He would catch up later. He stepped back and let people pass, trying to keep an eye out for Jhonate. He was hoping to talk to her as they traveled, but she was nowhere to be seen. He waited for some time, wondering if she had deliberately snuck by.

I see her. She is not far ahead, sent Deathclaw and Justan saw the image of her trotting up to join her academy friends.

Thank you. Justan smiled. *How are you doing up there?*

It is high, the raptoid replied. *But I will not fall. There are no sign of enemies up here.*

Justan trotted up the line, passing people until he saw the familiar line of her staff ahead. He edged between two horses and saw her walking next to Jobar and Poz, staring up at the edges of the cliffs on either side of the trail. Her eyes narrowed and Justan wondered if she had seen Deathclaw's head peering over the top. He trotted up behind her and only Poz saw him coming. The freckled warrior gave Justan an encouraging nod.

"Hello, Jhonate," he said, startling her.

"Why that has to be the first time I've seen her jump," Poz said with a boyish smile.

Jhonate sent a frown the student's way, then turned her eyes on Justan and said coolly, "Good morning, Sir Edge."

Justan moved up beside her. "I've been thinking on what you said yesterday and I have made a decision."

"Regarding what?" she asked.

"Your penance," Justan said. "For your inappropriate behavior."

"Why don't you just leave her alone?" Jobar growled protectively. "It's obvious she's trying to avoid you."

"I don't have time for you, Jobar," Justan said, his eyes not leaving Jhonate's. Her cheeks had gone red.

Jobar took a step towards him, his hands balled into fists, but Jhonate swung her staff in the student's way. "What do you propose?"

"If I remember correctly," Justan said. "My trainer used to make me run laps around the training grounds when she felt I needed correcting."

"I see," she said.

"I spoke to Lenny earlier and he said that the route to the caves is about eight miles long. That means we have about seven to go. I think that should be enough for someone with your strengths, don't you?"

She raised an eyebrow. "That could be dangerous, running around all these horses."

Something Jhonate often used to tell him came to mind. "If I did not think you could handle it, I would not tell you to do it."

A smile touched her lips. "Very well, Sir Edge."

Justan began to run forward. "Then come, Jhonate. I suggest you get going. You wouldn't want me to add another mile."

"Hmph!" she said and took off after him.

Justan ran past several of Faldon's men, old academy veterans carrying loaded packs, trying to see how long he could stay ahead of her. She was right behind him. He could hear her hastily mumbled "excuse me"s to the men as she ran past. He darted around some heavily laden horses, grateful that they were well-trained, but the next thing he knew, Jhonate was right beside him.

"Are we going to continue at this slow pace?" she asked. "Or are you a better runner than you used to be?"

Justan chuckled. "How fast can you go?"

"We shall see if you keep up," she replied and sped ahead.

Justan followed behind her with a grin. He had never seen Jhonate run like this. She ran leaning forward, her arms hanging loose at her side, her staff clutched in one hand. He had forgotten she had been raised in the forest, but it was easy to see in her movements. Jhonate moved with fluid grace, dodging people and animals with ease as if they were trees standing still.

He was hard pressed to stay with her, his strides not quite

so fluid as hers. It was kind of embarrassing. He had thought that his practice racing Deathclaw had made him a lot better.

You think wrong, Justan, said Deathclaw and Justan knew the raptoid was running along the plateau above, keeping pace with them.

What do you mean? he asked.

You see the running as a game, the raptoid replied. *This is why I always defeat you. This is no game. This is a battle.*

"A battle . . ." Justan tried to wrap his mind around what Deathclaw meant. Was he saying he wasn't trying hard enough?

She understands, your Jhonate, Deathclaw said. *Watch her. She does not run like she is trying to be faster. She runs like a hunter.*

Justan watched her more closely and saw what Deathclaw meant. The way she ran kept all the pressure on the balls of her feet, allowing her to change directions quickly and the way her arms hung lose at her side allowed her to keep her staff parallel to the ground, ready to strike at any time.

He attempted to emulate her posture, but it didn't feel quite right; he was a little off balance, a little awkward. He lurched around one man and bumped him, causing the man to stagger. "Sorry!"

Now you try to act like it is a battle, Deathclaw said. *Don't just act. Think like it is a battle. Breathe in your surroundings like you would if an enemy was before you.*

Justan began to understand. When he was in battle, his senses were sharper. Everything was much clearer. He thought back to the night he faced Talon and tried to recapture that sense of awareness. He felt a tiny click within his mind and time seemed to slow. The people, the horses, they all moved like they were underwater. Everything but Jhonate. Only she was at one with the air around her.

Justan joined her fluid weaving, aware of each part of his body's relation to the space around it, careful not to touch the living obstacles in his path, acting as if any contact would cause injury. He gained ground and soon he was at her heels.

As they neared the seven-foot-wide squeeze Lenny had

warned of, the crevasse narrowed around them. The people they passed slowed, walking closer together and the path became even more difficult to navigate. Soon the people and horses walked in single file.

Good, said Deathclaw. *You near the end of the human line. Once you pass them, the way will be clear.*

Justan was having trouble finding a place to pass Jhonate, but he finally saw the opening he was looking for. She was coming up on a large warhorse as it approached the seven-foot gap of the narrows. He darted forward, forcing her to the right, the horse's wide rear end blocking her path. Justan surged ahead and as he passed its left flank, the horse moved to the side as it was trained, nearly brushing the cliff wall.

There was no gap for Jhonate to squeeze through, but she didn't slow. She dove between the horse's rear legs, her staff held out in front of her, keeping her body low to the ground and making sure that no part of her body touched the horse.

Justan passed the horse, proud that he had finally pulled ahead and was surprised when, out of the corner of his eye, he saw Jhonate dart out from between the horse's front legs right next to him. The horse reared and his driver swore, but Justan and Jhonate continued on. He promised himself to return to the man and apologize later.

The way opened up a bit and they ran past Justan's bonded. Fist waved and Gwyrtha wanted to follow but Justan asked her to stay back with the ogre. Then they finally reached the front of the line.

"Father . . . Lenny . . . Bettie." Justan said as he sped by.

"Slow down, dag-blast it!" Lenny called out.

"Beat her!" shouted Bettie.

"Don't let my son show you up, Jhonate!" Faldon shouted.

Justan and Jhonate were in the open. Despite the narrowness of the crevasse, there were no more obstacles in their way. It was just the two of them side by side. Justan looked over at her and smiled. She smiled back.

"Nice move through that horse's legs!" he said.

"You seem to have lost your awkward gait," she replied.

"I outgrew it!" Justan said. "And you, I've never seen you run like this. Is it new?"

"You were always too slow to see it!" she said.

"You're so graceful, even Deathclaw is impressed."

Her eyes glanced to the top of the cliffs above. "He keeps pace with us?"

"He finds it a challenge," Justan said. "There are more obstacles up there."

"Then let us make it more difficult for him."

Jhonate picked up speed and Justan matched her stride for stride. Finally, he felt Deathclaw's frustration as rock formations got in his way, forcing the raptoid to run around. He laughed. "We are pulling away!"

She gave him a curious smile. "What? Have you never beaten him before?"

"Not in a foot race!" he replied.

This does not count, Deathclaw complained. *You have the advantage of terrain.*

There are unfair advantages often in battle, Justan replied. *A leader recognizes this and takes the better path.*

Deathclaw gave a disgusted snort.

They ran on for a time, neither speaking, just enjoying each other's company. Then Jhonate edged close and nudged Justan's shoulder with her own. Justan stumbled to the side a ways, then nudged her back. She stumbled a bit herself, barking out a laugh.

Justan reached out and grasped her hand.

They slowed down slightly and she looked down at his hand, her cheeks reddening. "What is this?"

"I'm holding your hand," Justan said. They continued to run, though they slowed a bit more. She looked away, blinking and he asked, "Do you want me to let go?"

"No," she replied quickly.

Soon they were just moving along at a slight jog and Justan began to walk.

"Wait," she said. "We need to keep running. My penance-."

"There is no penance needed," Justan said. "I just wanted to be alone with you for a while. I wanted to talk."

"Alone? Even from your bonded?" she asked softly and Justan knew she was thinking of the way they had monitored his talk with Vannya.

"I have closed my side of the connection," he said. "We are truly alone. They cannot hear."

"I see," she said and then they were just walking, holding hands. "This is . . . enjoyable."

"Jhonate, I'm sorry about before and . . . and everything that happened with Vannya."

"Do not mention her, please," she said.

"Sorry."

"Do not apologize either. It is not your fault. You and I had not made promises and . . . you did nothing wrong. I . . . it is just that I never-." Jhonate shook her head. "Sir Edge, why did you give me the ring?"

"It . . . I wanted to give you something. You had given me so much and-." Justan swallowed. "You were dear to me. You had become my best friend, and it was the most valuable thing I had to give. I wanted you to have something to remember me by."

Her hand gripped his more tightly, but she kept her face turned away, unwilling to look at his eyes. "And why didn't you tell me about its magic?"

"I wasn't sure if the magic worked. Anyway, wouldn't you have refused it if I had?" he asked.

"I did not ask you to protect me," she said.

"I wanted to anyway," he explained. "Besides, it's only fair. Your gifts have protected me more times than I can count. Your training kept me alive and the bow defeated foes I would have had no chance against otherwise."

"Still . . ."

Justan let go of her hand and grasped her shoulders. He

turned her to face him, but her eyes still avoided his. His voice rose. "You don't understand. I've never felt this way before, Jhonate. Not about anyone! All these months we've been apart and I haven't gone a day without you being on my mind-."

She knocked his hands away and grabbed the front of his shirt in her fists, then pushed him backwards, slamming him into the chasm wall. She leaned in close, her eyes inches from his, her face trembling with emotion.

"Stop right now. I cannot take this. Just tell me, Sir Edge," her mouth worked as she struggled to get the words out. "Do you wish to court me?"

Justan blinked in surprise, his jaw slack. He saw fear welling in her eyes and somewhere in his brain a voice shouted at him not to hesitate.

"Yes," he blurted.

She sighed, the tension leaving her body. She leaned forward onto him, her head resting against his chest. He slowly brought his arms up around her and held her close. He wasn't exactly sure what he had just agreed to, but at that moment he didn't care.

"Very well," Jhonate said softly. "I will accept, but there are some conditions. We must do this properly."

"Of course," he said, knowing that her people had very specific traditions. "What are the rules?"

"First, the courting is not official until my father or guardian has given his permission. You have stated your intentions so we can see each other, but we are not allowed to kiss until it is a sanctioned courting," she said.

"That . . . will be hard," he said.

"We can touch and embrace," she qualified. "But our hands must not touch improper places. That rule is in place until such time as our courting is over."

Justan's pulse quickened. He hadn't thought that far ahead. About any of it. "Well, that is how my mother taught me to act anyway," he said.

"Good. That will make it easier." she said and snuggled in closer.

Justan smiled. It was nice. All this time worrying and here she was in his embrace. He felt Deathclaw trying to say something to him, but he ignored it. "Are you sure about the kissing part?"

"Yes," she said firmly. "It will be hard enough to get father to accept you as it is. If he learns that you have kissed me without his consent, he will most likely have you killed."

"Okayyy." It sounded like this was going to be more complicated than he thought. "I have a qualification of my own, Jhonate."

She pulled back and looked up at him, frowning slightly. "You do?"

"Yes," he said. "If we are courting, you can't continue calling me 'Sir Edge'."

"But that is your name," she said, puzzled. "The Bowl of Souls gave it to you. Sir Edge is who you are."

"No," he said. "Edge may be what I am, but Justan is who I am. The Bowl of Souls didn't make me. It just named me. My closest friends and bonded still call me Justan and I need that. Especially from you."

"But . . . I cannot just call you Justan in front of others. It would be inappropriate . . . in their eyes at least," she said, frowning.

Justan sighed. "Then I will make a compromise. You will call me Justan when we are alone and in front of others you can call me Edge. Not 'Sir Edge'. Just Edge. That is considered proper between friends and peers at least."

She nodded and leaned back onto his chest. "Very well . . . Justan."

Justan rested his chin on the top of her head. "Is it okay if I kiss you on the cheek or forehead at least?"

She thought about it for a moment. "Hmm . . ."

"Come on, you kissed me on the cheek the day I left you in Reneul," he reminded.

"That was different. I had no idea that we would court one day," she said. "We had better not risk it now. My father is very particular when it comes to the rules."

Justan chose not to quibble and just enjoy the moment. Deathclaw prodded his mind again and Justan reluctantly opened the bond back up. *What do you want?*

There are short ones watching you, Deathclaw said in irritation.

Justan whispered in Jhonate's ear and she gave a short nod.

Where? he asked.

One on the ridge above. He has an arrow aimed at you. Several more are standing around the corner just ahead.

Justan's eyes moved down the chasm and with his enhanced sight, he saw the edge of a helmet peering around the corner. He whispered to Jhonate again and her hand tightened on her staff.

Shall I kill the one up here before he fires? Deathclaw asked.

No. Stay hidden.

Shall I take his bow?

No, as I told you before, dwarves are not usually enemies. These are likely dwarves from Wobble that are hiding out in the caves. If they saw you they might think they are being attacked. Something Lenny said pricked his mind. *Show me its face.* Justan relaxed. The dwarf wore a full beard. *Just tell Fist to spread the word that the dwarves know we're here.*

He whispered to Jhonate again and she pulled away from his chest. Justan pushed away from the cliff wall and walked forward with his hands held out to show he was no threat. Jhonate walked behind him, using her staff as if it were a walking stick. *Tell me if the bowman looks like he's about to fire.*

"Dwarves!" he said. "We know you are watching. We mean no harm!"

A string of curses echoed down the chasm and ten of the most well-armored dwarves Justan had ever seen came around the corner. They were covered in platemail head-to-foot, yet strangely they made barely a sound. Two of them held crossbows cocked at the ready while the others had swords or axes.

"What're you doing here?" asked one of them with a

gruff voice.

"We are friends of Lenny Firegobbler," Justan said.

The dwarves looked at each other. "Bah! If you was friends, you'd know his name right."

"Wait, it's Len-uh. Lenawee Firegobbler," Justan said, trying to remember the nuance of how others pronounced it.

"You do not know how to say his name?" Jhonate whispered.

"It's kind of a long-running joke between us," he replied.

"Yer full of it!" cried one of the dwarves.

"Seriously, he's just a few miles behind us," Justan said.

"He is telling the truth," Jhonate said.

"Yeah right. Yer comin' with us," one dwarf said. The dwarves moved forward and surrounded them.

"I don't like this," Jhonate said and Justan could tell that both she and Deathclaw were a hairsbreadth from attacking.

"It's really not a big deal," Justan told her. "They are just going to take us to the caverns and we were headed there anyway. Lenny will be here soon. It's fine. No problem."

"Now hand over yer weapons," a dwarf said.

Now Justan knew it would be a problem. He could hear the wood of Jhonate's staff creak as she tightened her grip.

We come!

Justan smiled. "Gentlemen, if you will wait just a few moments, I believe we will soon have proof that we are not your enemies."

"What are you talking about, boy?" said one dwarf.

They could hear him coming before they saw him.

"Slow down! Dag-blasted dirt-lickin' grass-chewin' turd-ploppin' rock-sniffin' crab-snatchin'-!" Gwyrtha came into view, bolting along the smooth floor of the crevasse towards them. Lenny clung helplessly to her mane, his body bouncing up and down on her saddle, his feet having nothing to grab onto. His grip hurt Gwyrtha a little, but she was having too much fun to care.

The dwarves saw her and raised their crossbows in alarm.

Justan drew his swords and in one smooth motion cut down through the end of the crossbow in front of him, severing the bolt tip, then kicked out with his right foot, knocking the other dwarf's crossbow wide. The bow twanged, but the bolt skipped harmlessly off of the cliff wall. There was a cry up above and Justan knew that Deathclaw had been forced to disarm their dwarf sniper.

Gwyrtha roared and slid to a halt in front of them, throwing up a plume of sand and causing the dwarves to yelp and scramble back a few steps before brandishing their weapons again.

"-Corn-sniffin' leg-breakin'-!" Lenny realized she had stopped and glared over at Justan. "Confound-it, son! What's the blasted hurry?"

Justan gestured to the other dwarves. "They don't believe that I know you."

Lenny slid to the ground and dusted off his travel clothes, then pulled Buster off of his back, puffed out his chest and turned his glare on the armored dwarves.

They gasped in recognition and Lenny yelled, "Who the hell're you?"

Chapter Twenty Four

"We wait, you horrible thing. Yes-yes. We wait for her return," Ewzad told the witch. He flung the cell door open and reached out, his fingers writhing at the hissing spider within. The creature now frozen, he motioned at Hamford to bring it into place.

"She is dead, I tell you. Send your force now. The bonding wizards must be destroyed."

"No-no. If she were dead, I would have felt it, yes?" Ewzad walked into the large center chamber and ignored the large man's depressed grunting as he pulled on the spider's legs, trying to maneuver its large red body through the door. Ewzad cocked his head and looked at the other creature frozen in the room.

The giant tortoise looked ridiculous now. Its shell grown out of proportion to its body, its legs and head hanging limp. He had accidentally killed the beast while growing it. Such was a problem with haste. He had severed its spinal column, but as long as it remained frozen, its body remained useable. Not until the cells were dead was it wasted. That was something that Ewzad wished he had learned long ago, then he would have had many more servants like Talon.

"The seed of power I planted within her still glows. I sense her somewhere out there. Not far. No, not far at all," he said.

"But I felt it, Master," Mellinda insisted. *"I felt the power of his sword tear her to pieces."*

"Yes-yes. You've shown me," he said absently.

"And what of the dagger, then?" she asked. *"Are you not*

concerned it could be used against you?"

"It will not come to that," he said dismissively. "Not with the Battle Academy and Mage School paralyzed. No, they are hardly a threat."

"This isn't a threat?" Mellinda shoved the memory into his head once more.

Ewzad felt Talon's fear of the warrior's weapon, the one that stole her emotion. He felt the witch force her to attack, saw her dive at the man with a clumsy strike, felt the sword touch her arm. There was a roar of power and he felt Talon's consciousness torn away as the arm flew into the darkness. Then he saw that man, that Sir Edge, hold the damaged eye up to his face and he heard the promise the man made before tossing it into the fire.

"We are coming for you, Ewzad Vriil," said Sir Edge.

Ewzad found his lips moving to the words. He slapped the witch's thoughts away in anger. As if he would fear such empty threats. How dare she overpower his thoughts without permission! He reached for that part of her that was attached to him and throttled it, sending bolts of rending power through their link. "Enough, you filthy thing! If the Dark Voice didn't command me not to, I would tear your very mind to pieces. Yes! Yes I would!"

Mellinda cried out in pain, then went silent. Ewzad reached up to his throbbing temples and let his squirming fingers soothe away the beginnings of a headache. Every once in a while he had to hurt the witch to remind her who was in charge.

"That is the last time I let you do that," Mellinda warned. She sent him a mental image of the commotion his punishment had caused. Far away in the City of Reneul twenty of her children had fallen over dead, allowing a hundred trolls to run screeching into the nearby orc ranks. Many had died, both troll and orc as she tried to regain control. *"You disrupt our plans with your petty attacks. Next time you try, you will not withdraw unscathed."*

"No more of your empty threats, foul one." Ewzad snapped. A few dead orcs and trolls would alter nothing. Their presence around the academy was merely a delaying tactic until his own army of creations was ready to be unleashed. That moment was just days away.

He watched Hamford pull the giant red spider into the room and gestured for him to drag it next to the tortoise. The man did so glumly and tromped away to lean against the wall. Ewzad walked to it and noticed that the guard had torn one of its legs partially free while trying to extract it from its cell.

"Hamford, you fool!" He lashed out with his magic and the guard crumpled to the ground, clutching his stomach, his face red with agony. For a brief moment Ewzad considered ripping the man's guts out, but for some reason he stopped. What did it matter, really? He could repair the spider's damaged leg easy enough. Ewzad laughed. "Come, dear Hamford. Be careful next time, yes?"

"Yes, Master," the guard intoned and laid there on the filthy dungeon floor, not even bothering to stand.

Ewzad returned his attention to the shell of the giant turtle, wondering how he was going to attach it to the spider's body. He reached into the dark corners of his mind and released a flood of voices, each one promising answers.

The day he had received his true name, the Dark Bowl had forced the memories and knowledge of every previous incarnation of Envakfeer into his mind. There were four Envakfeers before him and each one had been a wielder of Stardeon's rings. Each voice had different experiences, different techniques. His head was full of them now, and they argued.

He weeded through the voices. Only two of his predecessors had modified a tortoise before and only one of them had done so successfully. Ewzad locked the other voices away, leaving the one to explain. Ewzad giggled. "Very clever. Yes, very clever, Envakfeer. Yes, I am clever indeed."

He reached out, both arms undulating as his fingers writhed in complex patterns. He tore away the body of the tortoise and cast it aside. It was unneeded. Strong, yes, but slow. He enlarged the shell slightly and added more openings in its side for the spider's legs. He then changed the shape of the shell to conform to the spider's central body and abdomen.

Ewzad reached towards the spider next, quickly repairing its torn leg. He slashed with one hand, his magic stripping off the spider's carapace, then thrust forward with the other hand, sliding its body into the shell. Though large, the spider was still small for the shell, so he spread both hands wide, expanding the creature's size until it filled the shell perfectly.

Then came the tricky part, attaching the spiders body to the shell and fusing its nerves with the shell's built in vertebrae. If done incorrectly, the new creature would not be able to move, but Ewzad did not hesitate. The minutiae of conflicting nervous systems was one of the hardest things to learn according to the past Envakfeers, but for Ewzad it had come almost instinctively.

Once satisfied, he tweaked his design, reinforcing the spider's musculature so that it could carry the extra weight, and hardening the chitin that covered the spider's legs to protect it from attack. There, he had finished it. He had enough spiders and tortoises to make three more. They would be the centerpieces of the wall breaker unit that would end the siege on the academy. The magic that held the creature together would only last two weeks after it left his side, but that would be just long enough.

Ewzad scratched his head. "That is the biggest puzzle, dear Hamford, isn't it? Yes, how to make the changes permanent?"

Ewzad knew how to plant the seeds of change within men, and as long as they weren't activated the power lay strong and dormant for long periods of time. But in a way, those changes were even more unstable. The previous Envakfeers did not know the answer. They were missing the most important holder of knowledge and that was Stardeon himself. But since the creator of the rings had never used the Dark Bowl, his memories were lost to time.

"What could it be, dear Hamford, hmm? The only successes have been Talon and her brother and your sweet Kenn. What is the common thread? Blast! What is it?"

"I don't know, Master," Hamford said. Tears began to fall from his eyes at the mention of his brother's name. The man hadn't moved from his position on the floor.

"You still lay there, Hamford? My-my, with the stunning

display of power I used to create this creature before us, you whimper on the ground?"

"Yes, Master," Hamford said.

"Stand, blast you! Yes, stand and tell me why I shouldn't just take you apart or better yet, make you one of my creations!" Ewzad truly wondered why he had suffered the man to live for so long. Hamford had failed in every important endeavor he had given him. "Tell me, why is it that you live while my better servants are gone? Sweet dear Rudfen killed by that horrid man. Sweet Kenn . . . also killed by that horrid man. Now Talon . . . surely she lives, but you. Why do I suffer your presence? Why Hamford? Why?"

The big man climbed to his feet and stood there, showing no concern for his safety. He let out a great sigh. "I have asked myself the same question many times, Master. You are right. I should have been the one to die."

Ewzad felt a twinge of affection for the man and then he understood. "Ah yes, I see now. I understand! Do you know why I kept you all this time, dear Hamford? Do you?"

"No Master," the big guard said, his shoulders slumped, his face a perpetual mask of sadness.

"You are a reminder." Ewzad grinned over his realization. "Yes-yes, it's true. You remind me of my old friend Blem. Look at you. Big? Yes. Strong and capable? Yes. Smart? No. My, you are so much like dear Blem."

"The friend you killed, Master?" Hamford asked, his face unchanged.

Ewzad's eyes narrowed. Was the man trying to put in a subtle jab? Surely not. The man had been cowed. Now he was boring. "Ah, well Blem's death was a necessity you see? Yes. But I find that I am tiring of you, Hamford. All the constant moping. Ugh, so depressing. No-no. That won't do. I find that I am not as fond of the memories of dear Blem as I once was."

"Will you kill me then, Master?" Hamford asked and his eyes actually looked hopeful. The impudence!

"Kill you?" Ewzad sneered. "It will not be so easy for you to escape, dear Hamford. No-no."

"Yes, Master," Hamford said.

Ewzad considered several ways of teaching the man a lesson, but an alarm rang out in the back of his head. He frowned. One of his wards had been crossed. It was at one of the secret entrances to the tunnels of Castle Dremald; one he rarely used. He raised his thumb and it writhed, causing an image to float above. He laughed when he saw Talon's form slinking down the passage.

"See, Mellinda! I told you. Yes-yes I did!"

"*Unbelievable. She lives.*" The sultry voice sounded truly stunned.

Ewzad snapped his fingers and the tortoise spider stirred sluggishly, its powerful legs raising its heavy body off of the ground. "Dear Hamford, put my new creation in the catacombs. It is too big for the cells, yes? Don't worry, it will be quite docile for a while."

Ewzad ran towards the entrance chamber of his laboratory, knowing where his sweet Talon would appear. He entered the chamber just before she did. She stood and blinked at him with uneasy eyes, gauging his response to her appearance. He saw that whatever terrible damage the man's sword had done to her had been repaired by her body's regeneration. Her newly grown arm was a bit thinner than the other, but the correct length. It would fill out soon and no one would be able to tell the difference.

He threw his arms wide. "Dear sweet Talon, you return!"

"Ewieeee!" she hissed and ran to his arms.

He wove a quick protective spell around his body, aware of the damage she could accidentally cause with her ardent hellos. Talon tried to be gentle with him, she had learned the punishment that could happen if she left a mark, but still her instincts were to rip and tear. Talon slammed into him, but his magic kept him upright.

"Ewwie! Ewwie, I come back to you," she purred. She wrapped her arms and tail around him and kissed him all over his neck with her new lips. He could feel the sharp edges of her teeth against his skin and shuddered with happiness. If not for sweet

Elise, she would have been the perfect girl for him.

"Oh yes, I am glad to see you too, sweet-sweet Talon, yes I am!" he crooned.

"*I am pleased that she lives,*" Mellinda said. "*You must reconnect us, Master. I have so much to teach her still.*"

"Oh? Must I?" Ewzad frowned.

"*I will sacrifice a more suitable child for her this time so that I can help her further. And we must place the eye somewhere inside where it cannot be torn away.*"

Talon froze and looked up at him fearfully. "Doess sshe talkss to you, Ewwie?"

"Oh yes," Ewzad said. "She wishes to be part of you again. What do you think? Hmm?"

"No, Ewwie! Please no," Talon whimpered. "She numbss me. Numbss me!"

Ewzad wasn't surprised that Mellinda had found Talon's weakness. The witch was a crafty one. "But Talon, dear. Without her, I don't have a way to watch your movements. Yes, how else can I know what you're doing?"

"But . . ." Talon's eyes quivered. "The moonrat mother hatess you. She wantss me to betray you."

"Of course she does," Ewzad said with a smile. "Don't you, you filthy thing?"

"*That's preposterous. You know I have no choice but to follow your orders, Master. She is only saying these things because she knows I can punish her.*"

"Oh what a sweet liar you are," Ewzad said.

"No, Ewwie. No liess. I never liess to you!" Talon said, and began kissing his neck again.

"No-no, I wasn't speaking to you, sweet Talon." Ewzad caressed her scaled head and pondered the situation for a moment. What to do? He had an urgent mission for her to perform but could she be trusted to return again?

"*You will need me to monitor her,*" Mellinda reminded.

He snickered. The witch's eagerness made up his mind for him. "Talon my sweet. I have a question for you."

"Yess, Ewwie," she purred.

"Have you ever failed me before?" he asked.

"No, Ewwie. I always killss the oness you want."

"Oh? Are the ones who killed sweet Kenn dead? Hmm?"

She paused in her affections. "They . . . live. But the female iss to blame. She wantss the dagger. Makess me attack. Ruinss my planss."

"Oh, I know," Ewzad said, "She showed me the memory, didn't you, Mellinda?"

"You should not mention my name around the beast, Master." Mellinda warned. *"You gave her speech and that knowledge is dangerous."*

"You try to distract me from your failure, don't you, witch?" he snapped. "Without your interference, sweet Talon would have found a way to kill them all by now." He ignored Mellinda's simmering anger. "Come, Talon, dear. I have an improvement to make."

"Yess!" Talon said and danced around as he led her down the hall past the rows of cells and into his experiment room. Hamford and Arcon had recently cleaned it for him and the round room was full of empty tables. Ewzad motioned to one of them and Talon jumped upon it, sitting in eager anticipation.

Ewzad removed a small wooden box from the desk where his many books of notes were piled and walked back to her side. He carefully slid the lid aside and froze the dangerous beast inside before it could strike, then dumped it out onto the table beside the raptoid. "Here, sweet Talon, is the weapon you will use to destroy those nasty bonding wizards."

She leaned in close, sniffing it. "Sso tiny. What iss it, Ewwie?"

"Ah, see this comes from the shores of the southernmost reaches of Khalpany. Yes, the people there call it a death whisper." He giggled and placed the creature on his palm. At first glance it resembled a spider, but with only six furry legs. Tan in color, its elongated torso was hairless and soft like human flesh. "Look closely, sweet Talon. Look at its head."

She smiled and whispered, "It hass a man'ss face."

"Yes-yes, terrifying, isn't it? But watch." He squeezed its abdomen and a long needle-like fang sprung from its mouth. A single drop of fluid formed on the end. "This pretty little thing is filled with a most deadly venom. They kill hundreds in Khalpany each year and assassins value their venom for its terrible and magic resistant effects. Sweet Talon, this is what I give to you."

"Yess, Ewwie. Please!"

Ewzad flicked two fingers and the death whisper's hairy legs fell away from its body. He then spread his fingers wide and the creature's torso grew. Once it became too heavy for him to hold, he laid it on the table next to him and giggled again. "Now Talon, would you give me your tail, please?"

She laid the end of her tail on the table and Ewzad flipped it over so that the underside was facing up. His fingers writhed and a blade of air sliced open the last foot of her tail, cutting it down to the bone. Talon gurgled with pleasure and he turned his attention back to the creature's body.

He dissected the death whisper's body carefully, exposing the long tube-like venom gland that ran the length of its torso. He enlarged the gland a bit more until it bulged out of the cavity, then detached it from the creature's fang. Careful not to spill the venom, he placed the swollen gland into Talon's tail.

He attached the gland to the base of her tail barb and opened up a channel for the venom to flow through. Talon hissed as he sealed her tail back up and began the intricate process of joining the cells of the gland to her bloodstream and nervous system. Finally finished, he squeezed the base of her tail, smiling as the poisonous fluid leaked from the tip of her barb.

"Ahh, there you are Talon," Ewzad said. "Yes, more deadly than ever. Enlarging the gland may have diluted the potency somewhat, but pump those wizards full of your new venom and not even magic will be able to save them, yes?"

"Oh, yes, Ewwie. I will kills them for you!" she cooed.

"*Perfect, Master.*" said Mellinda, sounding pleased. "*I am sending one of my most precious children now.*"

Ewzad ignored her. "Good, Talon. But this time you will not go alone. I wish you to lead."

"Leadss?"

"What are you planning, Master?"

"I will send you with a group of ten armored orcs and four bladecats. I will command them to follow your instructions and the moonrat mother will make sure they obey."

"Yes, Master," Mellinda's voice was pleased.

"No, Ewwie. Pleease, Masster," Talon begged.

"I will place the witch's eyes in all the members of your force, sweet Talon." He paused and enjoyed the look of anguish on her face. "Except for you. This way I can keep track of your progress and none of the orcs will defy you, yes?"

"Thank you, Ewwie!" she cried and began kissing his neck again. "I lovess you."

Ewzad giggled, then he pushed her away from him. "Yes, sweet Talon I know. I am a kind master, yes?" His smile faded. "But if you fail me this time, I will put an eye in you. I swear I will shove it right into your sweet-sweet skull between your own two eyes and then let the witch do whatever foul thing she plans. Do you understand?"

She cringed, "Yess."

"No, Ewzad, that is unacceptable. Wasting the lives of my sweet children on such disposable creatures," she spat. *"Your orcs will die within weeks, those cats perhaps sooner. I must have her."*

"I think not, you nasty thing," Ewzad sneered. "Talon has proved her usefulness to me. Whereas you . . . are a constant disappointment."

"Yess, the female disappointss." Talon gurgled and flexed the new toy within her tail, smiling at the narrow toxic stream that squirted from the end of her barb.

"Please, do this for me, Master. She is the only one worthy. The things I could do for you with her at my command," Mellinda cooed and for the first time in months, she reached out to stroke the pleasure centers of his mind. Her voice deepened and flowed with exquisite promise. *"I will be . . . very grateful."*

"Disgusting!" The time when such nonsense swayed him had ended long ago. Ewzad shoved her touch from his mind. "I will have none of your foulness!"

"*Disgusting?*" she growled. "*What I promise is-!*"

Ewzad laughed. "Oh my! You still think yourself alluring! Don't forget, I know what you really are. Why should I wish to be pleasured by a filthy old dead thing like you? Hmm, Mellinda?"

Rage bubbled through his connection to the witch and she growled, "*I have told you not to say my name aloud . . . Ewwie.*"

Ewzad's face contorted at her insolence, his anger building to match hers. His arms writhed, his forehead throbbed. "Do you think that was wise? No. No it wasn't."

Talon saw the danger coming and took a wary step back.

"*Go ahead,*" Mellinda taunted. "*Try and punish me again, Ewwie. Just be warned. This time I will not allow it meekly. I will strike back with my full power and do everything I can to wrest control of your insignificant little mind.*"

"Oh, will you? We shall see." Ewzad gathered his mental faculties, readying himself to strike. His predecessors had told him how to harm her, but he had to be careful not to overdo it. Though he hated to admit it, he needed the witch. A few dead among an army of tens of thousands was nothing, but if he destroyed her, the entire army would fall apart. If that happened, the Dark Voice would punish him and his enemies would be able to unite against him. He would be hard pressed indeed.

Ewzad could sense the moonrat mother mount her defenses. He was so focused in his preparations that he didn't even register the alarm telling him that another ward had been crossed. He called upon the memories of the past Envakfeers and listened to their instructions on how to build a barrier around his mind. He didn't notice the sound of the steel door latches open or see the queen enter the chamber.

"Ewzad, there are some difficulties with the nobles, and-. Oh." Elise's expression soured as she saw Talon standing near, and she said in distaste, "It's back I see. Ewzad, I really need your help with something."

She walked towards him and Talon thrust out her hand, hissing in alarm. "Ewwie's woman! You must sstay back. Ewwie preparess to fight the moonrat mother."

Elise's eyes widened. "Wait! Wait, dearest!" Ewzad snarled, so focused on his coming attack that he did not register her words. She rushed across the room and threw her arms around him. His entire torso was writhing now and she had difficulty holding on. "Not now, Ewzad. Please calm yourself. You know we need her. We have discussed this before. Her insolence is empty. The Dark Voice has commanded her to serve yo-!"

Ewzad's magic flexed. With a flare of power, Elise was thrown from his body. She flew toward the chamber wall, smoke trailing from her garment. Talon darted over just in time to embrace the queen and they slammed into the wall together, Talon absorbing the impact.

Elise was stunned. She stayed in Talon's arms for a few short seconds before realizing what had happened. Then she felt the raptoid sniffing her neck and pushed away in revulsion. She stumbled and nearly fell, but Talon reached out and caught her wrist.

"Carefull, woman. Must not let Ewwie'ss childss be harmed," the raptoid said.

Elise's face colored and she turned to look at Ewzad, but the wizard's eyes were already on her. Ewzad's anger and focus evaporated. What had he done?

"Elise," he said, his arms outstretched. "Dearest-!"

"You hurt me!" she said tearfully, holding out her arms so that he could see the redness of her skin. Blisters were already forming and the smell of burnt silk filled the air. "W-why? You have never hurt me before."

"I am so sorry. Yes, dear Elise, so sorry. Let me heal you. Let me soothe your burns, yes?"

He slid towards her and for a moment she looked as if she might run from him. She shook her head and backed away. He grasped her hand and panic rose in her eyes. Then she squeezed her eyes together and took a deep breath. She let the breath out slowly and her trembling stopped. When her eyes reopened, the fear had left her.

She licked her lips. "Thank you, dearest. Please heal me and . . . please be careful next time."

He examined the wounds, murmuring a string of sweet apologies. His fingers writhed as he healed away the burns. How could he have been so careless with his dear sweet Elise? He did a quick sweep of her body looking for further injury. The foul witch was at fault. She had made him so angry! But . . . something pricked at his mind. "Wait, yes. I am missing something. What were you saying as you came in, dearest?"

"I was simply saying that fighting with the woman that controls the armies could be disastrous to our cause," she said.

"No, not that. Not that." He glanced at Talon. "Perhaps it was what you said, sweet Talon. What was it?"

Talon cocked her head at the queen and Ewzad noticed Elise give the raptoid a pleading look. "I . . . ssaid."

"What was it, Talon?" Ewzad asked.

"The childss-."

"Childs!" Ewzad ignored the despair in Elise's eyes and focused his magic on her womb. Talon was right. She had sensed them. Children! Two heartbeats. Two perfect little forms. His own children. Ewzad embraced Elise. "Babies, dearest! Yes-yes! Twins!"

"Twins . . ." Elise said, her voice blank. She grew pale. "Two heirs?"

"No-no. Do you see what that means?" Ewzad laughed, the kind of deep throaty laugh he hadn't laughed in years. "The Dark Voice wants an heir, but that leaves us one. One child is ours alone, Elise!"

"One is ours?" she said, and a hopeful smile spread across her lips.

"Yes!" Ewzad beamed at her. "They are only a few months old. By the time they are born, the academy will be defeated and the Mage School destroyed. We will rule Dremald and conquer the known lands with our child at our side!"

Mellinda chuckled. *"Congratulations, Master. The Dark Voice will be pleased."*

Ewzad laughed again. "Yes! I think it is time for a

celebration! I am finished waiting. Prepare the troops and bring me your sacrifices. My creations are ready. It is time we end this siege, don't you think, Mellinda?"

"*Yes, Master*," The mother of the moonrats didn't bother to rebuke him this time. Finally the waiting was over.

Chapter Twenty Five

"Lenui, I can't agree to these terms without the support of the whole council and I know there would be resistance," Faldon said, looking miserable.

"Listen here, Faldon!" Lenny said pounding a fist on the stack of papers in front of him. "Yer wantin' our help now, ain't you? Well yer the only one here, confound-it! And we ain't gonna accept a promise that you'll 'talk it over after the battle' as a dag-gum answer."

Justan looked around the room at the crowd of dwarves bobbing their heads in agreement. He felt bad for his father. Negotiation had never been Faldon's strong point.

They had been surprised to find that the dwarves of Wobble weren't alone. Since Ewzad Vriil's rise to power, the caves had been inundated with a steady stream of dwarf refugees from all over the kingdom. Instead of the fifty or so dwarves they were expecting, there were seven hundred and they had been joined by nearly a hundred human refugees from Pinewood that had made it to Wobble after their town had been overrun by moonrats.

At first, the dwarves had been angry that thousands more outsiders had been brought to their hiding place, but Lenny had somehow convinced them that this was a business opportunity.

"I still can't believe it," Justan said to Pall, who was standing right beside him. "Just yesterday the other dwarves were angry with Lenny for letting us in. Now he's in charge."

"Lemme tell you somethin', Edge," said Pall. "If there ever was a king among dwarves, it'd be Lenui Firegobbler and everybody here knows it. He's more dwarf than any of the rest of us. Strong, shrewd. He's a hard worker and he can booze better and cook better and curse better and build a better blasted weapon than any other dwarf I know."

"Well, he definitely has my father outmatched," Justan said.

"Lenui's a businessman. Makin' contracts comes as easy to him as rippin' a fart and that's the honest truth," said Rahbbie.

The crux of the situation was that the academy needed what the dwarves had. Hidden in the back of the caverns were vast stockpiles of weapons and food that the people of Wobble had been storing away for decades in preparation for just this sort of situation. In addition, they needed the extra troops. There were over five hundred dwarves here with battle experience and an army of armored dwarves that large would be a huge advantage against ground forces on the battlefield.

Justan looked at Jhonate, who was standing on the far side of the room with the other academy students, and gave her an apologetic shrug. She gave him a grim nod in return. His father really had no choice but to comply with the dwarves' terms. In truth, it was probably for the best.

Their terms were simple. In exchange for the use of their stockpiles and their help in the battles ahead, they wanted a long-term exclusive contract to provide weapons and armor to the Battle Academy. It was something Wobble had tried to negotiate with the academy for years and their lack of success was the main reason Stangrove Leatherbend's vision for the city had failed.

Faldon understood the reasons why as well as anyone. "Lenui, if the Battle Academy were to accept these terms, we would have a difficult time keeping our regular contracts. Many of them pay us partially in weapons. If that option was taken away, some of them may not be able to afford us. We could lose the contracts to other battle schools."

"C'mon, Faldon. They pay you in apprentice work and gall-durn castoffs and you know it. Any contracts you lose would just mean you end up with a smaller junk heap," Lenny said and the crowd laughed.

It was a long running joke that the academy threw away more weapons than they kept. In truth, much of Forgemaster Stanley's job consisted of reforging and repurposing the inferior work pawned off on the academy. It was a constant complaint of his.

Lenny continued, "If you had Wobble-built weapons and armor on every soldier, and magic weapons fer each of yer commanders, you'd be worth lots more to any kingdom that wanted to hire you. I'm tellin' you, yer contracts would go up."

Justan found himself agreeing. Their clientele would adapt. Instead of weapons, the clients without the gold to pay would come up with different kinds of goods to pay with. Perhaps things that the academy could really use.

"You make some valid points, Lenui, but how is Wobble supposed to provide for the academy's needs?" he asked. "You have fifty townspeople and not even all of them are weaponmakers."

"I got signatures from four hunnerd dwarves that plan to stay in Wobble after the war if'n the academy signs the contract," Lenny said. "Dag-nab it, once word spreads, we'll have hunnerds more! Folks'll be proud to say they make weapons fer the finest warriors in the known lands. We'll make Wobble the place it was intended to be!"

"Even with those assurances-," Faldon began.

"And, I got somethin' to sweeten the deal," Lenny interrupted. He motioned to Rahbbie, who gave a quick nod and ran over to hand him a long leather-wrapped bundle.

Lenny sat it carefully down on the table beside the stack of papers and unrolled it, inside were a dozen arrows, each one with its own individual sleeve. He slid one out and showed Faldon the tip. It was in the shape of a half moon and looked dull and pitted.

"What is it?" Faldon asked, giving it a dubious stare.

"It's an explodin' arrow," Lenui said proudly.

"Exploding?" Faldon said and Justan's interest was piqued.

"That's dag-gum right." The dwarf grinned. "Shoot one

of these and whatever they hit gets blown to bits'n pieces!"

"How does it work?" Faldon asked.

"My stupid brother Chugk came up with the recipe," Lenny said, "I ain't tellin' the secrets of how they're made, but I'll tell you they're made from the metal what's leftover when a magic weapon's forged. We call it 'dirty metal' and it's charged with whatever element was in the ore. Usually the stuff loses its magic when it cools, makin' it useless, but Chugk found a way to get it to keep its charge. Problem is, it's unstable. If you break a piece, things get dag-burned nasty. That's when he came up with the idear of makin' arrows with it."

"Show us how one works, Lenny!" shouted Zambon from the back of the cave.

"And where're we gonna shoot it, confound-it? Can't shoot it in the caves or out in the crevasse. 'Cides, they're too dag-gum rare fer target practice." Lenny pounded the stack of papers again. "But I tell you they work! I seen it with my own eyes years ago; the first time Chugk made one. My ears rang fer hours."

"All this sounds impressive, Lenui," said Faldon. "But how many do you have?"

"Just over eight hunnerd," he said. "Any time over the last ten years that any dwarf in Wobble made somethin' magic, Chugk's been makin' arrowheads with the leftovers. While we've been runnin' around tryin' to gather fighters, the folks of Wobble have been sittin' in these caves busy puttin' 'em on arrows."

"That is a substantial number if they are as powerful as you say." Faldon ran a hand through his hair, glaring down at the contract in front of him.

Justan was thinking about the exploding arrows. The one Lenny was holding glowed an intense yellow to his mage sight. An explosion caused by air magic was a fascinating concept in and of itself. But what kind of effect would they have when shot by his dragon hair string?

Faldon sighed, knowing how badly this would be received by the rest of the council members, but he finally nodded. "It seems I have no choice, Lenui. But there are still many details to be worked out."

"We'cn work that out when the academy's freed. But there is one more thing," Lenny slid another sheet of parchment on top of the pile. "Since we'll be yer sole supplier, and since you'll be our sole client, we'll be dependant on yer treatin' us fair. That means we'll need a seat on yer council."

Faldon's jaw dropped. "I-I can't. This is asking too much."

Justan there may be trouble, Deathclaw sent.

No kidding, Justan replied, shocked by Lenny's request. He could understand why the dwarves would want a presence on the council. But one of the biggest regrets in academy history was allowing Dremald to have a seat. They didn't even allow the Mage School on the council anymore and the wizards had requested one multiple times.

Not there. Out in the town of the short dwarves, Deathclaw said.

What is it? At Justan's request, the raptoid had gone to make sure that there were no enemy troops in Wobble. The dwarves had left the village as soon as the siege began and they didn't even have scouts posted there. This was an oversight that Lenny had raged about as soon as he heard.

There are people approaching, Deathclaw replied. *Four of them. And one is very big.*

Justan frowned. *Show me.* Deathclaw had kept his distance, so he could not make out the figures' faces, but what he saw was enough to cause Justan concern. *I'm coming.* He asked Fist and Gwyrtha to meet him, then made his way towards the back of the crowd. He felt a little guilty for leaving while his father was in such a difficult position, but in all truth, there was nothing he could do to help. This situation was far more urgent.

Jhonate saw him leaving and followed him out of the crowd. She caught up to him as he reached the cave mouth and grasped his hand. "What is it, Justan?"

"Deathclaw sees a group approaching and I think one of them is a rock giant," Justan said. "I'm going to check them out."

"I will accompany you," Jhonate said firmly and Justan smiled.

The last two days had been wonderful. Jhonate wanted their relationship to be discreet so their time together had been limited somewhat, but in a way, that had made their brief moments holding hands or embracing that much sweeter. Knowing that Jhonate returned his feelings had been an enormous weight off his shoulders. The only bad thing had been breaking the news to Vannya.

When he told the mage that Qyxal had died, she had been very distraught. Justan had held her briefly, but when her needs had become more intense, he had been forced to back away and tell her that he was courting Jhonate. Vannya didn't take the news well. The mage had disappeared into her tent and he had not seen her since. That had left Wizard Locksher with the responsibility of comforting her, something the wizard seemed ill-equipped to handle.

Fist and Gwyrtha were waiting just outside. As soon as Justan came into view, the ogre asked, "Do you think it's Charz?"

"I don't know. I haven't seen any other rock giants, but this one seems to be about the right height. If it's him, that means he has made amends with his bonding wizard," Justan said. "Perhaps that's who he's traveling with."

"I hope so," Fist replied. "I do not wish to fight him again."

"If it's Charz you shouldn't have to. If it is another rock giant . . . well, you have your mace now," Justan said.

"What are you speaking about?" Jhonate asked.

"I'll tell you on the way." Justan closed his eyes and dove through the bond to Gwyrtha. She was quite excited when he asked if he could increase her size again. The changes came much easier to him now and she was soon twice her usual size once more.

I'm big! she said, prancing about happily.

"I'll get going," Fist said with a sigh. He grasped his mace and ran down the chasm, getting a head start.

Justan sent the ogre some extra energy and turned to Jhonate. "Would you like to ride with me?"

She was staring at Gwyrtha with wide eyes. "How . . . did . . . you?"

"Oh, right. You didn't know we could do that. I'll explain later. Come on." Gwyrtha squatted down so that Justan could climb into the saddle.

He pulled Jhonate up behind him. She laid her staff between them and wrapped both arms around his waist. "I must admit this is frightening."

"Wait until we get going," Justan said and grasped two handfuls of Gwyrtha's mane.

Gwyrtha leapt off at a run and Jhonate let out an uncharacteristic yelp. She buried her face against his back and her arms tightened until Justan found it hard to breathe. *Can you slow down just a bit, sweetie?* He asked. *I don't want Jhonate to be afraid to ride you.*

He could feel the rogue horse huff out a chuckle beneath him, but she backed off just a bit. The ride smoothed out and Jhonate's grip loosened. "Are you okay?" he asked.

She lifted her head and cleared her throat, "I am fine. Tell me about this giant."

They caught up with Fist and Justan asked Gwyrtha to keep pace with him as he told Jhonate the important details about their encounters with Charz. "I am not sure if his abilities were totally unique to him or if other rock giants have similar healing rates. Hopefully they are not enemies, but we should be prepared nonetheless."

She gave a quick nod. "I have fought giants and I have fought armored creatures. I know what to do."

Justan checked in with the raptoid. *Deathclaw, what do you see now?*

I am closer to them. Look at-! The raptoid hissed. *Somehow one of them saw me and fired an arrow.* Justan sensed that he hadn't been hit, but the raptoid had been startled. *I moved in time but that arrow . . . I think it tried to bite me.*

Show me what you saw.

The giant was accompanied by two humans on horses, one male and one female. Another person that also looked to be female sat on the giant's shoulder. Justan recognized the man on horseback at once and smiled. *Are they coming after you, Deathclaw?*

They have stopped and are looking this way. The female that shot at me has another arrow cocked.

Stay back. They are not enemies. We'll be right there.

"Jhonate, Fist, I don't think we need to worry," Justan said. "The giant does look a lot like Charz but the man that's with him is Sir Hilt!"

"Sir Hilt? I wonder what he is doing here." Jhonate said in surprise. "And why is he traveling with a giant?"

Justan reigned Gwyrtha in and asked Fist to stop. "I don't know, but he's also traveling with a woman that is quick with a bow, so once we reach the exit, you and I need to walk on alone. The woman might see Gwyrtha or Fist and fire."

I'm not scared of arrows. Gwyrtha said.

But these arrows seem to be magic, Justan said remembering Deathclaw's alarm. *It is better to use caution.*

The last hundred yards of the chasm sloped upward and curved to the right. They dismounted just before the exit and left Fist and Gwyrtha out of sight as they stepped out into the open.

The four visitors were no more than fifty yards away, staring in Deathclaw's direction. The rock giant stood with its back to them, a thin female figure standing on his right shoulder, her hands raised to her eyes to shade them from the glare of the afternoon sun. Sir Hilt had climbed down from his horse and had his hands on the pommels of his swords, while the woman with the bow still had an arrow pulled back and aimed unnervingly close to the raptoid's exact position.

"Sir Hilt!" Justan called out and the four of them turned, the woman's arrow now targeting his chest. Justan raised his hands. "We came to greet you!"

"You do not want to fire on us," Jhonate added.

Hilt laughed. "Well what a surprise! The infamous Sir Edge!" He walked over to them and gave Justan a warm embrace. "I must admit, I have been thrilled to hear the stories of what you've accomplished since I saw you last."

Justan returned the embrace, but his brow furrowed in confusion. What things had Hilt heard?

"Sir Hilt, before you ask, I am not yet willing to return to my father's side" Jhonate said firmly.

Hilt gave an amused shake of his head. "We'll talk about that later. As for right now, I'll just say I'm happy to see you too." He gave her a quick embrace.

"Sir Edge," said a deep voice.

Justan looked at the rock giant. "So that is you, Charz. I'm glad to see you're free."

The giant nodded. "I did as you suggested and my master released me."

He seemed to have recovered completely from his fight with Kenn. He looked much the same as he had the first time Justan had encountered him except for one thing. He was wearing a necklace made out of thick iron chain with a crystal shard pendant that glinted red and pink in the sunlight.

"Is your master nearby?" he asked.

"No," Charz said. "He's back at the Mage School."

"Why aren't you with him?" Justan asked.

"He has other stuff for me to do right now," said Charz. "Besides, I still think he's not quite sure if he can trust me yet."

"Can't say I blame him," Justan said.

The giant smiled. "Can't say I do either. But I'm doing my best to bring him around."

Justan called out to the woman with the bow. "Um, miss, could you put the arrow down? He's a friend. He's not going to harm you."

"That lizard thing's with you?" the woman asked, raising an eyebrow at him. She slid the arrow back into her quiver, slung her bow over her shoulder, and slid down from her horse. She walked towards him, her lips pursed in thought.

The woman was perhaps in her mid-thirties with long dirty-blond hair tied back in a ponytail. She wore a long-sleeved blouse with leather bracers on her forearms and odd baggy trousers tied tight at the ankles. A gray-handled dagger in an ornate sheath hung from her hip.

"Hold still," the woman said, and to Justan's surprise, she began poking and prodding him. She turned him this way and that, lifted his arm and felt his biceps. She grasped his face and thumbed open his eyelids to look into his eyes, then leaned in and shoved her ear right into the center of his chest, listening to his heart.

"Uh, what are you doing?" Justan said.

"Just humor her," Hilt replied.

"Hah!" she said pulling back from his chest, her ear covered in frost. She rubbed her ear. "That one's cold and it doesn't like being interrupted." Justan's hand rose to the frost rune on his chest and she looked him in the eye once more. "So that's what a bonding wizard's like. I see what Yntri liked about you."

"Who are you?" Justan asked.

"You were right, Hilt! He's a good one," she said and startled Justan with a sharp slap to the behind. "Now go ahead and call out the others."

Justan rubbed his stinging cheek in confusion for a moment before calling out to his bonded. This woman was strange, yet there was something comforting about the confident way in which she handled herself. He felt he could trust her.

She walked up to Jhonate, "Now you, girl."

Jhonate's cheeks burned and her glare was icy, but she lifted her arms as if she had done this many times before. "Did Yntri teach you this?"

"Yes, Yntri among others," the woman said and began to do the same kind of poking and prodding she had done with Justan.

"You will not be smacking my behind," Jhonate said stiffly.

"Somehow I don't think I'll feel the same inclination," the woman replied and leaned in to listen to her chest. She stayed that way for a few moments. "Your breastplate was in the way, but I think I got a pretty good read on you," she said, then looked back to Justan. "You're good with this one."

Justan and Jhonate shared embarrassed glances. Gwyrtha and Fist walked up to them, confused about the mixed feelings they were getting from Justan.

"Ogre," the woman said. "What's your name?"

"Uh . . . Fist," Fist said hesitantly.

"Well, come here, sweetheart. I haven't tried to listen to someone as big as you before, but let's give it a shot," she said.

Justan edged over to Hilt and whispered, "Who is that woman?"

Hilt smiled. "Oh, that's Beth. She's my wife."

"Your wife?" Jhonate said. "When did that happen?"

"We were married about a year ago," Hilt said.

"You were crazy enough to marry a listener?" she asked incredulously.

"I had no choice really. She insisted on it. And I . . ." Hilt chuckled and shook his head. "It ends up I was happy to relent."

Justan looked back to see Fist patting Beth on the back awkwardly as she had her arms wrapped around him, her ear against his chest. She had a wide grin on her face.

"Oh, you are just a big cuddly wonderful ball of muscles aren't you?" she said, her voice sounding almost drunk. "Mmm, I could just hug you all day." She pulled back and placed a finger on the center of his chest where her ear had just been. "I am so happy you have left your pain behind."

"I . . . have a new tribe now," Fist said.

"Yes you do." She peeked into the pouch at his side. "Come here, you." Squirrel peeked his head out, then ran up to stand on her shoulder. She smiled at him and he chittered at her.

"Yes, I know, big guy," she replied, nodding her head at him. "Yes. You are sweet too and no, I do not want a seed, thank you."

Squirrel planted the seed back into his cheek and climbed back to Fist's shoulder.

What is that woman, Justan? Deathclaw asked.

I'm not sure. But she is on our side.

"Alright, scaley!" she bellowed, crooking a finger in Deathclaw's direction. "Come out from behind that rock and get over here."

Then Justan realized. She could see the bond. Somehow Hilt's wife was using spirit magic. What was it Coal had told him about the four types? Bonding, binding, blessing, and bewitching. What was this woman using?

"How long is this going to take, Sir Hilt?" Jhonate asked.

"Not too long," he assured her. "I know it seems like a pain, but she only has to do this with the major players."

"What does that mean? Major players?" Jhonate asked.

"I don't know," he shrugged. "That's just her name for certain people. There isn't much of a rhyme or reason to it that I have been able to tell."

Beth had somehow coaxed Deathclaw out of hiding and had just finished poking and prodding him. The raptoid was quite frustrated by the time she laid her head on his chest. After a few moments, she leaned back and reached up to caress his scaled head.

"Oh, you are a survivor, aren't you? And a thinker," she sighed and patted his chest. "You have such a long way to climb. But you're in the right hands."

"Why does she like you all so much?" Charz grumbled. "She just scowled at me and said I had a lot to make up for."

Gwyrtha padded up to Beth and nudged her.

"And you?" Beth let out an excited gasp, her hand moving to her mouth. "Oh you are just beautiful, aren't you?"

Yes! Gwyrtha agreed.

Beth laughed and threw her arms around Gwyrtha's neck. "Oh, you are a sweetie! Yes you are!" She laughed again and Justan wondered if she really was drunk. Beth kissed Gwyrtha several times on the top of the head then looked at Justan. "Oh, this is unfair! How can you stand it? She is like a bunch of beautiful spirits all smashed into one!"

"Uh, actually, you're not too far off," he said.

Ride? Gwyrtha asked eagerly.

"Can I?" Beth asked as if she had heard Gwyrtha ask the question.

"Uh . . . sure," Justan said.

Beth leapt into Gwyrtha's saddle and laughed as the rogue horse took off, Gwyrtha thoroughly enjoying the attention. Jhonate had a slight frown on her face as she watched the woman ride off.

Justan looked to Sir Hilt. "Can she actually hear them?"

"What do you mean?" Hilt asked.

"Excuse me," said a voice from above and Justan looked up to see that it was the girl standing on Charz's shoulder that had spoken. She jumped down nimbly, making it seem as if a ten-foot drop was just a step. She then folded her arms and looked up at Justan with large expressive eyes, her pert little nose wrinkled in irritation. She was so petite she barely came up to Justan's shoulder. "All this time you've been walking around as if I weren't here. Don't you remember me?"

Justan's brow furrowed. She did look familiar. "I'm sorry, but-." She tucked her hair behind one pointed ear and Justan gasped in recognition. "Antyni!"

"Yes, thank you." She looked up at Charz. "Am I so unnoticeable?"

"You are pretty light," the giant grunted. "Sometimes when you're standing on my shoulders I forget you're even there."

The elf gave him a cute little scowl and slapped the giant's leg.

"I'm sorry, Antyni," Justan said. "It was your hair. When I saw you last it was so much shorter."

"My people were forced to leave our homeland almost a month ago," she said. "My hair grows until we return to seed our homeland again."

"You were overrun?" Justan asked in dismay.

"We fought, but the moonrats were not alone. They had trolls and beasts this time," she explained.

"I am so sorry to hear that," he said. "Where are your people now?"

She opened her mouth, then blinked at him and frowned. "You ask more questions. Are you not going to tell me about Qyxal's death?"

Justan felt ill. He had been dreading this part. "You knew?"

"Of course," she said with a sad little nod. "He is my Elqala. I knew the moment he died. I asked Charz about it, but he didn't see what happened. Tell me."

"I'm sorry. I . . ." Justan sank to one knee in front of her. "Antyni, it's all my fault. Qyxal was only there because he was my friend. If I hadn't dragged him with me, he would still be alive."

"Justan, that was not your fault," Fist reminded.

"I . . . still can't help but feel it was."

"Tell me. How did he die?" Antyni asked.

Justan looked down and related what happened, telling her about Qyxal's brave attack on the bandham and how they had been unable to save him. She listened without comment, her face full of sorrow, but no tears fell. When he finished, she placed her hand under his chin and tilted his head up until their eyes met.

"Thank you for taking his pain at the end," she said. "What did you do with him afterwards?"

"We brought his body with us," he said. "We cleaned him and wrapped him in leather to preserve him until we could return him to you."

She closed her eyes and let out a sigh of relief, her hand pressed against her heart. "The prophet was right." She smiled. "You must bring me to him."

"Of course," Justan said. "He's back at the caves . . ."

They were interrupted as Gwyrtha came thundering back towards them. Beth clung to her mane giggling like a small girl. Gwyrtha skidded to a stop, which seemed to have become her preferred method of stopping. Beth slid off the saddle and hugged the rogue horse around the neck, peppering her head with kisses. She then staggered over to lean against Hilt.

"Oh, Hilt! Can we take them home? I want to keep them all!"

Hilt chuckled and shot a glance at Jhonate. "I don't think they would follow."

"That depends on how determined I am," Beth said, her voice slightly slurred. She raised a hand to her temple. "Oh, I am going to have such a headache after this."

"We've been speaking with you this whole time and I forgot to ask," Justan said. "What are the four of you doing here?"

"We bear the lodestones," Antyni said.

"What does that mean?" Jhonate asked.

"The prophet told us to come to Wobble," Hilt said. "He said the resistance would be here."

"He was right," Justan said. Why did it seem that every event came down to instructions from the prophet? "We are camped in the caverns beyond. The leaders are planning our attack."

"I must speak with them," Hilt said. "Things are far more dire than you know."

Chapter Twenty Six

"He is here?" Antyni asked as Fist gently laid the treated leather bundle in front of her.

"Yes," Justan said.

Everyone who knew Qyxal had gathered around them. Antyni had insisted on it. She wanted to give him a proper elven burial and that meant that everyone who knew him needed to be there. She said it couldn't wait until a return to her homeland. It needed to be done right away.

She untied the leather strips that bound the bundle together and carefully began to unwrap it. Justan swallowed. He wasn't looking forward to this part. He had seen it enough in his dreams; the way that his friend had looked at the end, his body charred and burnt, only one half of his face left whole . . . Justan didn't want to see what he looked like after several weeks tied behind Gwyrtha's saddle.

Antyni pulled back the leather to expose his head. To Justan's relief, the elf's face looked unchanged from the moment he had drawn his last breath. There wasn't even any smell.

Tears fell from Antyni's large eyes and she caressed Qyxal's hair. "Elqala, I missed you."

Antyni opened a pouch she carried at her side and brought out a tiny bottle. She pulled the cork stopper and dipped her finger inside. Then softly, she began to sing a murmuring chant in elvish as she traced a pattern on Qyxal's forehead with a glittering golden oil. The air was filled with the scent of spring leaves.

Justan had never been to a funeral like this. He didn't know if there was something he should do. He looked at the others but none of them seemed to know any more than he did. They simply stood, hands clasped in front of them, and listened.

Antyni's voice grew louder. It had a surprisingly thick alto tone that made the mournful melody yank at Justan's emotions. He wasn't the only one so affected. He saw tears streaming down the faces of many. Vannya was clinging to Locksher's arm, sobbing.

Antyni finished her design and began to paint a similar pattern on her own forehead. Justan switched to mage sight and saw that the oil burned a deep black. He looked at Qyxal and was surprised to see a white wisp of spirit magic rising from the elf's forehead.

Antyni's song rose in volume. The melody quickened. White cloudy vapors of spirit magic formed on her forehead as well. Then she leaned down and brought her head next to Qyxal's until the tendrils of spirit magic tightened and intertwined, joining together in one solid cord.

Her song faded and the spirit energy disappeared into Antyni's head. She touched her forehead to Qyxal's and kissed him gently between the eyes. She reached down and ran her hand through the ground beside her, gripping a handful of sandy earth. Antyni pulled the rest of the leather back and spread the sand over his body, then covered him back up and stood.

"My Elqala has joined me. His thoughts are with me now," Antyni said, turning to face the rest of them. "He has words for each of you."

She walked towards Justan and embraced him, then said, "Qyxal wishes for me to thank you for being his friend."

"Please tell him I'm sorry," Justan said.

She cocked her head. "He does not understand why you feel guilt. If he had not traveled with you, he would not have found the magic needed to help our people."

She moved past him to stand in front of Fist and embraced the ogre. "He valued your friendship and wanted you to know that you are smarter and wiser than most humans he has known."

"Tell him . . . thank you," Fist rumbled.

She nodded, then embraced Lenny. "Qyxal liked you, Lenui. He is sorry he was not able to properly use the gifts you gave him." She kissed him on each cheek and on the forehead. The dwarf sputtered with embarrassment and she added. "The kisses are from me. Thank you for caring for his body. Otherwise he would not have been able to hold on for me."

Lenny's face went red. "Well, uh, it was the thing to do."

She smiled, then moved on through Qyxal's friends, embracing them all and giving each a kind word, thanking Master Coal for his teachings, thanking Coal's bonded, and thanking Gwyrtha and Zambon. Then she stopped at Vannya.

The mage was in as sad a state as Justan had ever seen her; her eyes red and puffy, her hair and robes disheveled. Antyni gazed at her for a few moments, her nose wrinkled in confusion. She looked down at the ground for a moment.

"I . . . Qyxal wants me to say . . ." The elf reached up and placed one hand on each of Vannya's cheeks. Her brow furrowed for a moment, then she leaned forward and planted a tender kiss on Vannya's lips. "He loved you. He truly did, but he was never able to tell you so. He doesn't wish this knowledge to cause you pain, but he wanted you to know. He has some things among his belongings at the Mage School that he would like me to give you after we return."

Antyni swallowed and returned to stand at Qyxal's body. Vannya stared after her in shock, one hand raised to her lips. Justan saw a tiny wisp of spirit magic clinging there for a moment before it slowly evaporated away. She turned and buried her face in Locksher's robes, her shoulders shaking.

Justan felt horrible for her. Vannya had been though so much in the last few days and a lot of it was his fault. He wished he could help, but anything he did at this point would just make things worse.

Antyni asked Lenny and Fist to come and help her rewrap Qyxal's body. Once they were done, she thanked everyone once more and it was over. It was both the most touching and sad funeral Justan had been to. To know that Qyxal wasn't angry with him helped ease his mind, yet at the same time it felt like he had said goodbye all over again.

He walked to the elf's side and asked, "Antyni, is he still with you?"

"His presence fades," she replied. "He has left certain knowledge in my head, but his feelings about the knowledge will soon be gone."

"I could see his spirit communicating with yours," he said.

She seemed surprised. "It is a rare gift among our people to see the heart magic."

"It is part of being a bonding wizard," he explained. "I . . . saw that you left some trace of his thoughts on Vannya's lips."

Her cheeks reddened. "That was Qyxal's kiss, not mine. His feelings were very strong towards that woman and I could not resist him."

"I was surprised," Justan said. "I had no idea he felt that way about her."

"He should have told her," Antyni said. "My Elqala always was shy about his feelings. It is too bad. They would have had beautiful children."

"Uhh . . ." Justan didn't know what to say to that. She was probably right though. "I hope you don't mind my asking, but what does it mean when you call him Elqala?"

"In the tongue of my people, qala is sibling," she explained. "Elqala means a sibling that shared your womb."

"Oh. He was your twin," Justan said in understanding. "I wouldn't have guessed. You look so different."

"He was tall and dark of hair like mother. I am short and fair like father."

Justan nodded. "What will you do with his body now?"

"I have given him to the earth," she said, miming the way she has spread the dirt over him. "His body will now become soil and I will bring him back to the Mage School with me. When my people can return to the forest, he will help us grow the homeland."

"That reminds me. I brought the things he left for you," Justan said, picking up Qyxal's pack.

A smile touched her lips. "Yes, Elqala is almost gone now, but he was eager for me to see these things." She opened the pack and sifted through the items inside, pulling out Qyxal's notebook and the bulging pouch of honstule seeds. "These . . . honstule seeds are special to him."

"Qyxal felt that that book and those seeds would give your people the edge they needed to defeat the rot of the forest," Justan said.

She opened the bag and stuck her head in, inhaling the aroma. "The seeds are powerful." Antyni closed her eyes and gripped Qyxal's notebook. "He wants me to take his place."

"I told him I'd help when this was all over," Justan said. "I will extend that promise to you as well. I'll help drive the moonrats out of your land so that you can put his knowledge to use."

"Then I accept your offer on behalf of the Silvertree Sect. The moonrat mother is a foul and cruel enemy and we will need many friends to help us defeat her," Antyni said.

"I will help too," Fist promised.

Me too.

"Gwyrtha too," he added.

"An ogre helping elves . . . Thank you Fist." She shook her head in amusement. "This is an odd time for my people. Lenui gave me Qyxal's bow and arrows earlier and even though they smelled of iron and fire I accepted them anyway. Perhaps that's what is needed to win our homeland back."

"Qyxal felt the same way," Justan said. He placed a hand on her shoulder. "The meeting should be starting any moment. Are you coming with us?"

Antyni turned Qyxal's notebook over in her hands. "No. You go. I have much to do."

Justan and Fist walked back to the cave where the meeting would be taking place. As they neared, he heard a cry of pain. They trotted into the main chamber just in time to see Beth fall to the ground at Tamboor's feet. The warrior reached down to help her, but Hilt was already kneeling at her side, whispering something.

Beth grasped Tamboor's offered hand and allowed him to pull her to her feet. She held her stomach and looked at him, wincing as if in great pain. Then, standing on shaky legs, she reached up and cupped Tamboor's cheek.

"So angry . . . the horrors you've seen. Your soul hangs by a thread, Tamboor. Please don't let your memories break you." She kissed two fingers and laid them against Tamboor's chest, then turned to Hilt. "Ohh. I may be sick. Can I listen to you, love?"

Hilt nodded and pulled her close, holding her ear to his chest. He stroked her hair and she let out a long sigh.

Justan looked at Tamboor. The man's lips were quivering, but he closed his eyes for just a moment and clenched his jaw. When his eyes opened again he was stone-faced as ever.

"What happened, father?" Justan asked.

"She went around groping everyone and listening to their hearts, saying odd things," Faldon said. "But when she got to Tamboor, she cried out and fell."

"She's using magic," Justan explained. "I don't know how it works, but she can take measure of a person's spirit."

"That's what Hilt said. But I don't know. She told Lance that his time was nearly finished and well . . ." he rubbed his backside. "She smacked me a good one."

"What did she tell you?" Justan asked.

"She . . ." Faldon began, his brow furrowed in thought, then said, "I'd rather not say."

"Beth, honey," Hilt said and his wife lifted her head from his chest. "I need to get this meeting started. Are you alright now?"

She rubbed her head, still looking quite pale. "Not quite, but I won't delay you further. I know you have important things to say."

She pointed a finger in Justan's direction. "Fist, dear, would you come here, please?"

Justan, relieved that she hadn't been pointing to him, moved to the side so that the ogre could walk past him. Fist stood before her, uncomfortable with the way everyone was staring at him. "Yes?"

"Would you mind holding me for a moment, dear?" she asked.

The ogre scratched his head in embarrassment and looked at Hilt.

The warrior nodded. "It's alright, Fist. She just wants to listen."

He still looked hesitant and Beth said, "I know I may be a stranger to you, but to me you're like an old friend." She crooked her finger at him. "Come on. Please. It will make me feel much better."

It's alright, Fist. I think she just finds you comforting, Justan said

The ogre finally bent down and reached out for her. Beth wrapped her arms around his wide neck and drew up her legs and when he stood back up, he was cradling her like she was a child. Squirrel left his pouch to curl up on her stomach and Beth stroked the creature's fur.

"Thank you, Squirrel, that's much better." She smiled and snuggled her head into Fist's chest. "And thank you Fist. I might fall asleep if that's alright with you."

"Uh . . . okay," he said.

Jhonate moved to Justan's side, tugged on his shirt and whispered, "What is wrong with that woman?"

Justan looked at the frown on her face and shrugged. "I'm not sure."

Hilt turned back to Faldon. "She'll be okay now. We can begin."

Faldon nodded. "Very well, Sir Hilt. The first thing I must ask is why the four of you are here. My son says the prophet told you where we would be?"

"Perhaps I should start from the beginning," Hilt said, "About a month ago, Beth and I traveled west from Malaroo. Our intent was to visit the academy, but we heard about the siege while we passed through a small village on the way. The people there were confident that the Mage School was putting together a force to break the siege, so we changed our plans and headed there instead. We had hoped to see what we could do to help. But when we arrived, we discovered that the school hadn't done anything yet."

"As I thought," Coal said with a shake of his head. "We had hoped to try and convince them ourselves."

Locksher cleared his throat. "I know it is hard to understand, but the High Council is made up of wizards with differing viewpoints. Regrettably, this means it can take a while to get any decisions made."

"That's exactly what happened," Hilt said. "They were nice enough to let us in the gates while they deliberated, but by the time they agreed to send a force to help, the wards around the forest road had collapsed and there was an army of men blocking the road to Sampo."

"Ewzad Vriil's men," Justan said.

"Yes, Edge. The council was readying themselves to march against the men when the prophet showed up," Hilt said. "He took charge immediately and told them that an attack on the men at that point would mean defeat. He had an alternate plan." Hilt reached into his shirt and pulled out an amulet on a chain. "The lodestones."

The amulet was made of silver, perhaps two inches wide and four inches long. It was covered in runes and in the center was a dark gray stone cut in the shape of a triangle.

Faldon and Tamboor shared a look and Faldon said, "I have heard of them, but to be honest, I didn't think they would be used again. The Mage School took them back from the academy sixty years ago when the council had all wizards removed from the grounds."

"I hadn't heard of that," Justan said.

"Well, the two schools have clashed many times over the years," Coal said. "This time I believe was actually the Mage School's fault. It took twenty years before there was another accord between us."

"And the lodestones were never returned," Faldon said.

"It wouldn't have mattered anyway," Locksher said. "The lodestones can only be operated by those with magic and the academy no longer had wizards on staff."

"What do they do?" Justan asked.

"The lodestones are four amulets that act as keys to open a portal from the Mage School to a cave southeast of the academy," Hilt explained. "One was given to each of the four original members of the Battle Academy Council at the end of the War of the Dark Prophet. The portal was a secret and was meant to be used only in case of emergency."

"So the four of you came here from the portal?" Justan asked.

"No," Hilt said. "For the portal to work it must be activated from the academy's side. The four of us traveled here from the Mage School for that purpose."

"But how did you get through the forest?" asked Sir Lance. "It's crawling with moonrats."

"We were able to avoid them," Hilt replied.

"I have a question." Locksher said. "Why you four? It seems like an unlikely group for the council to send."

"They needed a group that was small enough to get here without notice, strong enough to fight if they needed to, and in order to use the lodestones, each person needed to be able to use magic. The four of us met the criteria. We all have magic in some form, we can all fight, and Antyni knows the Tinny Woods as well as anyone," Hilt said.

"I still can't see why the council agreed." Locksher replied. "There are at least one or two war wizards at the school at any given moment and I can't imagine them agreeing to send a party without at least one wizard as part of the group."

"Well, I wouldn't exactly say they agreed," Hilt said. "While they were busy arguing about it, Wizard Valtrek gathered us at the front gate and handed us the amulets."

"Of course it would be Valtrek." Justan found himself smiling. It seemed the wizard was used to going behind the rest of the council's back.

"He said he was doing it on the prophet's orders," Hilt added.

"So that's the plan," Faldon said with a look of triumph.

"I love it. We open the portal. The wizards come out and join us with their forces and together we break the army besieging the academy."

"Well, not exactly," Hilt said with a wince. "The wizard's are planning on coming out to help. But . . . this isn't an attack plan. It's an escape plan."

"What are you saying?" asked Captain Demetrius. "Escape for whom?"

"For everyone," Charz said from the back of the cave. The giant was leaning against the rear wall, his arms folded. "They're ready for you, Hilt. Go on, show them the mirror."

Justan wondered just who the giant's bonding wizard was. They had to be pretty powerful to reach him all the way from the school in the middle of the day.

Everyone's eyes returned to the named warrior. Hilt picked up the pack that he had brought to the meeting with him and reached in. He pulled out a gilded hand mirror. It was oval shaped with a handle about half the length of Hilt's forearm. The frame and back of the mirror was made of gold and encrusted with runes.

"We'll let the wizards explain," Hilt said. "This will allow you to speak face-to-face with them."

He turned the mirror towards Faldon and Justan saw his father's eyes widen as a voice issued from within, "Greetings, Faldon the Fierce. This is Master Latva speaking."

Everyone crowded around Faldon to get a look for themselves. Justan squeezed in with them and was relieved to see a familiar set of piercing blue eyes in the other side. Just seeing the master there made him more confident that the wizards were going to help.

"Master Latva! It is good to see you," Faldon said guardedly. "We are grateful that the Mage School is offering its help to free the Battle Academy."

"Of course, Faldon. Our schools have ever been allies. I just wish that we had found a way to help sooner," Latva said.

"We were all caught off guard by the siege. I am sure it couldn't be helped," Faldon replied, but diplomacy was something he never had a taste for. He got to the point. "So how is it that you propose to help? Sir Hilt mentioned an escape plan?"

"Yes, that is true," Latva said. "I understand that Hilt told you about the lodestones?"

"Yes," Faldon said with a nod.

"If we had the means, we would prefer to join you in an attack. However, the situation is worse than you know," Latva said and with an apologetic look said, "I am sorry to say it, but we will not be able to save the academy."

The cave was filled with angry voices as everyone began to speak at once. Faldon raised his arm to quiet them. "I would have to disagree. What do you know that we don't?"

"We recently acquired a source inside the palace in Dremald. Just a few short days ago, we learned that the stand-off is about to end. Ewzad Vriil has unleashed an army of his creations. They are on their way to the school now," the wizard replied.

"How many does he have, Master?" Locksher asked.

"Their raw numbers don't matter, I'm afraid. It's what they can do that makes them so formidable," Latva said. "They are specifically designed to overcome the walls and cause as much damage inside as possible."

"You are suggesting we give up and leave the academy to be slaughtered?" Faldon said.

"Not at all. We will help you get the people out," Latva said. "We are offering sanctuary. We have room for all of you. Once everyone is here safely with us, we can regroup and fight Ewzad Vriil and his accomplice together."

"Trade one siege for another is what yer sayin'," Lenny spat. "So we get to the Mage School. The army will just move down there."

"This is ridiculous." Faldon said. "We don't have the numbers for a direct assault. By the time we got to the front gates their thirty thousand goblinoids would close in and surround us. Even if we could fight our way to the gates and get the people inside the academy to the portal, we would take heavy losses. By the time those of us that survived got through the portal, we could be too few to help."

"There is a plan in place to help with-," Latva began.

"We already have a plan in place," Captain Demetrius interrupted. "We will spread out and strike in small units, melting away before the enemy can counterattack. We will bleed this army until the witch can no longer hold them and they retreat back onto the mountains. As far as Vriil's beasts go, they can be formidable, but we have fought them before and we can do it again."

There were cheers of agreement from around the cave and Master Latva let out a sigh. The wizard looked away and there was some muttering on the other end of the mirror. Their view of the master was jostled around, then moved away, showing first the ceiling, then the floor, then a pair of feet sticking out from under brown robes. Finally the view moved up and another face appeared.

Justan gasped. He knew this man.

Who is it? Fist asked. The ogre still stood on the far side of the cave with a sleeping Beth cradled in his arms.

He saw brown hair and kind eyes, but the rest of the man's features were difficult to focus on. He was sure of it. "It's the prophet."

"Hello, everyone," the prophet said with a smile. "So nice to see you all."

"Sir . . ." Faldon said with a look of awe and perhaps even fear. It was the first time in Justan's life that he had seen his father looked cowed by anyone.

"I wish I could take the time to speak with each and every one of you, but for right now I have some hard truths that apply to you all," the prophet said. "For I have seen a horrible vision.

"In my dream the sun dimmed and a vile tide of red-eyed beasts came in from the east. They swept over the hills and poured over the proud walls of the academy like they were nothing. Then the walls filled with blood until they burst like a dam, spilling across the land drowning all in its path."

There was a lot of murmuring but no one dared to argue

this time.

The prophet glanced around, his eyes seeming to rest on each of them before he continued, "I am sorry, but there is no way around it. If the academy is not evacuated in two day's time, everyone inside will be destroyed and then the monsters will find you in your caves and though your fight will be valiant, it will be brief."

The cave was silent as everyone absorbed the finality of the prophet's tone.

"Is this truly the only way, John?" Coal asked.

"Yes, Coal. I am sad to say it is," the prophet said.

"It won't be easy to convince the council," Faldon said.

"Nonetheless, they must be convinced," the prophet said. "You have people inside. Tell them it is time for boldness."

Faldon's face was filled with sorrow. "But to just abandon the academy to those creatures . . ."

"Faldon, I understand your sentiments, but they are ill placed," the prophet said. "The academy is not just some border land fort that became a fortress that became a school. The academy is what it has always been; a group of warriors that have banded together to protect the lands from evil. Master Latva was wrong when he told you that the academy could not be saved. The people inside those walls are the academy. By rescuing those people, saving the academy is exactly what you are doing. Walls can be rebuilt. People cannot."

Faldon's jaw tightened. "Yes, sir."

The prophet gave them a kind smile. "Don't worry. You have everything you need to succeed in this plan. I look forward to seeing you soon."

The prophet's eyes moved away and the mirror went blank.

"I . . . still can't believe it," Demetrius said. "We come all this way just to retreat."

"No," Justan said. "We came to fight and that's what we'll be doing. Say what you will, but the task the prophet has given us is anything but easy."

"A dag-gum frontal charge and retreat," Lenny said with

a slight shake of his head. "That's a massacre waitin' to happen."

"We will have to coordinate our attack with the people inside," Locksher said, rubbing his chin. "They will have to be ready to come out and join us at just the right time."

"You heard what the prophet said. Willum and Darlan have to convince the council to evacuate," Faldon replied.

"Yes and that will be a tall task," Coal said, his face filled with concern.

"To succeed, we will need to break the army's spirits," Lance said. "Strike 'em hard. Scare the hell out of 'em."

"The witch has too tight a grip on them," Jhonate said. "They will not break easily."

"Perhaps, but we have something the mother of the moonrats doesn't know about." said Sir Hilt. He inclined his head towards his sleeping wife. "We have a witch of our own."

Chapter Twenty Seven

Sweat trickled down Willum's back as his father told him of the prophet's warning. He sat in the council waiting room with the other assistants, his heart racing. *Father I don't know how we're going to do this.*

The wizard was sitting astride Samson on the outskirts of Wobble while Faldon's army made preparations in the darkness behind him. It was the first time they had been close enough to speak to each other without both of them laying still and meditating. *The prophet said it is time for boldness, Willum. You and Darlan have no choice but to act right away.*

It will be difficult. We've made little progress.

Anything new since last night? Coal asked.

Darlan met with Swift Kendyl this morning. Every member of the War Council that can be ruled out as the traitor is now on our side. Darlan had been working on the Training School Council members for days. Tad had been suspicious even of them, but Darlan felt they were all easy to rule out since none of them had been part of the day-to-day operations inside the academy until after the siege.

So it is down to Sabre Vlad, Hugh the Shadow, and Stout Harley then? Coal asked.

Or their assistants, Willum replied, eyeing the other occupants of the room. There were three of them and they were all possible suspects.

There was Silent Josef, Hugh the Shadow's assistant. He was fair faced, red haired, and wore black leather armor, the standard uniform of the Assassins Guild. Rumor had it that he carried more blades secreted around his body than anyone but

Hugh himself.

Then there was Kathy the Plate, Stout Harley's assistant. She had a pretty face, but did her best to hide it. She kept her blond hair short and painted a thick black stripe across her face that ran from temple to temple and covered her from nose to eyebrow. When she had her helmet on, it made her a terrifying sight, giving the illusion that there was no one inside the armor.

Finally there was Lyramoor, Sabre Vlad's half-elf assistant. He wore scalemail over light chain and a leather weapon sash filled with throwing knives. He was one of the deadliest swordsmen in the academy and fiercely loyal to Vlad, but he was also known as the most ill tempered and hard to deal with graduate in the school. Willum had always wondered why Sabre Vlad had picked him. The two men couldn't have been any more different.

All three of the assistants were staring back at Willum. Or more accurately, they were staring at the axe he wore on his hip. Word had gotten around that Tad had left the axe to him, but this was the first time he had worn it around the others.

"Hey Willum," said Silent Josef. Hugh the Shadow had given him the name as somewhat of a joke. While on a mission, he was silent as death. Otherwise, he was the loudest mouthed graduate in his guild. "We've been debating over here and we hoped you could settle something for us. Why did Tad the Cunning leave you his axe?"

"I guess he liked me," Willum said with a shrug. He didn't blame them for wondering. He hadn't been Tad's brightest student. "All he said in his letter was that he thought I could handle it."

"But you aren't even an axe guy," Josef laughed. "It's totally different than fighting with a scythe."

"Then I suppose it's time for me to learn," Willum replied. In truth he was wary about using the axe at all. Tad's instructions had been very specific.

"Let us see it, then," said Kathy the Plate, an axe user herself. She was one of very few women in the academy, but no one doubted she was as tough as any man. She wore the heaviest heavy plate armor in the Defense Guild just to prove it.

Willum understood their curiosity. Tad had always kept his axe sheathed and most students had never seen it before. He was hesitant, though. He was getting enough attention over the axe as it was.

Go ahead. Show it to them, Coal said. *I want to try something Edge did the other day.*

Willum thumbed open the clasp around the handle and slid the axe from its halfsheath. He laid it on the table before them so that they could take a look. Even Lyramoor stepped closer.

The half-elf had seen a lot of battle. He had a puckered scar that ran from just under his right eye down to his upper lip, the pointed tip of one ear had been cut off, and a chunk of his left nostril was missing. Willum had heard whispers that the rest of Lyramoor's body was a heavily scarred mess. Swen had seen him bathing once and told him there was no way that so many scars could have come from battle alone.

"Just don't touch it. Tad says it has been known to bite," he said, hoping they would be cautious, but if anything, the assistants looked even more curious.

"Ooh, that thing is wicked!" said Josef, leaning in closer to the axe, but to Willum's relief he didn't try to touch it. "What does it do?"

"I'm still figuring that out," Willum said. The runes on the side of the axe didn't just look painted red anymore. They glowed. To Willum the axe felt hungry. It was as if it was sending out a signal begging someone to use it.

Is it really that dangerous? Coal asked in concern.

I was exaggerating, Willum said. In truth he wasn't sure. Tad's notes on the axe had been quite intimidating, but he didn't think it could do anything to someone who hadn't claimed ownership over it. He hadn't dared try to communicate with it yet himself for just that reason.

"It's gorgeous," Kathy said, her eyes reflecting the red of the runes. Lyramoor's eyebrows rose.

Now, Coal sent. *I am going to change your sight so that*

you can see if any of them are wearing magic. Are you ready?

You can do that? Willum asked.

The mere fact that you are bonded to me means that you have some small magic ability. From talking to Locksher and Edge, I should be able help you shift to mage sight. I tried it earlier with Bettie and it worked just fine.

Alright. Do it. Willum said. He felt a little pressure between his eyes and his vision shifted. The axe glowed a blaze of yellow and red.

Air and fire magic, Coal said. *And very powerful.*

Willum's eyes darted to the others. Each of them had magic somewhere about them. Kathy's breastplate glowed a dark blue, Josef had multiple magic knives glowing from within his armor, and Lyramoor . . . The half-elf's whole body shimmered with a yellow haze.

That one has himself protected from mage sight somehow. We can see he has magic, but we just don't know what it is. Very interesting, Coal said. Willum thought it made him even more likely to be the traitor.

Kathy the Plate leaned closer to the axe, her finger's twitching. The runes glowed even brighter. "Are you sure you won't let me hold it?"

That seemed like a very bad idea. Willum picked the axe up off the table. "Not yet. Not until I know what it can do."

She frowned in disappointment, but didn't press the matter. Weapons were a personal thing. There was a standard code in the academy. You didn't touch a another warrior's weapon without their permission and it wasn't considered disrespectful to refuse a request.

Now I'll help you shift to spirit sight, Coal said. *You are looking for a sphere a little smaller than the size of your fist.*

That moonrat eye you warned me about, Willum said.

Yes, Coal replied. *Watch.*

Willum felt as if something very fine had been drawn across his eyes. His vision shifted again.

The axe in his hand burned even brighter as if white light was trying to break free from within the red and yellow magic.

Binding magic, Coal said. *Willum, that axe is very dangerous indeed. I would rather that you didn't mess with it.*

Willum didn't answer, but put the axe back into the half-sheath at his waist and looked at the others. He didn't see anything on Josef or Kathy and didn't expect to be able to see past Lyramoor's yellow haze, but to his surprise, there were two things on the half-elf. An earring in his pointed ear shimmered white and there was something near his abdomen that had a shape hard to define. It looked to be a bit smaller than Coal had said to look for, but he couldn't be sure.

Ah, his protection doesn't cover spirit magic, Coal said. *But then why would it? Few have spirit sight anymore.*

Do you think he's the one? Willum asked.

It is hard to tell, Coal replied. *I don't think that was a moonrat eye. You should keep a close watch on him though. See what Darlan thinks.*

There was a sharp rap on the door, signaling them that the council meeting was over. The four of them stood at attention waiting for the council members to file into the room. The atmosphere was a bit tense at first as Dann Doudy barged through. He seemed so upset that he didn't have so much as a sneer for Willum as he walked past him and into the corridor behind. Stout Harley was next, the wide man giving a jerk of his head to Kathy the Plate as he passed. She followed him out of the room, trotting to keep up. Willum noticed that they headed down the corridor in the opposite direction of Doudy.

The rest of the War Council seemed in high spirits as they walked in, talking to each other and laughing. Darlan wore a wide smile, something which told Willum she had achieved some sort of victory. The men clapped Oz the Dagger on the back and Willum understood.

The council had been talking about electing a member to take Tad's place as strategy teacher. Oz had been the obvious choice. He had been the strategy teacher in the training school for years after all, but there had been several other names up for consideration and the debate had been fierce.

Willum followed Darlan out of the room and down the

corridor towards the rear entrance of the council hall. They didn't speak until they were out of the building and then Darlan cast a privacy bubble around them so that no one could overhear.

"So Oz won?"

"Yes!" she said. "Now we have someone we can trust that isn't just part of the War Council, but part of the Battle Academy Council as well. If we're lucky some of them will start confiding in him or Dann Doudy will make a move and we will have the proof we need."

Willum sighed. "Darlan, things have changed. We're out of time."

He told her about the prophet's vision and the Mage School's offer of help. As he spoke, her steps slowed and her smile faded.

"You can speak with your father right now?" she asked and Willum nodded. "Ask him when Faldon's army plans to attack."

"They are planning right now," he said. "They will finish preparations tomorrow and get in position to strike early the next day."

She ran a hand through her hair and frowned. "That is close to the prophet's two day deadline."

"I know, but father says they need every second they can get to make sure everything goes as smoothly as possible," he replied.

"Well, so do we, so I suppose I can't complain," Darlan said, then stamped her foot. "Damn, it's going to be hard to get the council to abandon this place!"

"Well, I think if we-."

She stomped her foot again. "Blast it!"

"You know, Sir Edge was quite surprised to hear that you swore so much," Willum said, then winced, immediately regretting his words.

Her face colored, but she forced a smile and waved at some people that called out her name. "You told him I swore?"

Why did you tell her that? Coal asked.

"Well, no. I just repeated what you said to my father. I didn't know it would be a surprise," Willum said hurriedly.

What? Blame it on me? Coal said in surprise. *I haven't even met the woman yet.*

Sorry, Father! I wasn't thinking.

"A mother doesn't swear around her children," she said, continuing to force a smile on her face for the passers by. "And what the hell do you mean, I 'swear so much'?"

"Those were my father's words. Not mine," he said.

Willum! Coal snapped. *Don't tell people every thing you hear.*

"Don't try to shift the blame to your father," she said, this time shooting him a glare despite the people watching.

"Shouldn't we be discussing how we're going to convince the council?" he asked, hoping to change the subject.

Then don't bring such things up! Coal sent.

"Fine, but I'm not forgetting this discussion," she said. They entered the door that led down to the temporary Reneul Mayor's office and she stopped briefly when she saw no one was in the stairwell. "It is getting late, but I suppose we'll need to gather together the council members we know we can trust and have a plan ready for the council meeting first thing in the morning."

"Do you know what you're going to say?" he asked.

"The prophet said it's time for boldness, so let's be bold," she replied and headed down the stairs.

Willum sat on his cot, the soft glow of the light orb illuminating the notebook in his hands. The council members had left and the plans were set for the morrow. Darlan had gone to bed and now there was only this one task left.

What do you think, father? he asked.

I think you have the right of it. I don't see what else the creature could be, Coal said, his voice sounding closer than ever. It reminded Willum of evenings as a child, his father sitting next to him with his arm around his shoulder, talking about their day before tucking him into bed. As always, Coal tempered his advice. *But it is hard to tell for sure. I understand why you feel you need to do this. Just please use caution.*

Of course, father, Willum said.

Good night then. I will monitor you and try to help if you have trouble.

That shouldn't be necessary, but thank you. Good night, Willum said. He flipped through the pages of the book again.

When Darlan had opened the lockbox with Tad's key, the book had been the only item inside. It read like a journal, but really it was more of an instruction book on how to use the axe. Tad had been meticulous, keeping track of every bit of information he had been able to wring from the creature bound to it.

More importantly, Willum had discovered that the creature monitored Tad's every move. It would have seen how he died. Willum needed that information. They would be facing Dann Doudy in the morning and they needed to know what they were up against.

He had read Tad's notes over and over until he was fairly confident he knew what to do. Still, he glanced at some of the key passages again.

. . . The main thing to remember is the rules. Always follow the rules if you wish to avoid punishment. The creature will never break the rules, but it will find ways to work around them. Finding a way to take advantage of the rules is its main source of entertainment I think. Other than that, be clever. The longer you are clever, the longer it stays amused . . .

. . . I have refused to name it, something the creature ridicules me for. Instead I have focused on trying to discover what it was before it was bound to the axe. This both excites and vexes the creature for I still have not figured it out. Twenty years of research have left me without the answer. . .

. . . seen glimpses of white skin and black claws as

it hands over the ledger. I have seen red eyes through the cloud from time to time and once I saw a narrow tail with a forked end when I won a challenge and forced it to reveal a part of itself . . .

. . . Reading these words, you might think the creature evil and yet I don't think it is. I have seen both cruelty and kindness from it over the years. I would label it insane if it weren't so cunning. Perhaps unhinged is a better word to describe it. It is quick to anger and quick to praise. Sometimes it seems melancholy and sometimes giddy . . .

Willum skipped forward to Tad's last words in the notebook. He had read them multiple times and they seemed eerily prophetic.

. . . I have come to tire of the creature. I used to see it as a friend of sorts, a nightly challenger I looked forward to battling, but its antics have worn me thin. Now I avoid using the axe so that I won't have to deal with it. I'm afraid that has made it become tired of me as well. It has become much crueler of late. I believe that it seeks a way to betray me. It yearns for a new master and truthfully it is probably time.

One day soon I shall find a new weapon and then I will need to decide what to do with this old axe of mine. I have not yet decided whether to pass it on or bury it away. The latter option would perhaps be for the best, yet I can't bear to do it. I think I understand the creature better than ever now and it makes me sad . . .

Finally he sat the book to the side. Willum tapped the orb of light and the room plunged into darkness. He reached down to pick up the axe and the moment his hand touched the grip, the runes glowed red again.

Willum took a deep breath and let it out slowly, then laid back on the cot, holding the axe against his chest. "Alright axe, let's have a chat," he said and closed his eyes.

There was a brief unpleasant sensation like he was falling. Then he was no longer laying down, but standing up. He was somewhere high up in the sky, standing in the center of a rain cloud. Or at least that was his first impression.

He came to realize he was actually standing in a chamber of some sort. A chamber with walls, ceiling and floor made up of black and purple mist. The area was lit by sparkling shards of electricity that danced through the ceiling. Despite the look of the place, the air didn't feel moist. It was dry and very hot. Willum realized that the room wasn't made of cloud at all, but smoke.

"Are you here?" Willum asked.

A portion of the smoke cloud pulled away from the wall and wafted over to stand in front of him. A pair of red eyes glowed from deep within and Willum readied himself for the battle that would take place. He went over the rules in his mind. Be clever, Tad had said. Be clever.

"*Who is it that seeks my power?*" Its voice was both thick and raspy, high pitched and low, like two voices speaking together as one. "*Hmm, you smell like a warrior, but your thoughts . . . Are you an innkeeper? A stableman, perhaps?*"

Willum knew it couldn't read his thoughts. Tad's notes said so. It was mocking him. Trying to gauge his reaction. He kept his face from betraying his emotions.

"I wish to see the list of rewards due," Willum said.

"*Due? Ho-ho, and due to whom?*" it asked.

"To me," he said. "I am Willum, son of Coal and Tad the Cunning has bequeathed you to me."

"*I have been bequeathed to you?*" The thing yawned from within the smoky haze. "*Bequeathed, bequeathed. I hate being bequeathed. I much prefer being won in battle. Ho! Yes a battle to the death with me as the prize. So much more fun that way.*"

"Nevertheless, Tad's account is mine. I wish to see the ledger," he said.

"*The ledger? Ho-ho, did Tad leave you instructions then?*" it asked.

"The ledger please," Willum said and held out his hand. The ledger would be full of Tad's winnings and losses in the creature's games.

"*Hmph,*" it said and a long thin arm reached out of the cloud. Its skin was smooth and white and it had a book grasped in its hand. Its nails were pointed and red.

The book was bound in white leather that matched the color of the creature's skin. In flowery writing, the lettering on the front cover said, 'Tad The Cunning, Debts And Powers Owed', but Tad's name had been crossed out and 'Willum, Son Of Coal' had been scratched in above it, clawed directly into the leather. He opened the book to find that the pages were covered in the same flowery script, the ink a deep red.

Be clever, he reminded himself. Make it interested.

"Nice handwriting," Willum said, one eyebrow raised. "But I have to say, bound in your skin and written in your blood? That's going a bit far to impress me."

"*Would you prefer it bound in your skin and written in your blood?*" it threatened.

"You can't do that. Not unless I agree to it," Willum said and flipped through the pages. They were filled with rows of columns. On the left side were the axe's debts and on the right were Tad's. On each page so far they were all crossed out. "So a crossed out debt is a debt paid."

"*There are rules regarding questions,*" it said.

"You don't have to answer but if you do answer, you must state the truth," Willum said. "I didn't ask a question though. I made a statement."

The red eyes narrowed. "*You are correct. A debt crossed out is a debt paid or a debt bargained away. Either way a debt no more.*"

"Thank you," he said and flipped quickly through the pages. In the beginning of the book, the debts had been evenly skewed both ways. As he moved farther along they had become heavily skewed in Tad's favor. He sped through to the last pages and saw that in the last year, the results had swung in the axe's favor. When he reached the final page and frowned. The last crossed out debt on Tad's side said 'protective/mental' in the creature's flowery hand.

"*You start out with debts,*" the creature said with a chuckle.

"One," Willum said. "I owe you an answer to a question."

"*And do you know the rules?*"

"That is a question and here is my answer. I must obey the same rules as you. I must speak the truth at all times and I must always make good on my debts. If I attempt to do otherwise there are consequences," he said with a smile. "Debt paid."

"*Oh ho! A clever move for the new wielder. This is all a bit annoying, but still, new is fun, or can be fun. Hmm . . . Are you fun, Willy?*"

"That's Willum."

"*I prefer Willy. Or Willyum. Yum-yum-yum, Willy Yum!*"

Willum frowned. "Tad did say you would be tedious."

"*Ho-ho! Tedious? And you said bequeathed earlier. Such fancy words for someone so obviously less smart than the late Mister Cunning.*" It chuckled. "*I'll give you a point for that. One point for Willy Yum.*"

"Oh, good. One point for me." Willum said, irritated at the thing's obnoxiousness. "That means I gain a power."

The thing grunted. "*I suppose. What do you want?*"

"I shall think on that," Willum said. "But first I wish to make good on one of your debts to Tad."

A long white finger tipped with a red nail pointed from the shifting black cloud. "*The ledger has been updated, Willy.*"

He looked down to see that all debts under Tad had been crossed out and that the name on the top of the next page was his. The debts had been transferred over.

"Good. First I have a question," Willum said.

"*Ho ho, you wish to use a question?*" it said. "*Old Tad horded those like they were gold. So cautious with his questions, that Tad.*"

"It says here that I have four questions and five, no-, six

powers due," Willum said, noting that the power he had gained earlier had already been noted along with the date and time.

"Do you know the rules about a question debt?"

"You don't have to answer a question unless you have agreed to it in advance. Otherwise you can answer any other question I ask and consider the debt paid." Which is why he had been avoiding asking questions so far. He noticed that since he owed it no answers, the creature was asking questions whenever it wanted.

"True, Willy. True." The thing huffed. *"And I have agreed to nothing yet. What is the nature of the questions you wish to ask?"*

"I wish to find out how Tad was murdered," Willum said.

"Oh ho! I see. Willy Yum Yum wants to know how poor Mister Cunning met his end, does he?"

"Yes I do," he replied.

The smoke swirled as the creature laughed. *"I will refuse to answer."*

Willum had thought it might come to that. "Then I have an alternate deal."

"And what does Willy have to offer me?" it asked.

"A game," Willum said. "I will guess what you are."

"What-what?" the thing laughed. *"You would guess that? After knowing me these few minutes?"*

"I believe I have a good idea," he replied.

"And how many guesses do you need?" it asked.

"One," he said.

"Ho-ho! One guess? Yes, I will agree to that. If you make that guess, I will tell you all about Tad's death."

"But that's not all. Since I am about to attempt something Tad the Cunning couldn't figure out in twenty years, I want more." Willum found that he was getting used to the way this creature thought. "I have a big battle coming up. A war starts in two days. I want unlimited access to your powers until the fighting is over."

"Unlimited?" The creature spat. *"Oh Willy-Willy those*

are high stakes. High stakes indeed! Unfortunately, they are impossible. I don't have unlimited powers to give. You would use up my magic in a day or less. I would give you six hours."

"Twelve," Willum said. He knew how the axe charged. "You can feast on the blood of the goblinoids I kill."

"*Goblinoids? Ugh, Willy,*" it said with a chuckle. "*But done, if you agree to my terms upon your failure.*"

"If I fail, all your debts to me will be wiped clean," Willum said,

"*Ho-ho! That is so, and yet there is more,*" the creature said. "*If you fail I want three days of your life.*"

Willum frowned. Tad said nothing about this in his notebook. "And how would you take three days?"

"*Ho-ho! Question asked, answer given,*" the creature said happily and Willum winced, knowing that one of his answers owed had been stricken from the ledger. "*You will spend those three days in here with me while your body sleeps. Three straight days of play. Oh-ho how much fun!*"

Willum swallowed. "Agreed on one condition. I get to choose when the days start."

"*Done!*" The creature giggled, jumping up and down within its smoky cover. "*The pact is made! Now hurry! Hurry and fail, Willy!*"

Willum took a deep breath. This was the moment he had prepared for. Be clever, Tad had said. Be impressive. "I will begin with the clues. You have white skin, red nails, red eyes, and a forked tail. You are smart. You love to play games."

"*Yes, I know,*" the creature said, sounding bored. "*Tad knew this too.*"

"You have magic ability inherent within you that draws on air and fire," Willum said. "Two complimenting magics, but you are stronger in air."

"*Good, yes. Ho, a connection Tad probably knew but never mentioned,*" it said, its voice wary.

"My father is a wizard. I learned many things from him. When I was bored, he used to let me read some of his books. In fact, he had one book in particular that I loved as a child," he said. "It was one of my favorites because it had these beautifully painted pictures. It spoke about the different types of magic and magical creatures. I saw one that looked like you."

The creature said nothing.

"Once I read Tad's description I knew right away that you were a demon," Willum said with a smile and the creature quivered. "I thought back to that book I so loved and I remembered. There are four types of demons, one to combat each type of blood magic."

He quoted the book from memory. "'There are the kobolds, tough and hardy, made to fight the dwarves. Their strength is in earth first and water second and they are fairly common. There are the merfolk, full of life, made to fight the elves, but they are few in number. Their strength is water first and earth second. Then there are bandhams, very rare, made to fight the dragons. Their strength is fire first and air second.' And then there is you, the rarest demon of them all."

The smoke around the creature fluttered and it began to hiss.

"You are one of the demons made to fight the gnomes," Willum said with a smile. "You are an imp."

"*Impossible*," it said. "*How could you discover this when Tad could not?*"

"I had information he didn't. Tad was the best tactician in the academy, perhaps in the known lands. But he wasn't raised by a wizard."

The imp growled. "*You have the victory, Willum, son of Coal.*"

Willum opened the ledger to see that the debt had been noted. "Now you will answer my questions."

"*The debt will be paid,*" it said.

"Did Dann Doudy kill Tad the cunning?"

"*Dann Dann? Yes and no,*" said the imp.

Willum's lips tightened. Even in defeat the imp would be difficult. "Your promise was that you would tell me 'all about Tad's death'. So tell me."

"*Oh-ho. I was careless with that promise,*" said the imp.

It let out an irritated sigh. "*I only know what I saw. Tad, poor Tad came to me that night determined to win more powers. He played with more interest than I have seen from him in years. Oh-ho, even when he lost he settled for pain instead of loss of power.*"

Willum's teeth clenched. That's why Tad's face had looked so haggard that night. He knew there would be battles ahead and needed every ounce of help he could wring from the imp.

"*When I asked him what powers he wanted, Tad was very specific. He wanted protection from mental attack. That was rare. He had never asked it before. No, but it was something I could provide.*"

Willum nodded. "Tad thought that people were warming up to Doudy too easily and he was convinced that somehow he had some kind of mental power to control the whip beast that attacked us."

"*Ho-ho, well perhaps he did, but Tad made an error,*" said the imp. "*He asked for the wrong protection. Dann Dann didn't use a mental attack. No-no. Poor Tad backed Dann Dann into a corner and when the man turned to monster Tad was unprepared.*"

"What did Doudy do to him?"

"*It tore him apart. Tiny pieces. I was sad. So sad. Poor Tad. He picked the wrong power.*"

"Wait," Willum said. "You could have saved him if he had chosen a different power?"

"*The attack was not mental,*" the imp said. "*If he had asked for protection against paralysis, I would have been able to disperse the attack.*"

"So he couldn't move. That's how Doudy beat him." Willum's hand moved to his forehead. "He couldn't move and you just sat there and let him be torn apart? Tad, your companion for twenty years?"

"*He chose wrong.*" The imp's voice was defensive. "*I felt sorrow, yes. But the rules are the rules.*"

"You could have saved him!" Willum walked up to the

cloud. "There's no reason for you to hide anymore. Disperse this so that I can look in your face."

"*I will not. That wasn't part of the debt,*" said the imp, sounding irritated.

"It is time for the rules to change. Do you know why Tad left you to me, Imp?" Willum asked. "It wasn't because he died. He had planned to give you to me even before Dann Doudy killed him. He went to see Dann Doudy that night hoping to use your power for the last time."

The creature fumed behind the smoke. "*He tired of me. He told me so. I was bored with him anyway.*"

"Tad was tired of being taunted and hurt, that much is true," Willum said. "But he could have buried you in the earth or sealed you away somewhere you wouldn't be found."

The imp's baleful eyes glared at him through the smoke. "*Why didn't he then, Willy Yum?*"

"He had come to understand you over the years," Willum said. "Tad knew why you craved the games so much and why you were so upset when he let days go by without speaking to you. The last words in his notebook were, 'I think I understand the creature better than ever now and it makes me sad. To hide the axe away would be to doom it to solitude and that would be an unthinkable torture for this fiend. It is so lonely. Perhaps I can find it a new friend.'"

"*Ho ho, a friend? A friend for a fiend?*" the imp let out a bitter laugh.

"Tad chose me to be your new companion but it is up to you, imp," Willum said. "Do you want a master that only comes to you when he needs something from you? I can be that, like Tad was at the end. But I don't want to be. I can be your friend. I can play your games. I can keep you company when I have time to spare. But I won't be bullied and I won't be tortured. Do you understand?"

The imp grunted but this time it didn't bother to mock him. "*Go to sleep, Willy. If you survive tomorrow I will speak to you again.*"

"No, we speak now," Willum said. "I'm not finished,

imp. We have a lot to discuss."

Chapter Twenty Eight

"And Demon Jenn?" Darlan asked as they made their way towards the council hall in the dim morning light.

"Her death was a mistake as far as the imp knew," Willum said. "She must have seen Tad enter the room, because she barged in just as Doudy started to change."

"*You are going to tell everyone what I am now? That was not in the deal,*" said the imp. Their negotiations had taken up most of the night, but in the end it was agreed that he would allow the axe to monitor him and speak to him at any time. It couldn't read his indirect thoughts, so the only way he could communicate back without speaking aloud was when he was in direct contact with it.

Willum touched the axe's hilt. *It was never agreed that I wouldn't tell anyone. I am keeping no secrets from Darlan or my father. However I promise you now that I will be careful who I mention it to.*

"*Promise noted, but take care, Willy,*" the imp grumbled. "*Loose tongues, loose tongues.*"

I am surprised you allowed the thing access to you during the day, Coal said. *I'm not sure that was wise.*

I grew up bonded. What's one more voice in my head? Willum replied. *The thing is lonely, father. Believe me, it will be much easier for me to listen to its comments from time to time throughout the day than wrestle with it every night.*

"How sad," Darlan said, her brow creased with a deep frown and it took Willum a half second to remember what remark she was responding to. "Poor Jenn. Poor Tad. Hell, poor all of us if we make a mistake this morning."

"We'll be fine," Willum said, trying to sound encouraging. "Now that we know what we're up against, we'll be prepared."

"I'm not worried about Doudy," she said. "It's the rest of it that makes me nervous."

They walked in through the back door of the council hall and headed down the corridors, Willum keeping a hand on the axe. To Doudy and the traitor, this meeting should seem no more important than any other, but he still felt on edge, seeing possible danger in every shadow.

"*Ho-ho, how jumpy you are, Willy!*" the axe said. "*There is no one in this corridor but you and the scary wizardess.*"

You can sense that? Willum asked, relaxing a little. *Sense the people around me?*

"*Of course,*" it replied. "*Living things always give off a certain . . . flavor.*"

And you just give me that information freely?

"*We made a deal, did we not? Free use of my powers for twelve hours?*"

That doesn't start until tomorrow after the fighting begins, he reminded.

"*Oh-ho! I must have forgotten,*" it said.

Willum smiled. *I think you're just enjoying the extra freedom I've given you.*

"*The freedom I bargained for, you mean,*" it said.

Willum didn't bother to correct it. They were nearing the council chamber. Just before they reached the waiting room, Darlan turned to him.

"You know what to do," she said with a firm nod, then patted his cheek and walked inside.

At that moment Darlan reminded Willum of his mother. Not Becca, the woman who had raised him, but his real mother, the one that had been taken from him when he was four. It was the same firm but affectionate look his mother had given him the day she left him with his nursemaid and went to her trial.

Willum's sense of unease came rushing back. He

followed her into the waiting room and found it difficult to stay behind with the other assistants as she entered the council room proper. He stood right next to the door, waiting for the signal to come in.

Silent Josef laughed. "What was that little pat on the cheek about, Willum?"

He had hoped they hadn't seen that. Kathy the Plate was giving him an amused smile and Lyramoor rolled his eyes. Willum's cheeks colored. "I don't know. She says I remind her of her son."

"Oh?" Josef said. "Does she tuck you in at night too? Maybe sing you a lullaby?"

"No, but she does make me stand there and hold her yarn while she knits me a sweater," Willum said.

"No way! Really?" Josef guffawed.

"No," Willum said, straight faced.

Josef's smile faded and this time Kathy laughed.

"*Ho-ho! Willy with a stinger!*" said the axe.

Father can you switch my eyes to spirit sight again? Willum asked. He felt that click within his mind and the magic objects in the room started to glow again. There was nothing new to be seen. Lyramoor was still the only one with spirit magic on him. Willum rested his hand on the axe handle. *Imp, can you sense anything of interest on them? Anything that might link them to the mother of the moonrats?*

"*No, Willy. But the elf is covered with protective charms.*"

He's a half-elf, Willum sent as he glanced at Lyramoor.

"*Oh? Is that what he tells you? Ho-ho, I can see why. His body has been carved on too many times for a fighter. I would say that one was a blood slave.*"

Willum swallowed. Keeping an elf as a blood slave was one of the darkest of crimes. *Wouldn't that make him a likely accomplice to a dark wizard like Ewzad Vriil?*

"*Not likely. Those scars are old and his charms would protect him from any sort of spirit influence.*"

There was a shout of alarm in the council room and Willum threw the door open. The assistants sprung to attention and the four of them rushed inside, hands on weapons. The councilmen were sanding around the large square council table staring at Darlan. She was giving them a pointed look in return.

"I didn't like his attitude," she said.

"How did you do that?" Sabre Vlad said, pointing at Representative Doudy.

The man was on the far side of the table sitting precisely upright and Willum could see thick bands of air magic binding him to his chair. Another wad of air had been shoved in his mouth so that he couldn't speak. To a person without mage sight, it would look like the man had been bound and gagged with invisible ropes.

"I have bound Representative Doudy so that he won't cause a commotion when I say what I have to say," Darlan said.

"I can see that, but how?" he asked.

"She's a wizardess, Vlad," Oz said. "I just learned the other day, but Tad knew about it."

"Does Faldon know?" Vlad asked.

"Of course he knows!" Darlan said.

"It wasn't that close kept of a secret," said Hugh the Shadow, who seemed completely unsurprised.

Stout Harley looked at the rest of them with wary eyes. "Looks like the Training Council representatives are unsurprised by this stunt of yours, Darlan. What is this about?"

"Come on in, assistants," said Oz the dagger, motioning the rest of them to come closer. "This involves you too."

Willum walked quickly over to Darlan's side, but the other three were more cautious as they moved to stand behind the leaders of their respective guilds.

"Alright, Oz. Darlan," said Hugh the Shadow, resting his elbows on the table and peering at the two of them over steepled fingers. "Tell us what you have to say."

"We have some very important things to discuss regarding the war," Oz said. "But before we can speak candidly, we need to root a traitor out from our midst."

"Doudy?" Harley snorted dismissively. "He's a blowhard and most likely a shill. But he's harmless. Even if he is spying for the enemy, there's no way he can tell them our secrets from inside these walls."

"Oh, we think he can," said Darlan. "But Doudy's the enemy we know about. Our first concern should be finding the enemy hiding among us."

"One of the rest of us?" Sabre Vlad said. "There's not another man or woman in this room I wouldn't trust the life of my wife and children with."

"That's what makes this so difficult," Darlan said. "It's the reason Tad never brought his concerns before the rest of you."

"Is this about Tad's death?" Hugh asked.

"Just spit it out," said Harley.

"Tad was convinced that someone in this room was telling the enemy the academy's patrol routes and troop movements long before the siege began," Darlan said.

"There's no way," said Silent Josef.

"Tad didn't want to believe it either," Oz said. "But the evidence is overwhelming. How else would an army this size be able to sneak up on us?"

"What Tad didn't know was how the traitor was getting his information to the enemy," Darlan said. "But just recently we learned what is controlling this army and that gave us the information we need . . ."

As Darlan told them about the mother of the moonrat and her capabilities, Willum was scanning the room looking for anyone with a hint of spirit magic.

Do you see anything father?

No, sent Coal. *If anyone here is holding a moonrat eye, they have it well hidden. However, Dann Doudy is undoubtedly one of the men transformed by Ewzad Vriil's power. He is pulsing with it, struggling to break free. Fortunately, Wizardess Sherl's binding spell seems to be keeping it at bay.*

What about you, imp? He asked, touching the axe handle. *Do you sense anything?*

"There is something . . . ho-ho, two signals! One is coming from Mister Dann Dann, the other is hard to see."

"A moonrat eye?" said Hugh. "Astounding. Imagine what we could do with that sort of long distance communication."

"So what do you want us to do, Darlan? Empty our pockets?" Sabre Vlad said. He stood. "Go ahead, search all of us. I'm telling you there's no way someone in this room would betray the academy." He gestured to Doudy. "Purple face over there excluded, of course."

"Even if it isn't on someone's person, they could have one back in their rooms somewhere hidden away," Swift Kendyl reminded.

"No, it's somewhere in this room," Willum said. "Representative Doudy has one, but someone else is hiding another."

"Willum here has a talent at being able to see spirit magic," Oz said. "That's why he was assigned to Darlan."

Willum was watching Lyramoor's reactions. The elf was eyeing everyone in the room with suspicion, his fingers twitching near the hilts of his weapons. The more he thought about it, the more likely it was that Lyramoor was the one. A blood slave would have been captured by a dark wizard. What if that wizard had been Ewzad Vriil. What if he had never truly been freed?

"What are you looking at?" Lyramoor growled. The elf's voice was low and ragged.

"Lyramoor has spirit magic on him right now," Willum said. "His earring is one piece, but he has something else. Something around his belt buckle."

The elf stepped back, his hands clutching his sword hilts. Now everyone was watching him, their hands on their own weapons.

Sabre Vlad raised a calming hand. "Lyramoor has nothing to hide."

"Then why is he acting like that?" asked Stout Harley, frowning in suspicion.

"Lyramoor," Vlad said. "Show them it isn't one of those eye things so we can move on."

"I refuse," said the elf and Sabre Vlad looked back at him in surprise. "I don't show that to anyone, Vlad. Not even you."

"Come on. I don't think he meant-." Vlad looked back to Willum. "What part of his body did you say it was?"

"His abdomen. Just above his belt buckle on his right side," Willum replied.

"What could possibly be so secret, I wonder?" said Hugh eyeing the elf thoughtfully.

"I will not say," said Lyramoor, his hands still clutching the hilts of his swords. "Only that it has nothing to do with this witch you speak of."

"That's it, half-elf," said Stout Harley, pulling his warhammer free of the straps holding it to his back. His hammer's name was Thud and it glowed black with earth magic. He took great pride in its ability to dent any armor he came up against. All of his armor radiated black, made of the same material as the hammer.

The men of the Swordsmanship Guild were taught not to draw their swords unless they were prepared to kill. Lyramoor slid his falchions half-free of their scabbards. "Please don't make me slay you, sir," he warned.

"Threaten me?" shouted Harley, his face red. He stepped towards the elf, his hammer raised. "I will pound you to jelly!"

"Stop it, both of you!" shouted Vlad, standing between them.

"No, it's not coming from him! Not the elf," said the imp.

"Wait!" said Willum. "It's not Lyramoor. He doesn't have it." Everyone turned to glare at him. "I'm sorry, whatever Lyramoor has, it's not a moonrat eye. It's here somewhere in this room though."

"No, it's-ah! It's him in the armor! Ho-ho! He is hiding something!"

"I see," Willum said in sudden understanding. That's why he couldn't see it. Stout Harley's armor was obscuring it. "Stout Harley, sir. Would you mind removing your breastplate? The magic is so thick it's distorting my spirit sight."

"What?" The large man turned on him, anger twisting his

face. "Remove my armor? For you? Are you insane? I'm the head of the Defense Guild. I have been for fifteen years. I don't remove my armor to sleep at night!"

I hope your axe is right, said Coal. *Stout Harley is a legend.*

They're all legends, father. It can't be helped, he said, then touched the axe handle. *You better be right about this, imp*!

"*It's no one else, Willy. It's him, old naughty Stout Stouty.*"

"You can't make him do it," said Kathy, brandishing her axe. "Who are you going to accuse next, Willum? You just going to go around the room hoping it sticks?"

"I'm sorry, Kathy," Willum said. "I wish it wasn't true, but I am sure of it. He has a moonrat eye hidden under his breastplate."

"Liar!" shouted Harley. "You lying pig!"

"Harley," said Sabre Vlad, shaken. "I have never heard you talk like that ever."

The council members gathered around the guildmaster and his assistant, their faces grim. Darlan was the only one whose look was sympathetic.

"How long have you had the eye, Harley?" she asked.

"He doesn't have nothing like that!" said Kathy the Plate.

"What did the witch promise you at first?" Darlan asked. "Companionship? Love?"

"She . . . You got it wrong. She's not like you think," said Harley, sweat pouring down his face.

"You didn't know what she would ask you for, did you?" she said.

"She just wanted to be close to me. I . . . didn't know she was listening to the meetings, I-!" He grimaced with sudden pain.

She's hurting him for disobeying, said Coal.

"I . . . I-I'm sorry, I . . ." he dropped his hammer and clutched at his chest, "Kathy!"

His assistant stared at him in concern, her axe hanging

loosely from her hand. "Yes, sir?"

"Unbuckle . . . my armor," he wheezed slapping at the buckle on his shoulder.

She swallowed, but sheathed her axe and loosened the upper and lower straps between the breastplate and backplate on his right side. Finally she worked them free and the armor swung open.

Harley reached his left hand up under his padding and sweat-stained shirt and grunted. When he pulled his hand back out, his fingers were clenched around a shriveled sickly-green orb. He extended his arm out over the table and tried to let go. His arm shook and he grit his teeth. He grabbed his wrist with his other hand and strained. Kathy the Plate reached for his arm.

"No!" he said "Don't touch it!" He slammed his fist against the table, then pryed his fingers loose with his right hand. Finally the eye fell to the table and rolled, coming to rest right next to where Willum stood.

The moment the eye left his hand, Stout Harley collapsed to his knees and took deep shuddering breaths, sobbing. "Sorry . . . so sorry. Poor Tad. I didn't know . . . didn't know."

Kathy knelt by her guildmaster's side, her face pale as she rebuckled his armor.

"How did you get the eye?" Hugh asked.

The large man hacked and spat. "A year ago . . . it was a gift from . . . a villager when we were out on patrol."

"All this time . . ." said Sabre Vlad.

"What do we do with the eye?" asked Mad Jon, glaring at the orb.

"Destroy it," said Darlan. "Nothing good can come from keeping it. It's just another way for the witch to spy."

"Can I?" asked Willum, an idea coming to his mind. He unsheathed the axe.

"With Tad's axe?" Hugh said. "It seems fitting."

The others nodded and Willum lifted the axe over the eye. *See if you can learn anything from this, imp.* He chopped down, slicing the eye neatly in two and the spirit magic faded away. Somewhere in the corner of his mind Willum heard a faint cry of outrage. He smiled in satisfaction.

"*Ho-ho, she was mad!*" said the imp.

Do you think you can sniff out her powers better now?

"*I'm no dog!*" it said indignantly. "*But yes.*"

"Perhaps we should be focusing on our friend, Representative Doudy," said Hugh the Shadow. "His face is not looking normal. Are you doing that to him, Darlan?"

Darlan's eyes widened. "This has nothing to do with my spell."

While they had been distracted, the man's face had grown a deep red and his nose had swelled and bulged until it hung from his face like a large overripe fruit almost as big as his head. It throbbed a deep purple and rippled as if something inside of it was moving around.

"Ugh. What is wrong with him?" Josef asked.

"I think we should throw him off the wall," said Sabre Vlad with disgust. "Send Vrill and his witch a message."

Doudy shook his head, swinging his enormous nose back and forth.

"Is your spell going to hold?" Willum asked Darlan.

"I don't know. So far it's keeping his transformation in check, but-!" Darlan gasped as Doudy's nose tore free from his face and hit the table with a plopping sound.

It sat there on the table for a moment, sagging slightly while something moved around within. Then from the jagged hole where it had torn free from his face, the sack of flesh that used to be Doudy's nose turned inside out, revealing a writhing mass of purple tentacles, each one with a hissing snake-like mouth on the end.

Two throwing daggers sunk into the center of the squirming mass as Hugh and Josef aimed their throws perfectly. Several of the tentacles wilted as if dead, but the thing didn't seem to notice. It lashed out at Dann Doudy and Willum saw through his mage sight that the tentacles were pulling on the bands of air binding the man.

"Darlan!" he shouted. But the thing had already ripped the gag of air from Doudy's mouth. The man hacked and coughed, his throat swelling.

Darlan gathered her magic for another spell and the council members ran around the table towards the man, weapons drawn. Swift Kendyl was there first, dagger in hand. Then a golden sphere appeared in Doudy's mouth and a buzzing sound filled the room.

Everyone froze.

Doudy spat the sphere onto the table and laughed at the dagger inches from his throat. "This was not the way it was supposed to go!" He grabbed Swift Kendyl's wrist with a swollen red hand covered in purple veins and twisted. Wllum heard the bones snap. "I was content to walk around in this place and stir things up until Ewzad's creations arrived, but you guys had to mess things up!

"**Look at my face!**" he shouted, his voice deepening as he pointed at the bony stub that was all that remained in the jagged tear that used to be his nose. "**I hate that!**"

He turned and threw Swift Kendyl across the room. His paralyzed form struck Oz the Dagger and both of them were slammed against the wall.

Now, imp! Now! Break the spell before he hurts anyone else! Willum called, watching in terror as Doudy continued to transform, his figure tearing free of his fancy clothing as he grew and distorting further, becoming bulbous and red and purple and warty.

"*I am, I am!*" the imp said. "*It's not the same magic he used against Tad!*"

I'm trying to help too, said Coal and Willum could sense his father prying at the magic running through his body. *But that is a tough spell and it is hard to overcome at this distance.*

"**I bet Ewzad finds this funny. He hated my nose. Used to mock me about it all the time!**" said the thing Doudy had become, now seven feet tall and almost as wide. He swung one bulging arm, knocking Sabre Vlad and Mad Jon tumbling across the floor like rag dolls, unable to break their fall. "**Why? It's a Doudy family trait!**"

Doudy grabbed the frozen form of Silent Josef with one

hand and lifted him over his head. A throwing knife darted through the air, sinking into one of the empty nasal cavities where his nose had been. Flame erupted from the wound and Doudy howled, dropping Josef to the ground.

Lyramoor leapt up on the table, twin falchions in hand, heading for the golden orb that contained the paralyzing spell. The tentacled thing, now three times its original size, rolled into his path. It lashed out at him with fang-tipped mouths. Lyramoor danced with his blades, slicing every hissing tentacle that came his way, but the beast rolled and lashed out with wicked attacks from every angle, keeping the elf on his heels.

He got free, Willum said, suspecting it was one of the elf's magic items that had done it. *What's taking you so long!*

"*I'm almost there, you . . . Ah!*" said the imp in triumph. "*Ho-ho, there you go!*"

There was a sound like the ring of a heavy bell and Willum felt the spell shatter around him. Everyone else remained frozen. *What about the others?*

"*I can't free everyone!*"

Break the sphere! Coal said.

Willum saw the golden sphere rolling and spinning along the edge of the solid table as it was jostled by Lyramoor's battle. Willum ran towards it, hoping to reach the sphere before Doudy saw him.

Doudy's swollen fingers had grown too large to grasp the small knife handle protruding from his face, but the fire had gone out and he gave up trying just in time to see Willum break free. He lunged forward and swung his heavy arm down in Willum's path.

Willum swung the axe to meet the giant fist, his mind flashing through his options. The axe had three different types of attack powers to grant; force, slice, and flame. Doudy was huge, so he didn't know how much good force would do, but Doudy's reaction to Lyramoor's flame knife made his decision.

Flame! Willum commanded. The blade struck between Doudy's first and second knuckle and the heavy bell rang out again.

A concussive wave of fire streaked up Doudy's arm, splitting and searing his flesh. But Willum had miscalculated the forces involved. The weight of the monster's punch knocked the axe back, driving its spiked end deep into Willum's shoulder. Both of them stumbled backwards, crying out.

Lyramoor had cut half of the thing's tentacles away, but it still rotated, bringing more tentacles to bear, keeping him from getting to the orb. He growled and went on the attack. With a flurry of strikes, he sliced away at the thing, cutting the tentacles as close to the center mass as he could.

It tried to turn and roll and rotate, but he didn't let up, slicing until quivering severed tentacles littered the table around him and the thing had no way to strike back. He lashed out with his foot, kicking it off of the table, and turned, swinging his sword. The falchion's edge caught the sphere dead center, shattering it to pieces.

The buzzing sound stopped and everyone was free.

Willum pulled the axe free from his shoulder and shifted it over to his left hand. He walked toward the monster, ignoring the blood pouring from the wound. Doudy clutched his ruined arm as his body continued to grow. Now at twelve feet tall, he had to hunch over, his shoulders touching the ceiling.

Just sit back and let them take care of it from here, Willy, said the imp.

He's right, Coal said and Willum felt his father's healing energies stopping the bleeding. *Just look at him, he has no chance.*

Tiny blades blossomed all over Doudy's body, causing various elemental effects, burning, freezing, and shocking as Hugh the Shadow emptied his arsenal of throwing weapons.

Stout Harley roared as he swung his hammer into the beast's knee, taking out the joint.

Doudy fell forward and smashed one massive fist into the man, slamming him into the council table with a loud crack. "**Traitor!**" he shouted and drew back his burned arm to strike again.

But the blow didn't connect. Sabre Vlad swung his sword

in a vicious blow that severed Dowdy's arm above the elbow.

"Get back!" Darlan yelled in warning and a jet of fire spewed from her fingers. It struck Doudy in his distorted chest and engulfed his body in flames. The council members dragged their wounded companions as far back as they could and Darlan clenched her fist, intensifying the heat as much as she dared within the confined space. Doudy screamed and fell forward, trying to drag his burning body towards them. He continued to grow even as he burned **"You can't kill me!"**

Protect me from the heat, imp, Willum said and walked towards the monster.

"Ho-ho, getting one more lick in, Willy?" it said. *"Done."*

What are you doing, Willum? Coal asked.

"Willum, get back!" Darlan yelled. She let go of the magic, but it was too late.

"I'm invincible!" said Doudy, dragging himself closer. **"I killed Tad the Cunning!"**

Willum stood in front of him, seeing the intensity of the flames, but not feeling the heat. "You cheated."

He swung the axe with both hands. *Force.* The blade struck the tiny handle of Lyramoor's knife that was still stuck in Doudy's nasal cavity and the bell rang once more.

Doudy's head blew to pieces.

The council watched as his body began to deflate. Darlan extinguished the flames that raged around Doudy's body, and they tended to their wounded.

Silent Josef and Mad Jon both had broken bones that Darlan was able to set with her magic. Stout Harley was battered and bruised. Doudy's blow had cracked the council table down the middle, but the strength of his armor had kept him alive.

Oz the Dagger and Swift Kendyl hadn't moved from their positions splayed in the corner. Luckily Oz only had a slight concussion and Darlan was able to revive him. But Swift Kendyl was dead. His neck had broken upon impact with the wall.

While they mourned their friend, Darlan told them of the prophet's vision and the Mage School's plan to rescue them.

They protested, but their arguments were half-hearted.

After fighting one of Ewzad's beasts, they now understood what it would take to face an army of them.

A loud knock on the council room door disrupted their debate. Bill the Fletch had sent a messenger from the wall. The goblinoid army had begun their attack.

Chapter Twenty Nine

There are no patrols or scouts, said Deathclaw. *They are too confident.*

Justan nodded. *I had hoped so. As far as the mother of the moonrats knows, there is no one in the area to oppose her.* And why shouldn't she be confident? If he had their numbers, he might be just as lax. By the academy's latest count, the besieging army numbered just over 36,000. *How far away are you from the others?*

Perhaps an hour, Deathclaw said. *The giant keeps up a good pace and the wizard and mage cast spells to keep the people from feeling fatigue.*

Since Hilt and Beth were needed on the assault, they had given their lodestones to Locksher and Vannya. The two magic users were accompanying Charz and Antyni as they led all of the noncombatants to the portal's location. The plan was to get everyone that couldn't fight to the Mage School and out of harms way before the fighting came anywhere near them. Sampo's fighters went along to escort them safely through. Then they would secure the area and be available to help the rest of the army escape when the time came.

Justan turned to his father. "Deathclaw has arrived at the hills near the portal. He says there are no enemy forces nearby."

"Good," Faldon said. "Let me know when the portal is activated. As soon as the people of Sampo start going through, we'll begin our attack."

Justan nodded, eager to get started. Their army waited in the hills just south of the City of Reneul and his sensitive ears could hear the shouts of the enemy forces already. "How are things going inside the academy, Master?"

Coal shrugged. "Nothing has changed since yesterday. The goblinoids throw themselves against the walls and the academy warriors slay them. The council has the people ready to flee as soon as we arrive at their gates."

The only real concerns had been the giants to the north of the academy and the orcs to the southwest. The orcs had constructed siege engines and battering rams and though the academy had been able to keep them from being used so far, the orcs would eventually figure out how get past their hail of arrows. The giants on the other hand had constructed crude trebuchets. So far they weren't very efficient and rarely threw anything over the wall, but they were starting to learn.

"That should be to our advantage," Justan said. "Hopefully it means they are watching the walls and not keeping an eye out for attack."

"That's the hope," Faldon agreed. He pointed to the map spread out on the ground in front of them, "Let's go over the plan one more time."

"We know the gall-durn plan," Lenny grumped. "We helped you make it."

"No, you didn't!" said Bettie with a scowl. "Captain Demetrius helped him make it. You just stood around and grumbled about every idea, ya loudmouth!"

Lenny winced. Bettie always groused at him, but for some reason the last few days she had been brutal. He couldn't say a word without getting shouted down. Justan wondered if she had heard about an old girlfriend among the dwarf women.

"I wasn't complainin'! The plans fine. It's a good one," Lenny said grudgingly. "But someone's gotta have the job to point out flaws just in case. It's dag-gum battle etiquette darlin'."

"I'll etiquette you right up yer face," she snapped.

"Please, Bettie," said Master Coal and from his facial expression, Justan could tell he was saying more through the bond. Bettie frowned and folded her arms.

"Fine, Faldon," Lenny said. "Let's go over it again."

Jhonate leaned in close to Justan's ear and whispered, "I

think the dwarf and half-orc must be in love. I have never seen anyone but a married couple fight like that."

"You have a good point," Justan whispered back. "And you're right about those two. But not all married people need to be like that. Look at Hilt and Beth." They were standing together, linked arm in arm. They reminded him more of the way his parents were.

"Alright," Faldon said. He pointed down to the map with a long straight stick. "We'll be striking from the south, right through the city of Reneul. The west side of the city is occupied by orcs while the east side is full of trolls and moonrats.

"We will split our forces in two. Captain Demetrius and his cavalry will charge through the center of the troll-occupied side of the city. Beth and Sir Hilt will accompany them. She should be able to disrupt the witch's command of the trolls somehow, and if we hit them hard enough, we can scatter them into the rest of her army and create havoc."

"I can do it," Beth said and Hilt nodded.

"The rest of us will drive through the center of the orc-occupied side of town. It has far fewer buildings and is better suited to an army on foot. From the academy's count, the orc force is about four thousand strong which means we will be about even in strength-."

"Ha! Even?" said Pall with a laugh. "You have five hundred armored dwarves. We're worth at least ten orc a piece. With yer forces added in, we outnumber them two-to-one!"

Faldon smiled. "We can only hope. At the very least, we should have the advantage of surprise on our side. Our scouts tell us they haven't even bothered to fortify their rear against attack. Our two forces will meet together at the main gates and the academy's four thousand will come out to join us.

"This is where it will be tricky. We must then fight our way back through the city and out to the plains where we'll need to travel a three mile stretch before we reach the portal. Sampo's thousand fighting men will be waiting there with wizard help to aid us in our escape, but this stretch is where we will be the most vulnerable."

"It's always hard to fight on the run," Lenny agreed.

"I've been thinking about that," Justan said. "This part is where Captain Demetrius' troops could be most helpful."

"How so?" the captain asked.

"While the bulk of the army will be retreating on foot, you can remain on the attack, charging back and forth along our rear flank, wiping out enemy pursuit," Justan explained. "We can keep some archers at the rear with explosive arrows to provide you support if you become hard pressed."

Captain Demetrius nodded. "That is an excellent point."

"Good, son." Faldon said with a smile. "A solid addition to the plan."

"See, Lenui," Bettie said. "That's why you go over a plan one last time!"

Justan felt Jhonate grasp his arm. She pulled him down until his ear was at her lips and whispered. "It is just as I said. I told you to speak up more last night, Justan."

"They were doing just fine without my input," he replied, a bit embarrassed. He was standing among veterans and legends. It had seemed naive to think that his strategies could have been better than theirs.

"Edge has a few more notes to add," she announced and nudged him in the ribs.

"Do you?" his father asked.

He scratched his head. "Well, I had a few ideas . . ." Justan squatted down next to the map and noted a few strategic moves that he felt would make their solid battle plan even better. To his surprise, no one questioned him. They listened appreciatively. His father even patted him on the back. When he was finished it seemed everyone was just a bit more confident in their roles.

"See?" Jhonate said, poking him firmly in the chest. "You seem to forget that strategy was your strong point even before I trained you."

"Yes, Ma'am. I'll try not to forget again," he said with a smile.

Jhonate stared into his eyes for a moment, her lips

twitching. Finally she grabbed his wrist and pulled him over to where Hilt was standing.

"Sir Hilt," she said. "Would you mind speaking to me in private for a moment?"

"Uh, sure, Jhonate," he said in surprise. "But do we have time?"

"They just reached the cave where the portal is," Justan said. "You should have a few minutes before we begin."

"Alright, what do you wish to discuss?" Hilt asked.

"Come," she said, and didn't let go of Justan's wrist, but led both of them around the edge of the hill until they were just out of sight of the others. "Sir Hilt, what did my father tell you when you left?"

Hilt's brow wrinkled in surprise. "Now you want to talk about that? Can't that wait until after this is over?"

"I wish to know now," she said sternly.

"Okay," Hilt said, puzzled. "Xedrion wanted me to try to convince you to return with me when I came back. He said that I could promise a high command position, maybe even in his personal guard."

Jhonate sighed, looking a bit troubled, but she shook her head and said, "What where his precise words? Did he ask you to accompany me back?"

"Yes, if I could. He asked me to take you under my care until such time as I could return you to him," Hilt said. "But I told him that I couldn't promise anything. You have made your feelings known to me in the past and . . . Why are you smiling, Jhonate?"

She was beaming as she wrapped one arm around Justan's waist. "Edge, Sir Hilt has been commissioned by my father to be my acting guardian. Do you have something to say to him?"

Justan shared confused looks with Sir Hilt until it dawned on him the significance of what she had just said. "Oh! Uh, Sir Hilt, since you are Jhonate's acting guardian, I wish to announce my intention-." She elbowed him in the ribs. "I mean, ask for permission to court the daughter of Xedrion Bin Leeths."

Hilt blinked for a moment, then smiled broadly. Then his smile faded and his eyes went wide as he thought of the implications. He shook his head. "Wait just a moment, Jhonate. He never said-."

"He put me under your charge, Sir Hilt. That counts," Jhonate said.

"You do understand that he could very well kill me for this," he said. "Edge is an outsider and you are an heir-."

"I am nowhere near an heir. You know that even if my father refuses to acknowledge it," Jhonate said. "The joining of our two cultures would be good for my people, you told me so yourself."

Justan swallowed. This sounded much more complicated than he had bargained for. Jhonate an heir? An heir to what exactly? He realized that he knew very little about Jhonate's father or her people in general. He had understood long ago that she didn't wish to speak about them, so he had taken a position of accepting her peoples' traditions without question. Just what was he getting into?

"You and I may agree on that point," Hilt said. "And don't get me wrong. I am very happy that you two like each other. Beth noticed it right away and she thought it was a great match. But to give approval in your father's name would be more than presumptuous on my part."

"So your own approval and the approval of a Roo-tan Nation sponsored witch is not enough?" She noticed his surprise. "I noticed the sheath that Jharro dagger of hers is in and my father does not give them out lightly. I do not know what she did to earn that level of respect, but whatever it was, she is a listener and that should be good enough."

Hilt frowned in exasperation. "You put me in a bad situation here."

"We are going into battle," Jhonate said. "I wish to take care of this now just in case something should happen."

He reached up and grabbed a handful of his hair. "Fine. Sir Edge, you have my permission to court Jhonate, daughter of Xedrion Bin Leeths."

Justan smiled, but he was troubled by Hilt's reluctance. He turned to ask Jhonate what to expect, but before he could speak, she reached up with both hands and grabbed him by the back of the head. The next thing he knew, her lips were pressed against his.

He blinked in surprise and saw that her eyes were closed, her brow creased with the intensity of her emotion. Then he felt the tip of her tongue grazing his teeth.

He wrapped his arms around her, pulling her in tight and returned the kiss with fervor. Everything else vanished; the concern for his mother, the anxiety over the pending fight, the worries about Jhonate's father. There was only the moment; only the kiss. It was official. Jhonate wanted him as much as he wanted her and nothing else mattered.

Hilt chuckled and shook his head. "Maybe I'll get lucky and die during this battle and I won't have to face him."

Justan lost track of time. It could have been only a few seconds, it could have been minutes. To him it was just a perfect moment; one which would be burned in his mind forever. He was oblivious to everything else until he heard his father clear his throat.

Jhonate pushed away from him, her face flushed, her mouth hanging slightly open, looking as frazzled as he had ever seen her. She was gorgeous. Justan wanted to kiss her again right then.

Faldon stood there with an amused grin on his face. "I was, uh, checking on their progress with the portal."

"Father, Jhonate and I are courting," Justan said. He knew how strange that sounded, but he didn't care. "And it's official."

Faldon laughed and walked up to embrace them, kissing both of them on their foreheads. "I am so happy for you two. I knew this had to happen. Your mother will be glad to hear it!"

The portal is open, Deathclaw interrupted. *They are sending the people through now.*

Justan's smile faded just a little. "They have started, father."

Faldon nodded and stepped back. "Then it's time we split up."

Justan looked to Jhonate. She had regained her composure, standing as perfectly poised as usual. "Jhonate, since I'll be riding with the cavalry, I am sending Fist with you. Not that he needs it, but would you please watch after him for me? He would be of much more help afoot with your group."

"Of course, Justan. I . . ." She swallowed. "I will see you at the academy's front gates." She started to walk back around the hill towards the others.

"Wait, Jhonate-." She turned back and Justan didn't know what he was going to say. This battle suddenly had so much more at stake for him. The idea that something could happen to her was very real in his mind. He wanted to tell her to be careful, but she might see that as a lack of trust. Instead what came out was, "I love you."

She smiled, her cheeks flushing once more. "And I you." Then she turned and ran around the hill.

Fist, he sent.

I am happy for you, Justan, the ogre sent.

Me too! said Gwyrtha.

Don't tell Jhonate I said this, and she probably won't need it, but would you please watch over her for me?

Of course, Fist said. *She is part of our tribe now.*

The siege was nearing its end and both sides knew it. Arrows flew from the walls in a steady stream as the goblinoids continued their pathetic attempts to scale them. Unknowingly, they threw away their meager lives so that the mother of the moonrats could keep the academy busy until Ewzad Vriil's army arrived.

Inside the walls, the academy was a swarm of activity. The council members had left the hall and actively participated in the fighting alongside the other teachers and students. Stout Harley and Mad Jon were atop the south wall facing Reneul and repelling the siege machines of the orcs. Sabre Vlad was heading the defense of the north wall against the giants with the help of

Bill the Fletch, while the assistants were on the western and eastern walls leading the fight against the lesser threats.

Oz the Dagger, Hugh the Shadow, and Darlan stayed at the base of the stairs near the front gates. Oz coordinated the defensive efforts, while Hugh oversaw the movement of supplies and intelligence information, and Darlan organized the escape preparations. All three of them stood at the command table issuing orders while a steady stream of runners brought information to them from the four walls and all over the school. To an observer it may have looked like chaos, but in truth the three of them had everything under control.

Willum stood behind them, pacing back and forth, his fingers twitching. He wanted desperately to be standing on the wall fighting alongside his fellow students, but since he was their only contact with Faldon's army, he was stuck at the command table, away from the action.

"The portal has been opened." Willum said. "Their attack should start soon."

"Alright. Let's give them some help." said Oz the Dagger he motioned to the runners, gathering them together. "We need to intensify our attacks on Reneul and the giants! Keep them focused on us. There is no need to conserve any longer. Use it all! Arrows! Oil! Ballistae! Everything we've got! It ends today!"

And just like that, months worth of siege supplies were uncrated and put into use. The attackers were driven back under a sea of weaponry.

On every wall but the south, catapults had been brought up from storage and lobbed thousands upon thousands of sharpened iron caltrops into the enemy ranks. They would pierce through even thick leather boots but they were most effective on the north wall where the giants and ogres went barefoot or merely wrapped their feet in leather.

From the interior of the academy, clay pots full of flaming oil were loaded onto enormous trebuchets and fired into the enemy camps. The effect was immediate and crippling as the movement of the enemy forces slowed to a crawl.

The defenders on the south wall, however, were stuck with more traditional means of defense. Caltrops and burning oil would hamper the incoming army just as much as the enemy. Willum was concerned that the mother of the moonrats would notice and realize that something was planned, but Oz assured him that she would think they were only trying to keep the city of Reneul from becoming uninhabitable when the battle was over.

We are closing in on the outskirts of Reneul now, Coal said. *As crazy as it sounds, the enemy doesn't seem to have realized we're here yet.*

"They've started," Willum announced.

"Good. How are the traps coming, Hugh?" Oz asked.

"My men are almost finished," the Assassins Guildmaster said with a grim smile. "The magic reinforcing the walls will be broken with explosive effect. We will have to rebuild everything when this war is over, but the enemy is up for a big surprise if they think they are going to be able to use this place against us."

"*Ho-ho, that will be a sight to see*," said the imp with a giggle.

I hope we aren't here to see it, Willum said. The thought of the academy's destruction made him sick to his stomach and yet he saw the necessity of Hugh's plans. *If we are, that means we failed. But on the bright side, once they fished you from the wreckage, your next master could be a goblin, maybe even a gorc if you're lucky.*

"*Ugh. Not that, Willy*," it pleaded. "*If you have to die, die next to something intelligent.*"

If I make that promise, you have less incentive to keep me safe, Willum said.

Talon was furious. She ran through the empty streets of Wobble, her subordinates at her heels. They had wasted so much time finding a way down to the caverns only to discover that they were empty. The wizards had gone and worse, they had an even larger number of soldiers with them.

Something brushed her tail.

"Commander Talon!" said a voice behind her.

She stopped and turned on the armored orc with a hiss. He was one of only two under her command that could speak. The other orcs had been too heavily modified. She ached to kill them. She ached to kill them all actually. Ewwie had made each of them a challenge. But the two talkers she wanted to kill most of all. She probably would have already done so if Ewwie hadn't told them to call her 'Commander Talon'. She kind of liked that.

"The mistress wants to know how many," said the orc. "The bladecats can smell large numbers, but their scents are jumbled."

"It doesn't matterss to uss," she said. "We hunt the wizardss."

The orc would have frowned if its face were still capable of movement. "The mistress wants to know if there are enough to be a threat."

"Tell the female I don'tss care," Talon said. In truth, she wasn't sure how many there were. The encampment they had discovered at the base of the cliff had been quite large, but she wasn't sure how many had passed through into the caverns. In fact, she wasn't sure how they had gotten in there in the first place. If she had not found traces of her brother's scent ascending the cliff face, she might not have found them at all.

The trail at the bottom of the chasm was so narrow that it was impossible to calculate how many had marched out of there. "The numberss were large, but they ssplit here. Some wentss that way," she said, pointing to the east. Then she pointed to the north. "But the wizardss went thiss way. And that is where we headss."

The orc hesitated. "Mistress feels that some of us should follow the others and see where they went."

Talon didn't deny that she was curious too. Her brother had traveled with them after all. "No! Ewwie said to killss the wizardss sso that iss what we do."

The others gathered around her. One of the bladecats let out a growl and Talon rounded on it, her tail at the ready, poison dripping from its end. Ewwie had made the bladecat by combining a porcupine with a mountain cat and turning its quills into bladelike razors. So far she greatly preferred them to the orcs, but this was the first time one of them had turned on her. She could see the shriveled moonrat eye embedded in its forehead and wanted to rip it out.

But it didn't attack. Instead, one of the armored orcs jumped on its back and it sped off in the direction Deathclaw had gone.

She darted at the orc that had spoken to her and grabbed his neck with one hand, digging her claws into his armored skin. "I leadss! I!"

"We . . . cannot deny the mistress!" it said. "She made those ones go. The rest of us follow you . . . Commander Talon!"

Oh how she wanted to kill it. Take it apart. Watch it melt like Ewwie's creations always did. But Ewwie asked her to kill the wizards and now she was one orc and one bladecat short. She might need the rest of them.

Talon released his throat. "We go!" she said and ran to the north, following the wizard's trail. The others followed at her heels, the extra speed Ewwie gave them allowing them to keep up. Once the wizards were dead, if any survived, she would kill them too.

Chapter Thirty

I'm big-big! Gwyrtha said for perhaps the tenth time, taking great joy in the fact that she towered over the warhorses and chargers that made up Captain Demetrius' cavalry.

We know, sweetheart. Justan had increased her to three times her normal size this time. Justan looked like a child sitting on her saddle. He had wanted to grow her even larger, but Master Coal had advised against it. Increasing her size too much would reduce her energy and limit the other modifications he could make. The wizard had a point. Making her larger would increase the fear she would strike into the enemy, but it would also make her a bigger target.

So Justan had held back on her size and instead spent some of her energy hardening her scales and toughening the various other skin patches that made up her hide. Now that he was done, her reserve energy was only a quarter of what it usually was. It was a dangerous balance. There was no telling how long the battle would last or how much energy he or the other bonded would need.

"You ready?" Hilt asked. The named warrior trotted up to his right, Beth sitting right behind him. "She's impressive enough I think!"

"I've done all I can," he replied. He wished he could tweak the changes a bit more. But there wasn't time. Everyone was ready to start.

He leaned out as far as he could over the saddle and reached out his hand to help Beth climb aboard. Beth had said that riding on Gwyrtha would help her concentrate and Justan hoped it was true because she had perhaps the most important role in the attack. She sat high up on Gwyrtha's shoulders, straddling the rogue horse's neck and holding on to her now thick and wiry mane.

"You going to be okay sitting up there?" Hilt asked.

"I can't think of a better place!" She laughed and leaned forward, wrapping her arms around Gwyrtha's thick neck. "Oh, you are such a good girl! Yes you are!"

I know! Gwyrtha agreed.

"We're ready, Captain!" Justan shouted.

Captain Demetrius unsheathed his longsword and held it high over his head. "Charge!"

Now, Fist! Justan sent, knowing that the ogre would give the signal. Both armies would attack at once to further disrupt the enemy.

The cavalry surged forward, Gwyrtha taking the lead. Captain Demetrius rode on her left flank and Sir Hilt on her right, Samson right behind them.

The centaur had grown in size as well, much larger than Justan had ever seen him. He held one spear in each hand and was fully armored. At first Justan had been confused because he hadn't been able to see Master Coal, but then he had realized that the wizard had fully immersed himself in the bond. His body laid forward flat on Samson's back, partially submerged in the thick bony plates of the centaur's skin and covered by the centaur's stiff wiry pelt.

The east side of Reneul soon loomed ahead. Justan could already see a few trolls standing in the streets, swaying back and forth under the witch's control. He pulled Ma'am off his back and drew an explosive arrow from one of several leather quivers strapped to the side of Gwyrtha's saddle. The arrowhead glowed a sinister red.

"Beth, are you ready to start?" he asked.

"I already have," she replied.

Justan switched to his spirit sight and didn't see anything at first. Then he saw something so faint he wouldn't have noticed if he hadn't been looking for it. A thin white haze poured from Beth, flooding ahead of them faster than the horses could run.

Beth had figured out how to create a spirit cloud that would muddy the spirit magic of another witch. When she had first explained the concept to the rest of them, Justan was concerned that her powers would disrupt the bond, but she had assured him that she could tune it specifically to the mother of the moonrat's signal. It was how the four bearers of the lodestones had traveled through the Tinny woods unnoticed.

As Justan watched, the white haze flowed over two trolls in the streets ahead. They broke into a run, one of them jumping into the shadows and tearing into a confused pair of moonrat eyes.

It was time to begin. Justan focused in and took a deep breath. Time slowed down and his senses increased three-fold. He had been preparing for this moment for weeks and now it he was ready.

Justan pulled his feet from the stirrups and stood on Gwyrtha's back, his body fully aware and adjusting to Gwyrtha's every movement. He drew back the explosive arrow and smiled at the familiar buzz of the dragon hair string that filled his ear. Ma'am was eager to fire. He saw his first target, a troll, running out of the doorway of a two-story house. He fired.

The arrow shot forward faster than most eyes could have followed and struck the troll square in the chest. There was a sharp crack and the troll's tall form was jerked back into the house and exploded into an enormous fireball, flames bursting from every window.

The effect was more devastating than he had imagined. Justan drew another arrow. This was going to be fun.

Jhonate spun, sweeping her staff behind her, and the orc commander's head fell from his shoulders. She glanced to her left and saw the ogre, Fist, cave in the helmet of one of the other orc leaders with one swing of his wicked mace. She nodded in approval as she saw that Poz and Qenzic had made short work of their opponents as well. Only Jobar was still having a hard time.

The orc he had chosen was a big brute covered in a mismatched set of heavy armor looted no doubt from fallen warriors. Jobar had managed to disarm it and had gotten in a few good strikes with his daggers, but he had also managed to get his face bashed in pretty badly.

Fist went to help, but Jhonate grabbed his arm, holding him back, and yelled, "Qenzic! Poz! Go check on the others. Jobar, the rest of us are done here. Are you coming?"

The squat man growled and sheathed his daggers. As the large orc swung another fist, Jobar ducked the blow. He dove under the orcs arm, then slid behind it and jumped up, grabbing it by the neck. The orc twisted and grabbed at him, trying to throw him off, but Jobar got an arm around its throat and wrapped his legs around its waist.

He clenched his arm and arched his back. The orc threw punches over its shoulder right into Jobar's face, but it had no leverage and as Jobar strained, the punches grew weaker until finally it collapsed. He rolled off of it, breathing heavy, and Fist walked over and bashed its head in for good measure.

Jhonate held out her hand and pulled him to his feet. "Idiot! Next time do not take on the biggest one, Jobar. You slow us down."

Jobar spat out blood and grinned at her with a split lip. "Whatever you say, Daughter of Xedrion."

"Come. We have fallen behind," she chided and they ran out of the tent to catch up with the others.

While the original plan had been for the entire force to charge directly to the front gates, Justan had noticed that the orc leaders had set up command tents in the outskirts of the city far from the walls of the academy. Even better, they were just off of the main road.

As the rest of the force fought their way to the academy's gates, Tamboor's howlers had charged into the orc forces in front of the command tents, screaming in full battle fury. While they caused chaos within the orc ranks, Jhonate's strike force, consisting of Faldon's graduate class and twenty retired members of the Assassins Guild, had made a beeline for the tents.

Poz ran up to the tent as they exited. "The attack was a success, Daughter of Xedrion. Every orc in the command tents is dead."

"And our losses?" she asked.

"Two," he replied. "Retirees."

Jhonate's brow tightened, but she let no emotion show on her face. "Call in the howlers. We need to catch up with the others."

"And the dead?" Poz asked.

"We must leave them." The words felt like ashes in her mouth, but this was one mission where they wouldn't be able to lay their fallen to rest.

"But . . . it was Melo the Dash and Smiling Ty. They were-."

"We will never make it to the Mage School with the bodies of our comrades weighing us down," she insisted. "The best we can do perhaps is take up their weapons so they don't go to the enemy."

Poz frowned, but nodded and ran to carry out his orders.

She felt Fist's large hand rest on her shoulder. "A leader's burden is not enviable," he said.

"Is enviable your word of the day?" she asked.

"Yes," he said in his deep voice. "It's a terrible word for today."

Tamboor and his howlers had decimated the orc sub commanders and their staff, but now the orcs were fighting back. The advantage of a berserker force was creating surprise and terror. If their force was large enough and fast enough, they could wipe out enough of the enemy in the first few minutes to cause a rout. The disadvantage was that their fighting style was almost exclusively offensive. Warriors adapted during battle and after the initial surprise was over, the enemy often figured out how to fight back. If that happened, a berserker force could take heavy losses.

This was where academy berserkers were superior. Each one of them was trained to obey a signal that would snap them out of their rage and allow them to retreat. Every group of academy-trained berserkers had a caller, whose job it was to determine when the tide of battle had shifted and reel them back in. Tamboor's men had chosen Zambon for this task.

When Poz signaled him that it was time to move on, Zambon raised two fingers to his mouth and let out the piercing whistle that called them back. The men rushed back to join Jhonate's group, but Tamboor was not among them. Zambon had to let out the call three times before Tamboor reappeared, covered head to toe in orc blood.

The man twitched, breathing heavily, barely keeping himself under control. Zambon tried to trade swords with him, but Tamboor pushed his hands away and ran to catch up with the rest of Faldon's army. The berzerkers followed their leader, Jhonate's team at their heels, passing hundreds of orc dead along the way.

Lenui Firegobbler let out a stream of curses as he stood at the forefront of the dwarf formation, bashing the orc front lines to jelly. "Garl-friggin' frog-eatin' nose-pickin' sons-of-goblins!"

He hadn't worn a full suit of armor in nearly fifty years. He hated the stuff. Didn't even like making it. Plate armor was stifling and heavy and hampered his movements. He had hoped to avoid it this time around but his stupid brother had showed Bettie his old suit of armor from the War of the Dark Prophet over two hundred years ago. Of course she had insisted Lenui wear it again. The durn woman was moodier than ever lately and she had shouted him down until he finally let her help him into the suit. The dwarf forces had cheered when they saw her strap the breastplate on.

At least he was bashing orcs. It suited his temper.

"Yer lookin' like the Lenui of a hunnerd years old!" Shouted Pall, who was fighting to his right. The old dwarf stabbed a tall orc through the groin with his sword and let the dwarf behind him take it out with a spear to the neck.

"Shut up! I hate this dag-burned crab suit!" Lenui snarled, planting Buster between one orc's bulgy eyes with a satisfying thud. Why had Chugk insisted on keeping the stupid armor anyway? He had asked him to sell it years ago before the other dwarves went and put it in a museum or something.

The armor had been one of Lenui's youthful exuberances, forged during the time when he first caught the smithing fever. His daddy had laughed and encouraged him, pointing out techniques to make it better. Lenui spent a year's worth of earnings getting the ore magicked and spent months more of his precious time shaping and runing and coloring the metal.

He had been so proud when he finished it. Every piece shone like polished silver, the runes filled with red iron. On the breastplate was a large F made of gold-colored steel on an oval background of red iron. He had placed an even larger version of the same symbol on his shield and a smaller one on his helmet.

It was a suit of armor fit for a king, but Lenui in his stupid pride had worn it into battle himself. The old timers had laughed at first, saying that the F stood for Fancypants. But Lenui had showed them what a Firegobbler could do in battle. The armor withstood the toughest blows and shone bright no matter how much blood was spilled on it. It helped him survive some of the worst defeats and proudest victories of the war. In some ways he supposed he should be grateful for it. The armor had been the way Lenui had made his name, but it was also one of his greatest mistakes.

He could see it even now in the eyes of the other dwarves. He had crafted a hero's armor and the others still believed in it after all these years. Bettie had no idea what she'd done by making him wear it. They were seeing him as the hero of Thunder Gap once again. He could only hope this battle wouldn't have an ending quite so tragic.

With Lenui's shining figure leading them, the dwarf front lines moved steadily forward over the bodies of the orc dead, dwarf shieldbearers in front with short weapons followed right behind by dwarves with spears and poleaxes to keep the enemy from climbing over them.

Edge had known the value of a dwarf army. Their lines were firm and rigid, good at moving an enemy, and he had placed them on Faldon's right flank pushing the orcs towards the troll infested side of Reneul where Beth had disrupted the mother of the moonrat's magic.

It was working. Lenui could hear the screeches of trolls

tearing into the rear of the orc forces. The orcs began to panic, pressing in on the dwarf line in an attempt to get away. Their lines began to buckle.

"Hold firm, dag-blast it!" he shouted, busting orc heads and hands and kneecaps and whatever came close enough for Buster to hit.

"You heard him! Hold!" shouted Pall and the call went down the line as the dwarf troops did just that, planting their feet and felling every orc that tried to get past them. Soon the orcs learned to fear them just as much as they did the trolls and the dwarf line began moving forward again.

"Arrows!" came a call from down the line, and Lenui saw a black cloud streaking down on them from the orc camp ahead.

He got his shield up just in time to deflect several that might have hit his face and he still felt two skip off his helmet. He looked around and saw that the most of the other dwarves had done the same. The orcs weren't as fortunate. They went down in heaps all across the front lines, their bodies filled like pincushions.

"Hah!" shouted Rahbbie to his left. "Friggin' orcs decided to give us a breather!"

"Durn right," Lenui laughed. He turned and punched Pall in shoulder but the older dwarf didn't respond. That's when Lenui noticed the arrow fletchings sticking out of his friend's throat.

"Close the gap!" He shouted and tossed his shield to another dwarf that moved to take his place. "Nobody moves back, you hear that Rahbbie? Forward!"

Rahbbie nodded, his face ashen as Lenui pulled Pall's staggering form away from the front lines. He barked at the fresh-legged dwarves in the back ranks, "Get a blasted healer!"

Lenui tossed his gauntlets to the ground and Kile ran up to help him unbuckle Pall's breastplate. Kile wasn't much of a healer, but more of a field medic and he had plenty of experience from past wars.

When they got the armor off, the damage looked much worse. The neck wound had soaked Pall's shirt and armor padding with blood and they found the fletchings of a second arrow, previously hidden by the armor, that sprouted from just above his collarbone.

Lenui checked Pall's back, but the arrowhead hadn't gone through. It was embedded somewhere in the core of him.

"Damn!" Kile said. "Arrow had to have hit just right. Probly deflected off his helmet and down through the gap in his breastplate and backplate."

"Dag-nab it, Pall!" Lenui snapped. "Always wearin' yer armor too loose!"

"You hear me, Pall?" Kile said. "Can you hear me?"

Pall blinked, his eyes darting between the two of them and his jaw worked but no sound came out. Kile broke off the arrow head that protruded from the back of Pall's neck and pulled out the shaft. There was a quick rush of blood, but Kile shoved some herbs in the wound, causing the blood to harden instantly.

The neck wound was nasty, but dwarves were hardy. Lenui knew Pall could survive that. It was the other arrow that worried him. "What 'bout the other'n, Kile? What 'bout the other'n?"

"I'm looking, Lenui!" Kile fingered the end of the fletchings and pulled on it slightly. Pall cried out. "It's stuck in there good. I couldn't yank it out without taking his innards along with it. Blast it, Lenui, he needs a master surgeon, and even if one was standing right here . . . I mean look at the size of that wound. I'm pretty sure it was a broadhead."

Lenui swallowed. He knew what that meant. Pall lifted his hand and placed it on Lenui's shoulder. His voice croaked, "It's fine. I'm done . . ."

"Cow turds! You got another two hunnerd years left at least."

"Five hu- . . . nerd's enough fer me," Pall said with a grim smile. "My Sweet Patty's gone. My sons . . ."

"I know, Pall. They're a waitin'," Lenui said.

"Help me . . . sit up," Pall gasped and Kile helped push him upright. No dwarf wanted to die laying down. "Do . . . me one favor, Lenui."

"Whatever the hell you want," he promised.

"Hold . . . still." Pall drew his arm back and threw a surprisingly stiff punch right into Lenui's face.

Lenui clutched at his nose. "Dag-burned son of a-! I think you broke it!"

"You . . . dag-gum liar . . ." Pall chuckled and went still.

Lenui closed his old friend's eyes. His heart felt empty, yet there were tears dripping down his cheeks. He reached up and felt them. They were old man's tears, earned by experience at watching his friends die. He slammed his fist into the ground. He was too blasted young for old man's tears.

Kile coughed and Lenui noticed for the first time that smoke was filling the air, blown their way by a westerly breeze. He turned and felt the heat of the flames on his face. Their line was steadily moving forward as ordered, but they were hard pressed by screaming orcs and trolls, some of them on fire.

Eastern Reneul was burning.

Justan swore as the heat intensified. Troll trails! He couldn't believe he had forgotten to account for troll trails! The east side of Reneul had been occupied by trolls for weeks and in that time the trolls had trailed their flammable slime everywhere. His fire arrows had started a conflagration.

Hot! It's hot! Gwyrtha complained as she ran down the center of the street, trying to stay as far away from the burning buildings as possible. The air was filled with the screeching of flaming trolls and the screams of pained and terrified horses.

The cavalry had been forced to split up to avoid being burned alive and now that there was no need to fight, they were all merely searching for a safe route to the academy walls where the open space would bring them relief from the fire.

Samson led one large group, Master Coal using his magic to help part the flames. Justan led another column through the widest streets, hoping that by staying in the middle they could avoid the worst of the heat. So far he had only been partially right. The troll slime crisscrossed the streets as well and though most of it had guttered out fairly quickly, there were still places where the horses had to run through open flame.

"You okay, Beth?" Hilt shouted from the horse behind him.

Beth had laid forward across Gwyrtha's neck and buried her face in the rogue horse's mane, ignoring the heat. She lifted her head briefly to yell back, "No questions! Concentrating! The witch is fighting back!"

Justan knew Beth was putting all her effort into keeping her cloud of interference going. Gwyrtha's energy levels had dipped suddenly a few minutes before and he had realized that she was somehow pulling what she needed from the rogue horse directly.

Hot! Hot! Hot! Gwyrtha complained and Justan could sense that her feet were blistering.

I'm sorry sweetie, I'll heal you as soon as we get out of here, I promise, he sent.

The front gates were only a few blocks away. Just one more turn and they would see the market square. They were nearly there.

They turned the corner, Gwyrtha trampling a couple burning trolls that ran in the way and Justan noticed with alarm that the square ahead was completely blocked by fire. They were going to have to run through it. They had no choice. There was no way to backtrack now.

He quickly pulled out an arrow tipped with a blue glow. Hoping that this element worked as well as the others had, he fired into the street ahead. A torrent of water exploded into existence where the arrow struck, flooding the street in a ten yard radius.

"Yes!" Justan cried and picked through the quiver, looking for more. He found two and fired them ahead in succession, clearing a path through the blazing market bazaar.

The arrows left deep impressions in the ground hidden by the water. Gwyrtha slipped a couple times. Justan winced as he heard one of the other horses go down behind him, but he couldn't stop. He fired every water arrow he had until the way was clear. The academy gates rose just ahead.

As they approached, he heard shouting and cheering from the wall above and a smile spread across his face. They had done it. They had broken through. He stopped before the gate and turned, watching as Captain Demetrius and Coal's columns of cavalry rushed out of the burning city streets to join them.

Faldon's forces on the other hand were still making their way to them, hard pressed by orcs on every side. Captain Demetrius shouted and led the men west, rushing to Faldon's aid. Justan wanted to go with them, but Hilt called out.

"Stop, Edge! Beth should stay right here, keeping the witch from knowing what's going on at the gate."

Justan nodded reluctantly. Hilt was right and Beth needed Gwyrtha right now as much as she needed anything else.

"Don't worry," said Coal, who had withdrawn from the bond and sat up on Samson's back once again. "Captain Demetrius knows what to do."

There was a great shuddering sound and Justan turned to see that the great portcullis that stood in front of the gates was being raised. Once it had disappeared into the wall above, the gates slowly swung inward and Justan's heart caught in his throat. The first person to walk out was his mother.

Chapter Thirty One

Darlan led a flood of warriors through the front gates of the academy. While they ran to secure the area, she headed for her son.

"Mother!" Justan jumped down from Gwyrtha's back and met her in a fierce embrace. "I'm so glad to see you!"

"Oh, I've missed you so much!" she replied and hugged him back just as fiercely. Then she held on a bit longer.

"Um . . . mother." Justan said, feeling a bit self conscious with all the other warriors around. A couple of them smiled and shook their heads. "We're kind of in the middle of a battle."

"Oh, shut up, I haven't seen you in two years. A mother gets to embarrass her son when it's been that long." She gave him one more tight squeeze and pulled back. "Justan, you've grown. My, you look so much like your father, I can't believe it. Why if it wasn't for your hair and eyes I would have no idea there was any of my side of the family in you."

"Except for the magic, you mean?" Justan asked.

Darlan's smile faded slightly. "Yes well, we'll have plenty of time to talk of that later, won't we?"

"Yes we will," Justan said, then hugged her again. "Mother, I have so much to tell you and so many people to introduce you to, I-."

"Justan, where is your father?" she asked in concern, pulling back from him again.

"He's still fighting his way here," he replied. He could hear their explosive arrows going off in the distance. "But he's fine. A few scratches maybe, but Fist says they will be here soon.

Captain Demetrius has cleared the way for them."

"Good," she said, looking relieved. "Fist is your ogre friend, right?"

"He is my bonded," Justan clarified. "I assume Willum told you what that means?"

"I grilled him about it thoroughly," she assured him. "I must say, though. An ogre? What odd luck."

"It's not luck, mother. There was a reason we bonded, and believe me once you meet him, you will adore him," he said, watching as she walked toward Gwyrtha.

"Oh, I'm sure I will. And this is your rogue horse?" Darlan reached out to touch her enormous head hesitantly. "You must be Gwyrtha."

Gwyrtha nodded excitedly. *Mother*! She recognized Darlan's look and scent from Justan's memories.

Darlan smiled at the intelligence in those large eyes and ran her hand across the scales on Gwyrtha's snout to touch the horse-like pelt at the top of her head. "My you are . . . different, aren't you?"

Yes! she replied happily.

Darlan blinked and stepped around her to look at the woman laying along Gwyrtha's neck. Her hand went to her mouth. "Why Beth Puddle! What are you doing here?"

Beth raised her head and her eyes widened. "Wizardess Sherl?"

Then they both said at once, "I don't go by that name anymore."

Beth's brow wrinkled in confusion, her eyes going in and out of focus. "Not sure if this is a dream. Can't talk now . . . later," she said, and buried her head back into Gwyrtha's mane.

Darlan gave Justan a questioning stare.

"I didn't realize you knew each other. Beth is here to-!" Justan saw Gwyrtha's eyelids droop and reached out through the bond in alarm, seeing that her energy levels had dipped deeply. Beth was taking even more energy than before. *Gwyrtha are you okay*?

Tired, she said. *My feet hurt. I like your mother*.

Right! He had forgotten about her burns. *Hold on, sweetie.* Justan closed his eyes and soothed her feet, healing the burned tissue as well as he could. He was going to have to reduce her size or get rid of her armor if he was going to make up for the energy that Beth was siphoning away. Justan wished he had known Beth was going to do that.

It's okay, Justan, Gwyrtha said. *She asked nice.*

I'm glad to hear it, Justan sent and focused on reducing Gwyrtha's size just enough to increase her energy to a comfortable level.

Sir Hilt walked up and placed his hand on Beth's forehead. He frowned and whispered something in her ear. She gave a slight nod and his frown faded. Hilt looked at Darlan. "Wizardess Sherl. I'm glad to see you're here. No one told me that you're Edge's mother."

"That's because no one knows," she said, eyeing him a bit dubiously. "Sir Hilt, right?"

"Yes, we met at the Mage School years ago when I went before the bowl," he said. "Sorry, but Beth is a bit busy right now. She's concentrating."

"So Beth Puddle is the wizardess that Willum was talking about? The Beth who's your wife, that's supposed to be disrupting the mother of the moonrats?" Darlan looked as confused as Justan had ever seen her. "But how can she do that? Beth was quelled. And what happened to that boy she left the Mage School for?"

"Well, Beth's not using elemental magic. She's using spirit magic and . . . It's a long story," Hilt said.

"I'm sure he'll have plenty of time to tell you about it when this is over," Justan said.

One of the academy warriors ran up to them. "Mayor Darlan! We're ready! The area is secure!"

"Tell them to get moving," she said. "The evacuation starts now."

The soldier ran back through the gates and people began to stream out.

"There's one problem with that, mother." Justan said. He pointed to the conflagration behind them. "Our escape route is on fire."

"That's not a problem, honey. In fact, that's perfect!" she said with a smile, the fire reflecting in her eyes. Then her smile faltered just a bit. "Though I am going to miss our house."

"How is that perfect?" Justan asked.

She turned and waved as Captain Demetrius' cavalry rode back up the streets towards them. Faldon was riding right beside the captain and when he saw Darlan, a wide grin spread on his face despite the jagged wound that ran across his cheek from nose to ear. He leapt down from the horse and ran to scoop his wife up in his arms, twirling her around.

Darlan laughed out loud the same way she did whenever he came home from a long campaign. To Justan watching them was like reliving a memory from his childhood. Except this time as she kissed his father, Justan saw elemental magic leave her lips and enter Faldon's body to stitch his wounds closed.

When she broke off the kiss, Faldon reached up to feel the smooth skin where his wound had been. "It's been a long time since you did that, Darlan."

"Well, I missed you," she said. "Now put me down. We don't have time to dally."

Faldon let her down and looked at the inferno that was eastern Reneul. "Oh, that's a shame. Still I suppose it's perfect for our escape."

"And how is that perfect?" Justan asked.

"The enemy won't be able to follow us through there," Faldon explained. "By the time the mother of the moonrats figures out what has happened, she'll have to send her armies around the flames, buying us precious time."

Darlan patted Justan's cheek.

"I know this is going to surprise our neighbors, but it's time I came out of hiding anyway. Faldon, dear, can I borrow your horse?"

He helped her into the saddle. She yelled to the academy warriors to have the people follow her and led a column down to the streets. The people following slowed as they neared the fire, glancing at each other in concern.

The flames parted before Darlan like great curtains. Justan switched to mage sight and saw a protective barrier of red and black magic pushing the fire to either side of the street. He stared at his mother in awe. His father had said she was powerful, but the forces involved here were stunning.

"Sherl was always a genius with fire magic," Coal said.

"But how is she going to be able to keep a spell like that up long enough for everyone to get through?" Justan said. "Surely she's not that powerful."

"She doesn't have to be. Don't you see what she's done?" Coal said. "She's set the structure of the spell so that it feeds off the energy of the fire burning around it. As long as the buildings continue to burn, the barrier will stay active."

"Amazing . . ." Justan shook his head slowly. All of the new things he was learning about her made her seem different than the mother he knew and the thought gave him chills.

He looked back towards the front gates. His father was speaking with Oz the Dagger and Hugh the Shadow while people poured out of the gate in a steady stream. To the west Justan could see the rest of Faldon's army coming up the road towards them. Fist and Jhonate were somewhere near the back of the group.

They are finished, said Deathclaw. *The people who cannot fight have gone through the portal. Only the warriors and wizards stay.*

That's good to hear. Justan smiled. It looked like everything was going to work out just fine.

What do you wish me to do now? Deathclaw asked.

Keep an eye on the perimeter of the area. Make sure that the mother of the moonrats doesn't see what we're up to, he said.

Very well, Deathclaw replied.

Now they just had to get to the portal themselves. Justan ran to his father, dodging through the citizens of Reneul to get to him.

Hugh the Shadow was speaking as he arrived. " . . . The

fall of the portcullis will seal the traps. As soon as it is raised or broken, the magic that reinforces these walls will be broken and they will all go off."

Faldon shook his head solemnly. "Such a waste."

"We have no choice," Oz said. "We can't just leave it here for them to use against us."

"I agree with you. It's just . . . the history here." Faldon said. He noticed Justan standing there. "Any news, son?"

"Yes. The people of Sampo have gone through. They're ready for us." Justan said, though his enthusiasm had been trampled by the conversation he had overheard. "Are we burning the academy behind us?"

"It's more than that," Hugh said. A grin split his face. "By the gods you have grown! You've been named I hear?"

Hugh shook Justan's hand and turned it over to look at the rune. He gave Justan an appraising stare and Justan felt that familiar twinge of unworthiness return. How could he stand in front of this legend and pretend to be worthy of his runes? Justan pushed the guilt away. The bowl chose him. That was a fact whether he understood its reasons or not. "Yes sir. I am Edge."

Hugh the Shadow nodded. "It's a good name, Edge. And you don't need to call me sir. Just Hugh."

"I knew you were special the day you beat me in the Strategic Games," said Oz the Dagger, leaning forward to shake his hand as well. "I'm glad you're here with us."

"Thank you," Justan said. "So what's the current situation?"

"The orcs have been routed," Faldon replied. "Captain Demetrius' charge broke their lines and with their commanders dead and no way to hear the witch's commands, they've scattered."

"Sir Hilt's wife must have a long reach with that magic of hers," Hugh added. "Our scouts atop the walls say that the goblins are milling about, unsure what to do, while the gorcs are dealing with the trolls and fires that have spread to the training grounds."

"The only ones that seem to be able to hear her orders are

the giants. They keep throwing their rocks but their movements are so hampered by our caltrops . . ." Oz shook his head. "I tell you, if not for the prophet's warning I would think we had this war won."

The reminder gave Justan a chill. He watched as the dwarf troops, led by Lenny in shining armor, followed the citizens of Reneul through his mother's flame corridor. "How long is it going to take us all to get away?"

"It shouldn't be long. Faldon's retiree army goes through next," Oz said. "The trainees and students will follow and the academy graduates will be the last to leave. We plan to keep fighting from atop the walls until the last possible second to keep the mother of the moonrats confused and give us the best chance to get away."

A messenger ran up from inside the academy. "Sirs, there's a problem. Stout Harley is refusing to leave the wall. He says he's going to stay behind."

Oz pointed at Hugh. "I told you he was going to do that."

"I guess that means I have to talk him down?" Hugh said with a tired roll of his eyes. "I'm of half a mind to leave him."

"I'll go talk to him," Faldon said. "He won't be expecting me."

As Faldon jogged through the gates, Jhonate arrived. She ran up and kissed Justan quickly. "Fist said that you made it through unharmed."

Justan smiled. "You know you just kissed me in front of everyone."

Her face colored and she took a step back. "Many things happen in the heat of battle, Edge."

Fist ran up to them followed by Zambon, Bettie, and a hundred of Tamboor's berserker troops. The ogre held a large bloody form in his arms, his worry flooding through the bond.

"Father is hurt badly," Zambon said.

Tamboor hung limp in the ogre's arms, his eyes rolling and his mouth moving but no sound came out. His sword was still clenched in his fist, the tip dragging along the ground. The man was so covered in gore he was almost unrecognizable and it was hard to tell how much of it was his own.

"Is that Tamboor the Fearless?" asked Hugh in surprise. "What happened?"

"He gave in to the rage," said one of the berserkers, a short gray-haired man who was heavily scarred and covered in almost as much blood as Tamboor was.

"He was amazing," said Bettie with a look of admiration on her face, her long handled hammer resting over her shoulder. "He must have killed a hundred orcs on his own."

"I don't know what to do." Zambon said. "Even in this state he refuses to hold my sword and won't let go of Meredith."

Beth says to take him to Coal, Gwyrtha sent. Sir Hilt was at her side with his arm around Beth, whispering in her ear.

Justan scanned the crowd of people leaving the academy and found the wizard not too far away tending to a warrior with a broken arm. "Bring him over here."

They brought Tamboor to the wizard and Coal whistled in surprise.

The wizard ran his hands over Tamboor and shook his head. "It's pretty amazing, He has a dozen wounds, but each one stops just short of a major vein."

"That's berserker training for you," said Hugh with a chuckle. "Tamboor always knew how to take a hit."

"We may have to carry him out after I'm finished," Coal said. "This is going to take a lot out of him."

"I've got something for that." Hugh pulled a small stoppered vial from under his leather armor. He tossed it to Zambon. "Here. Have him drink this when the wizard's done."

"Thanks." Zambon turned it over in his hands and Justan saw that it glowed black and blue.

Justan felt a tap on his shoulder.

"Have you seen Lenui?" Betty asked, looking around anxiously.

"I saw him go through with the rest of the dwarves a little while ago."

"Idiot didn't wait for me?" She scowled and climbed up

on Stanza, then took off after him.

Justan and Jhonate and kept an eye out for attackers as they watched the steady stream of people entering the flame corridor. The last of the retirees went through, followed by the trainees in quick succession.

"Wait. Wait, I'm not done!" Coal protested. Tamboor pushed himself free of Fist's arms and stood. Tamboor looked as if he had regained some control of himself. His eyes were focused and his face calm. The wizard gripped the berserker's shoulder and began closing a deep gash.

The berserker nodded at the wizard in thanks and pulled the vial from Zambon's hands. He downed its contents in one gulp and strode over to Hugh, who was giving instructions to some of his guild members who were working on something at the base of the portcullis track. Tamboor tapped Hugh's shoulder and held out his hand expectantly.

"Tamboor! That was fast. Oh-." Hugh's smile faltered and he reached into his armor to pull out another flask. "Fine, but you know what that's going to do to you at the end of the day."

Tamboor swallowed the vial's contents, smacked Hugh's back, and ran towards Darlan's flame corridor, the rest of the berserkers at his heels.

"Justan can I go with them?" Fist asked and Justan felt the ogre's concern.

"Yes, go ahead. Make sure Tamboor gets to the portal safely," Justan said and the ogre ran off after them, one hand on the pommel of his mace.

"That man is lucky I was done with the major tissue repair or he could have done himself serious damage. I-!" Master Coal frowned. "Stubborn boy."

"What is it?" Justan asked.

"Willum doesn't want to leave yet. He's back up on the wall."

Willum stood next to Swen on the center of the north wall and fired an arrow at an ogre far below. The stupid thing had sat down in full range of his bow to pull caltrops out of its feet. The arrow plunged into its back and the ogre fell over, clawing at the arrow and howling as it rolled over more caltrops.

"Ho-ho! Good one!"

Willum nodded in satisfaction. As much as he knew his father would rather have him by his side, it felt good to be back up on the wall with the others and helping. He glanced back into the empty academy grounds behind him and his mood faded a bit. This could be his last chance to protect the school. No one knew what the academy was going to be like when the war was over.

"Gods on fire," said Swen beside him. "Look at that."

A large figure walked around the edge of the nearest hill. The giant was enormous and gray, naked but for a loincloth and its body had been tattooed all over in strange patterns. Its eye sockets were empty, but a single orange orb had somehow been stitched to the center of its forehead.

"It's that same gray giant," Willum said.

"Ho! And that's a moonrat eye, sure enough." The imp sounded impressed. *"I can feel her presence from here."*

A large group of giant leaders followed behind him, stooping and bobbing their heads, only whimpering softly as they stepped on the pieces of sharpened iron. The gray giant's feet were clustered black with embedded caltrops but he didn't seem to care. He stood just outside of the bowmen's range and raised his hands to his mouth.

"The mother can't see the front walls, but she can see you!" the gray giant shouted. The giants around him chanted and stomped.

"Ballistae!" Sabre Vlad commanded.

"He's square in the middle, sir!" said one of the men. The ballistae had been mounted at each corner and the giant had picked the perfect place to stand to stay out of their range.

"Can you hit it, Swen?" asked Sabre Vlad.

"Just," Swen said and cocked an arrow. He pulled it back until the wood creaked.

"The mother knows you are up to something in there!" the giant yelled.

"Whose mother?" Sabre Vlad yelled back. "Yours?" The men laughed.

"The mother is the wife of the Barldag and she demands your death!" the gray giant boomed. The giants howled.

"That's enough from him." Swen said and fired. The arrow whistled through the air and plunged into the giant's chest. The chanters flinched but the gray giant didn't seem to notice.

"The mother says that your plans don't matter!" The arrow had to have pierced a lung, but his voice didn't falter. "Whatever you are doing in there, today is your end!"

"*Ho-ho she sounds scared!*" said the imp. "*Do you wish to start your twelve hours now, Willy?*"

Why? Can you do something from here?

"*Perhaps,*" it said.

"Hit him again," said Sabre Vlad.

"This one's going right through his new orange eye," Swen promised and notched another arrow.

Willum hesitated, wondering what the axe could do at this range. *Fine. The battle should be over in twelve hours one way or the other anyway.*

The imp giggled. "*Good! Done! It begins now! Rub me on that arrow.*"

"Just a second, Swen," Willum said and stuck the axe out in front of the man's enormous bow.

"What are you doing, Willum?" asked Sabre Vlad.

"Trying something," Willum replied. He rubbed the axe's edge against the tip of the arrow and Swen's eyes widened as the arrowhead began to glow with an orange heat. "There. Fire now!"

"They come! They come! The destructors come!" the giant boomed. "Your death is nigh! The destructors come!" The others took up the chant.

Swen fired and the arrow hurtled through the air, fire blooming around the tip as it went.

"*Ho-Ho! Burner burner burner!*" laughed the imp.

"They come! They're he-!" Swen was good to his word

and the giant didn't finish his sentence. The fiery arrow burst through the orange moonrat eye in the giant's forehead, the magic in the arrow burning through to the back of its skull. The giant stood there for a moment longer its mouth still hanging open. Then steam poured from its eye sockets, nose, and mouth. The grey giant fell.

The chanting stopped as the other giants stared at the corpse in disbelief. A victory shout echoed along the north wall and Vlad laughed, pounding Swen's broad back.

"Sabre Vlad, sir!" said a messenger from the top of the stairs. "The students have gone through. It's time for the graduates."

Vlad nodded. "The front and side walls will be evacuated first. We'll be the last ones out."

Willum looked behind him and saw the walls emptying as the graduates left through the front gate.

"*Huh-oh*," said the imp, panic in its voice. "*Something bad comes! Bad bad! Ooh, I can feel it!*"

The giants at the back of the hills began to shout in excitement. The others turned and pointed and the chanting began again. "They come! They come! The destructors come! Your death is nigh! The destructors come!"

"We need to fall back," Willum said. "Something's coming."

"We stay until everyone else is through!" Sabre Vlad said. "Don't let their chanting scare you."

"Look," said Swen and Willum saw them. Dark forms came over the far hills, various shapes and sizes but all moving fast.

"It's Vriil's army," Willum said. "Just like the prophet said."

Sabre Vlad swallowed and grabbed two messengers. "Make sure this place is cleared out. Tell everyone its time to go. No more pretenses. We'll hold them off as long as we can."

"*That won't be long,*" the imp warned. "*Best go, Willy Yam!*"

I'm not leaving just yet. He watched the oncoming army

and sent his father exactly what he saw.

There were smaller figures, green-armored orcs and hairy man-shaped things that ran on all fours, mixed with gargantuan monsters; snake-like behemoths with red-glowing lines on their backs and spinning teeth and giant spiders with turtle shells. All of them rushed forward toward the north wall.

"*They have eyes!*" said the imp. "*Ho-ho. All of them have moonrat eyes and moonrat mommy feels angry!*"

Get out, Willum! Coal sent.

Not until everyone else is out of the academy, he said

Almost everyone is out already. There's just you and a few stragglers.

"Sabre Vlad! Father says that nearly everyone is clear," he said.

"Then we'll give them a few volleys before we go," he replied and raised his arm. "Fire as soon as they get in range!"

"Can you do that magic thing again?" Swen asked, pulling an arrow back. Willum nodded and reached out with the axe. *Do it.*

"*You are crazy, Willy!*" said the imp as it enchanted the arrow. "*Go or y*ou'll be dead.*"

Then you'll just have to protect me however you can, he replied.

The creatures streaked over the final hill, unaffected by the iron spikes that littered the ground. The graduates fired but the arrows bounced off of them ineffectively. The snakes with the glowing backs began to burrow at the base of the wall while the turtle-spiders started to climb. Armored orcs jumped and clung to their shells. Huge deformed mixes of ape and crab stood at the top of the hill and tore great boulders out of the ground and flung them.

While the graduates fired down at the beasts climbing towards them, the boulders crashed into the academy behind them, destroying buildings and crushing siege equipment. If the place hadn't already been emptied, hundreds of people would have been crushed by that opening attack alone.

"Fall back! Make for the gate!" Sabre Vlad yelled. More

boulders crashed into the interior of the academy and he added, "Keep to the top of the walls!"

Swen fired the burning arrow right into one of the eyes of the turtle-spider that had neared the top of the wall closest to them. Steam shot from the wound and it reared back, screeching. It fell, taking several armored orcs down with it.

Willum grabbed the big man's arm and they ran for the west corner of the wall. Silent Josef and Lyramoor had ignored the evacuation order and were running towards them. Willum motioned frantically. "The other way! The other way!"

"Go on," Lyramoor said and the two assistants jumped up to the wall's edge to let them pass.

"*On your right, Willy!*" shouted the imp and Willum turned just in time to see a round black ball the size of a wagon wheel appear above the wall right next to Silent Josef.

It rolled over the edge and rose above them, propelled upwards by four rope-like legs that shot out from its central body. It stood there like a spindly spider and a wide smile full of straight teeth opened in its side. Silent Josef threw two daggers in quick succession, burying them into the ball, and it quivered, then let out a high pitched giggle. Lyramoor slashed out with his swords, severing two of the legs, but before it could fall, two more legs shot out from its body to replace them.

"Force!" Willum shouted and swung the axe at the center of the ball's creepy smile. There was a heavy bell sound and the black ball was blasted off of the wall, its thin legs flapping behind it.

Two turtle-spiders had gained the top of the wall now and as Willum watched, Sabre Vlad stood on one of their backs and swung his sabre in a vicious arc, slicing an armored orc in two. The other orcs came at him but stumbled when the shell tipped as the spider started down the other side of the wall. Vlad spun and shoved one orc off the edge, then dropped to his stomach and clung to the shell with one arm as it went vertical. Lyramoor ran and jumped off of the edge of the inner wall. The elf latched onto the shell next to Vlad, kicking another orc loose.

"Come on!" Swen yelled and Willum ran after the tall

archer. Silent Josef, no longer hesitating, ran right behind them.

They turned at the corner and ran along the western wall, boulders still crashing into the buildings below. Willum looked back over his shoulder and saw more beasts climbing over the north wall, some running down the stairs into the interior. There was a rumble at the base of the wall and one of the giant glowing snake things burrowed up from underneath.

"*Behind you*!" cried the imp and Willum looked back.

"Watch out, Josef!" he yelled, seeing one of the hairy beasts running on all fours along the top of the wall behind him.

It leapt just as Josef turned. The hairy thing grabbed onto him, knocking the assistant off balance. His lower back struck the outer wall and Josef started to topple backwards. Willum reached out for him, but he wasn't quick enough. The weight of the beast pulled the assistant off the wall.

Hurry! Coal said.

Willum looked down as Silent Josef fell and saw even more of Ewzad Vriil's beasts running along the base of the wall outside. Swen yanked at his collar and they ran on towards the stairs at the southern corner.

Faldon the Fierce and Stout Harley stood at the bottom yelling and motioning at them as they rushed down the stairs. They hit the ground and the two warriors shoved them towards the front gates where Hugh the Shadow waited, the great pin to the portcullis in his hand, ready to pull it as soon as everyone was through.

There, just outside, stood Samson, Coal on his back with his hand outstretched. Willum stopped under the portcullis and took one last look back. Boulders fell, some even striking the giant monsters that crawled across the grounds. On the south wall, one enormous shape larger than the others rose up and flowed over the wall like a living river of quivering black jelly.

Willum backed up and Coal grabbed his arm. His father yelled something as he pulled him up on Samson's back behind him, but Willum didn't hear. He saw Lyramoor drag a limping Sabre Vlad through the gates, followed by Faldon and Stout Harley. Then Hugh pulled the pin and dove, just clearing the great portcullis before it crashed to the ground.

More of Ewzad's creatures came around the outside of the western corner, heading right for them. The men climbed on horses and Willum wrapped his arms around his father's waist. Samson rode away, the others close behind him. Then somehow they entered a tunnel of fire, riding through the blackened streets of Reneul. Flames surrounded them but he didn't feel any heat.

Willum looked back and saw that Ewzad's creations had entered the tunnel after them. There were armored orcs and black balls on skinny legs and large cats with swords bristling from their bodies and they were right on the heels of Hugh the Shadow's horse.

Hugh threw some things on the ground behind him and plumes of colored smoke rose up, causing some of the creatures to clutch their throats and stumble. Then he turned in his saddle and threw tiny blades and stars and other items he had hidden throughout his armor. Each projectile caused a different effect as it hit; freezing, burning, exploding. The creatures directly behind him scattered, some collapsing to the ground, some falling into the fire. A few others dodged or simply slowed down, but either way, none of them were on his heels anymore.

Then Samson burst free of the fire corridor and out onto the path beyond that led into the grassy hills. Darlan stood at the exit with her arms raised, a look of pure concentration on her face. Coal reined Samson in and waited as the others escaped.

The moment Hugh darted out, Darlan threw down her hands and shattered her spell, releasing all the pent up energy at once in an explosion. A plume of flame shot upwards along the corridor from where they stood all the way through to the entrance by the academy. Everyone paused for a moment, watching as something came out. One armored orc took three stumbling steps towards them before collapsing and deflating. Nothing else left the corridor alive.

Willum swayed in the saddle, the edges of his vision dimming.

"*Willy! Breathe stupid! Breathe!*" shouted the imp. Something hit him like a punch to the gut and Willum gulped in a deep gasp of air.

"Willum, are you alright?" Coal asked.

"Yes," Willum gasped.

"*What kind of warrior forgets to breathe?*" asked the imp

I don't know! It was an old habit of mine. Something I used to do whenever I got too excited as a child, but I haven't done that since I was ten.

"*Ho-ho, until today, Willy!*" the imp laughed. "*Wee Willy back again!*"

Shut up, imp.

"I was afraid the traps were going to go off before we could get out of the way," Hugh said with a smile.

"Look!" said the Daughter of Xedrion, pointing back at the school.

Everyone stared back at the south wall of the academy as two giant turtle-spiders climbed to the top of the wall, orcs and other beasts clinging to their shells. The enormous glistening black thing flowed up and over the wall beside them.

"What if they don't try to break through the portcullis?" Faldon asked. "What if they all just climb over the walls?" His concern was rendered moot as something heavy and red and full of teeth struck the portcullis and crashed right through it.

They saw it happen before they heard it. The walls of the academy bowed inward as if sucked in from the inside. There was a flash of light somewhere within the center of the place and the walls blew outward, the individual stones scattering into smaller and smaller pieces, taking Ewzad's creatures along with them.

The blast radiated outward, leveling the closest half of Reneul's buildings, then pushing their debris outward in an expanding circle. Willum knew that the same thing was happening all around the academy, thousands of goblinoids being tossed like motes of dust in a windstorm.

Then the shockwave struck them.

The wizards threw shields up hastily. A bright red one came up around Darlan and the academy council. A blue and gold shield appeared around Sir Edge and his enormous rogue horse. Coal threw up a much weaker black shield of his own and

Willum saw a line of gold magic shoot from his axe to help bolster it.

Debris and dust blew past them followed by a wall of fire.

Chapter Thirty Two

Deathclaw froze against the side of the hill as Justan's emotions flooded his mind. There was fire and light and fear.

"What is it, lizard?" asked Sir Lance, crouching next to him. Why the grizzled named warrior had decided to scout with him, Deathclaw had no idea. "What's going on with yer master?"

Deathclaw hissed. "He's not-."

The ground was rocked by a big thump and a sound like a long peal of thunder. They turned to look back in the direction of the academy and saw a great plume of smoke rising into the air.

"By the gods . . ." Lance said, his mouth hanging open. "What just happened?"

"The school is . . . gone," Deathclaw said. "Justan is not dead."

"Gone?" said Lance in disbelief.

He started to stand, but Deathclaw caught his shoulder and pulled him back down.

"What?"

Deathclaw shook his head and placed two fingers over his mouth and pointed towards the other side of the hill they were on. They crept up slowly and peered over the top.

There, standing in the plains, was a large cat-like creature with long flat quills sprouting from all along its body. Sitting astride it was a green orc covered in armor much like the one Deathclaw had fought before. It was staring towards the plume of smoke that rose from the academy.

Sir Lance reached up and grabbed the pommel of the great two-handed sword that rose from his back. But before they could make a move, the cat ran on past their hill. "They'll see the cave!"

Deathclaw and Lance ran after it, but they were too late. The cat stopped at the top of the next hill and crouched. The orc climbed down from its back and watched the line of academy retirees that had just arrived entering the cave.

Deathclaw raced up the hill after them, his sword drawn, and they did not notice his approach until the last second. The orc turned and time slowed. Deathclaw brought Star down in an overhead chop and the orc brought its arm up to block. In the full light of day Star was at its weakest, and Deathclaw knew that the blade would not penetrate through its armor. So he hit the crease in the orc's armor at its wrist.

The blade made it most of the way through, cleaving through bone before binding up in the skin on the far side of its wrist. It screeched and rolled to the side, tearing the sword from Deathclaw's fingers.

It stood and reared back to release a stream of acid just as the tip of Sir Lance's sword caught the back of its head. The edge of Lance's blade cracked with energy and sliced clean through, sending the top half of its head spinning through the air. Leaving the rest of the body to collapse and melt.

The cat hissed at them and ran towards the line of warriors. They saw it coming and pulled their swords, but before it reached them, it was struck by a gust of air. The cat was bowled over, then swept up into the air. The beast rose, soaring higher and higher, spiraling upwards until it was but a small dot.

"Don't you think that's high enough, Wizard Beehn?" Locksher asked, his hand shading his eyes from the sun as he watched its ascent.

"Oh, I suppose," said the squat man in the wheeled chair. He cut off the spell. "It's just that I never get to fight beasts. It's such a rush."

Deathclaw watched the speck above grow larger as it fell until the cat struck the hill behind them with a thud, sword-like quills spilling everywhere before smoking and beginning to melt.

"Are there more?" Beehn asked eagerly.

"We didn't see any," Lance said. The warrior folded his arms. "How'd you get so fat Beehn? Last I saw you, you were trying to get the other wizards to keep their bodies in shape."

Beehn scowled and Deathclaw didn't stay to hear them argue. He left to return to his scouting and noticed Locksher examining the body of the melting orc. He walked closer and watched the wizard pull a knife from within his robes and cut a piece of rubbery armor from the corpse. Locksher turned it over in his hands, rubbing the sticky residue between his fingers, and wrapped it in treated leather before stowing it away back in his robes.

"You want that?" Deathclaw asked.

"It may help me to figure out the process that Stardeon's rings use to create these creatures," he said and he eyed Deathclaw. "In fact, you may just be the secret to this whole thing. If I had a small piece of you to study, I just might be able to understand it better."

Deathclaw took a step back.

"Uh-oh!" Locksher said, looking back at the melting body. He moved the orc's rubbery arm to the side and stabbed into its armpit with his knife. When he pulled the blade back out, a shriveled green orb was stuck on the end. "Deathclaw, I think you should tell Sir Edge that the mother of the moonrats now knows where everyone is heading. He needs to hurry."

Jhonate got to her feet, coughing, the air full of dust and smoke. Fire burned in the hills around them in patches, but she didn't expect it would last. The new growth of spring grasses wouldn't let the fires spread quickly.

"Jhonate!" yelled a voice from the smoke ahead of her. She barely heard it over the ringing in her ears. Gwyrtha's huge form soon appeared out of the gloom. Justan jumped down from the beast's back and rushed over to embrace her.

He pulled back. "I'm so glad you're alright. I didn't have a way to throw a shield around you."

"I am fine," she said, holding up her hand. "Once again it seems your ring protected me."

"It's not my ring. It's yours," he said, grasping her hand with his own. "Let's make sure the others are okay."

They didn't need to search long, a great gust of wind swept past them, pushing the smoke away and they saw the others standing pretty much where they had been when the academy exploded. Master Coal dropped his hands and released his wind spell in relief. The shields thrown up by the wizards had protected them.

"That was much bigger than expected," Oz said.

They stared sadly at the place that used to be their home. The academy was gone. Not a wall stood, just torn and blackened ground. The same was to be said of most of Reneul. The few houses still standing on the outer edges of the city were in shambles and from where they stood, the training grounds were unrecognizable.

"You are kidding me," said Hugh the Shadow. He pointed to the Scralag hills and they could see movement. Large lumbering forms were making their way out of the hills towards them. "They're still coming?"

"That blast had to have killed most of the army," Faldon said. "There can't be many."

"There doesn't have to be," Stout Harley said. "You saw what they could do."

"Wizardess Sherl!" said Sir Hilt. He ran over to Justan's mother, his wife hanging limply in his arms. "Beth isn't responding. Her heart is beating and she seems to be breathing fine, but I need to make sure."

Darlan placed her hands on the woman's head and chest. Jhonate switched to mage sight and saw black and red energies passing through her into the witch.

"She is just asleep, Sir Hilt. She's exhausted," Darlan said with a smile. "We just need to get her to the Mage School. She'll be fine."

"That means we're no longer protected from the mother of the moonrat's gaze," said Oz.

"We need to go!" shouted Justan. He climbed atop his enormous rogue horse. "Deathclaw says that one of Vriil's monsters just appeared at the cave. It had a moonrat eye with it."

"She knows where we're going," Jhonate breathed. Everyone mounted their horses, and Hilt put Beth in the saddle in front of him. Jhonate tightened her jaw and jogged over to Gwyrtha. She hated to admit it but she found the beast frightening. It reminded her of stories her nursemaids had told her as a child. She pushed those silly feelings away. "I am riding with you, Justan."

Justan helped her up behind him and she held onto his waist as they galloped up the path towards the cave. It wasn't long before they saw the line of pursuit coming after them, but they had a good lead on the enemy and the first two miles of the journey went rather well. Then Jhonate heard Faldon swear from the horse just ahead of them.

"How did they get ahead of us?" Justan asked and spurred Gwyrtha forward.

Jhonate leaned as far out of her saddle as she could and saw a group of students including Jobar, Poz, and Qenzic in a fierce battle with a group of four orcs in overlapping green platemail. There were already two students down and Jobar looked pretty beat up. Poz was the only one that seemed to be having any success against his foe. The orc facing him was missing one arm from the elbow down.

"Those are armored orcs. They're fast! Fast and strong and their armor is part of their skin!" Justan shouted. He started to pull the bow off his back and groaned. "All I have with me are explosive arrows and everyone is fighting too close!"

Lyramoor and Coal's son Willum jumped down from their horses, running to help. Faldon jumped down too. "Let's make this quick! There are more coming up behind us and I want to be long gone before they get here."

No sooner had he spoken than five more armored orcs ran out of the grass, followed by three huge mountain cats with sword-like quills. Everyone else slid down to join the fight.

Jhonate jumped down and ran towards Qenzic, who was hard pressed by one of those orcs that carried a longsword. Qenzic was able to get his shield up in time to block each blow, but every strike he got in just bounced off the orc's armor.

Sabre Vlad arrived there before her. He was limping, but still spry enough. A savage upward swing of his blade sliced the orc open from hip to shoulder like its armor was nothing. The wound wasn't fatal yet, but Qenzic saw the opening and thrust his sword through the gap his father's sword had made and the orc collapsed.

A sound rang out like a deep bell behind her and Jhonate twirled to see an orc tumble away from Willum, its head rent in two. Stout Harley faced off against one of the cats with blade-like quills, smashing at it with his hammer while quills bounced off his armor like they were nothing.

Jhonate ran back and forth, looking for her opportunity to strike. Justan was down off the rogue horse's back with his two runeswords drawn. She stepped towards him but heard a roar to her left. Gwyrtha had faced off against one of the cats and had a face full of quills.

Justan ran to her aid and Jhonate turned to do the same, but another cat appeared in front of her, growling and bristling.

She twirled her staff and assessed the beast. It was almost the same height as her and likely three times her size. It would be quick, strong, and it had plenty of ways to attack. It was best fought at range or by someone who was heavily armored which meant it was probably too much for her, but Jhonate didn't mind a challenge.

She struck first, using her staff like a spear, its tip narrowed to a fine point. She jumped forward and jabbed several times in quick succession, scoring hits on its nose and forehead, narrowly missing its eye. The cat roared. It spun and sidled towards her, its sword-like quills bristling outwards.

Jhonate backed out of its range, thrusting in with her staff whenever she had an opening. She struck several times, but couldn't get in close enough to do real damage. She was starting to consider testing the strength of her ring and chancing a close attack when a dagger spun past her to bury itself in the cat's side.

"Need some help, daughter of Xedrion?" Jobar asked, another dagger ready in his hand.

The cat roared and came at him. Jobar dodged at the last moment, throwing a dagger as he did so. The dagger plunged into its shoulder this time and it roared again. It began edging towards him, quills bristling.

"What are you going to do now, Jobar?" she asked. "Never throw your weapon away unless you know the attack is going to be fatal!"

"I have more," he said with a grin and pulled out two more blades. "Picked them up from the Wobble dwarves."

"Just keep its attention. It can only back towards one of us at a time," she said and edged around towards the cat's face. Jobar threw another dagger and as it roared, Jhonate darted forward, thrusting her staff down its throat. With a mental command, she caused wicked spikes to sprout from the end of her staff, piercing deep into its flesh.

The cat responded by leaping towards her. Jhonate backpedaled but it bore her down under its weight. It could have seized her head in its jaws and killed her right there if her staff hadn't been in its mouth. Still it tried, blood and drool pouring down on her, the staff in the way. Luckily, its underbelly was free of quills.

To her surprise, Jobar jumped in from the side and wrapped his arms around the cat's bristling head. He cried out in agony, but ignored the hundreds of quills that pierced his flesh and got a firm hold under its neck. He pulled back and lifted it away from her, the Jharro staff still protruding from its mouth. Jhonate scrambled out from under it as he twisted its head more and more. Finally there was a crack and the beast began to steam.

Jobar stumbled back, his whole left side covered in quills. Jhonate grabbed her staff, returned it to normal, and pulled it from the melting cat's mouth. As she looked around, she saw that most of the fighting had shifted further away.

Jobar fell to the ground, crying out in pain. "Gah! That hurts!"

"Healer!" Jhonate shouted and knelt next to him. "Jobar you idiot! What were you thinking?"

"Heard you kissed that Edge guy," Jobar said with a grin.

"Couldn't let him show me up. Always . . . kind of hoped that would be me."

"I know, Jobar," she said. He was that way with every female. The quills in his skin were loosening and turning rubbery. She pulled one of them out and a gush of blood poured from the wound. This was bad. She shouted again, looking around for help. "Healer! Warrior down!"

"Hey . . . daughter of Xedrion," Jobar said. He reached out with the arm not covered in quills and gripped her hand. His teeth were clenched against the pain, but still he asked, "Why not me? Why couldn't it have been me?"

"Do not call me that. My name is Jhonate," she said. "That is what you will call me from now on. Do you understand?"

He chuckled and winced. "I . . . guess that'll have to be enough . . . Jhonate. Nice to say it without you hitting me . . ."

Master Coal rode up and slid off of Samson to kneel beside her. The wizard placed his hands on the man and after a brief moment, shook his head. "I'll try, but it's not likely I can save him. Those are a lot of wounds."

"Please try." Jhonate stood while the wizard worked and turned away, wondering why she had tears streaming down her face. For Jobar? That didn't seem right. But then again, he was a comrade and even though he had never let go of his foolish infatuation with her, she had grown used to him. If he survived, she would have to . . .

Jhonate saw the quick gleam of scales in the grass ahead. A pair of cat-like eyes watched her. She twirled her staff and pointed at it. "You. Come, face me!"

"More coming!" Came a shout to her right.

She risked a glance to see what was coming and the thing in the grass came at her, all scales and teeth and claws.

Chapter Thirty Three

Justan worked within the bond, pushing the last limp quill out of Gwyrtha's face. He healed the wound. The cat thing hadn't died easily, but the blast from his right sword had cleared a space of quills large enough for his left sword to stab through.

"More coming!"

Justan opened his eyes and saw a large lumbering giant come over a hill towards them along with several hairy looking men that ran on all fours. He readied his swords.

Justan, she's here! Gwyrtha warned.

He turned just in time to see Talon streaking out of the grass towards Jhonate. He opened his mouth to yell, but no sound came out. Talon leapt, claws extended. Jhonate set her staff in front of her, forming the tip to a sharp point.

Time slowed for Justan and he watched as the tip of her staff punctured Talon's abdomen and continued on through to protrude out her back. But it didn't stop the raptoid. She struck Jhonate full on, her claws tearing through the graduate's hardened leather breastplate like it was paper. Talon's weight drove Jhonate backwards and she fell, the raptoid landing on top of her.

Justan ran to her, fearing the bite to the throat that would likely come next. But Talon didn't stay. She leapt off of Jhonate, her momentum pulling the staff out of her body and Justan realized that the raptoid had another target in mind.

Talon darted for Master Coal. The wizard was kneeling over the prone form of Jobar da Org and didn't see her coming.

Samson did, however. The centaur thrust forward with both spears. Talon jumped and spun in mid air, narrowly avoiding the attack and jabbed out with her tail.

The wizard looked up and raised his arms defensively. Justan saw the beginnings of a shield spell coming up, but Talon's attack went right through. Her tail barb thrust deep into his forearm.

Coal fell back, completely vulnerable, but she didn't continue the attack. The raptoid leapt back to avoid another spear thrust from Samson, then turned and ran right at Justan.

Justan narrowed his focus even further, letting his sword suck away his emotions as the world slowed to a crawl. Talon ran towards him, a wide grin of triumph on her face. Why was she so happy? Her first attack had taken Jhonate down, but surely hadn't been enough to do lasting damage and her attack against Coal had resulted in a single wound any of their mages could fix easily.

Was it just a distraction to get to him? She was a few feet closer now and Justan readied the defensive move he had been working on ever since their last fight. He was ready. And this time he would blast the head from her shoulders.

But something still nagged at him. Why hadn't she simply come for him right away. He had his eyes closed at the time. There was no need for a distraction. There was something else.

She was closer now but a large shape was looming in on her right. She jumped for him as expected and her tail was raised in striking position. The barb was red with Coal's blood. The shape on her right moved forward and something descended towards her. She turned her head slightly, her eyes looking at the incoming shape and Justan suddenly understood.

At the tip of the barb on her tail was a tiny hole. A single drop of clear fluid dripped from the end. Poison! Ewzad Vriil had given her poison.

Talon contorted in mid air but the shape descended too fast. It was dark and round with large spikes jutting from one side. It connected with the side of Talon's face, shattering teeth to splinters with such force that it spun her whole body in mid air. One spike tore her jaw free on one side as the mace head continued its downward path.

Justan's world rushed back to normal speed.

Fist's strike threw her body to the ground with bone crushing force. Talon bounced and rolled a few times, then contorted and convulsed, clutching at her face and screeching, her tail thrashing about.

Fist started towards Talon again and others rushed in to help.

"*Stop!*" Justan said aloud and through the bond. "No one come any closer! Her tail is full of poison."

How did you get here anyway? He had been so focused, he hadn't sensed the ogre coming.

I came with the captain. I rode on Albert. He is tired, but I touched him with my mace so he could move faster.

"Jhonate, get my mother. Tell her to come help Master Coal right away. Talon got him."

While he spoke, a throwing knife darted in, plunging into Talon's side. Flame shot from the wound. The pain seemed to jolt her to her senses, because she stopped thrashing and rolled to her feet. Talon gurgled at them from her ruined face and ran into the grass. Lyramoor started after her.

"You won't catch her." Justan stabbed his swords into the ground and took Ma'am off his back. He pulled an arrow from his quiver and pulled back. The explosive arrowhead glowed a bright blue. This time he would not let her survive.

Time slowed again and he tracked her movement through the tall grass. The power hummed in his ear. It would be a tricky shot. He took a deep breath and let it out slowly.

A cavalryman charged through his field of vision and in that brief moment he lost sight of her. No. Not again. Not after this! He scanned the grasses for the slightest sign of movement.

A large giant over twelve feet tall rumbled past, chasing the men on horseback, disrupting his sight again. Justan snarled and fired, the arrow hitting the giant in the neck. The force of the strike knocked it stumbling off balance. Its neck swelled and burst in a flood of water and the giant fell, its head rolling into the grass beyond.

Justan slung his bow over his shoulder, grabbed his swords and sheathed them as he ran to Coal's side. To his relief, Darlan was already there and Jhonate was on her feet standing beside them.

"Jhonate are you okay?" he asked.

"Jobar is dead," she said, looking down at the graduate, her eyes pained and red. "Your master was trying to help him but that creature hit him first and I did not stop it."

"What about you? Are you okay?" Justan asked, taking her face in his. "Are you wounded?"

"There is just one small puncture," she said, poking her finger through a hole in her breastplate. "But it is small. The ring absorbed the rest."

"But you're feeling okay? No dizziness or anything?" She shook her head and he embraced her in relief. "I'm sorry about Jobar. Really I am. But don't blame yourself. You couldn't have been prepared for her." He slammed his fist into his leg. "Blast it, I should have prepared you for her!"

Justan knelt at his mother's side. Coal's face was pale and he was sweating profusely. He was bleeding from both nostrils and a small bead of blood had formed at the corner of one eye.

"He needs more than me," Darlan said. "I'm more of a battle healer and it isn't even my specialty. This is poison . . ."

"You can do it, Darlan," said Willum, who knelt across from her. "The i-. The axe says that it's a tough one, but I know you can do it."

"Oh Willum, I'm sorry but whatever this poison is, it's resisting all my attempts to root it out. I have him stabilized but barely," she said, her face pained.

"We are only a mile from the portal," Justan said. "We need to get him there. Willum, is Bettie there? Can you tell her to get the best healers she can ready?"

"Coal can hear you," said Willum. "He's just not responding because he's trying to move as little as possible. He says . . . No, Father! No . . . He says it won't matter. He can't do anything about it, but he used his mage sight to look inside his own body . . . he knows it's too late."

Darlan's eyes widened and she focused in, her energies moving more intricately. "Wait-wait. Blast it, that poison's persistent!"

Tears ran from Willum's face. "He has things to say. Sir Edge, he says that when he's . . . gone, we are all going to collapse, all of his bonded and you need to get us to . . . Master Latva. Coal says take us to Master Latva. Do it fast. There's not much time, but he'll know what to do. The bond has to be passed on . . . no, father. No. I don't want someone . . ."

"No, Coal," said Samson.

Willum shuddered, his eyes clenched closed, nodding as he heard his father's request. Finally he opened his eyes and looked at Justan pleadingly. "P-please . . ."

Coal let out one last breath and was still. Willum fell forward across him and Samson started to fall, but Fist was there, straining as he helped ease the rogue horse to the ground.

Justan sat there stunned, staring at his master's body in disbelief. His mother wrapped her arms around him. Jhonate squeezed his hand.

"Too many deaths," Fist said. "Too many."

"We need to . . ." Justan's mind went blank. "We need to . . ."

Run! said Deathclaw. *We are waiting for you but you need to run. The wizards say the portal has only so much energy left.*

"Run." Justan stood and looked back towards the academy. There was a steady stream of creatures still coming. "We need to take Coal and his bonded to the cave and we need to do it quick. The mother of the moonrats knows we're here and knows we're vulnerable and she will keep throwing these monsters at us until we're all dead."

"How do we take him?" asked a tall man with an enormous bow slung over his shoulder. He gestured at Samson.

Justan scratched his head, unsure what to do. Samson was heavy normally, but now he was huge. If he wasn't so big, Gwyrtha could do it.

I will take him, said Gwyrtha. *Make me big big big.*

Maybe if he undid all the armor changes and used up most of her energy it could work . . . Justan shook his head. "It's ridiculous. He's just shaped wrong for that."

Make me wide.

Justan shook his head in exasperation.

"We pull him," said Fist.

"On what?" Darlan asked.

"On that," Fist pointed to the corpse of the dead giant.

"It's not quite big enough," said Jhonate. "His legs will hang off the end."

"We'll heal him afterwards if he gets bumped up too much," Fist said. "Coal made him tough."

Justan hesitated, the ridiculousness of the situation making it a difficult decision to make. Finally he shrugged. "Okay."

It took ten men and Fist with Gwyrtha's help to load Samson on top of the giant's body. Justan increased Gwyrtha's size, then wrapped ropes around her chest and shoulders and tied them to the giant's feet. The large student named Swen took Willum on his horse and Justan laid Master Coal's body across Gwyrtha's neck much in the way Beth had been.

Faldon rode up to them alongside the cavalry and the other council members. They all looked battle weary and many of them were wounded. "We need to go now! We drove off that last bunch but another large group is right behind us."

"We're ready," said Justan. He looked to Jhonate. "Hurry, take Albert. I don't think he can handle Fist's weight on the ride back. Fist climb up! Let's go!"

They started off at a gallop but their burden slowed Gwyrtha down. Fist touched his mace to her side, but Justan had been forced to use up the last of her energy to make the changes and she was tired in a way that Justan had never seen her. They fell to the back of the group. The others slowed down, looking back in concern, but Justan waved them on.

"Keep going, sweetie," he coaxed, patting Gwyrtha's neck.

"They are coming," Fist said. "And there are many of them."

"Will you hold on to Master Coal for me?" he asked the ogre and stood in the saddle, pulling Ma'am from his shoulder. He focused and turned, stepping around Fist, then stood on Gwyrtha's haunches, assessing the situation.

They ran forward in a steady stream, beasts of many types ranging from modified orcs and cats to enormous centipedes with mouths wide enough to swallow a man. Justan drew an arrow and focused on slowing them down.

He fired strategically, blasting groups of smaller creatures into the air with fire or air arrows, and bursting larger creatures with water or earth. It was working. They were falling back. Then he realized he had just two arrows left.

"How much further, Fist?" he asked as the enemy surged forward.

There was a great boom and a lightning bolt fell from the sky stunning several beasts. Fireballs exploded into the midst of them, followed by several volleys of arrows. Justan turned. Wizards and elves stood atop the hills on either side of the road, raining death upon the remnants of Ewzad's horde while the warriors of Sampo stood protectively in front of them.

"We're here," Fist said.

The cave looked like a wide crack that opened into the hill before them. Several wizards stood nearby, ushering people in. The cavalrymen were already dismounting and leading their horses in.

Justan climbed down from Gwyrtha's back and found Deathclaw standing there waiting for him. Justan swallowed. "Deathclaw, I'm sorry. I almost had her again, but she got away."

I know. Fist told me, said Deathclaw, but the raptoid didn't seem angry. *Don't worry, Justan. I will kill Talon soon enough.*

From the intense feeling coming through the bond, Justan didn't doubt it.

"Sir Edge!" said a familiar voice and Wizard Beehn

rolled towards him, propelling his chair with tightly controlled gusts of wind.

He ran forward and embraced the man. "It's good to see you, but-."

"You have a burden for me to bring over," Beehn replied. "He didn't know what it was going to be, but prophet wanted me to be there for just that purpose. Where is it?"

Justan blinked in surprise and gestured to the centaur that was tied down to the giant corpse. "He's unconscious. We need to get him to Master Latva."

"That is a surprise," Beehn said. He frowned, but the sounds of approaching battle got louder. "I'm sure you'll explain later."

He stuck out his hands and made a lifting motion and Justan saw an intense amount of air magic pool under the centaur's body. The ropes around it fell apart and the centaur rose about two feet into the air.

"Would you mind pushing me?" Beehn asked. "I can't seem to do this spell and push the chair at the same time."

"Of course," Justan said. He turned the chair and Samson's body swung with them.

Justan pushed the wizard to the mouth of the cave and went inside. The portal opened up along the back wall of the cave. It brightened the cave with a shimmering light and a steady mist flowed out of it, but Justan could not see what was on the other side. He pushed Beehn forward, but stopped right in front of the portal.

"I'm not going through yet. Not until the others are through." He stopped and looked back. "Uh, Poz, would you help push the professor through?"

The freckle faced graduate nodded and took his place. Justan ran back outside the cave to see wizards and elves running towards them.

"We've held them off as long as we can!" Shouted one wizard that Justan recognized as Munsey, the council fire wizard. "They'll be right behind us."

Justan realized that Gwyrtha wasn't going to fit through

the portal. He rushed to her side and reduced her back down to her normal size. The rogue horse let out a sigh of relief as her energy rose back to its regular brilliant levels.

I'm small again! she said happily.

People crowded into the cave until only Justan, Jhonate, and his bonded remained.

"What do we do?" Fist said.

"We go in," Jhonate said, grabbing Justan's hand.

Justan's parents appeared at the mouth of the cave, urging them in.

"I'm just waiting for Deathclaw," Justan said.

"What if he doesn't want to go?" she asked.

"He's coming." Justan backed everyone down to the cave entrance.

Go! The raptoid ran over the hill in front of them. The head of a large centipede-like creature rose above the hill behind him, followed by bulky greenish creatures with large slavering mouths that dripped slime as they moved.

"Trolls!" Jhonate yelled. "Modified trolls!"

"Get in and get behind me!" Darlan shouted from the entrance behind them, her arms raised as she prepared a spell. They ran inside and the moment Deathclaw darted in, she thrust out her hands.

A column of fire burst from her palms, extending outward in a large cone shape, covering the hill in front of them. Rock burst upward from the ground beneath the cone and melted, swirling around and scattering everywhere immolating everything within its range.

It lasted maybe fifteen seconds, but when she lowered her hands the area in front of the cave glowed white hot, the hill in front of them sinking as it melted.

Faldon was there to catch her as she released the spell and he pulled her back towards the portal. "That bought us a few minutes." He looked around at them. "Well what are you waiting for?"

"We have an issue," said Sir Hilt. Beth and Charz stood

beside him.

"What is it?" Justan asked.

"Four people have to stay behind and release the lodestones so that the portal closes. The four people on the other side are already ready with theirs."

"But?" Justan said. "You mean to stay behind to face these monsters alone?"

"There is a back way out of here," Beth said. "The four who stay behind won't die today. I have foreseen it."

"Why can't we all go through and just have them pull the stones on the other side?" Faldon asked.

"The portal location is permanently fixed," Beth said. "Even with the Mage School side closed, the council is worried that with the forces at Ewzad's disposal, he could find a way to force his way through. We can't give him a back door into the school."

"The three of us have been ready to stay behind all along," Hilt said. "The Mage School is going to need eyes that can report back to them and Charz can send messages back and forth. Whoever stays behind will remain outside the school until the war is over."

Charz snorted. "Antyni was gonna stay, but she says she can't do it now that she has a responsibility to her people or whatever."

"We need someone else to stay with us," Hilt said.

"I'll stay," said Darlan trying to push away from Faldon's arms. "You all get away."

"No," said Faldon. "You're too weak to resist me and I'm taking you in there with me."

"Surely there's someone else who can do it," Jhonate said.

"No," said Hilt. "The prophet said it would be one of the last five who entered the cave."

"Then it has to be me," Jhonate said.

"No," Justan said.

"No," said Charz. "It has to be a magic user."

"I will stay with you," said Fist, walking forward and Justan's heart sank.

"Oh!" said Beth with a smile. "That would be so nice, but no. It doesn't feel right."

Justan swallowed in understanding. Of course it would be him. How was he going to leave his bonded without him at the Mage School? He just saw his mother again after so long. He looked at Jhonate, his heart heavy. He didn't want to leave her. Not now.

"I will," said Deathclaw. *I have magic.*

"But Deathclaw I don't think you-,"Justan began.

"He's the one," Beth said with a nod. "I feel it."

I do not wish to be stuck around all those people anyway. Deathclaw said. *I will be your scout outside the school.*

Justan hugged him. "I'm going to miss having you around."

Deathclaw froze. He had never been hugged before. Finally, Deathclaw patted his back and Justan felt his affection returned through the bond. *I will miss you too.*

Justan stood back and Fist picked Deathclaw up in a mammoth hug of his own. "I'll miss you too!"

Me too! said Gwyrtha

Don't make me scratch you, the raptoid said in irritation. *Put me down.*

Fist did so reluctantly and Deathclaw walked over to Hilt's side. The four lodestones were set in the back wall, two on either side of the portal, and Beth showed him which one to take.

Faldon and Darlan entered the portal, followed by Jhonate and then Fist and Gwyrtha. Justan paused just outside and looked back.

I will contact you each night, Justan sent.

Deathclaw nodded in response and Justan walked into the misty light.

Chapter Thirty Four

Justan stepped into the mist and a moment later walked out of the portal into a large ornate hall. The floors were made of polished marble, the walls painted white with gold filigree. Enormous pillars rose to the ceiling, each one covered in colorful murals. The hall was full of people, academy students and refugees, some being healed, others being guided away by Mage School students in work robes.

There was movement behind him and Justan saw four wizards remove their lodestones from gold inlaid circles in the wall. The portal vanished and behind it was a mural depicting the portal. He found that distantly funny somehow.

Deathclaw's presence was now very far away. Justan had no idea of the raptoid's thoughts or feelings, but he knew exactly which direction he was in. Justan looked around and realized he didn't see Coal's bonded anywhere.

"Big John!" bellowed Fist. Standing a short distance away, talking to Oz the Dagger, was the prophet. He nodded in response to what Oz was saying a sad smile on his kind face. The ogre rushed forward and picked the man up in a mighty hug.

The prophet didn't seem surprised at all. He laughed and returned his embrace. "Fist! You have grown quite a bit since you last called me that. We should have to come up with something else, don't you think? Now would you please set me down?"

The moment Fist put him down, Gwyrtha nudged him. *John!*

The prophet embraced her shaggy head and scratched behind her ears. "Yes, Gwyrtha, I am glad to see you too."

Everyone pressed in, each of them with things to say to the prophet, but he raised his hands. "I will speak to each of you later. Right now I have some urgent business to attend to. Edge and bonded! Follow me and hurry. We don't have much time if this is to work out right!"

He took a few steps and paused, then pointed to Locksher and Jhonate. "Oh, and you and you too. Come along!"

The prophet walked quickly through a set of doors and up a curving stairwell. Justan grabbed Jhonate's hand and followed.

"Sorry, I know it is a tiring climb after all you have been through today." The prophet didn't look back as he spoke but he didn't have to, his voice reverberated up and down the stairs. "Unfortunately it is necessary."

It was a long climb and the ceiling in the curving stairwell was low enough that Fist had to hunch over as he walked. The ogre's back was aching by the time they reached the top. Gwyrtha had the toughest time of it though, her long claws making it difficult for her to find purchase on the polished marble.

When they arrived at the top of the stairs, the prophet opened a gilded door with a crystal knob. They walked into a long, elaborately decorated hallway. The prophet shook his head. "You know when this place was first constructed, everything was so clean and austere. But wizards get bored. Leave them alone too long and they start gussying up the place."

The floor was covered in a plush red carpet that stretched the hall's entire length. Flameless torches were mounted into the wall every ten feet between detailed paintings. On the right side were portraits of named wizards and on the left were portraits of named warriors. Justan knew where they were now. They were nearing the Bowl of Souls.

"Ah, there you are," said Master Latva, coming in from the door at the end of the hall. He wore his familiar blue robe.

"Where is he?" The prophet asked in concern.

"He just walked through," said the head wizard. "I delayed him as long as I could, but he's not exactly a talkative man."

The prophet jogged past him and pushed open the doors into the Hall of Majesty. Justan ran forward and followed him inside.

"STOP!" John shouted with a voice of such authority that everyone froze in their tracks. Tamboor the Fearless stood in front of the Bowl of Souls, his body covered in drying blood, his sword Meredith held high in the air. He turned his head to look at them, his eyes troubled and unfocused.

"Stop, Tamboor! The bowl will not accept you as you are," said the prophet.

Tamboor's arms fell slowly to his sides and his sword slipped from his fingers. His mouth opened and he stepped towards the prophet, his arms outstretched. "John . . . John, they're-."

Tears rolled down his cheeks and he fell into the prophet's arms, sobbing. "Efflina, Cedric, Lina . . ."

John held Tamboor in his arms and patted his back gently. To Justan's surprise, tears rolled down the prophet's face as well. "I know, Tamboor. I'm so sorry that happened. Come, please. I must speak to you for a moment."

The prophet led Tamboor to the far corner of the room and spoke to him in soft whispers. Justan couldn't make out what was being said, but tears were still falling from the Tamboor's face and he nodded, responding in soft words of his own.

"He is talking," Fist said and the ogre had tears rolling down his cheeks too.

The doors behind them opened once again and Professor Beehn wheeled in floating the still forms of Coal and his three bonded on a plush carpet before him. His wheelchair was being pushed by the gnome Alfred who was trailed by Lenny and Zambon, both of them looking quite confused about their surroundings. Zambon stared up at the unending tiers of chandeliers hanging from the arched ceiling, while Lenny marveled at the statues of named warriors and wizards that lined the room.

"I'll be dag-gummed." Lenny was still wearing his full suit of shining platemail and pointed with the helmet he held in his hands. "That there's the Bowl of Souls itself."

The prophet looked back at them and motioned. "Zambon, would you please come here for a moment. What we're discussing concerns you too."

The guard shared an uneasy glance with Justan and walked across the hall towards the prophet, his eyes lingering at the Bowl of Souls on its pedestal. The prophet placed his hand around the guard's shoulder and talked to the two men together.

Professor Beehn set the carpet down gently next to the rest of them and looked at Justan. "I'd like to speak with you later, Sir Edge."

"Of course," Justan replied and watched as Alfred wheeled the wizard back out of the hall. He turned to Latva, who was kneeling at the head of Master Coal, looking down on him sadly. "Master Latva, Coal said that you would know what to do to save his bonded."

The wizard blinked and looked up at him. "I am sorry, Edge. That is the prophet's realm, not mine."

"But he said to come to you and mentioned something about the bond being passed on," Justan said.

"I suppose I can see why he might think that," Latva said hesitantly.

"I apologize, Sir Edge," said Alfred, the tall gaunt gnome having just rejoined them. "We are still getting used to being able to talk freely about this. The prophet just released the ban on teaching spirit magic earlier this week."

"He did?" Locksher said, one eyebrow raised. "How interesting. So you two are bonded then?"

Latva and Alfred looked at each other. "Yes," Latva said finally.

"I wondered if that was the case," Justan said. "Ever since Charz said his wizard was at the school, I've been going over it in my mind and the way you two acted, always seeming to know what the other was doing . . . It just made sense."

"Yes, well we try not to make things that obvious," Latva said. With a smile, he added, "But I do so enjoy putting the other council members on edge with how much I know about things going on outside the room."

"So you were Master Coal's master." Justan said.

Master Latva shook his head. "I'm not the bonding wizard, Sir Edge."

Justan's brow furrowed. "So . . ?"

"I am," said Alfred. "Gnomes aren't usually wizards, but when our master died about one hundred years ago, his magic was passed to me."

"But why didn't you say something when I was named and the other wizards captured Gwyrtha?" Justan asked. "Why send me away? Why not just teach me here?"

Latva looked at Gwyrtha. "The rogue horse was the problem. Alfred could have taught you in secret as he did Coal, but we had to get her out of the school. We would not have been able to keep them from experimenting on her without explaining the bond and we were not allowed."

"Surely, the rogue horse would have been protected," Locksher said. "After all, there are so few left."

"We were mainly worried about you," Alfred said.

Locksher sputtered indignantly.

"The time of keeping these things secret is at an end," the prophet said, walking back up to them. He stood next to the still forms of Coal and his bonded, then sat down cross legged at Coal's head and rested his hands on either side of the wizard's temples. "Now if you'll excuse me, I must speak with Coal for a moment."

Justan pondered that for a moment. The prophet was speaking with Master Coal's spirit? Could he do that at any time or was it just because his death was so recent? No one really knew the extent of the prophet's powers. Even the histories were vague about the prophet's feats.

Fist gasped and Justan looked up to see Tamboor standing in front of the altar again, his sword held high. With Zambon standing next to him, Tamboor dipped the tip of his sword into the bowl. A white light rose from the bowl and Justan switched to spirit sight.

A tall white figure stood behind Tamboor with one hand

placed on his head. The figure's mouth moved and Tamboor's mouth moved along with it. A low chant echoed from Tamboor's mouth, rising and building, the language unrecognizable to most, but Justan remembered the chant. He could almost repeat it himself. He didn't quite understand the meaning of the words and yet he felt that if he heard it enough times, he just might.

Tamboor's voice grew louder and louder until with a booming voice he yelled, "TOLIVAR!"

"Good one," the prophet said with a nod, still holding Coal's head in his hands.

Tamboor stumbled back and collapsed on the floor, sobbing as Zambon knelt next to him. Fist ran over to them.

"Uh, John, sir. What about my Bettie?" Lenny asked. "Can you wake her up?"

"I can negotiate the process, yes, but ultimately the decision isn't mine," he replied.

"Coal said there has to be a transfer," Justan said. "Can the bond be transferred to one of his other bonded?"

"I am afraid not," John said. "The bond has to go to someone who was born with spirit magic."

"I would like to volunteer," Justan said. "I already like them all. I would be happy to include them as my bonded."

The prophet looked up at him briefly and smiled. "That is so kind of you, Edge. Coal is touched with your offer. Unfortunately you are not a candidate for the transfer. You already have bonding magic and so I cannot move Coal's bond to you, it would most certainly drive you crazy."

"Then what can we do?" Alfred asked.

"Tolivar!" the prophet said.

The man whose name had been Tamboor rose from the stairs and walked towards them. Fist and Zambon followed.

It seemed strange to Justan that the man was walking towards them newly named, yet still covered head-to-toe in orc blood. Only his cheeks were washed clean and that was from his tears.

Tolivar stood before the prophet and Justan noticed that the sword on his back wasn't his, but Zambon's. A naming rune had appeared on the pommel, but there wasn't a rune on the back of his right hand. So he wasn't a named warrior? Now that Justan thought about it, Tolivar didn't sound like a name given to a warrior, but how could Tamboor be a wizard?

"Yes, John?" Tolivar asked.

"I spoke to you about giving up your vengeance and starting life anew."

"Yes, sir."

"I know it is soon, but we have no choice. Here is your first opportunity to become something different," John said. He motioned to Coal's bonded. "These people have lost their bonding wizard. They will die in the next sixty minutes if their bond is not transferred."

"But I am not a bonding wizard," Tolivar said.

"No, but you do have spirit magic and that makes you a candidate. I can transfer Coal's bonding ability to you. I have spoken with Coal and he finds you acceptable," John said. He placed his hands gently on each of the bonded's heads. "Now look at each of them closely. This is not something being forced on you. You can choose to refuse. The bond is permanent. Your mind and soul would be linked with theirs forever."

Tolivar's eyes moved over each of them and Justan noticed them linger on Bettie. The edge of his lip curled up and a look of pain passed over his eyes.

Will he do it, Fist? Justan asked.

I don't know, Fist said. He placed a heavy hand on Justan's shoulder. *Every time he saw her, he would remember what happened to Efflina.*

"Please," Lenny said. He held Bettie's hand in his. "Just 'fore she fell, Coal made Bettie tell me . . . she was gonna wait, but-." Lenny looked into Tolivar's eyes. "She's gonna have my baby. First new Firegobbler in a hunnerd years. Please!"

"Oh, Lenny," Justan said.

Tolivar looked at her again and his countenance changed.

That's right, Tamboor, Fist thought, his hand tightening on Justan's shoulder. *She's not an orc, she's a mother.*

Tolivar closed his eyes for a moment and when he

opened them again, he said, "I'll do it."

"Very well," said the prophet. He lifted his hands from Coal's head and to Justan's spirit sight, it looked like he lifted a white crown from the wizard's brow. He stood and walked to stand behind Tolivar and as he did so, Justan saw the trails of the bond linking from each prone figure to the crown in the prophet's hand.

"Tolivar, the bond is yours," The prophet said and placed the crown on Tolivar's head.

Tolivar's hands flew to his head. His face twisted in pain and he cried out, then fell to the floor next to the rest of them. As he hit the ground his hands opened and Justan saw the wizard's rune on his left palm.

"Will Tamboor be okay?" Fist asked in concern.

"Tolivar will be fine," the prophet said. "The process of bonding can oft times be a painful one as I am sure Sir Edge and Alfred can attest. Right now all four of them are getting used to it. This may take a while."

"You sure she'll be okay now?" Lenny asked.

"Yes, Lenui. She is perfectly healthy as is your child," John said. He folded his arms. "Now for the main reason that I have gathered you all in this room with me today. Today was a victory and a defeat for both sides, but the war has just begun.

"I am usually not allowed to take part in wars or disagreements. However, this time the Dark Prophet is involved and since he has gathered his champions, I have been allowed to gather mine. Now before I send you forth to vanquish these enemies, I felt it would be best to tell you the truth about them.

"You see, this war isn't Ewzad Vriil's war. No, the seeds were planted thousands of years ago. It's Stardeon's war. If only I could have foreseen what his actions would bring about, I could have stopped this long ago."

Father . . . Gwyrtha thought.

The prophet smiled sadly and patted Gwyrtha's head. "You have some partial knowledge, but it is incomplete. It's time I told you the true story of Stardeon and his wife Mellinda."

Epilogue

"Speak to me, you horrible thing. Speak!" Ewzad said, paced back and forth outside the entrance to the dwarf menagerie. He had to know what happened. Had to! There had been nothing but silence from the mother of the moonrats for two solid hours.

Several dwarves within the menagerie were staring at him, fingering magic talismans. Hamford and Arcon stood behind him, sharing uneasy glances. The last he had heard, his beautiful creations had breached the academy walls. Then Mellinda had screamed so loudly that Arcon had fainted and Ewzad himself had nearly collapsed.

"Speak, blast you! Or so help me, I will reach through this nasty little eye and tear you to pieces! Would you like that? Hmm?" His arms and fingers writhed. His head throbbed. But there was no answer. Whatever had caused Mellinda to go silent had to be bad for him. "Arcon!"

"Yes, Master," said the mage, looking pale and drawn. The mage had been unresponsive for nearly a half hour and Ewzad had been forced to heal a hemorrhaged vessel in his brain in order to wake him.

"Yes, Master? Is that all you have to say?" Ewzad spat. "Tell me what you know!"

"Nothing," he said. "I only know that my mistress has been greatly wounded. She is too focused to the situation at the academy to be able to respond. She hasn't spoken with me either."

"What did they do? Did the Mage School find her lair? Did they-!"

"*Gone*," said Mellinda in his mind, her voice weak and

wracked with pain. "*All of them gone.*"

Ewzad stopped mid-stride. "All of whom, my dear? Hmm?"

"*A third of my sweet children . . . and over half of their precious gifts . . . all gone. Destroyed by the wizards and their vile tricks,*" she moaned.

"Destroyed you say?" Ewzad shouted. Several of the dwarves ran for their ringmaster. "And the academy?"

"*Gone,*" she whispered.

"Show me, witch! Yes, show me! Show me all of it!"

She pushed the vision into his mind. Ewzad saw his creations climbing the walls, saw that the interior of the academy had been emptied, and saw the great explosion and the smoking hole where the academy once stood. She showed him the ragged chase of their remaining forces against the fleeing academy survivors and Talon's attack and the death of the bonding wizard. Then he saw the wizard's arrival and support of the enemy's escape. Finally she showed him the empty portal they left behind.

"They fled to the Mage School," she said. "I don't know why I did not hear of their plan beforehand, but my eyes inside say the grounds have been flooded with refugees."

The wizard quieted as the enormity of it hit him. Two thirds of his goblinoid army dead. Three quarters of his army of creations gone. He giggled.

"Oh my! Dear Mellinda, you had me frightened for a moment."

"*Why are you so happy?*" she growled.

"Today was a success, of course! Yes-yes, the academy gone. All went to plan!" He turned to his two assistants. "You hear that, Hamford? Arcon? It's gone!"

"*But they got away.*"

"Some escaped, true. But their losses must have been heavy yes?" Ewzad said.

"*It is hard to say. I saw many fall, but the destruction was so complete . . .*" Mellinda paused. "*And what of our losses?*"

"Losses? Oh my, no. They were fodder!" he said. Ewzad began pacing again, but this time in excitement instead of worry. "Goblinoids and moonrats? Easily replaceable don't you think?

You have more of your children breeding than ever before and once the goblinoid survivors spread the word that we destroyed the academy, worship of the Dark Prophet will spread and recruits will pour in. Yes-yes, this is a battle won!"

"*And what of your army of creatures?*" she asked.

"Yes, it is too bad about my creations. I so wanted to watch them kill more, but they would have died in a few days anyway, don't you think?" he reminded her with a shrug.

"*Yes, of course,*" she said and his excited attitude began to cut away at her gloom. "*What do you wish done with your creations that survived?*"

"So sad. They will melt away before we have a chance to use them again, yes? Hmm . . . even if I wanted to throw them at the Mage School just for fun, they wouldn't survive the journey. No-no. Send them to the place where you build your troll horde and let them be devoured. The magic your trolls absorb should give you another useful generation or two."

"*An excellent suggestion, Master,*" she said and he could sense that she was pleased.

"It was, wasn't it?" He giggled again. "Now I want you to tell Talon to come back to me. I have another adjustment to make before I send her into the Mage School."

"*I . . . cannot find her,*" Mellinda admitted. "*She ran off after she was gravely wounded. She is either hiding or-.*"

"She lives," Ewzad said, unconcerned. "Yes, sweet Talon will return soon enough. Until then, bolster our presence around the school. Just don't get too close, no. We will let them sit while we prepare our final assault. Yes-yes! All our enemies cowering in the same place. This war is almost over!"

"Hey, Lord Protector!" said a gruff voice and Ewzad whirled to see the dwarf ringmaster standing at the entrance, his beefy arms folded in front of him, his face twisted into a scowl. "You done bein' crazy so we can do some gall-durn business?"

Ewzad heard Hamford swallow and the big man grabbed his sword in preparation. But the dwarf's insolence flew right past Ewzad's ears for once. It was a good day. "Lead on, Ringmaster. But your delivery had better be good this time, yes? I shall be quite perturbed if you made me wait out here for nothing?"

"I wasn't makin' you wait, dag-gum it!" he grumbled. "But come on in. I think you'll like what we got fer you."

Ewzad followed him in, excited to get started on a new series of creations. The walls of the Mage School would provide an even greater challenge. The ringmaster led past the wary eyes of the other dwarves to the rear of the menagerie.

"Got a present fer you, yer lordship," said the ringmaster, giving his black handlebar moustache a twist. He turned and walked to stand before a row of six cages covered in tarps. Screeches issued from within and Ewzad could see that the tarps were punctured and torn. "Show 'em what we got, boys!"

The tarps came off and Ewzad squealed, clapping his hands in delight. "Excellent! Excellent! Oh yes!"

"You was right about these things," said the dwarf. "Meaner'n hell and hard to control. One of 'em even resisted the paralyzin' orb just like you said it might."

"They are beautiful!" Ewzad cooed. "Yes, Hamford. Don't you think?"

The large man's eyes were wide with terror. Standing in the cages were six raptoids.

The Bowl of Souls series will conclude in:

MOTHER OF THE MOONRAT

Coming fall 2013

See www.trevorhcooley.com for updates and details.

In the meantime, to get your Bowl of Souls fix, follow @lennyswears on twitter for daily adventures and excerpts from the personal diary of our own Lenui Firegobbler.